Wildfire

Skye Malone

Wildfire

Book Three of the Kindling Trilogy
Previously Published as The Children and the Blood Trilogy

Cover design by Karri Klawiter
www.artbykarri.com

ISBN-10: 1-940617-41-3
ISBN-13: 978-1-940617-41-1

Join Skye Malone's mailing list to hear about new releases!
www.skyemalone.com/mailinglist

For Avery

Prologue

roken lights flickered, sending off occasional sparks as they dangled over the rubble-strewn floor. Pounding her fist on the metal storage room door, Tanya Bartlow swallowed down the urge to sob and cast another glance to her daughter huddled in the corner.

"We're getting out of here," she promised for the hundredth time, hating the fact stupid reality was probably going to make her a liar.

Clutching her stuffed bear, Missy nodded, believing her mother with all the faith her five years of life could hold.

Fighting renewed tears, Tanya turned back to the door. Early on, she'd tried blowing the damn thing up, to the near destruction of the whole room. The supports above the door could be holding the weight of the entire factory for all she knew, because when her magic hit the door, things had gone horribly wrong.

Half the room was on the ground. Concrete, steel and rebar from the levels above had been their unwelcome companions for the better part of half an hour, ever since the sounds of explosions had faded from the building above. They'd been lucky – insanely lucky – to survive the ensuing cave-in, though doing so put them no closer to escape than they'd been before.

And meanwhile, the damned, dented, useless door remained.

The hallway had collapsed, she was fairly certain. And the door-frame itself was far too shallow to hold a portal, had she been any good at forming them anyway. But she couldn't tell that to Missy. She was all the girl had left, no thanks to the royals, the war, and her husband's blind faith in the former that led to his death by the latter.

Or whatever the story was these days.

Cursing under her breath, she slammed her fist into the warped metal again, begging no one in particular to finally start playing fair.

Magic roared down the hall.

She stumbled away from the door. Hurriedly, she motioned for Missy to scoot behind the chunks of concrete. With her round face nearly the same color as her curly blonde hair, the little girl quickly did as she was told.

The door jerked as someone pulled at it from the other side.

A voice grumbled in annoyance. Another voice, colder and infinitely more authoritative, murmured in response.

Magic hit the door and spread, chasing the length and breadth of the steel. Heat began to radiate into the room while, with alarming speed, the gray metal shifted to orange.

Tanya retreated, the sweat slipping from her brow only partly the fault of the oppressive warmth baking the room. Like syrup, the metal door slid down and pooled on the ground, where it rapidly began to cool.

She barely noticed it. Her gaze was locked on the men in the hallway.

Taliesin. At least a dozen. Without hesitation, she struck out, throwing everything she had at them. The Taliesin staggered back, their hasty shields barely holding against her furious assault. Gasping, she whipped her hand toward the next few, succeeding in sending them toppling against the wall.

A wave of magic slammed into her, and then she was on the floor. White lights and darkness danced across her vision as footsteps pounded into the room.

Missy's screams sent her surging blindly to her feet. Blinking frantically, she scanned the blurred chaos for her daughter, only to stumble as the girl barreled into her.

The shadows faded, revealing the Taliesin. Red-faced with fury, one of them grabbed her and wrenched her around.

"Try that again and you're both dead," he growled.

She glared, seething with the desire to spit in his face, though she knew it'd only give the bastards an excuse to finally make Missy an orphan. Satisfying herself with a sneer, she pulled her frightened daughter toward the door.

"That was all?"

The dry voice drew her attention from the Taliesin. By a blockade of concrete and steel at the end of the corridor, a man leaned calmly against the wall. Slender and tall like some kind of elf from a fantasy book, with prematurely gray hair pulled back into a long ponytail at the nape of his neck, he raised an eyebrow and then shrugged away from his support, ignoring the guards as they retreated from his path.

Despite herself, she shivered. The man looked human. There wasn't a trace of magic on him, nor any sense of what side he was on. He was just ordinary.

And the Taliesin deferred to him without question.

Her heart pounded harder at memories of the guards' whispers and the snide comments from the Council bastard, Sebastian. The mad teenage queen of Merlin swore there were wizards out there no one but cripples could detect. Wizards more powerful than anyone on either side of the war.

Wizards who'd actually been responsible for everything that'd happened the night Howard died.

"A woman and a girl, with the door heavily bolted from the outside?" the man continued. He regarded her curiously. "What on earth did you do to earn such fear?"

She couldn't breathe enough to bring the words into the world, but at her silence, he simply smiled and then jerked his chin at the Taliesin. Without a sound, the men pushed her toward the stairs.

Fire lit the factory floor and poured black smoke through gaping holes in the ceiling. The walkways were on the ground, though their warped supports still protruded from the walls like broken bones. Chunks of the roof lay everywhere, with crushed beds and curtain frames sticking up like insect legs from beneath the car-sized debris.

Other things pinned by the destruction came into view.

Her gorge rose and swiftly, her hand dropped to cover Missy's eyes.

The Taliesin shoved them onward. Rubble shifted beneath her shoes, threatening to roll her ankles with each step as she circled an enormous chunk of concrete with bolted-down parts of rooftop machinery still attached to its side.

Her breath caught. On a space of cleared ground ahead, people were kneeled with their hands clasped atop their heads. Men and women alike, they waited, their bodies trembling and their eyes locked on the floor.

Unbidden and utterly out of place, a sense of satisfaction hit her, almost ludicrous in its strength. Council guards cowered among the prisoners. Fear etched their faces, the expression so similar to the one they'd always brought to Missy's face that the sight nearly made her laugh.

The ponytailed man strode past. Her satisfaction withered as quickly as it had come.

As the Taliesin shoved her to her knees next to the other Merlin, she watched the man cross the open space in the center of the factory floor and approach a small group on the opposite side. A pale-haired woman stood beside a giant, their backs to the prisoners and their attention on a third man seated on a block of concrete. Watching the far end of the factory, the man ignored them, giving no sign he noticed the fires or the destruction all around.

She followed his gaze. Against the wall, crumpled walkways formed a rough tent over what had once been a door, though only a shattered hole of soot-covered concrete remained.

Motion caught her eye and she turned back toward the group. But for the man inexplicably staring at the wall, the other three people were looking at her.

Involuntarily, she flinched from the sight of the giant's face. Scarred was too mild a term.

The man looked like a monster from one of Missy's nightmares.

She swallowed hard, cursing herself for the reaction. She was better than this. Stronger than this. The bastards who might have killed Missy's father had no more right to her fear than the Council who'd vilified her husband for crimes she knew Howard would never commit.

And she'd be damned if she let them see her cowering like the spineless scum at her side.

Clenching her teeth, she forced herself to look back and run her gaze over every inch of his twisted face.

The giant gave no sign of caring about the attention. Expressionless, he glanced to the man on the concrete slab. Upon receiving no more notice than before, he turned and started toward the prisoners, the other two with him falling in behind.

His wounds became more apparent as he came closer. In the melted horror of one side of his face, a milky white eye stared out, moving as though it could still see. Vicious scars cut across one wrist and hand to climb past the buttoned sleeve of his shirt, hinting of greater damage hidden above. Ignoring Missy's small noises of fear and the sobbing of a wizard farther down the row, he came to a stop, surveying them all.

"We require information," he said quietly, his tone leaving no doubt that the need would be supplied. "Safe houses. Places of refuge. Any location where your allies and your queen will try to hide."

His mismatched eyes skimmed them again and then came to rest on the guard kneeled at his feet. "Have you nothing to say?"

"Go to hell," the man growled.

For a moment, the giant was silent. And then the guard collapsed dead to the ground.

Tanya stared, her ragged breaths doing little to fill her lungs.

"We will only ask once," the giant said.

His gaze ran down the rows of wizards and then caught on her. A hint of curiosity flickered across his face and, with a quick glance to the blonde woman waiting like a ghost behind him, he started toward her.

Tanya struggled to keep breathing as he drew closer. Unconsciously, her fingers tightened on her daughter till Missy whimpered with pain.

"Simeon tells me you were locked in the basement," the man said. "Bolted in from the outside, in point of fact." Dry amusement touched his expression as his gaze slid from her to the cowering wizards and back. "Am I correct to assume your compatriots placed you there?"

She could feel the Merlin watching her, daring her to answer, and she trembled.

"Yet," the giant continued when she didn't speak. "You're familiar."

His deep voice nearly turned the words into a question, and for a moment he looked almost mystified, as though he sought to place a memory.

She swallowed hard. The Merlins' gazes were physical pressures. Fighting the urge to curse the bastards, she kept her focus on the giant, knowing the judgmental, baseless hatred she'd see in the other wizards' eyes anyway.

"You knew my husband."

The giant's brow twitched downward.

"You killed him."

Eyebrow rising again, he regarded her skeptically and then glanced to the blonde. Hints of disgust showed through the woman's glacial expression as she shrugged a slender shoulder.

"And who was your husband that we would bother killing him?" the giant asked, the dry amusement returning.

"Howard Bartlow," she said, looking hard into his nightmare eyes. "The man you framed for selling out the king."

The giant paused. "Howard," he repeated. His gaze flicked down the line of wizards thoughtfully.

And then his face cleared.

"Tanya," he said, his tone warming as he fitted her name into the blank that had obviously been in his mind. His gaze dropped to her daughter. "And… Missy. Howard had a photograph of you both." He nodded to himself and then made a baffled noise. "My dear lady, who told you we killed your husband?"

"You killed the royals."

He shrugged an eyebrow. "Well, yes," he admitted as though the statement was obvious. "But by no means did we kill your husband." He smiled at her briefly, and then turned the expression on the Merlin kneeling nearby. "They were the ones who did that."

She stared at him.

"Howard was helping us," the giant continued. "The Children and their Council had decided to do away with your family. To be rid of the liability you presented. Howard turned to the only help he could find. They killed him for trying to save you."

He glanced back to the Merlin, calm certainty in his eyes. "Or haven't they threatened you since he died?"

One of the guards opened his mouth furiously.

Like a striking snake, the blonde woman's hand wrapped around the man's throat. Choking, he lurched in her grip, his face slowly beginning to change color.

The giant ignored them. "So tell me, Tanya. Can you help us? Will you work with us to make sure Howard's sacrifice for you wasn't in vain?"

For a long moment, she couldn't pull her gaze from the other Merlin. In the blonde's hand, the guard twisted. With red-rimmed eyes, a sobbing woman stared down the row, her expression everything Tanya had known it would be.

Tanya drew a ragged breath. She needed to consider that the

giant's words could be a lie. After all, she had to be smart. Missy was counting on her to be smart, even when everyone else was always so damned dumb.

And yet… and yet…

For eight years, Howard had treated the youngest princess for whatever happened to her at the beginning of the war. But to do so, he'd needed to know where the royal children were, even while in hiding.

And that had been always such a threat to the royals. Such a terrible threat.

So maybe, when the princess didn't show improvement, the Council and the king had started to wonder why they needed him. Or her. Or Missy. For Tanya's part, they'd only kept her alive after Howard died because she might have had information on the ones to whom her husband had supposedly sold out. She'd lived in terror for months, hearing over and over how they'd kill her or Missy if they became a problem, or if more 'evidence' against her family came to light.

How she'd dreaded their lies…

She stared at the wizards, a shiver running through her that, for once, had nothing to do with fear. Because she loved her husband, she'd done whatever the Council asked. She'd followed their edicts and obeyed their rules. After the war started, she'd moved and moved, living in so many safe houses, she'd lost count in the first year. And sure, it meant she'd left everyone she'd known, and sure, it meant her own daughter had spent so much time in basements, Missy had been three before she'd gotten her first glimpse of the sky.

But the Council had to protect the royals. Regardless of what it cost, regardless of how much it hurt, she and her family still had to be locked away.

Because the Council had to protect the royals.

Tanya paused. Her lip twitched.

How they'd feared what she knew…

"Safe houses?" she repeated.

Her mouth curved as she looked up at the giant, and the shivering strengthened with the feeling of her own smile.

"I think I can help."

Chapter One

—————◆·————

"I'm just saying, we should head back to the city. Give the bastards a piece of our mind."

Ashe closed her eyes, fighting the urge to yell at the portly man. For most of the past half hour, she and Elias had been arguing with the remnants of the Merlin Council, with precious little to show for the effort. Stubbornness wasn't the half of it. After months of hiding in Darius' shadow, the survivors were desperate to prove they weren't incapable of being leaders after all.

"Arthur, didn't you hear us the first time?" Elias asked tiredly. "These aren't just a couple of random wizards we're dealing with here. They're incredibly organized and they run *Taliesin*. We go after them ragtag, we'll get killed. We need to regroup."

"They just got lucky today," Arthur insisted, turning to the others rather than answer. "Now that we know they're out there, they've lost the advantage. We can get the drop on them."

Ashe rose from her seat on the mobile home's steps as several councilors began to nod at the man's words. "Excuse me," she muttered.

No one seemed to notice as she walked away.

They'd be leaving soon, regardless of whether the Council agreed. Neither she nor Elias wanted to be anywhere near Croftsburg when the Blood solidified their hold on whatever remained of the factory and any other wizard hideouts in the city. It was only a question of how soon the wounded could be moved and where they were going to go. Everything else was just nonsense she was amazed anyone was taking time for.

Sighing, she ran a hand through her hair and glanced around the yard in the twilight. Several acres of grass and trees surrounded them, centered around a dilapidated blue mobile home and an equally dilapidated blue garage. All of it belonged to yet another friend of Elias', though unlike Joe's restaurant back in Croftsburg, this place looked as if it'd been abandoned for years. The survivors had quickly turned the property into their camp, however, and with the help of her assistant, Ermengarde, Katherine had methodically sorted the worst wounded into groups looked after by those still able to walk. Nathaniel's guards encircled them, watching the country road beyond the property while, by the far side of the garage, several teenagers kept the littler children distracted with games invented on the spot.

Ashe paused as she caught sight of Lily. The center of attention whether she realized it or not, the girl sat picking at leaves beneath a young oak tree a few yards from the garage. Cornelius stood some distance off, watching Lily as he'd done since the moment they arrived, and it was anyone's guess what was going on behind his eyes. Nathaniel waited closer by, as protective as Ashe had asked him to be, while Cole sat beside Lily and studied them all as if taking odds on whether the wizards would suddenly attack.

"What do you *think* is happening, you old fool?" Elias barked, causing several people to glance over at the noise.

Ashe shook her head, not bothering to turn around.

"He's going to get himself killed," Katherine murmured, coming up beside her.

"Tell me something I don't know," she retorted. A heartbeat passed and she closed her eyes, regretting the sharp tone. "How's it coming?"

"The wounded should be ready in another few minutes. Ermengarde and I will stay with the worst injured, but the rest should be able to travel with friends, families… whoever remains."

Ashe glanced to her.

"Most hope their relatives escaped through other portals," the woman supplied. "And for those who know their loved ones did not…" She sighed. "They go on."

By the steps, the overweight councilman snarled something incoherent at Elias and then stormed away.

"Guess that ends the debate," Katherine commented.

Ashe looked over, taken back by the closest thing to a joke she'd ever heard the woman say.

The suggestion of a smile hovering on her lips, Katherine bowed her head. "Whenever you wish to leave, your majesty."

Turning, she headed for the injured.

"Of all the stupid, incompetent…" Elias muttered, stalking across the yard.

"So how'd that go?" Ashe asked dryly.

An annoyed breath escaped him, degenerating into a scoff by the end. "They say they'll run, though I'd not recommend putting them in any group that wants to stay away from Croftsburg for long."

She sighed.

"Katherine got the others ready to travel?" he asked.

"In a few minutes."

Elias nodded. "Then we need to decide what to do about…"

He trailed off skeptically.

She followed his gaze to Cole. "What?"

"He presents an issue for transport," Elias said carefully.

"He still needs to come with us."

"Your highness–"

"No, Elias," she cut in, exasperation hitting her. "He's coming with us."

The man grimaced.

"You know why," she said.

"He's a cripple."

"And we need his help to identify Blood wizards."

"So we bring him wherever you go. We can't put you and Lily in danger by traveling slowly on his account." He paused. "Your highness, the city was one thing. But we need to get you both as far from this part of the country as we can, and the time it would take–"

"Is better than the possibility of going someplace and having no one to point out the Blood wizard waiting there." She paused, the edge in her voice fading. "We stay together, Elias."

He looked away.

"So you can get us a vehicle?"

A moment passed and then he closed his eyes. "There's a van in the garage that should give us enough room."

"Thank you."

He bowed slightly and then headed for the garage. She sighed as he walked away. Of its own volition, her gaze slid back to Lily and Cole.

They needed him. With Crystal and Ghost dead, and Mud

betraying them, Cole was the best shot they had at identifying the Blood. Everything she'd told Elias was true.

To a point, anyway.

She bit her lip, disquiet moving through her. Something was off about Cole. And it wasn't just that he kept watching the wizards as though all the reassurances in the world of their trustworthiness wouldn't make him relax. The look on his face the moment before she dragged him through the portal in the factory was nagging at her, leaving an increasingly uneasy feeling she couldn't seem to shake.

He hadn't looked scared by the Blood wizards. Horrified at what was happening, yes. But that hadn't been the only thing.

Lost. That was the only word she could think of to describe it. Like someone had taken something from him. Or possibly had, anyway. Like, if he could have, he almost might've stayed to see if he could get it back again.

Her brow drew down as she watched him. She wanted to ignore the way the memory of the look on his face made her feel. Whatever she thought she'd seen, Cole was on their side. He'd rescued them the night the Blood came to their farmhouse and he'd obviously been keeping Lily safe ever since. That should've been enough to end the discussion.

Except she couldn't quite let herself be that naïve anymore. Not after Darius and the Council and the way she'd let herself believe them too. Fact was, she barely knew Cole. His actions on the night her dad had been killed notwithstanding, she'd only met him for a few minutes before she'd thought he and Lily died, and she had no idea what he'd even been doing at their farm in the first place. He'd helped Lily, sure. And for that she was incredibly grateful.

It was just everything else that neither he nor her sister had yet explained.

She couldn't bring her discomfort up to the others, though. Since the factory, Nathaniel and Elias seemed to have fallen back on a view of her safety that shared a lot in common with a scorched-earth policy. Wary enough of Cole on their own, there was no telling what they'd do if she mentioned she had misgivings about the boy too. And then there was Lily, who clearly trusted Cole implicitly and wouldn't take well to the idea that her sister didn't feel quite the same.

Though really, that was only one of the issues with the little girl.

Never particularly comfortable around any wizard she'd seen since Ashe found her again, hearing that the portal could have killed Cole had left the girl practically glued to his side. For the past half hour, Lily had regarded every wizard on the property with near-rabid defensiveness, as though daring them to try to force either her or Cole to go anywhere near magic again.

But that hadn't stopped the Merlin's interest. Curiosity about Lily was rampant, and nothing short of having Nathaniel stand guard over the girl had thwarted the wizards from trying to prod Lily for answers to the question plaguing them all. The girl looked human. And after seeing the equally human-looking Blood lay waste to the factory, no one was content to just idly wonder why.

Her lip slipping from between her teeth, Ashe tensed as yet another group made good on her thoughts and started toward Lily again. Nathaniel shifted position warningly, bringing the wizards to a halt. The closest said something, at which Nathaniel's face darkened, but after a moment's consideration at his silence, the wizards scowled and then retreated.

Ashe exhaled, trying to calm down as she watched them go. The whole mess was getting upsetting. More so, anyway. And that was without bringing into it the issue of the staff or why Lily'd had it when Ashe found her and Cole outside Chaunessy Tower, or even what the hell they'd been doing there at all. Between the two of them, they presented so many questions she didn't know where to begin.

Assuming she wanted to, anyway.

From the grass, the little girl tugged out a peculiarly shaped leaf and showed it to Cole with a comment too quiet to be heard over the distance. At her words, the young man's mouth twitched in a smile and Lily grinned.

Ashe's brow drew down.

Cole glanced over, catching sight of her watching them. The little girl followed his gaze, and her face clouded with confusion at whatever she saw in her sister's eyes.

Quickly, Ashe turned away, cursing internally. She was slipping. Letting herself get distracted by everything that had happened over the past half hour, let alone the past half year, and it was showing.

But she'd be damned if she allowed it to upset Lily.

"Your highness?"

The words broke into her thoughts and she looked over sharply. Across the yard, Katherine stood beside a group of guards, a few of the wounded already supported between them.

"We're ready," Katherine called.

Taking a breath, Ashe nodded. Pushing the thoughts aside, she strode over to help the woman, determined to at least address the problems she knew how to solve.

———— ◆ ————

Cole watched as Ashe faltered and then hurried toward the wizard who looked like a schoolteacher from hell. Katherine, he thought Ashe'd called her. Yet another one to keep track of.

He grimaced and then buried the expression, careful not to let Lily or Nathaniel see. The man was starting to remind him of Geoffrey Carnegean, his ostensible uncle back in Washington who'd tried to kill him, and the implicit threat that seemed to live on the wizard's face wasn't helping dispel the similarity.

And Lily had enough worries for ten people. He didn't need to go making her think there was reason for more.

Exhaling, he looked over at the girl. Her black hair glistening in the fading sunlight, Lily was spinning a misshapen leaf between her fingers, the unease on her face deepening as she watched her sister walk away.

"Hey," he whispered to her, surreptitiously checking Nathaniel. The man had turned his gaze on a few wizards who, at the look in the guy's eyes, immediately reconsidered walking anywhere nearby.

"It does kind of look like a cat," Cole said, nodding to the leaf.

For a moment, a ghost of the little girl's grin resurfaced. "Like that big one. Candle."

"Yeah," he agreed, though he couldn't place the name among the innumerable cats roaming Ben and Sue Summers' farm.

Lily's gaze dropped to the leaf, her smile fading. "Do you think we could go back there?"

He hesitated. "It's not really–"

Nathaniel shifted behind him and Cole cut off, struggling not to scowl. He could anticipate the man's expression. He didn't even need to turn around.

Her brow furrowing, Lily's gaze twitched toward the wizard and then away. Slowly, she began spinning the leaf again.

Safe, he finished silently. Not anymore.

A headache flared briefly at the base of his skull. He glanced up in time to see a wizard run his hand down the doorframe of the mobile home.

By his side, Lily made a small noise. "You don't think they're going to make us use those things again, do you?" she whispered, her gaze on the door and her hand frozen on the leaf.

He didn't answer, watching the doorway. Across the yard, Ashe crouched to help Katherine hoist a woman to her feet. Together, the two of them walked the wounded woman to the steps, where a man hurriedly took the woman's weight from them and then headed through the door.

The pair vanished. Slowly, Cole exhaled.

"Cole?"

"No," he said without looking at her. "I…"

He trailed off as the wizard atop the steps ran his hand over the doorframe again and then glanced back at Ashe a second time, saying something Cole couldn't hear. The girl nodded and then motioned to the people gathering behind her. A half dozen more wizards hurried through the door and disappeared.

"I don't think so," he finished.

Lily nodded, her expression still troubled. Ignoring Nathaniel, she scooted closer to Cole and wrapped her arm around his own. Gently, she lay her head against him. In her fingers, the leaf began to spin slowly again.

Cole swallowed. They wouldn't send him through one, anyway. He couldn't say anything about what they might try to do with her.

Because portals killed his kind. Or, at least, they had until Ashe hauled him through one with the aid of a fiery staff that'd since disintegrated into dust. So if the wizards wanted to leave using those, it meant he wasn't coming along.

And maybe that wasn't such a bad thing.

Guilt rose at the thought, though it was tangled up with a bunch of other junk he couldn't sort out. He didn't want to abandon Lily, especially now, here, in the midst of a group of wizards who were probably as safe as rabid dogs. Ashe could be okay, but before today, every other wizard he'd seen made backstabbing Hollywood house-wives look saintly by comparison.

And when it came to Ashe…

He shook his head, everything descending into insensibility again. There'd been this shell-shocked girl who, barely half a year before, he'd tried to save from a bunch of wizards hell-bent on killing her. And then there was this girl who, barely half an hour before, had decimated a bunch of wizards like they were nothing in a display that rivaled the Fourth of July.

And he couldn't see a trace of the former in the latter or figure out how the hell she'd so dramatically changed.

Admittedly, what she did at the factory saved his life. Probably the lives of everyone here. But it also left God knew how many other wizards lying dead in her wake. And those wizards worked for his dad. His dad who Cole'd thought had been dead for eight years, and who had just brutally taken out over a dozen wizards of his own.

Cole closed his eyes. His head hurt, and it had nothing to do with the portals opening and closing in the mobile home's doorway. The people who worked for his dad had murdered Lily's entire family, Ashe aside. For that matter, according to the Taliesin wizards, Victor Jamison had spent the better part of the past eight years killing a whole lot of people, including Lily's grandparents, Cole's wizard caretakers, and pretty much anyone else who'd gotten in the way of whatever it was he wanted.

And Cole's mom.

He let out a breath, fighting to remain calm as he drove the thought back into the category of absolute bullshit he refused to believe. The rest of the confusion filling his head might be up for debate but, whatever the Taliesin said, nothing could've made his father hurt Clara. Nothing.

Behind him, Nathaniel shifted again, and the pair of boys creeping along the length of the garage toward Lily paled and backpedaled swiftly.

Cole watched them retreat, his expression darkening.

He'd go, but he couldn't leave Lily. He'd stay, but then he wouldn't ever know what really happened with his dad.

So for novelty's sake, he'd just go insane.

Scowling and unable to hide the expression, he looked away as the kids disappeared behind the garage. There had to be an answer to all this. Something he wasn't seeing. Something that could explain who the hell was actually the bad guy in this situation.

Something.

The sound of the garage door opening pulled him from his thoughts. With a shuddering succession of clunks, the chains winched the door up, revealing a dusty brown van with cobwebs on its wheels. The muffler growled as the vehicle crept forward, and when Elias brought the van to a stop and shoved open the door, the hinges creaked loud enough to make Lily flinch.

"Ready?" the man called.

His wife nodded and then returned to directing the wizards who remained to carry the lame and wounded toward the portal. Shutting the door behind him, Elias headed over to help.

Cole glanced to Ashe, but the girl wasn't paying attention to the wounded anymore. Tracking her gaze, he spotted a tall wizard leaning on the side of the mobile home. As Elias strode away from the van, the man shrugged off the wall and began walking toward Lily. Immediately, Ashe descended the stairs to intercept him, while beside the little girl, Nathaniel turned, blocking the other man's path.

"Stay behind me," Cole murmured, rising to his feet and drawing Lily with him. Dropping the leaf, she obeyed.

"Cornelius," Ashe called, jogging briefly to catch up to the man as he neared the little girl.

The wizard looked over at her. Cole glanced between them cautiously, fairly certain he could cut the tension there with a knife.

"You should go with Katherine," Ashe said.

"I am coming with you."

There wasn't a request in the tone, and at the words, Nathaniel made a soft growl of disapproval.

Cornelius' gaze slid over, pinning the man with a look that spoke volumes, despite being utterly impassive.

"Hey, Cornelius," Elias called as he walked up, seemingly oblivious to the tension. "They're ready to go."

"I will be traveling with her highness."

"Just decided that on your own, have you?" Elias chuckled.

Cornelius regarded him coldly. Elias met his gaze with a look whose edge probably could have cut steel, for all its apparent calm.

"I am coming with you," Cornelius repeated, turning back to Ashe as if the other man didn't exist.

The girl glanced between them. "Cornelius," she said again, her quiet tone uncomfortable.

She fell silent at the look in the wizard's eyes, and for the life of him, Cole couldn't read it. But after a heartbeat, Ashe dropped her gaze away.

"Alright," she agreed.

Elias glanced to her in alarm, but Ashe didn't take her eyes from the grass. For a moment, the man seemed to heavily consider arguing, but he wrestled the impulse back. Looking to his wife, he jerked his chin toward the doorway.

Katherine's eyebrow twitched up, but after a heartbeat, she nodded. Turning swiftly, she disappeared through the portal.

The magic faded, taking Cole's headache with it.

"Let's go then," Elias said, the humor gone from his tone.

"Where?" Ashe asked, still looking discomfited.

"South."

The brief glance he gave Cornelius made it clear he wasn't about to say more.

Seeming distracted, Ashe ignored them. "Where'd you find the staff?"

Cole froze, the question taking him by surprise for all that he'd known she'd ask eventually. Faltering, he fought to keep his gaze from darting to the other wizards.

"Uh…" he started inanely.

Internally, he cursed as she waited. He could tell her the truth. After all, she was probably trustworthy. But the others…

And the fact it was his father they were fighting…

And all the other potential weapons the Carnegeans might own…

Not to mention the fact wizards were bastards as a rule…

"Homeless guy out west."

Lily looked up at him. Silently, he begged her not to say a word.

"He had this collection of junk," he continued, making up the story as he went. "At least, we thought it was. But he seemed okay, and he let us stay with him for a while at this, um, abandoned gas station he lived in. And one day, Lily picked up the staff and…"

Cole shrugged, and then faltered again when he saw the questions rising in the others' eyes. "But yeah," he pressed on. "It was great. Until these Taliesin showed up. I think maybe they were looking for us. But they killed him. Burned the station to the ground. We barely got away."

"What was the man's name?" Cornelius asked, his tone unreadable.

Cole paused, wracking his brain. "Old Bill," he said and then winced internally. The name sounded like a character from a cheap western. "But that's just what he said to call him. I don't know if it was anywhere close to the truth."

Silence followed his words, and he wouldn't have dared put odds to whether they believed him. Elias and Nathaniel merely glanced to one another while Cornelius kept studying him with a lack of expression that made him feel like a dissected bug. For her part, Ashe just glanced to Lily, and a hint of doubt crept onto her face when the girl wouldn't meet her eyes.

Heart rate spiking, Cole shrugged. "What?" he challenged quickly. "You think Lily and I are lying?"

Arching an eyebrow in a display of affront he knew was theatrical, he tried not to feel a touch of victory when Ashe blinked in surprise.

"Of course not," she said. The words were too quick, but with an efficiency he was coming to associate with wizards in general, she instantly buried any trace of discomfort and just glanced to Elias.

"So," she continued, dropping the topic entirely. "South then."

Cole drew a careful breath, trying to bring his pulse back to normal. At Ashe's words, Elias nodded and then raised an eyebrow at Cornelius, clearly waiting for the wizard to precede him. Smoothly, Cornelius started toward the vehicle, giving no sign he'd noticed the man's glare.

Elias shook his head and followed.

Nathaniel looked back, his gaze fastening on Cole. "This way."

Tightening his grip on Lily, Cole trailed the wizard toward the van. Nathaniel tugged the rusting side door back and turned, waiting for Ashe. A few steps away, she hesitated, her eyes flicking over the length of the dusty vehicle and then back to the door. She drew a steadying breath, suppressing whatever emotion had threatened to emerge onto her face, and swiftly pulled herself into the van, leaving Nathaniel to follow.

Cole's brow drew down, wondering if she was expecting the thing to explode.

Pushing Lily ahead, he let her precede him inside. Bracing herself on the door, the little girl climbed up to the middle seat and then paused, realizing there wasn't enough room for the three of them on the bench. Worriedly, she glanced to Cole and then to the seat behind her.

He didn't move, suddenly struck by the overwhelming compulsion to just turn and run for the city, wizards be damned. Because staying here was stupid. Mind-numbingly stupid. Lily was fine. Ashe was her sister, for pity's sake. Regardless, the girl would protect her. Hell, she'd probably incinerate anyone who threatened to give the child so much as a cold.

And thus there was no point in the whole damn world for him to take off with a bunch of wizards when, after eight years, his dad was only a few miles away.

In the rear of the van, Nathaniel looked over, saying nothing.

Cole met the man's gaze, fury rising. Ashe wasn't the problem; those other three wizards with itchy magical trigger fingers were. Trying to leave would only provoke questions, the kind whose answers wouldn't go well. After all, even if Ashe was some kind of royalty to them, they obviously only listened to her so far. Which meant the minute they learned about his dad, they'd probably kill him. Apologize later. If at all. The big guy had made that abundantly clear with every glance, and the news about Cole's father would only serve to shorten the man's obviously already microscopic fuse.

He was still trapped. Four different groups of wizards from two different sides, and he was still trapped.

"Cole?" Lily called.

Swearing to himself vehemently, Cole gripped the door of the van and climbed inside.

Chapter Two

The van rattled in the darkness, and its broken muffler provided accompaniment in the form of a dull roar. Bits of foam rained past tears in the ceiling with every pothole, while beneath the threadbare fabric of the seats, ancient springs complained over being put into service again.

For the hundredth time in the past few hours, Ashe glanced to Lily. Looking terribly small with her thin legs dangling over the seat's edge, the girl sat at the far end of the bench, her attention locked on her interlaced fingers atop her dirt-smudged jeans. Worry drifted across her face in time with thoughts passing through her head and, as though feeling the pressure of Ashe's attention, she tucked her chin deeper into her chest as if trying to hide.

Brow drawing down, Ashe let her gaze slide back to Cole, but the young man gave no sign of noticing her glance. Lily's worries had something to do with the staff, of that much she was fairly sure. The little girl had retreated into herself ever since the mention of the artifact, though that could have just been natural. Bringing up the place they'd been staying must have been hard, especially since God knew what the girl might have seen when the Taliesin came, which went a long way toward justifying why Lily was so shut down.

Of course, it didn't address the other possible reason. The one she'd really rather avoid.

Cole had been defensive about what he said, but maybe that was just his personality. She couldn't really know, seeing as how they were a few steps shy of total strangers anyway. But the alternative was that he'd been lying, which opened a whole other host of issues. His lies meant Lily'd lied too, if only by her silence, and that's where things became truly upsetting.

Her stomach quivered. Lily wouldn't lie. Not to her. At least, she wouldn't have a few months ago.

Drawing a breath, Ashe pulled her gaze from the young man. Maybe it wasn't what she was thinking. Maybe Lily was just tired. Maybe Cole hadn't lied. Maybe she'd been imagining things when they fled the factory, and maybe the hours of running and fighting and seeing people die were pushing her over the edge.

Right now, she'd almost prefer to think she really was going insane.

Grimacing, she looked back toward the window, her gaze catching on Cornelius as she moved. Already shaky, her stomach clenched again.

In the shadows, he looked so like Carter.

She shoved the thought down hard as she turned to the countryside. The sooner they got out of this van, the better.

Without the light cast from the moon, the darkness beyond the glass was nearly complete. Lonely farms dotted the horizon, distinguishable only by their security lights blazing against the night. Hours slid past, blurring into cities and towns with endless stretches of darkness between. Sleep tried to come, though it brought vivid flashes of the days before that sent her starting back to consciousness every time.

Lily shifted on the seat, and she glanced over to see the girl studying something out the front window.

The growl of the muffler faded and the headlights went dark as Elias turned the van up a gravel drive toward a country church situated beneath towering trees. A flurry of birds burst from the steeple, the screeching animals abandoning their night roost to the wizards coming near, and the bells clanged as they were bumped by the panicked flight. Elias' eyes flicked upward in annoyance at the noise, and the van sped up as he guided it around the building and then stopped just shy of the light cast by a lamp above the back door.

The van clunked as Elias shoved the gearshift into park and, a moment later, the noise of the engine died. "Stay here," he said, glancing at her in the rearview mirror.

She nodded. He cast a quick look farther back to Nathaniel, and then climbed out.

Minutes slid past.

Elias emerged from the back door and waved a hand for them to follow.

Shoving open his door, Cornelius got out and then stepped back to the side of the vehicle. The door ground open, the old track beneath it protesting loudly as the rust gave way.

"Come on," Ashe said, nudging Lily ahead of her. Nervously, Lily looked to Cole, meeting his eyes where she wouldn't even look at Ashe's own, and she only climbed from the van when the young man nodded as well.

Ashe's stomach clenched and, angrily, she ordered herself to calm down. She was better than jealousy, especially when there wasn't anything going on. Lily was just worried the boy wasn't coming too.

She was being ridiculous to let that bother her.

Pushing the discomfort from her face, she glanced back as Nathaniel forced the door closed. As he moved past her toward the church, she stepped aside and looked to Lily.

The girl was watching Cole, and trailed him instantly when the boy headed after Nathaniel.

Ashe tried to keep breathing.

Cool air laden with the smell of dust and polished wood pressed against her as she followed Elias into the building, and above the short flight of steps on the opposite side of the entryway, shadows obscured the hall. Elias lifted his hand and Lily gasped as electricity crackled around his palm, the sparks racing in tight circles till they gathered into a sphere of sustained blue glow.

"It's alright," Ashe told her as Nathaniel followed suit with a light of his own.

Appearing as utterly unconvinced as ever, Lily said nothing. With a barely repressed grimace, Ashe motioned for her to follow Elias. Beyond the steps, an oak door sealed off the end of the hallway, though an inset window gave a view of the room beyond. The hinges moved soundlessly when Elias pushed open the door, and the light in his hand played across the long rows of pews. Leaded glass windows lined the sanctuary, their colors muted to near black by the darkness outside, and the thick maroon carpet swallowed their footsteps as Elias led the way into the room.

"Bathrooms past the doors on the far end," he said quietly. "And an emergency exit to the left there."

He jerked his chin toward a narrow door halfway down the length of the sanctuary and then turned back to them. His gaze swept Cole and Cornelius, and then landed on Nathaniel. His eyebrow twitched up in the faint blue light.

The larger wizard tilted his head briefly toward Cornelius.

"Come on," Elias said to Cole. "Help me get food and blankets."

Without waiting, he headed for the doors at the end of the sanctuary. Jaw muscles jumping, Cole glanced toward Lily and then followed.

Ashe didn't look away from the young man till the doors closed at his back.

Time crawled by. At her side, Nathaniel eyed Cornelius, keeping the man at a distance. Shadows hung strange and heavy in the ceiling arches, and the silence echoed with the residual energy of people, motion, and sound.

She shivered, the seconds creeping past with almost physical pressure.

The doors swung open as Elias came in carrying crackers, jelly, and bottles of water. Loaded down with brightly colored fleece blankets, Cole trailed several steps behind. Twitching his chin toward the pews, Elias left him to put down the blankets while he crossed the distance to her.

"Dinner's served," he said with a rueful glance to the rough sandwich ingredients.

Ashe paused.

"I left money in the kitchen," he supplied, reading her hesitation.

She took the food. Herding Lily ahead of her, she walked over to the steps to the altar.

The crunching of the crackers broke the silence as, a few minutes later, she sat with Lily on the carpeted stairs. Small though it was, the meal dulled the hunger she hadn't known was gnawing at her and gratefully, she closed her eyes.

Lily shifted uncomfortably on the dense carpet.

Ashe glanced over and then tracked the girl's gaze to the rest of the sanctuary. Nathaniel leaned on the banister several feet away, while Elias rested a shoulder against a window frame. Radiating aplomb, Cornelius sat on one of the pews, looking for all the world as though he'd chosen the centrally visible spot of his own accord. Watching them all, Cole quietly ate a sandwich near the rear of the room.

Lily never took her gaze off the boy.

Drawing a breath, Ashe set her bottle of water aside. "Lily?" she asked softly.

The little girl didn't answer.

"Are you okay?"

Lily looked down and Ashe's stomach clenched.

"Is it what happened with Old Bill?"

The girl fidgeted, her eyes twitching from Cole to Nathaniel. Half-formed answers flitted across her face, none of them making it all the way to the open.

Nausea moved through her and Ashe drew a short breath, trying to quash the feeling. She wanted to hope that whatever happened, Lily wouldn't have seen it. That Cole might have been able to spare her, or perhaps that it hadn't been as bad as she feared.

Because given what she knew wizards were capable of, the possibilities were truly frightening.

"You can talk to me, Lil," she said, worry filtering into her tone. "Whatever it is."

The girl's face crumpled. Sharply, she shoved away from the steps and ran from the room.

Cole rose quickly and disappeared out the door after her.

Speechless, Ashe stared.

"What the–" Elias started.

He cut off as Ashe stood, her eyes still locked on the swinging sanctuary doors.

"Your majesty?" Nathaniel asked, clearly torn between following them and staying with her.

"G-go," she stammered, too surprised to hide her confusion. "Make sure they…"

Nathaniel let the partial order be enough. Swiftly, he strode after the girl.

Stunned, Ashe watched him leave.

———— ◆ ————

He knew the wizards would be after him in a heartbeat, but he didn't care. As he burst through the swinging doors to the lobby, Cole saw Lily stumble to a halt and cast a lost look down the halls stretching away on either side. Moving fast, he crossed the distance between them and took her arm, pulling her along as he jogged down the hall and slipped into the nursery where he'd found the blankets. Without pause, he headed for the closet and tugged her into the shadows, closing the door behind them.

The light switch surrendered to his fumbling. Blinking in the glare, he yanked a dusty towel down from the heights of the shelving and kicked it swiftly into place around the base of the door, praying it blocked the light.

"What was that?" he asked, turning to Lily. "She asked about the staff, didn't she?"

Swallowing, Lily nodded.

"What'd you say?"

Anger tinged the anguish on the little girl's face. "You lied," she said desperately and then she shook her head, as though she couldn't get past the idea. "To *Ashley*. Why?"

He exhaled sharply, knowing they had moments till the wizards found them.

"It's not Ashley, okay? It's the others. Lily, they…"

Cole grimaced. He didn't want to lie to the kid. And truth was, it really wasn't about Ashe, or even Lily. It was about holding the wizards and this whole damn mess at bay till he could figure out who the bad guys were.

And keeping them both safe till then.

"We don't know if we can trust them," he continued honestly. "Any of them. Even if Ashe says we can… they could be lying to her too."

Lily looked away.

"You can't tell them the truth, Lily. Not even Ashe. Not yet."

"Why? If they're lying to her, then–"

"Trust me," he said, feeling like a bastard for all that he knew there wasn't any other way. "Please. You have to do this, to keep Ashe safe as much as anything. These are the Carnegeans we're talking about, remember?"

The girl hesitated. "They'll hurt her?" she asked, her voice small. "We–"

The door nearly ripped from its hinges as Nathaniel yanked it open.

"Get out," the man snarled, glaring daggers at Cole as Lily shrank back.

Cole didn't move. He could see the dilemma raging in the man's eyes. More than anything, the wizard wanted to tear the girl away from him.

But she was some kind of royalty, same as her sister. And Ashe wouldn't take kindly to the kid being hurt, or scared more than she already was.

It was strange how even that tiny amount of vicarious power made things ever-so-slightly better.

Cole reached down and took Lily's hand. "In a sec," he said neutrally.

Nathaniel's face darkened. Deliberately taking his eyes from the man, Cole looked at the girl, forcing his face to give no sign of how his heart was pounding.

"Okay?" he asked her quietly.

She swallowed again, her gaze darting to the wizard. She nodded.

Cole glanced back to Nathaniel. "After you."

The man's expression could have cut stone. With rigid control, he stepped away from the door, letting Cole lead Lily from the closet.

As Cole pushed the sanctuary door open, Ashe surged to her feet, her face flashing through a gamut of fear, confusion, and relief with a speed he would have thought impossible. Smothering the expressions with almost equal rapidity, she cast a hurried glance to the others.

His eyebrow twitched with irony, though he stilled it quickly lest the linebacker see. He wasn't the only one busy hiding everything from the wizards.

The girl was scared to death they'd see her have a damn emotion.

"You," Nathaniel growled, putting a hand on Cole's shoulder to stop him from going farther. "Over there."

Jaw muscles jumping, Cole contemplated the odds of shrugging off the man's grip and concluded he'd probably just get his shoulder dislocated for his trouble. If not worse. Taking a careful breath, he glanced to Lily and nodded.

Hesitantly, she headed toward her sister, looking back every few steps. Exhaling, he started for the far side of the room, obliquely grateful when the wizard's hand fell away.

This couldn't last.

Cole grimaced at the thought as he sank onto the slick wood of the pew. He knew he wouldn't be stuck here forever. His dad was going to be looking for those girls and him, same as always. And given that he knew Cole was with them, he wouldn't expect them to travel fast, since portals were–

He stopped, true shock taking the breath from his lungs for the first time in – well, a few hours, anyway. But he couldn't believe he hadn't thought of it. Hadn't considered that…

Oh God. His dad probably thought he was dead.

Victor had seen them go through the portal. And of course he knew Cole was a cripple. So he must've thought that when Ashe had tried to save his life, she'd actually…

Cole managed a rough breath as his gaze slid to the wizards. Silently, Elias disappeared back into the lobby, pausing only to still the swinging door behind him as he went. In the shadow of the windows, Nathaniel stood watch while, with the same expression that made everything look as though it was his own intention, Cornelius lay down on a pew. Ashe was spreading a fleece blanket on the floor by the baptistery and, on the steps to the altar, Lily sat, her petite form small on the wide stairway.

The Blood would be coming, and not just because of whatever they'd wanted the girls for in the first place. And while he didn't exactly care about anyone out there besides his dad, or trust anyone here besides the kid and possibly Ashe, that wasn't really the point.

Cole swallowed, his gaze moving to the darkness beyond the fractured view of the leaded glass.

There wasn't a chance in hell he'd be getting any sleep tonight.

———— ◆ ————

Sunrise crept across the windows, gradually setting the myriad colors of the stained glass alight. Like a retreating tide, the shadows slunk beneath the pews and into the corners of the room, taking with them the heavy silence of the sanctuary.

With her back resting on the wood-paneled wall of the baptistery, Ashe sighed. The sunlight felt strange after so many hours of darkness, but she knew it was only exhaustion. She'd spent enough all-nighters in the library at the factory to know. But she hadn't wanted to sleep. Every time she started to drift off, the shadowy figures of the artificial trees and various podiums around her had transformed into shapes to populate her nightmares.

It had made for a long night.

She glanced up as the sanctuary door swung open, admitting Elias back into the room. For the better part of the night, he'd stayed in the lobby, watching the world through the broad glass double doors fronting the church, while Nathaniel stood guard on the sanctuary.

Though he hadn't been the only one. She hadn't seen Cole stir from his surveillance of the windows all night.

"We should get going," Elias said as he came near, his quiet voice breaking the stillness. "Church office'll be open in a few hours."

She nodded and then eased away from the wood paneling. Electrified numbness tingled down her legs with the motion and she hissed through her teeth, freezing as she waited for her muscles to wake up. With a sympathetic wince, Elias reached down and helped her to her feet.

On her bed of rainbow-patterned fleece blankets, Lily groaned and opened her eyes. Blinking, she glanced around and then stopped moving as she caught sight of the wizards.

"It's okay," Ashe said at the intense caution that flashed through her sister's eyes, stronger than it'd been even the night before. "We're just heading out soon."

Lily turned away, her expression unchanged.

Ashe had to fight to keep from looking to Cole, though there wasn't much point. She could feel his stare pinned on them anyway. Lily hadn't spoken since coming back with him, and she could only conclude it was because of something the boy had said or done.

And all the excuses or alternate possibilities in the world weren't making that suspicion go away.

"Where are we going?" she asked, working to focus.

"There's a—" Elias started.

On a pew near the center of the room, Cornelius sat up. Tiredly, he ran a hand over his face and then glanced toward the altar.

She could see the anger in his eyes, though his impassive face gave almost no sign, and she could imagine the glares Elias and Nathaniel must've been giving him. His gaze flicked over them, landing on her last and for a moment, the anger faded into the same pained and nearly desperate look she'd seen by the van the day before.

But the wizards were watching, and she could tell he felt it. Without a word, he smothered the expression and rose, heading for the lobby.

Growling a curse under his breath, Elias glanced to Nathaniel and then started after him.

"It's okay," Ashe said, not taking her eyes from Cornelius.

The two men looked back at her.

"Just… watch Lily," she finished quietly.

The little girl made an anxious noise. Putting a hand on Lily's shoulder briefly, Ashe gave her an attempt at a smile, though she knew it probably wouldn't help anything, and then followed Cornelius from the room.

She could feel Cole's gaze tracking her the whole way.

In the lobby, Cornelius stood beside the glass doors, watching the empty road running past the church lawn.

"Hey," she called, pausing by the oak door.

He didn't move.

"We should really–"

"I know," he interrupted sharply.

She blinked, taken back for a heartbeat before irritation surged. Casting a half glance toward the sanctuary, she scoffed. "Then come back–"

His hand twitched up and then he looked over, a beseeching expression flickering across his face before he dropped his gaze to the ground, seeming for all the world as though he was struggling to find what to say.

Letting the rest of her words die, she eyed him warily.

"I…" He swallowed. "I was mistaken, your highness. About a great deal. And I…"

He trailed off, and when he spoke again, the formal tone was gone. "I'm sorry."

She stared at him. He didn't look up from the ground.

"How many of the… Blood… are there?" he asked, his voice strained.

Her brow flickered down and she glanced to the sanctuary again before stepping farther into the lobby, letting the door swing shut behind her. "I'm not sure," she answered carefully.

He nodded.

"Are they aware Lily is alive?"

"I don't know."

"We will not let them touch her."

His iron expression faltered as he registered the plural he'd so readily used. Regret flashed in his eyes, so fast she almost missed it, and he turned to the front door.

"Thank you," she said quietly.

He nodded again.

"We should go," she told him.

His gaze didn't leave the road.

"Which one was it?" he asked, his tone so careful it could have split the glass without leaving a trace.

She swallowed uncomfortably. "The one with the scars."

He glanced back and she could see the question.

"Yeah."

"Thank you."

She looked away.

"And… what you said," he continued. "About Darius and Sebastian."

Her stomach twisted at the memories, but she could hear the truth in his voice. He asked, but he only partly wanted to know.

"We need to get going," she said.

Hesitating briefly, he nodded. "As you say."

He walked back to the sanctuary entrance, and then bowed. "After you, your majesty."

She looked up at him, reading the formality drawn back around him like a coat. He wouldn't ask again. Her answer had been clear. And as for the rest…

The tension of the months of arguments, hurts and lies finally coming to an end pushed on her, making it hard to breathe, and she felt her face mirror his impassivity to protect her from giving any sign. With a tight nod, she headed back into the sanctuary, leaving him to follow.

"So where are we going?" she asked Elias as she neared the stage.

His gaze flicked from her to Cornelius. She waited.

Elias grimaced. "Atlanta. The Council and some of the others have safe houses in the city. Plan is to lay low. Decide what to do from there."

"I can offer a few locations in that area as well," Cornelius said.

Elias regarded him. "Good to know," he allowed.

Cornelius gave an incremental nod of acknowledgement.

"So clean up and get going?" Ashe said briskly.

Elias pulled his gaze from the man. "Yeah."

Without another word, he went to gather the blankets.

At her side, Ashe could feel Nathaniel's glare, but Cornelius gave no sign of noticing. Calmly, he walked to the pew and collected his coat from the seat.

"Your highness," the wizard murmured.

"He's on our side, Nathaniel," she said, watching Cornelius. "He just never believed about the Blood till now."

Unable to look at him for fear of what he'd see in her eyes, she headed after Elias and tried to ignore the feeling of Nathaniel's disagreement following her across the room.

Chapter Three

———◆———

With the blankets returned to the nursery and the sandwich ingredients packed for the van, they emerged into the early morning sunlight. Mist hung over the fields across from the church, adding to the morning's silence and, as the van pulled back onto the country road, no other cars could be seen.

Miles and cities rolled past, accompanied by the rumble of the muffler and the occasional shower of foam from the tears in the ceiling. After a while, Lily started braiding the tattered threads of the seat fabric and interspersing her weaving with larger bits of foam, though ultimately even that distraction proved too boring to continue for long.

As the clock on the dash ticked past three and traffic clogged the highway around them for miles, Elias sent the van down an off-ramp into Atlanta. Rolling hills covered in cement and asphalt surrounded them, interspersed with leafy trees and buildings of gleaming steel and glass. Signs for loan stores gave way within a few blocks to fresh new cafés and salons, which vanished almost instantly into neighborhoods straight out of suburban fantasies. Apartment complexes followed, each built into the bones of older buildings or on top of them.

The van pulled over.

Wincing at the screech of the rusted door, Ashe climbed out into the oppressive heat and then circled with Lily to the other side of the van. By the driver's side door, Elias waited for them, and when Nathaniel and Cole appeared as well, he wasted no time.

"Anything?"

A hint of a glower showed on Cole's face, but he glanced around the street nonetheless.

"No."

Elias' mouth tightened, but without any option except to take Cole's word, he headed into the brick apartment building. A narrow stairwell wound up through the six stories of apartments, and steel fire doors sealed off any sound from the halls beyond. At the top floor, Elias tugged open the door and strode quickly toward the far end of the hallway.

Eggshell-white walls and pale hardwood floors greeted them as they entered the apartment, and the twenty-foot high ceiling made their every step echo. A stiff white couch sat in the center of the room, facing a flat-panel television affixed to one wall, while dust-covered chrome appliances with their manufacturer's stickers still attached waited in the shadows of the kitchen to the left of the entryway. Twin doors of light wood stood open on the right, leading to bedrooms, the only occupants of which were bare mattresses on steel-framed beds.

Ashe glanced down to see Lily blinking blearily at the apartment. "Come on," she said to the girl, casting a quick look to Nathaniel and then heading for the nearer of the two bedrooms.

"Blankets and pillows in the closet," Elias called.

She nodded without turning around. Leaving the girl sitting on the mattress, she pulled open the closet door and then hauled down the plastic storage bags holding the bedding. A wave of dust cascaded down with the blankets and she retreated, coughing.

While she made the bed, she could hear Nathaniel ordering Cole to stay away from the room, though if the young man had a response, it was too low to make out. Seated on the couch, Elias was calling Katherine on his cell as, across the room, Cornelius investigated the kitchen cabinets one by one.

"Here you go," Ashe said, folding the coverings down. Wordlessly, Lily tugged off her shoes and then climbed beneath the blankets and laid her head on the pillow with a tired sigh.

Ashe sank onto the edge of the bed and then brushed a piece of Lily's dark hair from her cheek. "You doing okay, kiddo?"

The relaxation vanished from Lily's face and her eyes skirted the open door. In the living room, murmurs from the television rose, obscuring the wizards' voices.

"They're friends, Lil," Ashe said, a touch of pleading creeping into her voice. "We're safe with them."

The girl didn't appear reassured.

Ashe paused, thinking. "Do you remember the stories of the night Mom died?"

Lily nodded warily.

"Cornelius was there." Lily blinked at the words. "He watched over us both because Dad asked him to. He made sure we were safe. Elias and Nathaniel…" Ashe hesitated. "That man at the factory, the one who said I was crazy? He did a lot of horrible things, and when I found out, he locked me up. Nathaniel and Elias helped me escape, even though he probably would have killed them for it."

She bent slightly, trying to catch the little girl's eye. "They're not bad people. No matter what he says, they're not."

Lily looked away.

"What's going on, Lil?" Ashe asked quietly.

Conflict twisting her face, Lily squirmed beneath the blankets. "It's just–"

In the other room, Elias swore vehemently.

Ashe spun, but nothing else followed. Through the doorway, she could see Cornelius frozen by the kitchen, staring into the living room.

"Stay here," she told Lily. She rose to her feet and crossed to the door, peering cautiously into the room beyond.

To a person, everyone's eyes were locked on the television.

Flames engulfed the skeletal remains of a three-story building, making the arcs of water rushing from the firemen's hoses seem to exist for nothing more than show. Red and blue lights chased themselves in circles above ambulances, and fire trucks and police cars were scattered throughout the building's parking lot. Dense smoke darkened the midday sky and in the strange twilight, the reporter in her lime skirt suit and matching jewelry looked grossly out of place.

The woman's commentary was nonsensical as well, filled with empty hypotheses of children playing with firecrackers or candles left alone. After the first few words, Ashe ignored her, looking instead to Elias as he rose from the couch. Distractedly, the man paced across the room, thumbing on his phone as he moved. She swallowed hard, watching him wait as the other line rang.

"Councilor," Nathaniel said.

Elias turned, looking from the large wizard to the screen. The cameras cut to the studio, only to switch quickly to shots of a small bungalow in ruins, its soot-stained and crumbled walls long since abandoned by the firemen.

The phone still by his ear, Elias growled a curse. Drawing a breath, he waited a moment more and then hung up. "Felix isn't answering," he said shortly as he dialed another number.

Nathaniel's jaw tightened. He glanced to Ashe and then strode across the room, heading for the window beside Lily's bed. Swiftly, he scanned the street and then tugged the curtain closed.

"Laurence either," Elias continued, fury simmering in his tone.

"Does anyone know of this location?" Cornelius asked.

"No."

Cornelius took out his phone.

"What's going on?" Lily called worriedly.

Ashe's heart jumped at the sound of the little girl's voice. Regrouping quickly, she pasted the most reassuring smile she could muster onto her face and looked back into the bedroom. "Nothing, kiddo. Just try to get some sleep, eh?"

She glanced to Nathaniel. Swiftly, she twitched her head to Lily and then toward the closet door. Face darkening, he balked, unwilling to consider leaving without her, and then finally nodded at the insistent look in her eyes.

Fighting to keep from showing how she was trembling, she turned back to the living room. From the corner of her eye, she could see Cole by the second bedroom, his hand gripping the doorframe and his gaze locked on the screen. In the kitchen and by the sofa, Cornelius and Elias had gone silent, their faces telling her all she needed to know.

They'd been sold out. Someone, somewhere had known enough of where the Merlin would run to exchange their own safety for the information.

And now the survivors were paying the price.

She swallowed hard, her stomach quivering as the television played on, showing flames twisting to the accompaniment of the reporter's endless questions while telephone calls rang without anyone on the other end of the line.

———— ◆ ————

He knew it was his dad and he could tell the others did too.

Fingers digging into the doorframe, Cole watched as the perfectly coiffed reporter babbled on, her expression emitting the false intensity of someone who wanted to convey empathy while having lost nothing at all. Staging left, she turned to a fireman and began asking inane questions of the blaze's origin that Cole knew were bound to be answered wrong.

The camera cut to footage of a sobbing toddler clutching his blanket while the building behind him burned.

Cole thought he was going to be sick.

Drawing a rough breath, he retreated from the screen into the empty bedroom. Cold white walls and steel stared back at him, and through the window, the pale blue sky gave no hint there were fires burning somewhere in town.

The Blood would find them, whatever Elias said.

Grimacing, Cole scrubbed a hand over his hair. There were easily several dozen innocent people in this building, and whether it was the wizards or the Blood who started the fight, those innocents would undoubtedly get hurt. And that didn't even bring into it the eight-year-old in the next room who'd probably have to watch her sister or a lot of other people die.

He had to do something.

His gaze returned to the window. Placed on the adjacent side of the building from the window in Lily's room, the view overlooked the narrow alley between the apartments and the shorter building next door.

And just beyond the glass pane, a rusting fire escape clung to the brick wall.

He had to believe his dad would listen to him. Eight years couldn't have changed the man that much, regardless of the war and everything else they'd been through. And thus he could explain to him that, whatever the hell was going on, Lily had nothing to do with it and Ashe wasn't like the rest. Hopefully, anyway. Whatever started this mess, it could end without another building in flames or a bunch of innocent people getting killed.

Swallowing hard, he looked back through the doorway. Elias was pacing, one hand clenching into a fist while the other clutched the phone. By the kitchen, Cornelius hung up and then began dialing another number. Elias glanced to him.

"William?" he asked shortly.

"Alive. Getting out of town."

Elias nodded and resumed pacing.

Cole exhaled slowly and listened for sounds from the next room, though Ashe and the linebacker had barely budged since the news came on. He doubted they'd leave Lily's proximity any time soon. Carefully, he slid toward the window and thumbed the dusty lock. Hot air pressed against him as the window opened and nervously, he cast a glance to the living room.

For the moment, the wizards were out of view.

A pang of remorse hit him, despite the fact he knew there was nothing he could do. He couldn't have explained this to Lily or warned her that he was going to leave, and not only because, thanks to Nathaniel, he couldn't even get into the same room with her anymore. Explaining meant telling her the truth about his dad, and he couldn't do that. Not now. Maybe not ever.

He just hoped she'd forgive him when he saw her again.

Swiftly, he swung a leg over the windowsill and climbed onto the fire escape, only to freeze as the grating creaked under his weight. A heartbeat passed. The metal didn't move again. Remembering how to breathe, he hurried down the switchbacks of ladders to the ground. Hitting the concrete, he paused, taking the barest second to glance at the empty window above.

And then he ran.

❖

Ashe let out a breath as the news mercifully cut to a commercial and brought an end to the litany of disasters no one could seem to explain. A man had been found dead outside a local eatery, while nearby, a four-car pileup on the interstate had resulted from a woman flinging herself off an overpass. Police were asking residents for tips, though preliminary evidence suggested a lovers' quarrel that led the woman to kill herself after she'd murdered the man.

It was painfully neat. And while the police hadn't released names, it didn't really matter. Survivors of the ambush by the restaurant had already called Cornelius with word that both victims were Merlin anyway.

Raking a hand through her hair, she looked away from the screen.

In the living room, Elias was still trying to reach the others, though Cornelius had switched a few minutes before to taking the calls coming in. Between the two men, communication now consisted of terse comments of names and statuses as they ran through a list of everyone they could think to reach.

Katherine was okay. Ermengarde and the most seriously wounded were as well. The groups with the youngest of the children had still been on their way here, as the little ones couldn't travel by portal after portal for long without becoming ill. A couple phone calls ago, the kids had all been successfully diverted elsewhere. Of the Council, half of them were on the run again, bringing their constituencies in tow.

The rest were on the way to the morgue.

A shudder ran through her and she fought to keep it from being seen. Elias said no one knew of this place and she was working hard to let that be a comfort. As much as it could be, in any case.

Across the room, Cornelius gave a look of annoyance to a cheerfully loud commercial. Swiftly, he muted the volume with the remote before returning to his call, bringing silence to the apartment for the first time in what felt like a year.

Or near silence.

Her brow furrowed as she glanced to the next room. The sound of traffic carried through the door, far louder than it should've been, and as she stepped from the bedroom, she felt the brush of warm summer wind drifting into the apartment. Pulse quickening, she rounded the door.

The other bedroom was empty. The window by the fire escape was open. She swore under her breath as she rushed across the room and caught herself on the sill.

Nothing moved in the alley. Her gaze raked the rooftops and streets, but of the few pedestrians strolling down the sidewalk, not one glanced her way.

"Your highness?" Nathaniel called.

She shoved away from the frame and raced back to the door. "Cole's gone," she said to the room at large.

Elias cut off midsentence, with Cornelius a heartbeat behind.

"What?" Lily cried.

Scrambling out of the bed, the girl stared at her.

"What do you mean 'gone'?" Lily asked, clutching the footboard as if to steady herself.

Ashe looked between the wizards and her sister. She strode into the bedroom. "Cole left, Lily. He climbed out the window and he left. Why?"

The little girl's expression melted from horror to worry, and her eyes darted to Nathaniel. Ashe followed Lily's gaze and then twitched her head toward the door. Reluctantly, the wizard left the room, closing the door behind him.

"Lily," Ashe pressed.

The girl eyed the door. "It's those bad people, isn't it? They're making the fires the people on the news are talking about."

Ashe hesitated and then nodded. The worry deepened on Lily's face.

"We have to stop him," Lily pleaded as she grabbed her shoes and tugged them on.

Ashe's brow furrowed. "Stop him from what? Lil, answer me already. Why'd Cole leave?"

"He's going to try to stop them. To protect us. He must be. But they'll hurt him and maybe–"

The girl cut off, breathing hard.

Ashe stared at her. "Why would he do that?"

"Because they're *horrible*!" Lily cried as though it was desperately obvious. "And he's so… he always… he knows his dad was a king so maybe he just thought he needed to…"

Her face crumpled with fear. Ashe barely noticed.

"His dad was…" she repeated slowly. "Wait. What?"

"They killed his dad too, just like ours. Only his was the Taliesin king."

Ashe trembled.

"Elias!" she yelled, spinning and ripping open the door.

Magic flared around the wizards as she tore into the room.

"Get us out of here now!"

Without hesitation, Cornelius threw a hand toward the other bedroom door and darkness swirled instantly in the opening. Elias looked from him to the portal and back.

"Safe house," Cornelius snapped. "Go!"

"What are you doing?" Lily cried.

Ashe didn't answer. Rushing across the room, she grabbed the little girl's arm. "I'll explain later."

Lily tugged away. "I'm not leaving! What if he comes back? We can't–"

"His dad killed Mom!" Ashe snapped.

The girl's face went slack with shock. Taking advantage of the brief lapse in resistance, Ashe hauled on Lily's arm, dragging her from the bedroom. Regrouping, the little girl balked, shaking her head as she dug her heels in. "But–"

With a snarl, Ashe swung Lily up into her arms and then raced into the void.

Dense shag carpet caught her feet as she hit the other side and she stumbled, already looking around. Wood paneling lined the walls of the windowless room, and cobwebs hung in the corners. Only an ancient television occupied the space, its cracked screen giving little hope that it was usable, and through the bedroom door, not even that much furniture could be seen.

"What's going on?" Elias demanded.

Letting go of the struggling girl, Ashe glanced back as the portal spiraled and disappeared. "Where are we? How far is this from the other apartment?"

"A few miles," Cornelius said.

"Can we get farther?"

"Your highness, what the hell is going on?" Elias asked.

"Cole's dad is king of Taliesin."

For a heartbeat, the wizards froze. A curse escaped Elias.

"Does anyone know about this place?" she asked Cornelius.

"No."

"Can they track the portal at all?"

Cornelius shook his head.

Exhaling, she ran a hand over her hair as she looked to the other side of the room. Eyeing them all, Lily had backed herself as far into the corner as she could without running into the cobwebs.

Elias cleared his throat. "How much does Cole know?"

Ashe didn't turn around. "Not sure."

Ignoring the wizards, she headed toward Lily.

"I don't believe you," the girl mumbled.

"Come on," Ashe said, jerking her chin toward the bedroom.

Grudgingly, Lily went. Ashe glanced over her shoulder as she followed.

"You're sure no one can find this place?" she asked Cornelius.

"We'll keep watch," he answered.

She nodded and then pushed the door closed behind her.

"Has Cole been in communication with his dad?" she asked.

The girl looked away.

"Lily!"

Turning back, Lily treated her to a baleful glare. "He's not bad."

For a heartbeat, Ashe couldn't determine if she meant Cole or Jamison, and then she decided it didn't matter. She knew the look Lily was giving her. Drawing a breath, she paused, forcing herself to slow down and try another tack.

"I'm not saying he is."

"Yes, you are!"

"No," Ashe responded carefully. "I'm not. I… I'm just worried, Lil. And I need you to help me not be. Okay?"

Lily wouldn't meet her gaze.

"Has he been talking to his dad?"

The girl shook her head. Ashe drew a breath for what felt like the first time in minutes.

"Are you sure?"

The brief glower was answer enough.

"What can you tell me?"

Lily clasped her arms behind her back and shifted her weight from one foot to the other.

"I need your help, Lily. Please. What's going on?"

Shrugging a shoulder, the girl didn't meet her eyes. "He can't talk to his dad. He died a long time ago."

Ashe paused. "Okay," she allowed, setting aside for the moment the fact the statement wasn't true. "And Cole told you that?"

Lily nodded.

"So when you say he's gone to help us," Ashe continued, "what's he doing?"

"What I *told* you," Lily replied, her voice trembling. "He's going to try to stop the bad people. He always… he always protects me. He doesn't let bad things happen. And those Blood…" She trailed off, fear derailing her thoughts. "We have to help him. They might… they could…"

Biting her lip, Lily struggled not to cry.

"They're not going to hurt him, Lil," Ashe said quietly.

The girl looked up.

"Cole's dad… he's more than the king of Taliesin. He's the leader of the Blood. And…" She paused, nausea spinning through her stomach as the look on Cole's face at the factory finally fell into place. "I'm pretty sure Cole knows this."

Her brow furrowing in horror, Lily stared.

"His dad's name is Victor Jamison, and he's not dead. He pretended that people killed him so no one would come looking for him, because some wizards took Cole away and Jamison wanted him back."

She wetted her lips. "And he killed Mom. Grandma. Grandpa." She drew a breath. "Victor Jamison tried to kill our whole family."

Silence fell between them.

"I don't believe you," Lily whispered.

"It's true. I wish it wasn't, but–"

"Cole said his dad was a good person!" Lily protested. "And he wouldn't lie to me. He wouldn't!"

Ashe paused. She couldn't push the girl much farther. "Maybe Cole just thought he was."

Lily floundered and then looked away.

"Did he tell you anything about where he was going?"

The girl shook her head.

"What about getting in touch with him? Did he say anything about that?"

Sorrowfully, Lily shook her head again.

Ashe looked away, trying to marshal her thoughts. "Okay," she said, nodding as much to herself as the girl. "Then this is what we're going to do. We're getting out of here. As far from Atlanta and all this as possible. But I need you to promise me something. If Cole tries to contact you or if you see him again—" She bent to catch the girl's eye. "—you can't talk to him, okay? And you stay away from him. Just for now. Alright?"

The little girl looked like she felt sick.

"Lily?"

"He's not bad," she mumbled.

Forcing herself to breathe, Ashe fought down the responses that rose to mind. "Okay," she agreed.

Lily eyed her.

"He's going to be fine, Lil. It's us I'm worried about. I need you to promise you'll stay away from him."

"But—"

"Lily."

The girl dropped her gaze to the floor. "Okay."

Ashe hesitated. "And," she continued carefully. "I need to know if he was telling the truth about where you found the staff."

Exhaling in frustration, Lily looked away.

"Please," Ashe urged. "It's important."

Lily's gaze went to the door. Her lip slid between her teeth as anxiety gradually subsumed her expression again.

"Lily?"

"Where he said," she answered softly.

Ashe paused. "Really?"

A desperate noise exploded from Lily. "What?" she cried, her voice breaking. "Are you calling me a liar too? He's not a bad person and neither am I, but you just keep–"

"Okay!" Ashe yelled.

Breathing hard, Lily cut off.

"Okay," Ashe repeated more calmly. "I'm sorry. I just… you seemed…" She regrouped, shaking her head at herself. "I'm sorry."

Lily looked up, her expression more anguished than enraged. "I just don't want you to get hurt," she whimpered.

"I'm not going to get–" Ashe started, and then the automatic response caught up with her. She swallowed, trying not to feel the phantom twinge where Harris' bullet had torn through barely a week before. "I'm careful, Lil," she amended quietly. "More than you know."

Lily's lower lip trembled. Wordlessly, Ashe crossed the room and kneeled down, wrapping the girl in her arms.

"I just… I can't… with Daddy, I just…"

Pained, Ashe closed her eyes, bullets having nothing to do with the tightness in her chest. "Shh," she whispered.

Lily buried her face in her sister's shoulder.

"We're okay, kiddo," Ashe told her.

When the girl didn't respond, Ashe pushed her back gently and looked into Lily's teary eyes. "Hey. You calling me a liar?"

Lily sniffled and shook her head, an uncertain smile hovering around the edge of her lips.

"Good," Ashe said.

Taking a steadying breath, she climbed back to her feet and then ruffled the girl's hair, producing a cry of protest from Lily, who instantly started smoothing her black waves. Her lip twitching, Ashe looked away and her gaze caught on the door. Outside, she could hear the faint sounds of Elias and Cornelius talking.

The nascent smile died. "Wait here for me?" she asked Lily. "I just need to tell them what's going on."

Lily looked as though she'd rather Ashe didn't, but she just nodded.

"I'll be right back."

The girl didn't answer.

Running a hand through her hair and trying to school her features back into something resembling impassivity, Ashe headed for the door.

"So?" Elias demanded immediately.

Ashe glanced to Nathaniel. Without a word, the man disappeared into the bedroom.

"She doesn't know where he's gone," Ashe said once the door closed. "She thought Jamison was dead."

Elias let out a breath slowly.

"Will Cole try to reach her?" Cornelius asked.

"She promised she'll stay away from him if he does," Ashe replied. Her mouth tightened at their expressions. "And yeah. I know. But it's the best I could get from her. She refuses to believe he isn't just trying to protect her."

For a moment, no one spoke.

"Could he be?" Elias asked finally.

The wizard held up his hands at the look she gave him.

"Hear me out," he said. "I'm just trying to think this through. He had your sister with him for over five months, and he never delivered her to his father in that time. He showed up like a bat out of hell, according to you, on the night your father died, and the Blood nearly killed him for it. He was running *away* from Chaunessy Tower when you met up with him and now…" Elias' brow furrowed at his own thoughts. "What if Lily's not wrong?"

Ashe stared at him.

"We can't take that chance," Cornelius countered.

Elias drew a breath, his expression clearing. "No, you're right." He glanced to Ashe. "What do you want to do?"

"Besides get the hell out of here?" Ashe replied. Exhaling, she paced a few steps away, trying to focus.

"I have numerous connections throughout the Carolinas," Cornelius offered. "It would provide the chance to keep moving for a while."

From the corner of her eye, she could see Elias nod. "Most of the others have headed west and, I hate to say it, but that might lead the Blood to believe we've gone that way as well."

Ashe ignored them as they continued talking. Between the two of them, they could figure out where to go better than she could. And, for the moment, she didn't care anyway.

Cole helping them. A few minutes ago, she'd have readily considered the idea. He'd risked his life to save them at the farmhouse, after all, and he'd obviously taken care of Lily to the point where she wouldn't believe a word against him no matter what his dad had done.

Of course, that was then. There was no telling when he'd found out about his father and things had changed. The look on his face at the factory as much as said he'd wanted to stay to see the man. For that matter, he'd been at Chaunessy just when his dad came to take over. He could have been trying to meet Jamison. He could have been trying to deliver Lily into his hands. He'd left her here for now, sure, but maybe he just hadn't known how to bring the kid along.

And maybe he'd be coming back for her, a dozen Blood wizards in tow.

"Your highness?"

She blinked at the realization Elias had called her several times. "Sorry," she said, struggling to push away the spiraling thoughts. "What?"

"You ready to go?"

She scoffed as she made a beeline toward the other room.

Chapter Four

After a half dozen blocks, he crested a hill and finally caught sight of the smoke on the horizon. Slowing his steps, he stared at the black clouds and tried not to curse the fact the wizards had chosen hot, hilly, and all together huge Atlanta of all places to hide.

Swiping the sweat from his eyes, Cole looked around, but other than a couple wary pedestrians, no one was paying attention to the young man running madly down the street. Trying to look casual, though he knew he was probably failing, he forced himself to slow to a walk.

Feeling every hour of his lack of sleep from the night before, he scanned the street, evaluating his options. He could keep walking, and probably reach the fires by the time the apartments had been rebuilt. Busses weren't much of a choice either, though he saw more than a few speeding past on their way to who-knew-where. Without knowing their schedules or routes, he could as easily end up on the opposite side of town as anywhere near where he wanted to be, and take three hours to get there as well.

Buildings grew in height and age as he walked, and every window felt like it held someone watching. Each glance from passersby put him on edge and he found his gaze darting to the fences and parking meters along the street, hoping to catch sight of an unlocked bike, though the impulse made him feel like a jerk.

He rounded a street corner and paused. A chuckle escaped him.

Before the opulent awning and circle drive of a twenty-story hotel, a trio of taxis waited. Swiftly, he checked the door of the hotel, but through the darkened glass, he couldn't see anyone coming.

He darted for the nearest taxi.

"You free?" he asked as he tugged open the back door and slid inside.

The driver looked back in alarm. "Where to?"

"That, uh, fire," Cole said, pointing in the general direction, though buildings blocked the view.

The man gave him a flat look. "Address, kid."

Freezing, Cole wracked his brain and then pulled an address from fragmented memory, hoping he got it right. The driver's eyebrow twitched skeptically, but after a moment's hesitation, he put the car into gear.

Releasing the breath he hadn't known he'd been holding, Cole sank back into the seat.

The cab twisted through town, weaving a path he knew he'd never be able to retrace. Time slid by, every second chewing away at the chance the Blood would still be nearby. After a century of stoplights and traffic, the cab rounded a corner and the fire trucks finally came into view.

"Just pull over here," Cole said, shifting around to get a better view through the windshield.

The driver eyed him briefly and then did as he was told.

People milled around on sidewalks. Beyond the cordons of yellow and red tape, firemen worked to quiet the smoldering remains. Fragments of the roof draped across the charred bones of the building, sporadically raining debris down on the indistinguishable ashes littering the ground, and below the trees on the far side of the parking lot, EMTs hovered over residents huddled beneath blankets.

But none of the people were glowing, and for the life of him, he couldn't tell if any of the onlookers seemed more like wizards than the others.

"Hey, kid, you going?" the driver asked impatiently.

Cole let out a breath. Somehow, he'd hoped it would just be that easy. Show up and everything would be, if not alright, at least closer to an answer than it'd been thus far. But the Blood were gone, and he had no idea where they were going next.

Though, he realized, he did know where they'd been. And perhaps more than here, in the Taliesin Council headquarters they'd have been inclined to leave people behind.

"Kid!" the driver snapped.

"Is there a bus station near here?"

The man blinked. "Huh?"

"A bus station," Cole repeated. "You know, Greyhound or whatever?"

"You want me to take you to a bus station," the driver stated. "What about this place?"

"My, um, my girlfriend will be there. I thought… it's just that her family lived here, and I was worried she'd come back to help them. But I don't see any of them here, and the bus station was always their emergency meeting place, so–"

The driver held up a hand, cutting off the rest of the explanation. "Whatever, kid." He put the car back into gear.

Cole sighed and sat back again. It felt ridiculous, on some level, to be traveling back across nearly half a dozen states to a place where his dad only might be. The Blood could have left. They could have their own places to hide, miles from anywhere he would think to check.

But as plans went, it was the best he could do.

Gridlock and frequent muttered cursing from the driver later, the cab pulled into the circle drive next to the brown block of the station. Coming to a stop behind another taxi, the man turned in his seat.

"You staying here or you want to head for the zoo next?"

Cole didn't bother to reply. Reaching into his pocket, he fished out the wallet he'd stolen from his uncle Geoffrey a day and a lifetime ago. Crinkled hundred dollar bills shared space with a handful of twenties between the folds and, glancing to the meter, he drew out several of the latter and handed them up to the man.

"Keep the change," he called and then climbed out before the man could respond.

Beneath the garish fluorescent lights, a few travelers glanced up as he peered around the door. Eyeing them, he held his breath, waiting for anyone to strike out.

Nothing happened. The travelers returned to their books and mp3 players, albeit with expressions that hinted they didn't want to be caught staring at the crazy kid.

He swallowed, trying to calm down. No one in the room had even the faintest hint of a glow, and he couldn't feel any suggestion of magic either. Which, on the latter account at least, meant absolutely nothing and he hated the fact. Slowing his steps, he drew a breath and worked to appear casual as he walked over to the ticket counter. An approximation of a smile pulled at his mouth as the attendant glanced up, but from the tired look on her face, his effort was wasted. Radiating boredom, she sold him a ticket for the only bus leaving for Croftsburg, and then raised an eyebrow, waiting for him to go away. Burying a grimace, he took the ticket and headed for the metal seats arrayed in rows down the length of the room.

The clock on the wall seemed to be moving backward and when the call finally rang out to board the bus, he was fairly certain the world itself had come to a screeching halt. Around the room, a motley collection of people stood and gathered their bags before making their way toward the bus. Running a hand over his face in a futile attempt to bring focus back to his bloodshot eyes, Cole rose and followed them out the door.

Brilliant colors lit the clouds as the sun sank behind the city skyline and to the east, darkness was already setting in. Headlights glared from cars hurrying home for the evening and in the deepening twilight, pedestrians faded into the shadows of the buildings.

He wondered if Lily was doing alright.

The thought hurt. Brutally shoving it down, he climbed aboard the bus.

———— ◆ ————

Lights played over the Savannah River and swayed gently above the decks of the boats tethered to the shore. From the street below the apartment, someone laughed before continuing along the sidewalk with their friends.

Sitting in the shadows beside the balcony window, Ashe watched the late night crowd. It'd only been a few hours since she and the others arrived in the riverside apartment, and they couldn't stay long. Halfway through renovations, the apartment would again be filled with construction crews bright and early the next morning.

But it was safe for now.

Ten more calls had come in over the course of the day, though only three had been to report additional attacks. But the surviving Merlin were scared, and as a result, some had begun cutting ties with every other refugee and going to ground in places no one else knew. As a people, they were fragmenting on their own, in addition to being picked apart by the Blood and, try as she might, on some level the diaspora was starting to make her feel like Jamison had already won.

She looked over as the hardwood floor squeaked. In the archway entry to the living room, Cornelius paused, catching sight of her in the darkness. With a glance to Nathaniel by the window on the other side of the room, he crossed to her side.

"I thought you were sleeping," he said quietly.

She didn't answer, returning her gaze to the street.

"We will be leaving early. You would benefit from a few–"

"I know."

Cornelius paused, and then sank down beside her and leaned back against the wall.

"Cole will not find her."

Ashe swallowed and said nothing.

"Lily will always trust you more than him. You are her sister. You cannot–"

"She's scared I'll get hurt," Ashe interrupted. "She's scared I'll die like Dad."

"We will not let that happen."

"You can't promise that."

"My lady–"

She glanced at him. His brow flickered down almost imperceptibly, and he looked away.

Silence fell between them. Somewhere down the street, a jazz band began to play.

"I didn't know what I was doing at the factory, Cornelius," she confessed. "I just…"

She trailed off. Over the past few hours, she'd had to admit it to herself. Taking Lily to the factory had been stupid. Emotional and stupid. She just hadn't wanted to be apart from the girl. And she'd wanted to keep her safe.

Those two things didn't exist in the same world anymore. They hadn't for a long time.

"You still did well."

She drew a breath. "And someone shot me last week."

He looked over at her. She dropped her gaze to the patterns of shadow on her jeans.

"She's scared I'll die," Ashe said. "I'm terrified she will. That someone will try to kill me and hit her instead. But I have to stop Jamison. I can't run. And if I go after the Blood–"

"I know."

His voice was cold though his face was not, and despite his gaze on the middle distance, he didn't seem to be watching the apartment at all.

She looked away. Music twisted and danced through the open window, interspersed with clapping from the crowd. On the couch in the center of the room, Lily rolled over in her sleep and sighed.

"You could send her elsewhere."

Air escaped her, despite the fact the suggestion had been hovering in the back of her mind. She'd just wanted another answer. Something.

But she knew there wasn't anything else.

Lily was a target. Equal or perhaps only slightly less so than her sister by benefit of Ashe's knowledge of how to bind magic. And whether or not she was with the little girl wouldn't stop Lily from being one. Not as long as Jamison was alive.

But if he was distracted…

If he thought there was a better chance of catching Ashe than of scavenger-hunting for the girl across the whole damn world…

Her eyes found Lily in the darkness.

Jamison hadn't won. Not with this. Not while Lily was safe.

She wondered if this was what her father felt like when he'd sent them both away.

"Could you do it?" she asked.

Protests rose on Cornelius' face, each fighting the others to be the first to emerge.

"My place is beside you."

She said nothing.

"Your highness," he pressed.

"She's the only family I have left, Cornelius. I can't let them take her from me too."

He turned away, his gaze catching on Lily asleep on the couch.

"Please," Ashe whispered.

"And what are you going to do, your majesty?"

She didn't answer. His tone left little doubt he was actually wondering anyway.

"I should be here," he said as though she'd spoken.

"You should be protecting the last of the Merlin's Children. One of them, at least." She paused. "How fast can you arrange something?"

A moment passed. "It would take about a week to put everything in place. Perhaps a bit more."

Ashe swallowed. In spite of herself, she'd hoped it would be longer. Several years, maybe. Or never.

She shoved the thought away. Across the room, she could feel Nathaniel watching them as much as he was keeping an eye on the street, and the pressure of his gaze was almost too much to bear. And Lily would be furious. Incensed. She'd never agree.

Assuming anyone told her.

Drawing a sharp breath, Ashe pushed to her feet, suddenly needing to be out of the line of Cornelius and Nathaniel's gazes.

"Do it," she ordered.

"My place should be here, your highness."

She ignored the words, unable to continue the lopsided debate. "Don't tell me where you take her. Just in case."

Her gaze darted to the girl and back. "And don't say anything to Lily."

Before he could respond, she strode from the room, desperately trying to convince herself she wasn't running away.

<hr>

Chaunessy Tower looked in better shape than last he'd seen it, though Cole supposed even quasi-invisible wizards wouldn't want to leave holes blown through the walls and windows forever.

"Keep the change," he said to the cab driver, pushing the money through the grill toward the front seat. Without waiting for the man's reply, and doubting there would have been one anyway, he climbed from the taxi and headed for the revolving door.

The cherry wood front desk in the center of the room was empty, as was the rest of the lobby. Chips and scars still marred the gray marble walls where debris had hit them, though the security cameras near the ceiling had obviously been repaired. In unison, they turned to the door as he stepped inside.

Cole hesitated. It wasn't quite the reception he'd been expecting. It wasn't quite anything.

"Hello?"

His voice bounced off the walls, sounding small in the cavernous room. Somewhere in the distance, the air conditioners kicked on, almost perversely deadening his call with their white-noise hum.

And nothing else happened.

Letting out a breath, he glanced to the cameras. Someone was here, anyway. Or else they'd left behind a perfectly good security system for no reason.

Still eyeing the cameras obliquely, he started across the lobby.

Marble squeaked beneath his shoes, accompanied by the whisper of the fabric of his jeans. The hum of the air conditioners pressed on his ears, impossible to ignore for being the only other sound.

His steps slowed as he neared the opposite side of the lobby. An island of elevators waited ahead, with a hall leading between them, but he barely glanced to the gleaming doors. At the end of the corridor, a black abyss gaped beyond the remnants of a decimated wall. Above the broken hinges of the missing doors, a few lonely brass letters dangled from shredded plaster, and in the darkness, the air-conditioned breeze sent small bits of something skittering down.

The ding of the elevator nearly made him jump out of his skin.

An elevator door rolled to the side. Magic spiked a migraine straight through the back of his skull.

"Hello, Cole."

Wincing, he retreated, but he wasn't fast enough. Three wizards rushed out and encircled him, leaving behind a monster who approached as if he had all the time in the world. Scars and melted flesh distorted half the man's face, though they did nothing for the glow emanating from his skin or the cold distrust in his one normal eye.

"Isn't this a surprise?"

The man could have been commenting on the weather.

Drawing a rough breath, Cole tried to keep all the wizards in sight at once, despite the fact it was impossible. Surrounding him on all sides, the men circled, cutting off any escape.

"Are you alone?"

Cole looked back at the giant who could've given Nathaniel a run for largest wizard he'd yet seen. "Where's my father?"

Humor twitched the man's lip. "Alright," he acquiesced. He stepped to one side, clearing a path to the elevator. "After you."

Cole hesitated, his gaze darting between the wizards and the distant street baking in the summer sun.

It was too late to back out now.

He walked inside the elevator.

———— ◆ ————

"He is not a threat to me, Mason."

Brogan glanced to Jamison. The man didn't turn from the one-way window taking up the majority of the wall.

"You know that's not the point, sir."

"It's been six hours."

"The Merlin would not have just let him leave. They must have an agenda."

Jamison exhaled. On the other side of the glass, the boy seated at the metal table in the center of the bare room shifted uncomfortably on his folding chair.

"Perhaps. But for the moment, I do not care. He is my son. He belongs with me. And I have been kept waiting long enough."

Without another word, Jamison headed for the door.

Brogan's mouth tightened as the door closed, but he made no move to follow. There was only so much arguing he would allow himself since, security issues aside, he couldn't help but understand the king's point of view.

He let his gaze slide to the boy in the other room. The boy who both Jamison and the rest of the Blood had assumed was dead. The boy who had somehow escaped a portal, and then dozens of wizards, only to arrive on their doorstep. They had no explanation. Cole hadn't said a word since they brought him up here, except to ask after Jamison. Any other question was met with silence and an expression that, whether the boy knew it or not, was patently his father.

It was interesting.

With a coldness that could have been cloned from Jamison, the boy glanced over as the door opened. And then he froze.

Sound vanished from the room.

Brogan sighed. The boy was a cripple and the king was no fool. Let Jamison have his privacy, such as it was. Cole didn't present a threat.

His Merlin captors, on the other hand…

Brogan drew out his cell phone. Simeon answered on the first ring.

"Expand the perimeter. You see so much as a Merlin baby, I want it reported."

He hung up. On the opposite side of the glass, Cole rose, sudden uncertainty in the boy's every motion.

Brogan's eyes narrowed.

It was all so very interesting.

Chapter Five

Cole shifted in the metal folding chair, succeeding in almost rocking himself sideways on the uneven legs for the hundredth time in however long it'd been. White walls devoid of anything as helpful as a clock stared back at him from all sides, save the one occupied by what could only be a one-way mirror. Blazing fluorescent lights burned on the ceiling, illuminating every mind-numbing inch of the room and making his reflection look like raccoon-black circles hung beneath his eyes – although the latter might've just been the truth.

He felt like he'd stumbled into a cheap cop movie somewhere between the elevator and here.

Hours had crept by, he was fairly certain. Possibly days. His stomach was gnawing at itself with a determination that left him feeling every single moment since the candy bar he'd snagged at the bus stop, and his head had long since begun to pound in dull rhythm with his heart. The restless night aboard the bus had left him aching all over, though the sharp edge of the chair on his spine wasn't helping anything. And meanwhile, the wizards and the Blood kept coming, asking the same questions about where the Merlin who'd sent him were hiding, as though expecting the sheer repetition to do anything other than drive him insane.

But they said nothing of his father. And thus they got nothing in return.

It was petty revenge and he knew it. But as each passing minute fueled the fear that his dad had died since he'd last seen the man, it'd become the best he could settle for, short of trying to see how the chair and his temper would fare against them.

Though that option was getting more tempting.

The door opened.

He glanced over, idly placing odds as to whether it would be a Blood or Taliesin this time.

"Hey, Cole."

His breath caught.

Gray touched Victor Jamison's temples and a suggestion of weathering showed around the corners of his dark eyes. A thin scar barely an inch long traced his cheekbone and his suit was nicer than anything Cole had ever seen him wear. With one hand on the doorknob, he stood motionless, the glow around him so similar to that around Lily and yet so inexplicably different at the same time, and then he carefully stepped farther into the room.

The door closed.

Air pressure shifted and the silence became deeper than before.

"It's been a long time," Victor said.

Broken syllables tried to order themselves in his mind, and all he could think to do was laugh, though the sound strangled itself before it could emerge.

The council chamber in the moments after his father's arrival flashed through his mind.

Beneath him, the chair rocked and his hand instinctively gripped the metal table. Drawing a breath, he tried to drive the image away. Steadying himself on the table, he rose to his feet.

"Dad," he said.

Victor paused and then crossed the distance between them. With infinite care, he reached out, wrapping Cole in a hug.

Cole froze. Uncertainly, his arms rose and embraced the man. A heartbeat passed, and then Victor pushed him back, holding him at arm's length and looking firmly into his eyes.

"I never stopped searching for you. I want you to know that. Not for a single day."

Cole forced a breath into his lungs. "I know."

Victor hesitated, but he only nodded in response. Still gripping one of Cole's arms, he turned and sank down onto the edge of the table.

Shakily, Cole returned to the chair.

The silence stretched with the awkwardness of a break in a script to which neither of them knew the lines.

"So," Victor said, a hint of tension leaking into his voice. "'How've you been' hardly seems appropriate, don't you think?"

Cole chuckled weakly. He couldn't quite bring himself to look at the man. And all he wanted to do was stare at him.

"They tell me you were in Utah," Victor tried.

"For a while."

"Ah."

Silence set up camp in the middle of the room.

Cole forced his gaze up from the table. "They told me you were dead," he said, a question wandering somewhere in the words.

"I thought you were too."

He tensed, and after a moment, his father looked away, dropping the implicit question.

"I'm sorry," Victor said awkwardly. "I should not have…" He grimaced, and then seemed to regroup. "The wizards. Were they… good to you?"

Cole couldn't figure out how to answer.

"They didn't hurt you?" his father pressed.

"No."

Victor nodded, seeming relieved. Silence returned.

"Did they say anything else about me?" Victor asked after a moment.

Cole's gaze hit the table hard. He could feel his dad growing tense as the seconds passed.

He closed his eyes. This was what he'd wanted. This was what he'd come here for. The chance to ask his father why. To find out the reason behind all the death and destruction from the one man who could tell it to him.

And all he wanted in the whole world was to change the subject, to pretend he hadn't heard or just say nothing, because in this moment, when his dad still hadn't confirmed or denied or done any of the things Cole was afraid he'd do… he didn't know. Not for sure.

Suddenly, that ignorance felt more precious than gold.

"Cole?"

He swallowed, his gaze still on the table. "They said…" An ache moved through him. "They said you started the war."

From the corner of his eye, he saw Victor become still. A moment slid by and then the man drew a breath, folding his hands carefully.

"I did."

Cole looked up.

"I killed the Merlin king," Victor said, his voice becoming meticulously matter-of-fact. "I broke the spell. When the guards came to his defense, an explosion I caused killed much of the Merlin royal family. And started the war."

He stared at his father as suddenly, the air began to share qualities with the concrete walls. Nothing of regret showed on the man's face. No shred of remorse either. Just the acceptance of a job that had to be done.

"Why?"

"You have spent the past few months among the Merlin," Victor stated, partly asking.

Feeling choked, Cole searched for an answer. "A bit," he allowed.

"And the Taliesin," his father continued in the same tone. "They told you I was a madman, or some permutation thereof."

Cole couldn't respond. His dad nodded anyway.

"They have their point of view. And without fail, it works in their favor. But you are going to have to decide for yourself what to believe. I cannot – and will not – try to make up your mind for you. All I ask is that you hear me out, see what I can show you of our side, and then go from there."

Cole nodded, not knowing what else to do.

"Thank you," Victor said.

Silence fell between them.

"I won't lie to you," his dad said finally. "That night the Merlin king died… I knew what I was doing. I knew it was murder, and I knew it would mean war. Mason and I, we intended to remove the Taliesin Council the moment our magic was returned, though at the time, arresting them was all we had in mind.

"Things didn't go the way I planned."

Victor gave him a hint of a rueful smile, but his gaze fell away before Cole could respond.

"At least," he continued. "Not overall. But in terms of killing the Merlin king…" His mouth tightened. "Yes. That went mostly according to plan."

A moment passed. "I don't know what the Taliesin or Merlin told you about Nicholas' death. I don't know what they said about my motives either. Mason and I pretended to be deliverymen and I shot the king when he answered the door. I hadn't ever killed anyone in my life and when I saw the look on his face…" He shook his head. "It was terrible. The worst thing I had seen till that night. And yet, I had no choice."

Cole looked down, his imagination struggling to compete with the memories of the past few days. Seconds crawled by, each one more uncomfortable than the last, till finally he dragged his gaze back to his dad.

"Why?" he asked again.

Victor paused. "Your time with the Merlin. It was spent with the remnants of the royal family, was it not?"

Cole froze. "Some."

"The younger one."

He gave a small shrug.

"And the elder?"

He hesitated. "Not as much."

"What did you think of them?"

Barely breathing, Cole searched for an answer. His gaze wanted to flick to the mirror, knowing someone was probably back there.

His father seemed to read the impulse.

"It's okay," Victor said.

Cole swallowed. The truth still seemed like a risk, for all that he didn't want to lie to his dad. But the idea had never been to give the Blood information on either of the girls. Not until he knew what the hell was really going on.

"They're just kids, right?" Victor said as though he'd answered. "A little girl and her sister, lost in the war?"

Cole said nothing.

"You didn't know their family. And you shouldn't believe everything you see."

The faint hiss of the air conditioner became the only sound in the room.

"I didn't start out intending to kill their king," Victor continued, picking up the previous topic as though the last exchange hadn't happened. "Until the week before Nicholas died, it'd never crossed my mind. To tell the truth, I'd even worked at reconciliation between our sides, if you'd believe that. It's how your mother and I met and, for a time, what I even thought was possible. But the one thing the Merlin's Children absolutely would not give, the one thing we needed above all else, was our magic. And while at first, it was simply a matter of equality with them, in the days before the war, it became a necessity for dealing with a larger problem I'd only just begun to understand."

He glanced to Cole. "We're royalty, you and I. The descendants of a leader who, while revered by his followers as a king, still lost his children any shred of real authority. That we were symbols of that legacy, I'd always known. That we couldn't live a life of our own, a life outside the Council's control…" His mouth twisted. "That I didn't appreciate. Not until your grandfather died.

"I never got along with Thelonious. He was…" Victor sighed,

clearly revising whatever he'd been about to say. "He was what they wanted me to become. A stamp on their authority. A broken man, cowed by the Council and dreaming of what might have been. Not that I saw it that way. Thelonious had, in his own manner, sheltered me throughout his life. I almost wish he hadn't. I would have been better prepared, at least. Or maybe I would have taken you and Clara far from this a long time ago. After all, the Council had never spoken to me. They acted like they scarcely knew I was alive. And I believed…" He shook his head. "I don't know what I believed. That the whole 'Taliesin king' issue wouldn't matter. That it was enough that I'd distanced myself from my father and everything else the moment I was old enough to walk out the door.

"And then Thelonious died.

"The Council summoned me before his body was even cold. And they explained the way things were going to be. I would leave your mother immediately. Taliesin *kings* didn't marry Merlin. As a cripple, you'd be kept permanently out of sight at a location they'd designate, and if I couldn't produce an heir with magical powers to take your place, then they'd be forced to see what could be done with you. Or really just your children. The magic in our line had to be preserved, you see. For what it meant to the people."

Old anger played through Victor's eyes and then he drew a breath, burying it. "I was sent to a safe house with bodyguards under the pretense of protecting the new king. My job disappeared, my phone was monitored, and everyone I knew stopped answering my calls. I was kept from home with 'Council business' day and night, giving me no chance to tell your mother what was happening. And meanwhile, the Council was preparing to take you both away from me."

He grimaced. "So I reached out to the only person I could. As a child, Mason Brogan had been a neighbor and close friend. When he grew up, he went into business with his father. 'Creative marketing and finance', I believe he once called it. But regardless, he wasn't on the Council's payroll and, through his work, he had resources. Contacts. Money. So when he came to pay his respects after Thelonious' passing, I begged the guards for a moment to speak with a fellow Taliesin, and they made the terrible mistake of agreeing.

Victor paused. "The Council ruled as long as there was no one with the power to oppose them. I had to change that. If I wanted to protect my family, I had to return magic to our people, and my ability to bind the same. No matter the cost.

"Mason assembled a team of people he trusted, people who were loyal to the crown and not the Council, to serve as backup if things went wrong. He located transport while I slipped the attention of the guards, and then we were on our way to the Merlin king's home."

His brow furrowed, memories playing out behind his eyes. "Nicholas knew we were Taliesin when he opened the door. Perhaps not that I was their king, though regardless, I doubt he'd have cared. Five hundred years of binding had left us beneath their notice. He simply turned to call his bodyguards to help with the packages, and that was the end. The silenced gun went off. I started a war."

He fell silent, studying the ground without seeming to see it. Cole swallowed hard. He couldn't find his voice, though he didn't know what he would have said anyway.

"I'm sorry," Victor told him quietly. "Saying it all so bluntly… it would be nicer to let the past die. But I need you to know the story, so that whatever they've said, whatever else you've been told… you can judge for yourself. You don't have to believe me. I just want you to have all the facts I can provide, no matter how unpleasant, so you can make your own decisions."

Cole managed a nod.

"And as a part of that…" Victor said. He shrugged off his suit jacket. Cole's brow furrowed in confusion, but his father didn't look up. Carefully, he unbuttoned the wrist of his dress shirt and then rolled back the sleeve.

Cole's eyes widened.

It looked like a tattoo gone horribly wrong. Jagged black lines radiated out from the inside of his elbow like an explosion beneath his skin.

"Shooting the king wasn't enough," Victor said. "We hoped if I did it, it would be. But when nothing changed and the guards were coming… I did the only thing I could think of. The only thing greater than 'simply' killing the king. I grabbed my pocket knife, soaked it in his blood and–" He gestured to his arm. "– took it as my own."

"Is that why…?" Cole asked, trailing off as he pulled his gaze from the charred veins.

"The Blood," Victor acknowledged with a hint of a wry smile. "It changed everything. And so did we."

He rolled the sleeve back down, leaving it unbuttoned. "The effect of the spell breaking was like nothing I could have imagined. Painful. Agonizingly so. I felt it rip through me, into the people near me, and outward like a tidal wave. And when, through the pain, I saw the guards… I just wanted to stop them. And then the house was gone.

"I didn't mean to kill them, Cole. Not the whole family. No one, in fact, but the king. I know it doesn't make it better. But… it still needs to be said."

Victor fell silent, his brow furrowing as though he was still trying to work through the memories.

Cole watched him. His own thoughts felt muzzy from lack of food and sleep, and in the midst of all he'd just heard, he didn't even know where to begin. He wanted to be furious. Indignant. To insist that whether or not you meant to kill God-knew-how-many people, it didn't change the fact you had.

But the regret on his father's face made the protests die.

"What happened then?" he asked.

Victor looked over and, at whatever his dad saw in his eyes, the man gave him a faintly relieved smile.

"We went back to the Council. We knew something had changed about us, that we didn't have the look of Taliesin anymore, though we didn't realize we were the only ones. We just rushed back, intent on disarming the Council before they had a chance to collect themselves, but we were too late. We'd been too late before we even reached the Merlin king.

"They had your pillow, covered in bloodstains. And just before I could kill them, they explained that you weren't dead. They'd simply enacted the next stage of their plan when the guards reported I'd gone. But now, if I didn't play nice and submit to the Council's authority completely–" His mouth tightened. "–the next time I saw you, you would be."

Victor paused. "I… wondered… as the years went by, if I should have just killed them then. Perhaps their guards would have tried to keep you as leverage. Perhaps the ones holding you wouldn't have learned the Council was dead before you'd already been found."

Cole swallowed, remembering Stephen and Vivian bringing him with them for exactly that purpose, right after his dad killed the

Taliesin Council. "They, um… they did."

Victor glanced to him.

"The guards. They kept me with them. A few days ago, when you…"

"You saw that."

It wasn't a statement and it wasn't a question, and when he looked up, he couldn't read the expression in his father's eyes.

"There was a room next to the Council…" he said, the words not wanting to come.

Victor dropped his gaze to the ground. "I lived for eight years knowing that on any given day, you could be taken from me. Permanently. That if they grew angry with you, or if their policies on our family changed, or even if something simply went wrong… you might die. And there was nothing I could do about it."

He looked back up at Cole. "I don't know if you can understand that, especially in light of how it must have looked to you. But please know that everything I've done has only ever been to keep our family safe. There is no other reason."

Cole watched his dad, and for the life of him, he couldn't think what to say. The memory of his father standing over the dying councilor came back to him. He'd been cold. So very cold. As though the death of the man in front of him was nothing more than the natural conclusion of events, long delayed.

And yet, if he'd gone through all that his father had, maybe he would have felt that way too.

"I should have stopped them though," Victor added quietly.

"Why didn't you?"

"I believed them too much," he answered ruefully. "And I wouldn't risk you." His brow furrowed, regret still strong in his eyes. "So I went home. I thought we could regroup. Track you down before they'd gotten far." He shook his head. "But in our apartment, I found five more guards, with your mother drugged at their feet and our home in shambles. The guards simply ordered me to ignore her and come with them, or else they'd have to do something about Clara too. And that was to be the end of it.

"Mason killed them," he said flatly. "They didn't even know what hit them, I think. But we made it seem like they'd been caught by Merlin vigilantes by scrawling death threats against Taliesin and other such garbage on the walls. And yet, even with that, we knew it wouldn't be over. As long as I was alive, the Council could use you as leverage. But if I was gone, you'd become the sole heir to the throne, making you infinitely more valuable and thus safe. So a few days later, we staged an internal power struggle, from which I ostensibly died. I went into hiding. And spent the next eight years looking for you."

He paused. "I never thought it would take so long."

Cole waited, but his father didn't say anything else. He wetted his lips, wanting to speak, and fearing what might come.

"And Mom?"

Victor didn't move. Briefly, his gaze slid toward the mirror.

"She was a victim of the war."

A quiver clenched Cole's chest. "What do you mean?"

His father didn't answer.

"Is she… dead?"

Victor looked away.

The trembling grew stronger. The air felt like soup, thick and hot and choking on his lungs, and more than anything, he didn't want to speak the words chasing themselves around inside.

"Dad, did you…?"

"No."

Victor pushed to his feet and headed for the door.

"But–"

"Please," his father interrupted, glancing back. "I… I will tell you about it. But not now. It was…" His mouth tightened, and then he dropped whatever he'd been about to say. "Come on," he finished brusquely, pulling open the door. "There's something I want to show you."

Cole hesitated. He wanted to press for more, to demand to know why people would claim Victor'd killed Clara if he really hadn't, but then it came back to him. Everyone in this mess said whatever they wanted to blame the other side.

Maybe, just maybe, this wasn't any different.

Clinging to the idea despite the doubts clamoring inside, he rose and followed his father. He had to believe someone was telling the truth in this situation.

He just hoped it was his dad.

Two guards stood on either side of the door. At the sight of Victor, they bowed and murmured 'your majesty' in solemn tones.

Victor glanced to Cole as the guards spoke. His eyes narrowed, a hint of suspicion in his gaze.

"They'd already told you that part, hadn't they?"

Cole hesitated.

"Which was it? Taliesin or Merlin?"

He swallowed, discomfort rising. His gaze went to the guards in an attempt to buy time.

"Never mind," his father said, dropping the question. "Perhaps later."

Victor motioned onward and then led the way down the hall. At his touch to the small arrow beside the elevator, the door hissed back. Victor stepped inside.

Warily, Cole followed.

A door opened in the hallway and he looked back as his father leaned over to push a button for a lower floor. From a room near the guards, the scarred giant emerged. The man's gaze flicked to the elevator before he headed in the opposite direction along the corridor.

And then the door slid closed.

"That was Mason."

Cole glanced over.

"The man you saw," his father elaborated. "Though most people just call him Brogan."

Gears and cables whispered as the elevator rushed down.

"What, um…" Cole asked quietly. "What happened?"

"His scars?"

Cole nodded as the elevator slowed and then dinged. The door rolled open.

Victor's face hardened. "Ashley."

It took Cole a moment to follow.

Striding down a colorless hall that could have been pulled from any office building on the planet, his father wasted no attention on the rooms beyond the open doorways lining the corridor. Reaching the double doors at the end, he glanced back only to check that Cole was still with him, and then pushed the latch and continued through.

It'd probably been a conference room once, though not much to designate it as such remained. Cots covered the floor and a handful of people moved between the wounded curled upon them. Wire racks were arranged along a wall, stuffed to overflowing with medical supplies, while against another wall, blankets were piled.

Beside one cot, the blonde Blood wizard from the factory straightened, and Cole tensed. Beautiful if she hadn't looked like a Nordic assassin waiting for the command to strike, she studied them, and only when Victor gave a nod did she bend down over her injured charge again.

"Isabella," his father said. "Our healer extraordinaire, among other things."

Victor watched her. "There used to be more of us. The Blood, I mean. But war and the retaliation of any who've learned of our existence has taken its toll."

He sighed. "But that's not why I brought you here," he said, turning back to Cole. "I know you can't see the difference, but there are cripples and Taliesin in here both. We even have a few Merlin and a human or two with us."

Victor met his eyes. "I need you to understand this. We're not like the wizards you've met so far. All these people, they aren't fighting for Taliesin's side, or Merlin's side, or any side. They're here to end a system that started over five hundred years ago. A system of dividing people into groups and putting one above the other, to the destruction of anyone below. And that's all. You, me, the Blood, we lead. But we listen to everyone. We're open to help from any who want to bring an end to what the sides of Merlin and Taliesin have done. And we don't care what people may have been in the past. Only what they can be in the future."

His gaze on the cots, Cole said nothing. The room looked like the lawn outside the mobile home, only with about three times as many wounded.

Wounded who'd been fighting Ashe, or the Taliesin Council, or both.

He swallowed, feeling strangely ill. It just seemed so stupid. The fighting. The killing. All of it, when this was the only result anyone had seen in nearly a decade.

But maybe all wars ended up looking that way.

The door behind them opened, interrupting his thoughts. Brogan strode through, a dozen people carrying more injured hurrying in after him.

"Council loyalists," Brogan stated succinctly as he passed.

Victor glanced back toward the door.

A hand on the handle, a man stood frozen. "You found him."

Cole paused, struck by a sense of familiarity he couldn't place. And then it clicked.

Harris dropped his hand from the door, coming closer. "Have you seen Ashley?" he asked, a note of interrogation pressing hard on his voice. "Do you know where she's hiding?"

Taken back, Cole stared.

"There will be time for all that, Detective," Victor said peaceably. "Cole has only just arrived."

Harris ignored him.

"N-no," Cole answered, fighting to keep from looking at his father. "I don't."

Harris was silent, his eyes weighing the response.

"The detective is one of the humans I spoke of," Victor supplied into the pause. "He has been helping us since Ashley set his partner on fire."

Cole blinked, trying not to feel punched in the gut by his father's casual tone.

At the reminder of his past, Harris' expression tightened. "I should get back." He glanced to Cole. "We'll talk more later."

Without waiting for a reply, he headed after Brogan.

Cole could feel his father's eyes on him as he watched the detective walk away.

"Did he… um…" he tried, the words slipping from his grasp. "Did he say why she, um…"

"They got in her way."

His gaze went to his father as Victor turned and headed for the door.

"What do you mean?"

Victor paused. "Merlin teach their charges to have little concern for those who cannot protect themselves," he explained carefully as he looked back. "Human, cripple, young or old. It does not matter. If they get in the way of the wizard's goals… they die."

"But were they… did they threaten her or something?" he asked desperately, knowing he was defending the girl he remembered from the farm more than anything.

His father studied him. "How much do you know about the young Merlin queen?"

Cole couldn't respond. Suddenly, all the hours of restless sleep and the pathetic excuses for food were making themselves known on his aching head. What did he know about her? Nothing, apparently. Or at least the tip of an iceberg he *really* didn't want to see.

He'd left Lily with this girl.

Swallowing hard, he shoved down the panic. Ashe would protect Lily. At what cost, he didn't know, but that wasn't the point. Lily's safety was more than guaranteed.

Everything else was just information to help him figure out where to go from here.

He gave his father a small shrug.

"I think it is difficult to describe how truly relieved I was to see you, Cole. And not just because of the years the Council kept us apart. Queen *Ashe,* as she has rather appropriately renamed herself… I thought she had killed you when she pulled you through that portal. And even if through the use of that staff she had somehow managed to keep you alive…"

Victor's mouth tightened. "She feeds on your kind, Cole. To strengthen her power. Queen Ashe, upon taking the Merlin throne, led a campaign of destruction against cripples the likes of which our world had never seen. No one knows how many died, though those who escaped to join us estimate hundreds, if not more. But 'Bloody Queen Ashe', as she's now known, summoned men, women, even little children to her side, all under the pretense of fighting *us*. And then she killed them. Brutally. Systematically. And without any but her fellow murderers the wiser. It wasn't until people began to question why they never heard from their friends that the ruse came to light, and even though the surviving cripples have fled…" He shook his head. "There's no guarantee she's stopped killing.

"I'm sorry," Victor finished. "I know she can make herself look like just a girl."

Cole didn't move, though he knew his father had fallen silent. It was all he could do to just take in the words.

She'd watched him ever since they found her again. What did she think? He'd turn her sister against her? Or that she couldn't kill him while Lily was there?

He saw her face again, bloodlessly pale and huddled over her little sister as he drove them away from their farm.

He wanted to be sick.

"Cole?"

Drawing a rough breath, he fought to push the horrific accusations aside. It was all just information. Just information to help him figure out how to deal with the situation. Or something. But it couldn't be the focus. Not right now.

Blinking, he dragged his gaze up to his dad.

"Why did you…" He swallowed. "Your men. Keller. I heard him. They tried to kill… on the farm, they tried…"

"We didn't want to hurt them. We just had to stop their father. He was…" Victor paused. "He wouldn't have ever given up the war. But we did not go there to harm his girls."

"You shot her!" Cole protested. He threw a glance to the rest of the room, trying to keep his voice down. "I mean, your people. They said they only needed one and they shot Ashley. And me."

Silence answered him and he looked over to find his father frozen still.

"What?" Victor asked quietly.

"One of them. I don't know who. They shot Ashley and me and…" He shook his head, his shock fading, though it was doing little for the clouds fogging his brain. "Lily saved me."

"Lily?"

He cursed himself, but there was nothing for it. And it didn't really matter anyway. "Yeah. Ashe's sister. She did something. She didn't know what. But she saved my life."

Victor seemed to remember how to breathe. "Then I owe her. Tremendously."

His dad paused, and then visibly drove the possibilities from his mind. "I don't know what happened that night. And I don't know what my men misunderstood that they would do such things. But I can promise you, killing you or the girls was never the plan. Not remotely."

Cole watched him. "Then what was?"

"To bring them with us. To see if maybe, as the last of the Merlin's Children and as the leaders of their people, they could be convinced to help us bring an end to this violence."

Cole looked away.

It sounded so much like what the Council had said to him, once upon a time.

"And if they couldn't?" he heard himself ask.

"We believed they could."

He glanced back to his father. Victor shrugged, a ruefully optimistic look in his eyes.

Cole's gaze fell away.

Footsteps approached and from the corner of his eye, he saw Brogan walk up.

"My apologies. You are needed."

Victor's face tightened with frustration, but after a moment, he drew a breath and pushed the expression away.

"I'm sorry. Duty calls." He glanced to Brogan. "Are the rooms ready?"

The man nodded.

Victor echoed the motion. "Then I'll see you later," he continued, directing the last to Cole. He reached over, clasping Cole's arm with a smile, and then headed for a door on the far side of the room.

"Come with me."

He glanced to Brogan warily. The man's voice was a growl and his one good eye pinned Cole with a stare that somehow made it clear how unfathomably easy it was for him to kill if he felt the need.

Without another word, Brogan turned and disappeared back out the double doors.

Breathing again, Cole cast a look after his father and then followed.

People cleared from the giant's path quickly as he stalked down the hall and, when the elevator arrived, the door seemed to open faster for fear of the man waiting for it. Striding forward, Brogan hit the button for a floor without giving it a glance, and then turned, silently waiting for Cole to join him before the door slid closed. The ride upstairs was no better and when the door opened, Cole fought to keep his pace slow as he fled the confines of the elevator.

Brogan made him feel like he was trapped in a box with a ticking bomb.

The giant strode by him. Continuing around the turn, he marched toward a pair of ebony doors and then shoved them open without a backward glance.

Cole trailed him cautiously into the room. Windows formed two of the walls, extending from the ceiling nearly to the floor, and beyond their glass, the glittering cityscape stretched to the horizon beneath the night sky. The black waters of the lake interrupted the expanse to the south, though the glow of a bridge bordered its edge and suburbs glimmered on the far banks. To the east, crowded highways formed a serpentine river of red and white light.

He swallowed, continuing farther inside. A sunken space in the middle of the floor was ringed by thickly padded seats of black leather, and glistening crystal lights dangled over the glass table in the center. Where the windows met, a black grand piano stood, and near the entry, a doorway led off to a bathroom with a Jacuzzi inside. A marble-trimmed kitchenette lay in the rightmost rear corner of the room, with a door open beside it. In the bedroom beyond, a bed the size of a truck waited opposite a flat-panel television wide enough to use as a surfboard.

The door shut behind him. Startled, he turned.

Brogan's stare made his blood go cold.

"Who sent you?" the man growled.

"What?"

The giant paced toward him and Cole backed up, catching himself before he stumbled over the edge of the sunken seats.

"You never answered the others. You will answer me."

Brogan's voice held no anger, just a quiet certainty more chilling than any rage could have been.

"Who sent you?" the man repeated. "I will not believe you escaped dozens of Merlin without assistance from their queen."

"I didn't–"

"I will not ask again."

Cole swallowed, his gaze locked on the warped skin of Brogan's face and the milky white eye staring at him as though it could still see.

"She…"

The giant's jaw clenched. Cole grabbed after the only thing he could think to say.

"They're afraid of you. They're running. They… they know you're hunting them. And…"

He faltered. Too much would endanger Lily. Not enough might get him killed, king's son or not.

"It wasn't a dozen Merlin. It wasn't even half that many. And the queen… I escaped because she was distracted. They all were. They saw the news about the fires, and while they were trying to reach their people, I…"

He hesitated, and then risked the truth. "I climbed out the window and down the fire escape."

Brogan's cold gaze took on a dry cast. "The fire escape."

"You think I'd make that up?" Cole cried.

"And this was in Atlanta?"

He tensed, but there wasn't anything for it. The giant wasn't stupid, and Ashe would've gotten Lily the hell away from there once she discovered he was gone.

At least, he hoped so.

Or maybe he did.

Fighting to stay focused, he nodded.

Brogan watched him for a moment and then stepped back, allowing him to gain distance from the edge of the seats.

"How many of the Merlin survived the attack on their hideout?"

Cole froze. At his silence, the giant's brow rose.

He grimaced uncomfortably. "I'm not–"

"How many?"

Brogan's stare was uncompromising.

Cole drew a breath, floundering. He didn't owe the Merlin anything. And it wasn't like a count was dangerous. It didn't say where they were, or what defenses they had. It meant nothing.

His conscience didn't buy his line of reasoning and his skin refused to stop crawling with guilt as he looked back into the giant's eyes.

"Maybe a hundred?" he hazarded. "But I'm not sure. I'm not!" he insisted as the man's face darkened. "I think there might've been more elsewhere, but I never saw them, so I don't know."

Again, Brogan studied him before finally turning and striding to the door. "I will have someone bring you dinner."

The giant paused, glancing back. "And if we have further

questions…"

He let the rest of the statement hang in the air.

Cole hesitated. "Okay."

Brogan's face gave nothing away. Without another word, he left.

A breath escaped Cole. Shaking his head, he scrubbed a hand over his hair, trying to drive away the adrenaline surge the giant caused.

He really didn't owe the Merlin anything. And a stupid count of how many had been at the mobile home lot was harmless.

At least, he thought it was.

Maybe.

He grimaced, turning from the door and walking to the window.

Hundreds of feet below, workers rushed home for the evening while the dinner crowd made their way into the restaurants lining the street. Taxis like golden fish wove between the other cars, racing the lights and traffic and each other for their destinations.

It didn't matter. They couldn't do anything with a count.

Except know how many were left to kill.

His eyes closed. The cold surface of the glass pressed against his forehead.

Wizards were bastards. That was one thing of which he'd been absolutely certain, long before he'd come to Chaunessy today. The Carnegeans were more than proof; they were wizard poster children. And even if his father had worked for peace, Ashe's family could have been the same.

He wondered what his mother had done.

A twist of pain burned his chest, carrying with it all the unanswered questions from earlier that day, and he scowled, forcing scorn into its place. Whatever Clara had done for peace, the Carnegeans had hated her for it, so it must have been good. And chances were,

Ashe's family had been just like his grandparents. After all, King Nicholas had maintained his grip on Taliesin's magic without ever considering a compromise.

Until Victor killed him for it.

Though it wasn't like he'd had much of a choice.

Cole grimaced. That wasn't the point. At least, possibly. But it didn't change anything about the destruction his father had caused since.

Except who had his father hurt? Edmund Vaughn and the Council, who'd kept Cole prisoner for eight years, apparently while being ready to kill him the whole time? The Merlin royal family, who stood every chance of being the monsters the Carnegeans had idolized them as?

And as for the rest…

He wanted to believe that his father didn't have to keep fighting the Merlin. Maybe that he didn't even *want* to keep fighting them, if they'd only stop too.

It hurt how much he wanted to believe that.

But it wasn't just on his father.

He wondered what she was telling Lily. Would she hide it if she felt the need to murder one of his kind, or would she simply spin it somehow? Tell Lily they'd been trying to hurt her, or that they worked for the so-called bad guys. Truth be told, she might not even bother. She didn't honestly seem to care if she killed people in front of the kid. The four dead wizards she'd left outside Chaunessy a few days ago showed that.

Maybe she'd just teach Lily to be the same as her.

His stomach turned and he opened his eyes, swallowing hard as he pulled his forehead back from the window.

She'd been accused of killing hundreds of people. That didn't make it true. He couldn't make a decision on rumors.

No matter how likely they appeared.

His gaze tracked a taxi through the traffic without really seeing the car.

Keller and Reece had looked so eager to find the girls the night they killed Vaughn, they'd nearly been salivating over the idea. And later, Reece's team claimed to only need one.

Maybe they'd just misunderstood the plan.

Maybe his dad didn't know Brogan's people as well as he thought.

Cole rubbed his fingers over his eyes and then turned from the window, pacing the length of the ridiculously nice apartment. Brogan's people had tried to kill him on the cliff that night. Ashe had burned a man alive just for getting in her way.

Hollywood never made choosing sides this hard.

A knock sounded at the door and he froze halfway across the thick, white carpet. A heartbeat later, the latch turned and a silver cart bearing covered dishes and a carafe of juice came in, followed by a suit-clad man who kept his eyes on the ground.

"Your dinner, sire," the man said deferentially.

Cole stared at him, his brow climbing at the title.

"Shall I put it on the table for you?" the man continued at his silence.

His gaze darted from the man to the small table in the kitchenette and back. "Um, that's really okay."

"It would be my pleasure," the man said, putting action to the words by wheeling the cart over and then carefully arranging the food on the wrought iron table.

"Will there be anything else, sire?" he asked when he finished.

Dumbstruck, Cole shook his head.

"Have a good night."

He stared as the man wheeled the cart away and shut the door.

His gaze slid back to the table.

The aroma of barbecue chicken and fries drew him across the room before his caution got to have a vote.

Ashe really was a threat to the kid, he decided as the last of the chicken disappeared from the plate. Even if he set aside all the things of which she'd been accused, he'd still seen enough to make how violent and brutal she'd been taught to be abundantly clear.

Though given the way Nathaniel and the others had been watching him, there seemed a good chance the accusations were real.

Drawing a breath, he pushed the thought away. He needed to trust his dad. Regardless of what the Blood may or may not have understood, he had to believe that the man he'd known, and the person who'd sworn to him today that he wanted to help those girls, could be trusted to follow through on his word.

He had to be able to put weight on that, at least.

A breath escaped him. But that wasn't the only issue.

Ashe would have run with Lily when she saw he'd escaped. He didn't know her well, but he knew enough to bet on that. And where they would've gone was anybody's guess. Elias hadn't exactly been forthcoming, and with an entire country full of places to hide, telling his father might not accomplish much.

His gaze returned to the window. His dad might have resources to help, though. And the difficulty wasn't important. He had to get Lily out of there. He couldn't let Ashe do to her sister what'd obviously been done to her.

He just needed to find a way.

———— ◆ ————

The man had stopped bleeding a while ago, though from the stains covering him it was hard to tell. Curled in a ball on the concrete floor, he whimpered as residual shocks of his own magic sizzled through his veins.

"Hartford then," Brogan remarked, glancing over.

Jamison nodded, turning away. The wizards behind him hurried to drag the man back into the cell.

Brogan ignored them, studying his employer. By the security station on the opposite side of the room, Jamison tapped the keyboard and watched the camera pan across the wide cell.

"They were close," he commented, not looking up from the monitor as Brogan came near.

Brogan said nothing. Jamison didn't seem to mind.

Locks clanked behind them. Hands clasped in military parade rest, the guards took up positions on either side of the cell door.

"Are you ever going to tell him you killed his mother?" Brogan asked quietly.

Jamison tapped another key. The monitor switched to another camera.

"No."

A key clicked. The monitor switched again.

"She never would have understood," Brogan said.

"I know."

Behind them, the wizard began to sob. Jamison glanced back.

Brogan followed his gaze. In a shadowed corner of the cell, an old man motioned to two prisoners. The pair struggled to their feet and shuffled over to comfort the weeping man.

"He's still alive," Brogan noted dryly.

Silent, Jamison watched the old man. From his corner, Charles Brentworth stared back, nothing in his eyes to give evidence of the fact his magic was long since gone.

Jamison's expression hardened.

"Six more of the Council's people hiding in Hartford?" he said, turning to Brogan. "Excellent. Tell Simeon he leaves within the hour." His lip twitched, the introspection of the moment before gone. "And bring out another prisoner."

Chapter Six

The first thing he saw was a purple cat, and then his vision cleared.

Blinking, Cole pushed away from the pillow and then rubbed a hand over his face. Cartoon felines danced across the massive television screen in time to muted music, and sunlight streamed past the curtains on the far side of the room.

He couldn't remember falling asleep. With the addition of food to his system, everything had gone blurry. He recalled asking the guards outside his door where his father could be found, at which he was told the king was unavailable for the time being, though they'd pass along that Cole wanted to speak with him. Without options, he'd gone back inside. The apartment yielded little in the way of things to distract him, considering he no more knew how to play piano than fly to the moon, and somewhere between flipping on the television and lying back on the mountain of a bed, morning had decided to arrive.

Stifling a yawn, he dug the remote from the pile of pillows and then sent the cartoon cats into oblivion. Even on mute, the creatures were disturbing. Climbing off the bed, he tossed the remote back into the jumble of pillows and then walked out of the room.

Sunlight poured into the apartment, giving everything a new and fresh look utterly at odds with how he felt. Wincing at the glare, he made his way to the bathroom and splashed water on his face, trying to drive away the cobwebs clinging to his brain.

This wasn't going to be easy.

The thought was clear despite his exhaustion, and he grimaced as he swiped a towel from the rack and then pressed it to his face. Last night, everything had seemed, if not straightforward, then at least manageable. Whether or not the Blood were trustworthy, his father could still help the kid and that was all that mattered. But now, other factors came to mind, making everything so much more complicated.

Ashe wouldn't let Lily go easily. Hell, she wouldn't let Lily go at all. She'd kill anybody who tried to get near the girl, to the destruction of anything else around her.

And that was just the start of the problem.

Roughly, he tossed the towel back at the rack. Avoiding his reflection in the wall-sized mirror, he headed for the door.

He had to find his father. Unavailable be damned, they needed to talk.

The two guards outside the apartment glanced over as he leaned around the door.

"May we help you?"

"My dad. Have you seen him?"

"I believe he is occupied at the—"

Victor walked around the corner. "They said you were looking for me?" he called, ignoring the guards' bows.

Cole nodded. Victor motioned toward the apartment and at the gesture, Cole stepped back inside.

"What's going on?" his dad asked as the door shut. Crossing the room, he headed for the couches circling the sunken area of the floor.

Cole paused before following, suddenly trying to find where to begin. Sighing tiredly, Victor dropped onto the black leather cushions and stretched his arms across the backs of the seats next to him.

"You okay?" Cole asked, watching him.

Victor shrugged. "Long night."

Cole's brow furrowed and at the expression, his father seemed to hesitate, as though deciding what to say.

"Prisoners," he admitted. "From the Council."

"What happened?"

"Oh, nothing. It's just… a process. When they're brought in, it's better if they can't hurt anyone, so I take their magic before we start talking to them. Things go smoother that way. But this bunch had gotten closer than most before we caught them, so we had a few more questions than usual."

"Closer?" Cole asked, lowering himself onto the couch without taking his eyes from his dad.

"To me. I have a house in upstate New York where I've been staying the past couple years and they managed to make it within a few hundred miles. But it's fine. They had no idea they were near us, and neither did their superiors, apparently." He smiled. "In any case, I'd love to take you there someday. I think you'd like it."

Cole wanted to smile at the idea, but the words just brought him back to the topic at hand.

At his silence, Victor's brow furrowed. "Are *you* alright?"

He hesitated. "Not really."

His father waited.

Cole grimaced. "It's Lily. Ashe's sister. She… she's just a kid. And I can't stop thinking about Ashe turning her into… or teaching her to…"

He looked away. "You know what I mean."

His father sighed and nodded, the ease of the moment before fading from his face.

"I just wish I'd tried to bring her with me. To… keep her from that or whatever."

Victor was quiet for a moment. "We still could."

Cole glanced up. A strange look of consideration was in his father's eyes, but at Cole's expression, sympathy took its place.

"I told you," Victor said. "We've wanted to find Ashley and her sister for years. You're not asking us to do anything we haven't tried already. After all, these are the girls who can help us end the war."

Cole nodded.

"Even if," Victor continued carefully, the considering look creeping back into his eyes, "it won't necessarily be that simple anymore."

His father's eyebrow climbed pointedly.

Cole looked away again.

And that was the problem, and the realization that, when it finally came to him last night, he'd wanted to do anything but entertain. Sending Brogan's people after Ashe wasn't a bloodless proposition. They couldn't just go in there and ask nicely for Lily to come back to Chaunessy. They'd have to use force. They'd have to start a fight.

And against Ashe, with her little sister at stake, there was no chance that would go well.

"We can try to separate her from the girl?" Victor offered. "Perhaps wait for a time when they're not together–"

"They're always together."

His father's mouth tightened. "And thus trying to separate them means—"

"I know." He didn't look back for all that he could feel his dad watching him. "Ashe might die."

The words were distant, and so much colder than he felt, and when he glanced up, he saw his father's eyes narrow with curiosity in response.

"If she will not surrender and it's the only way to save Lily," Victor allowed. "Yes."

Cole's gaze returned to the floor. He knew she wouldn't.

"Are you okay with that?"

A scoff escaped him. Okay? He was the farthest thing from, considering he was having a conversation he'd never planned on having in his life.

They were discussing the possibility of someone's death. And not just that, but someone he'd tried desperately to help. Someone whose life he'd nearly died trying to save. She'd just seemed like a kid. Practically his own age, yes, but that night at the farm, she'd looked just like a scared child, fighting to hang on while her world fell down.

He felt like breaking something and his stomach wouldn't stop churning. It didn't matter. It couldn't. That girl had been gone for a long time, if she'd ever existed at all.

And the present was what they had to deal with now.

"We have to save Lily," he answered tightly, struggling to focus on the words and ignore the way his stomach kept trying to rise.

His father nodded compassionately. "Whatever the cost."

Cole couldn't respond.

"If it helps," Victor said. "I promise we won't go into this trying to kill Ashley. We'll do everything in our power to avoid it. After all, if we can separate Lily from her sister without Ashley's death, having the girl with us will likely make the queen willing to listen to what we have to say. Perhaps even to cooperate with us, in the end. We want to negotiate for peace, Cole. Bloodshed has always been our last resort."

He swallowed, working to be comforted by the words.

"Do you know how many people Ashley keeps around her?" his father continued.

Cole drew a breath. This was part of it too. Just, thankfully, the one that was less hard.

The people with her were bastards. At a minimum, they'd supported Ashe's brutality. More likely, they'd taught it to her in the first place. If anyone was to blame for this, chances were it was them.

He owed them nothing. Nothing at all.

"Only three wizards, last time I saw," he said. "Nathaniel, Elias and Cornelius. Nathaniel's a big guy, some kind of bodyguard who could probably give Brogan a run for his money, and the other two used to be on the Merlin Council. I can give you descriptions, if you want. There was a woman with them for a while. Katherine, Elias' wife. Looks like some crazy schoolteacher. Whole bunch of guards and other wizards were running around as well, but those first three were the only ones Ashe kept close."

"Probably the ones who support what she's become the most."

He gave a dry laugh at his father's ability to read his mind.

"We can get descriptions when our people are ready to head out," Victor continued. "But in the meantime, do you know where they would have gone?"

"No," he admitted. "But I overheard Cornelius say he had some safe houses in the south, so they may stay in that area."

His father nodded. "Then we'll start there."

Cole echoed the motion and then looked away, the resolution of the moment before fading into the cold reality of what might happen.

Seconds drifted by.

"I should go tell the others then," Victor said, rising to his feet.

Cole glanced up, and his stomach clenched at the pride in his father's eyes.

"For what it's worth," his dad said. "You're doing the right thing. Unpleasant as the possibilities may be… this needs to come to an end."

He watched as his father climbed the short steps to the main living room floor.

"And it'll be good for her that you're here," Victor added optimistically. "Lily, I mean. We'll do all we can to keep her from seeing if things go badly. But no matter what, even if you're not her family or a wizard, you're still a familiar face. You'll be a tremendous help to her in understanding this as time goes on."

His father smiled and then left the room.

The door closed.

Cole didn't leave the chair.

And that was the other part. The one that couldn't possibly be more hard.

Lily'd know. The moment she got here… the moment she saw him in the company of the 'bad men' who'd just dragged her away from her sister…

Her dead sister.

His imagination tossed up images before he could stop it and his stomach lurched with the result.

Lily would know.

And she'd never forgive him.

He shoved away from the couch, his feet carrying him around the glass table as though it would get him anywhere.

There wasn't another option. They had to go after Lily, and Ashe had chosen what she'd become. He couldn't let her turn her sister into the same thing. And Ashe getting hurt wasn't inevitable. His father said they wouldn't go into this trying to kill her. They didn't even *want* to kill her. Bloodshed was their last resort.

Though it might be the only way…

The white walls stared back at him, cold and unsympathetic, and everything around him suddenly felt so stupid when people only a few floors away were prepping for the possibility of being forced to kill a girl his own age. And he'd have to explain to her eight-year-old sister why. He'd have to help her understand the death of the only family she had left in the world.

Because it'd been the only way.

His feet hit the steps and then he was across the room, unable to stand the silence and the lack of distraction any longer. He didn't have to like it. He didn't even have to tolerate it. But they had to save Lily.

Dear God, he wanted another way.

The guards looked up in alarm as he threw open the door. He ignored them, heading down the hall without the least destination in mind. The elevator didn't answer his call and after a few heartbeats, he abandoned it for the stairs.

Motion helped. It kept him from thinking about what he was running from.

He stopped at a random floor and bolted past the exit. People filled the hallway and stared at him in shock as he passed, and every one of their gazes seemed to ask him why.

Why he'd agreed to this. Why he couldn't have come up with something…

Anything…

He darted down a service stairway, escaping their scrutiny.

The floor below was better. Quieter, although that swiftly began to lose its appeal. Noise was better than anything, though if it could have not had people in it, that would have been even nicer. But the empty, gray hallway was anything but distracting.

A door opened behind him. He spun.

"Oh, hey," Harris said, pausing halfway out of what appeared to be a makeshift bedroom. "What're you doing down here?"

Cole froze, wanting to flee though there was nowhere to go.

Harris' brow furrowed at his silence. "Cole?"

"Uh…" He glanced down the hall. Blank doors lined either side, and short of running from the man, there wasn't anything to do but answer the question. "I needed some air."

Harris' skepticism didn't fade. "You alright?"

An incredulous laugh threatened to escape him. Seeming to read the impulse, Harris paused and then shut the door behind him.

"There's some chairs around the corner," he offered. "Nice view. Good place to think. I was just heading there, if you'd care to join me?"

Cole eyed him, knowing the latter words had to be a lie. The man had been starting in the opposite direction when he'd come out the door. But he found himself turning to go back down the hall anyway.

Two armchairs and a small pedestal table stood in an alcove at the end of the next hall, framed by plants so green they could only be artificial. Tall windows ran to the ceiling in front of them, looking out on the city and the bright blue sky.

Grabbing the leftmost chair, Harris moved it for a better view and then sat down.

Cole watched him, but the man never glanced his way. Warily, he took the opposite chair.

Silence filled the hall. Outside the window, a flock of birds spun through the sky.

"Not quite Monfort, is it?" Harris commented.

Cole looked over at him. The man's gaze remained on the window.

"No," he answered, returning to the view of the city.

Seconds slid past, and the clouds and mirrored sides of the sky-scrapers did nothing to help clear his mind.

"You weren't coming down here to think," Cole said finally, the silence wearing thin.

Harris glanced to him askance. "And this is the last place to look for much air."

Cole exhaled and pushed the chair back to leave. He didn't need this right now.

"Does she have the little girl with her?" Harris asked, his voice hard.

Halfway out of his seat, Cole paused. "What's it to you?"

Harris scoffed. "Oh, I don't know. Maybe it's just that I don't want to see one of the only innocents left in this situation get blown up in the crossfire." He grimaced. "Listen, whatever your history is with Ashley, you still seemed to be looking out for her sister so, like it or not, you've got a responsibility to the kid now."

Cole didn't move.

Exasperation flickered over Harris' face. "Come on, Cole. Help me help her, alright?"

Carefully, he eased back into the chair, not taking his eyes from the detective. "What're you going to do?"

"Well, that's partly up to you. Right now, you're the best chance I've got at information, since besides you, me and Mud, everyone else who's seen that girl is either on her side or dead."

"Mud?"

"Little guy. Looks like a walking advertisement for the necessity of basic hygiene. Barely made it out of Ashley's rampage against cripples and anyone else she felt like killing."

Cole swallowed, feeling shaken for all that Harris' words didn't confirm anything he hadn't already been told. "Did Ashe really set your partner on fire?"

Harris' face hardened and Cole suddenly found himself stifling a shudder at the look in the man's eyes. "Scott's in physical therapy. He hopes he'll get the okay for a part-time desk job with the department soon. If he's lucky, that is, and the rest of the office thinks they can stand the sight of his scars."

"I'm sorry."

The words sounded ridiculously inane, but at them, Harris turned back to the window, his rage seeming to slowly sink back inside.

"If there's *anything* you know..." the man sighed, frustration mingled with a sort of exhausted desperation in his tone.

Cole's gaze fell to the ground, his eyes tracing the patterns on the tightly woven carpet tiles. "Brogan's people are going after her," he admitted. "I gave my dad all the information I had."

Harris appeared to relax a bit. "Is the little girl with her?"

"Yeah."

At his tone, Harris glanced to him.

"You think she'll hurt the kid."

It was only partly a question, but at the words, Cole looked away.

"Ah," Harris said.

Silence fell between them.

"You know," Harris said. "It took me almost six months to track that girl down after what she did to Scott. And I'll tell you the truth. Every so often – even with everything I saw that she'd done – I still found myself wondering how it could be possible. She looks like a kid. Hell, she makes you think she *is* a kid. And she's responsible for more deaths than most serial killers can claim."

Cole shifted uncomfortably in the stiff-backed chair.

"It's not always easy," Harris continued. "Doing what you have to. Doing the right thing. Sometimes, it hurts like hell. But I can tell you… it's worth it. For every life that girl doesn't have the chance to take… it's worth it."

Cole was silent, uncertain how to respond. He remembered the girl at the farmhouse; the white-faced kid running as her world burned. But he hadn't witnessed the rest of it. The dead cripples or all the hell she'd wreaked in the months since. He'd only seen part of this.

And so maybe he needed to trust the calls of those who had. It'd be hard – unbelievably hard – to explain this to Lily, given what might happen when Brogan's men found her. But it wasn't all on them. Or him. Ashe'd made her choices and she'd keep making them, and he couldn't be responsible for that.

He could only do whatever it took to get Lily to the end of this safely.

"How'd you get involved with her, anyway?" Harris asked.

The question jarred him from his thoughts. He scoffed. "Long story."

"Do I look like I'm going anywhere?"

He glanced over. Harris raised an eyebrow.

Cole grimaced. "I got in a fight with my… with Robert and Melissa. And when I left, I ran into Brogan's men and overheard them say they'd found some guy and his girls. From their tones, I could pretty much guess what they planned to do. So I followed them. I was going to call the cops once I found out where they were headed, but instead, I got there too late. They'd already killed the guy. But I managed to get the girls into the car and drive the hell out of there."

He fell silent for a moment and then gave a small, humorless laugh. "And yeah. She just seemed like a kid. Just some scared kid."

A moment slid by. He looked to the man in the other chair.

Harris was motionless, his gaze lost in thought, but at Cole's glance, he appeared to unfreeze.

"So then what was all that about a diary and her plan to kill her family?" the detective asked, his tone giving no sign of whatever he'd been thinking.

"You mean the diary about how I was supposedly planning to sell a little kid for sex while getting her sister hopped up on drugs?" Cole replied, old anger threading through his tone.

Harris waited.

Cole drew a breath, letting it out slowly. "Brogan's guys wanted to find those girls, so they spun the fact they'd just killed their dad into a story that'd be sure to make the whole world try to track us down." He paused. "For all the good it did. But regardless, they fed the news a total crock. I'd never met Ashe or Lily before that night."

Harris returned his gaze to the window, saying nothing.

The detective's phone buzzed.

Blinking, Harris drew himself from whatever thoughts he'd been having and tugged the phone out.

"Harris," he said.

Cole watched, but the man gave no indication of what he was hearing.

"There in a minute." He thumbed the phone off and then returned it to his pocket. "Sorry to cut this short," he said, rising to his feet, "but I've got to run."

Circling the chair, he paused briefly and then reached into his sports coat.

"Listen," he continued. "If you think of anything else or just need to get some more air sometime…" He extended a business card. "My cell's on the back."

Cole took the card and Harris gave him a nod. "Good talking to you," the man said.

"Yeah," Cole replied.

The detective was already heading down the hall.

Shifting around in the chair, Cole tucked the card into his pocket and then looked back out the window. White clouds drifted across the sky, forming shapes his imagination was too tired to name.

Harris was right.

He sighed, hating the thought despite knowing it was true. It sucked beyond words and made his skin crawl, but Harris was right. Whatever happened, whatever it took, saving Lily and bringing this whole nightmare to an end would be worth the price.

Even if it meant Ashe might die.

———— ◆ ————

Harris reached the elevator before he remembered to breathe, and when he did, he felt his brain start buzzing like a bag of angry wasps.

Jamison's men had been at Ashley's home. Jamison's men had destroyed the farm. Jamison's men concocted the whole diary and its tales of Cole being her boyfriend, which meant they may well have fabricated the story of Ashley murdering her family too.

And they'd never once mentioned it to him.

He blinked, realizing he'd yet to summon the elevator car. Swiftly, he jabbed at the down arrow, and then had to hit it again when his fingers missed the first time.

It didn't make sense.

Unless they deliberately wanted to mislead him.

Or Cole was wrong.

Harris cast a glance down the hall, but no one was coming. The boy had obviously decided to stay where he'd left him.

There wasn't any reason for Cole to say he'd seen them when he hadn't. What could he gain by lying? But even if the Blood had been there, Cole could have misunderstood the situation. Or he'd missed part of it. He said himself that he'd only come in for the last few minutes, and he'd only assumed Jamison's people killed everyone based on what he thought he'd overheard.

But he could have misconstrued it. Jamison's men must have known what they were heading into. Cole could easily have mistaken their preparedness for intent, and come to the conclusion the Blood were the ones planning to kill the whole family.

Of course, that didn't explain the diary.

The elevator arrived and distractedly, he headed inside, scarcely sparing enough attention to find the button for the parking garage. He hadn't given much thought to the diary in the past months; everything she'd done since had driven it mostly from his mind. But when they first met, Jamison corroborated the story that Ashley killed her family. He'd been foggy on how Cole was involved, but about the murders there'd been no doubt of the girl's responsibility.

So…

Exhaling, Harris rubbed at his eyes as he worked to find stability amid the chaos inside his mind. Ashley could have imagined everything in the diary, though nothing he'd seen of her thus far seemed to indicate she was remotely delusional. A killer, yes. Cold as hell, absolutely. But delusional? Not so much.

Though, now that he thought about it, that last bit directly conflicted with the diary, which seemed to point squarely to a girl approaching terminal velocity for psychosis.

He dropped his hand back to his side. Cole had to be right. Jamison and his men made up the diary. But at the same time, the reasons may not have been quite what the boy thought. Ashley could have killed her family. Probably had, given everything else she'd done since that night. Meanwhile, Cole said he'd arrived late, so he had no evidence one way or the other as to what the Blood had found when they first arrived. And for their part, the Blood hadn't known who grabbed the girls. They'd just been trying to cover their bases, with the goal of protecting as many people as possible.

So just the part about Cole may have been a lie.

Except then there was also the part about her plan to burn the house down, which didn't fit with what Cole said he saw at all.

Harris dragged a hand over his hair as his brain tried to pull itself apart to make the pieces he'd thought he had in place suddenly fit again. Jamison's men needed to protect their people if they were going to accomplish anything. He knew that. So for them, burning down the house could have been a self-protective measure. They'd found the bodies. They'd found everything Ashley had done. And…

what? They covered it up for her? They didn't even have a reason for being there in the first place. Why would they…

He paused. Tanya. Or, more specifically, her late husband. Though most of the time, Harris avoided the widow on account of her being the angriest and possibly the most deranged woman he'd ever seen, he'd still overheard her stories of why Howard Bartlow died.

Howard had worked with the Blood. He'd hated the war and he'd tried to bring it to an end. But he was still from Ashley's side, originally one of the 'Merlin' group who seemed to be responsible for all this, and he'd been a doctor of some kind for the little girl. Tanya even said he'd been killed by Merlin the same night Ashley's family died.

So perhaps Howard had learned how brutal Ashley could be. Perhaps he'd gone to the Blood for help. Brogan had said they were trying to protect the little girl, that night in the police station six months ago. Howard could have learned of Ashley's plan to wipe her family from the face of the earth, and perhaps that was why the Blood had been there that night.

But Jamison's men would have needed to cover up their presence. Chances were, there would've been enough forensic evidence from their attempt to stop what Ashley did that if anyone found it, the Blood might have been exposed.

He exhaled as the elevator slowed. Fine. Dandy, even. Cole may well have misunderstood most of it, given that he didn't see anything but the end, but that still left one problem. Brogan and Jamison had lied. And they'd kept lying, even after it was clear he was helping them.

Harris grimaced. He'd known they weren't necessarily telling him everything, and to be honest, he hadn't really cared. They wanted to stop Ashley and the creatures like her from killing innocent people, and they'd financed his efforts to do the same. That'd been enough.

But this was different.

The elevator slowed. Dropping his hand from his hair, he forced the scowl from his face, though when the doors opened, the expression nearly slipped back again.

"Hey, buddy," Mud said, tromping into the elevator with a sub sandwich in each hand.

Harris didn't respond.

"Off again, eh? I gotta say, it's a pleasure watching you work. That last place ya'll hit…" He grinned, his teeth full of lettuce and tomato. Harris winced, looking away. "Beauty of a thing."

"Three of Jamison's people died."

"Eh, well," Mud allowed. "True."

"What do you want?" Harris asked tiredly, praying the elevator reached the parking garage soon.

"Who says I want anyth–"

He glanced to the little man.

"Okay, okay," Mud surrendered. "Look, I just thought, seeing as how you're so… useful, with your being human and all… maybe you could tell them they don't need me to go out there anymore? I could stay here; coordinate prisoners or something. I mean, you've got the whole stealth reconnaissance thing covered. Wizards never even know you're watching them. What do you need me for?"

It took everything Harris had not to comment on the last.

"So what do you say?" Mud pushed.

"It's not my call."

"Well, yeah, but I just thought that if you–"

"Ask Brogan yourself, Mud."

The little man paused. "Yeah, well…"

With a quiet ding, the elevator door opened. Harris struggled not to bolt through the gap. The little man reeked of month-old produce. And that was the best of his qualities.

The smell of metal and engine oil surrounded him as he headed into the parking garage, and the sound of traffic filtered down the exit ramp. A few wizards glanced back as he came around the corner, but their attention returned swiftly to Brogan upon realizing it was just him.

"…apartment building on the southern outskirts of Atlanta," Brogan said. "Tanya says there are at least three hideouts inside, though the Merlin may have added more since she was last there, so don't assume anything. This building doesn't connect to its neighbors, so we'll use a standard approach, but be ready in case they try to use portals inside. Questions?"

Harris looked away. It'd only taken a couple days of helping the Blood hunt down Ashley's hideouts to learn to hate apartment buildings, since they basically amounted to kids and families trapped in a box with wizards inside. The Blood had been lucky thus far, managing to take out the Merlin and keep them from harming their human shields.

But the chance that this would be the time an innocent got hurt always made his skin crawl.

"Good," Brogan finished. "Move out."

Grimacing, Harris headed for the car with Mud tottering behind in a cloud of stench and grumbling. The wizards ignored him as he swung into the back seat, though the disgust on their faces was damn near blatant as the little man followed.

His gaze returned to Brogan as the car started to pull away. Deep in conversation with another man, the giant paid the departing vehicle no attention.

Jamison and Brogan wanted to stop killers like Ashley, and that was good. With Cole back, their focus was now solely on ending the violence while protecting those caught in it, and that was good as well.

But they'd also lied to him. They'd misled him about their involvement the night Ashley murdered her family, and they'd kept him in the dark long after it became abundantly clear he was trying to stop her just as much as they were.

There had to be a reason. And when any sane person could see the Blood were the ones on the right end of this, he couldn't imagine what might have been so damaging about that night that it was something they needed to hide.

Chapter Seven

---◆◆---

Cole sighed as the sun climbed over the horizon to shine through his bedroom windows. Rubbing a hand over his eyes, he blinked tiredly and then snagged the remote from the nightstand and turned off the early morning program he couldn't remember a moment of anyway.

He'd managed five hours of sleep last night. At this point, it was practically a record.

Shoving the blankets aside, he climbed out of bed and then scavenged together the clothes he'd tossed aside the previous night, before making his way into the living room. The sun was even more obnoxious in there. Groaning, he held up a hand to block the glare. He had to remember to close the curtains at night. Blinding himself every morning was starting to get old.

He glanced over as the latch on the apartment door turned and the door swung open.

"Would you like some coffee, sire?"

"Phillip, don't call me that."

He followed the man as Phillip crossed the room with a tray of breakfast food on his arm and his gaze locked firmly on the floor.

"How'd you know I was up, anyway? You have motion sensors in here or something?"

A hint of a smile pulled at the man's face as he set the tray on the table in the kitchenette. "No, sire."

He gave the man a dry look.

"Cole."

"Thank you."

He looked to the tray as the smell of coffee hit him. "And thank you," he added more emphatically.

Phillip's smile widened.

"So seriously," Cole persisted, taking the carafe before the man could reach for it.

"You have gone to the cafeteria looking for coffee at this hour three times this week," Phillip replied. "We work to learn your schedule to better serve you."

Cole paused, glancing up with a coffee mug in one hand and the carafe suspended in the other. No expression touched the wizard's face.

"You really don't have to."

Phillip said nothing.

Uncomfortably, Cole finished pouring the coffee. They had the strange non-argument almost once a day. By now, he was starting to suspect that, even with little things like his own name, he wasn't ever going to win.

"If there will be nothing else, sire?"

Cole suppressed a grimace. And that was proof.

"No."

Phillip bowed and then left the room, shutting the door silently behind him. Shaking his head, Cole carried the mug back to the bedroom.

It was vital people saw him as next in line to the throne. That was what his father said. At least, whenever Cole saw him, anyway. For days, he'd been locked in his office, taken up with everything from skirmishes on the outskirts of town to full-scale battles in other parts of the country. And as a result, they hadn't had much chance to talk about how ridiculous being viewed as royalty made Cole feel.

Though, if he had seen the man, that probably would've been the last thing he'd have brought up anyway.

He took a sip of the coffee, feeling it spread through him with the wonderful promise of relative consciousness on its way.

In the two weeks since he'd arrived at Chaunessy, he'd heard nothing of Lily. For all intents and purposes, the girl – and her bloodthirsty sister – had vanished off the face of the earth. But other news had poured in, brought by everyone from the Blood to Harris to the creepy little man who insisted on being called Mud. Ashe's people were killing the Blood and Taliesin alike, though their capabilities were limited by their numbers, given that many of them had run for the hills when their Council fell. But rebel Taliesin had taken up the slack, and nearly every day another group of holdouts tried to wreak havoc on those who'd sided with his father when their own Council died.

Simeon had been seriously injured the week before. Isabella's skills had saved his life, though he still favored his right leg heavily. Meanwhile the death toll among the Blood's allies kept rising, to the point where Harris refused to tell him any details beyond an acknowledgement that people had died anymore.

Though, to be honest, the man had rarely said much of anything since they'd spoken that first day. True to his profession, the detective just seemed to be taking everything in, as if collecting data on a case he couldn't seem to solve, and that no one else could see.

It was annoying.

Mud made up the difference, though, with such relish that Cole had started avoiding him whenever he saw the man coming down the hall. From everyone else, he received silence, barring requests of what they could do to serve him.

But of Lily, there was nothing.

It hadn't taken long for the insomnia to start. With so many dying every day, it really wasn't surprising he couldn't sleep. Each new attack left him worried the wizards would return with news that they couldn't reach Lily before the Merlin got away, or that her sister had killed her rather than be captured, or simply that in the crossfire, the little girl had died. The waiting was making him crazy, especially since he'd started to feel like, for the past few months, his whole life had essentially been spent doing just that one thing.

He blinked and then lowered the mug, discovering it empty. A humorless chuckle escaped him. Crazy he might be, but right now, distracted was probably the more accurate term. Time seemed to creep every day, yet when night finally came, he couldn't remember a moment that'd gone by. Books held no interest and neither did the television, and plunking keys on the piano felt about as appealing as scraping his fingernails on chalkboard.

Something needed to change or he really would go insane.

Setting the cup on the nightstand, he glanced to the apartment, but the only solution was the same one he came to every day. The cafeteria on the plaza level wasn't much, but it was open early and provided the chance to overhear information, even if being there did mean the wizards would be watching his every move to learn how to serve their supposed future king.

But that was still better than sitting here all day.

He headed out of the room. Rupert and Jerome straightened swiftly as he opened the apartment door, their eyes locking on the end of the hall as though their attention had been there the entire time.

"It's alright, guys," he said as he strode by. "Next shift coming soon?"

"In one hour, sire," Rupert replied precisely.

"See you tomorrow then."

He turned the corner, hurriedly outdistancing the additional formality that was sure to follow his words. As two of the half dozen honor guards his father had placed on his room, the men were nothing if not proper, and typically made him feel awkward as hell.

The elevator was predictably empty, though sadly, the cafeteria nearly was too. Each small round table was unoccupied, save for one beside the kitchen where a woman was refilling a miniature army of salt and pepper shakers with their respective contents.

Her eyes went wide as he walked in. Giving her a tight smile, he made a beeline for the large coffee machine, praying she didn't follow. Filling a mug as full as it would go, he paused only long enough to add a splash of something purporting to be cream and then wove quickly through the seating area to a table in the farthest corner of the room.

Sinking onto the rickety metal chair, he turned his gaze to the window. The cafeteria overlooked the ostensible park that bordered one side of Chaunessy. Roughly the size of a basketball court, the expanse of gray concrete was dotted with cement benches and tables, though none of the early morning passersby seemed to notice the seats enough to consider stopping. Decorative trees fringed the space, each branch utterly devoid of birds or squirrels.

The Blood had to find Lily soon.

He grimaced, returning his attention to the dining room.

Motion caught his eye. He glanced back outside to see Simeon stride around the corner of the building, three wizards hurrying after him. Gesturing angrily, Simeon snapped orders without turning around.

Cole leaned closer to the window, watching the Blood march up to the exit directly below. Yanking open the door, Simeon spun, snarling something at the man behind him, and then disappeared inside.

The wizards raced back around the corner and out of sight.

Brow furrowing, Cole pulled away from the window and carefully set the coffee mug down. The Blood could have just been upset by another Taliesin attack. Or maybe by some warmongers who'd gotten away.

There was no guarantee this had anything to do with Lily.

His gaze slid to the cafeteria door.

He was so damn tired of waiting.

Rising swiftly, he winced as the chair legs scraped loudly across the tiles, but he kept moving. Ignoring the stare of the woman by the kitchen, he wove between the tables and then strode from the cafeteria.

The elevator took forever to answer his call, for all that no one else was probably using it, and when it finally arrived, he slipped quickly past the opening door. Scanning the buttons, he jabbed the one for the topmost floor and then scowled, waiting for the elevator to catch up with his commands.

There was absolutely no evidence that Simeon's hurry had anything to do with Lily, he reminded himself as he watched the numbers climb. Given the man's expression, he almost hoped it didn't.

With only a hint of motion, the elevator eased to a halt and, moving slower than seemed possible, the door drifted open. Skirting through the gap, he hurried toward the door halfway down the black marble hall. Thick white carpet grabbed at his feet as he crossed the lobby, and the glass chimes overhead spun gently when he passed. Sunlight streamed through the windows that circled the upper reaches of the space and cast splintered light across the stairway as he jogged up the steps to the dark double doors on the far side of the room.

His knuckles paused an inch from the wood. Muffled voices came from within the office, snapping back and forth as though in an argument, and then suddenly fell silent.

The door opened sharply. Brogan stared down at him, mismatched eyes narrowing.

"Let him through, Mason," Victor said calmly.

The giant stepped back, and warily, Cole moved around him. On the opposite side of the office, his father stood behind an ornately carved desk, his form silhouetted by the sunlight pouring through the bank of windows at his back. Bookcases lined the rightmost wall, interrupted only by a door to a conference room, while a sofa of hard, utilitarian design sat in the adjoining corner. A few feet from the couch, Simeon stood, something almost like impatient fury in his eyes.

"Everything alright?" Cole asked carefully, watching the gray-haired wizard.

"Of course," his father replied.

Simeon turned away, resting a hand on a bookcase nearby.

Victor's mouth tightened at the motion. "You have your orders," he said, his voice cold.

Simeon's gaze snapped from Victor to Cole. His face darkened and then, without a word, he strode from the office. Cole stepped quickly out of the way as he swept past, and neither wizard spoke as Brogan closed the door. The giant's gaze returned to Victor for only a moment, and then the Blood headed for the conference room.

Victor sighed, regarding his desk. "My apologies," he said to Cole, fingering a fountain pen on the desktop.

Still eyeing Brogan askance, Cole approached the desk. The large man was perusing the papers scattered across the oak conference table as though they were completely engrossing.

Cole wasn't fooled for a second.

"I didn't mean to–"

"You didn't," Victor said, holding up a hand to stave off anything further. He gave Cole a brief smile, gesturing to the chair in front of the desk. "Simeon needed to leave anyway."

Cole sat down, uncertain what to say, and he could see his father read the expression.

"We lost some supporters last night," Victor explained, sinking into the wingback chair behind the desk. "A pair of Taliesin who'd sided with us since the early days of the war. The Council loyalists are not going quietly and, even though we're making progress… it's costly. Add to that the fact Ashley has the same powers I do, as well as advantages I do not, and that we lack knowledge regarding the full extent of the resources at her disposal, or how close she is to potentially binding us all…" He smiled tiredly at the litany. "You can see how this takes a toll on people's morale."

"Resources?" Cole asked, watching him. Exhaustion seemed to press down on the man, leaving him suddenly wondering when his father had last slept.

Victor sighed. "The staff she carries, as well as any other artifacts in her possession." He gestured dismissively. "It's not something to concern yourself over, and Simeon should not have let those same concerns get the best of him. We can't operate assuming she'll find a way to bind us again at any moment. We can only focus on now, and what we can do to stop that from happening."

Cole hesitated, fairly certain his surprise was plastered across his face, despite the fact his dad didn't seem to notice. He couldn't believe he'd forgotten, or that it'd never occurred to him that they didn't know. In all the waiting and concern for Lily, it hadn't even crossed his mind.

"She…" His eyes darted to Brogan. The man lifted a piece of paper to read, giving no sign he heard anything from the office. "She doesn't have the staff."

Victor's gaze snapped up from the desktop. "Excuse me?"

"Ashe doesn't have the staff," Cole repeated. "It was destroyed when she pulled me through that portal."

"You're certain?"

"I watched it disintegrate in her hands."

A short chuckle escaped Victor. "I hadn't thought anything could destroy something like Merlin's staff."

"Getting a cripple through a portal."

"Indeed."

Victor shook his head in amazement, but slowly, the humor faded from his face.

"What?" Cole asked.

"It's nothing. I'm grateful you told us, even if her sources will simply give her a new weapon since that one is gone."

"Sources?"

"The Merlin historians," Victor said, an edge to his words. "The ones that, unlike her, we have never managed to find."

Cole hesitated, glancing to Brogan again. "You're looking for the Merlin historians?"

Victor chuckled. "Seems ironic, I know. But believe me, those historians are the other piece to ending this war. Or, more specifically, their archives are. Merlin's historians kept records of everything, from fairytales of immortal wizards to progress reports on reconstruction after the last war. And while we might not need all that, we believe they do possess information that would enable us to defend our people in ways that haven't been possible for nearly five centuries."

"What do you mean?"

"Deterrence, primarily. As I've said, bloodshed is not our goal. But with the knowledge we would gain from the Carnegeans' archives, we'd be able to communicate to the Merlin and Taliesin perpetuating this war that, should they continue to do so, they will face an enemy with skills beyond their own."

"And if Ashe got her hands on those archives?"

His father paused. "She would do the same, in her way."

Cole looked down. He could feel Brogan in the next room, listening intently for all that he continued pretending to read. The tension of Simeon's departure still hung in the air, and he couldn't for a moment believe the giant wouldn't share everything he heard with the other Blood, if for no other reason than their apparently low morale.

But it didn't matter. He couldn't sabotage his dad, regardless of what he thought of the others. If the Carnegeans' records really were that important, his father had to know the truth, and now. After all, Lily might crack, or give away the information accidentally. For all he knew, she'd done it already, and everything his grandparents had was currently in the bloody queen's hands.

The possibilities after that were too terrible to contemplate.

"I don't think Ashe knows about them."

Victor's brow furrowed.

"Lily and I were the ones who found the staff, not Ashe. And the Carnegeans… my grandparents," he acknowledged with a grimace in his father's direction. "They hid from everyone, Merlin included. Had everybody convinced they'd been dead since the war began. We just stumbled across them by accident."

His father stared. Cole shrugged.

"You just *stumbled* across them…?" Victor repeated. "But the queen doesn't know where they are?"

"I don't think she knows anything about them at all," Cole said, hoping the words were still true.

"But what did you tell her about the staff?"

"I… I lied. I told her we got it from a drifter we'd stayed with for a while, until Taliesin killed him and burned his place down with everything inside." Cole paused. "I don't think Lily will tell her the truth."

"Because you asked her not to?"

Cole winced illustratively, but nodded. "And because she's worried the Carnegeans will hurt her sister if Ashe goes there."

"But you know where they are?"

He nodded again. "Washington state, north of the Kettle Falls area."

Victor exhaled, closing his eyes as a smile pulled at his mouth.

Shaking his head, he glanced to Brogan, who looked up from his papers and nodded shortly.

"Thank you," Victor said to Cole as Brogan strode from the room. "You have no idea how much you've helped us today."

Cole looked down uncomfortably.

A moment passed, but his father didn't say anything else.

"Have you heard anything about Lily?"

Victor blinked, drawing himself out of his thoughts. "My apologies. You didn't come here to simply listen to our problems."

He waited.

"We have a lead," Victor confessed. "That was part of what brought Simeon up here. And, if all goes well, we are hopeful it will result in finding Lily–" He paused. "–today."

Cole froze.

"A contact has informed us that the Merlin are attempting to relocate the girl. One of the queen's bodyguards will be meeting a pilot at the airport outside Banston today at two, after which he'll travel with Lily to an undisclosed location." Victor smiled reassuringly. "Don't worry. Simeon's team will reach her before the Merlin put her on the plane."

Cole exhaled, running a hand over his hair as relief hit him. Just like that, it'd be over. The waiting, anyway. She'd be here, safe.

And Ashe could be dead.

He paused, the relief melting like ice in a heat wave. Lily might have to watch her sister die today. And here he was smiling.

Glancing up, he swallowed, trying to push the discomfort aside. "So then what?" he asked, his voice tighter than he'd have liked.

"Then," Victor said, "after we get Lily settled and hopefully adjusted to what's happened... we see what she can do to help the

Merlin agree to negotiate."

Cole nodded, his gaze dropping to the ground. The first part would take weeks. Probably more. He wanted to believe she'd understand eventually, he just hoped his father was prepared for months to pass between now and that time.

"Do you think they're even going to listen to her?" he asked distractedly. "I mean…?"

He shrugged rather than finish, not really wanting to remind himself that negotiating hinged on getting a bunch of grown Merlin to obey a kid.

Silence answered him. He looked up to find Victor watching him. "They will."

"Are you sure?"

His father paused, a considering look creeping into his eyes. "The Merlin's Children," he began, as though choosing his words carefully. "They possess similar abilities to mine. I assume you know that."

Cole shrugged again, nodding.

"But their powers are not exactly the same," Victor continued. "In one, vitally important aspect, they are utterly distinct. The Merlin's Children can create a spell which binds an entire people. And based upon everything I've seen in my research… and in all the research I did with your mother before the Carnegeans disowned her… I am fairly certain I cannot. The ability was somehow tied to the Merlin's Children's bloodline and–" He chuckled dryly. "–despite my rather crude method of mixing that blood with my own, it remains something they alone can do."

Victor exhaled and folded his hands in front of him, humor fading. "Which is why we need Lily's help. Between her abilities and the information your grandparents maintained, we have a very good chance of binding those who oppose us. The spell operates on affiliation, that much was clear by the way it bound everyone associated with Taliesin's supporters in the first war. Using this spell, we could bind Ashe's allies and any Taliesin who resist us in a single moment. And if they still choose to fight…" He splayed his hands illustratively.

Cole eyed him warily. The hairs on his arms were raising and, for some reason, it was becoming hard to breathe. "What?" he asked cautiously.

"We are up against forces determined to enforce their worldview on us, no matter the cost. The losses we've suffered, you've already seen. But even without their magic, there is a strong possibility they will keep fighting. They are willing to do anything to continue this war, Cole. You've witnessed that. And you know the brutality monsters like Ashe are capable of. If she'd found your grandparents first, I do not want to imagine what she would have done. So, if we have no other choice… we may have to force the issue."

Cole swallowed. He couldn't have stopped the question if he tried. "How?"

Victor paused, as though deciding again precisely what to say. "If pushed hard enough," he allowed, "the spell does have the ability to end the lives of those it is used against. Merlin obviously never took it that far, but based on what some historians believe… he could have. Of course, we don't want to do that, and if it came to that point, we would only seek to eliminate those it would take to serve as an example to the others. I told you, bloodshed is not our goal. But you know the atrocities the Merlin queen committed, and that her people supported. If pushing the spell is what it takes to make them understand they must end the war…" He gestured regretfully.

"Then that is what we will have to do."

Cole wanted to blink, but he couldn't make himself move. Everything in the room seemed to have come down to the fixed point of his father's face and the small shrug of his hands. The world beyond the window was a white glare and his body felt strangely thick, as if he didn't know what to do with it anymore.

"But this is where we are going to need your help," Victor continued.

The words hit him like a blast from a fire hose. He fought not to choke.

"Lily will have trouble understanding this," his father said. "She is a child and she has not seen what you have. Or," he amended, his eyebrows rising and falling eloquently, "we hope she has not. But, regardless, she trusts you, and she will need your help to understand that this is not about hurting people as her sister has so willingly done. This is about securing peace. It always has been. And if, upon binding them, Merlin and Taliesin back down and negotiate with us for their surrender, so be it. That is what we would prefer. And if they do not…"

He sighed. "I promise you, she won't have to see it, or know the details of what you're asking of her. We can shelter her from that. We *must* shelter her from that; it's the only humane thing to do. And later, when she's older and this war is something for the history books… then hopefully she'll understand that through her efforts and those wizards' sacrifices, peace became a reality."

Cole shook his head, frantically trying to figure out how the man in front of him could be the same one he'd been speaking to only moments before. A breath entered his lungs, rasping his throat like sandpaper as it came. "She…" He swallowed hard. "Dad… she's just a *kid*. She…"

A compassionate expression flickered across Victor's face. "She's a weapon, Cole," he said gently. "In our hands or theirs. You need to realize that. Both those girls are."

Trembling spread up from his stomach and his forearms were glued to the wooden surface of the chair. His eyes searched his father's face, desperate for the joke, for the explanation that would somehow make this sane.

But there was nothing.

"Dad–"

A knock sounded behind him, and he flinched. On shaky arms, he twisted in the cage of the chair and looked back to see Brogan slip around the door.

"My apologies," the giant said, bowing slightly. "Keller needs to speak with you."

Cole heard his father sigh, and when he turned back around, he froze to see the man watching him.

"I know this is hard, Cole," Victor said. "But I also know we're the best hope Lily has for a normal life, given what she is. She can be safe and happy here, more than she'd ever be elsewhere. That's what you want, isn't it?"

A chuckle escaped Cole, the sound clinging by its fingernails to this side of hysteria. He could feel Brogan at his back and see the expectation on his father's face, along with the concern slowly growing in his eyes. His dad wanted him to agree. Needed him to agree.

And Cole couldn't even find it in himself to breathe.

Swallowing hard, he moved his head in something approximating a nod.

Victor smiled. "Then we'll talk more soon."

"Yeah," Cole managed.

"In the meantime," his father continued. "We have a place set up for her, if you'd like to see? It's the apartment down the hall from yours."

He wasn't sure if he nodded again. He wasn't sure of anything. His rubbery arms moved of their own accord, pushing him out of the chair, and he had no choice but to obey the distant commands of his legs as they carried him across the room. As he neared the giant, his gaze twitched up to see Brogan staring him down.

Swallowing again, he glanced to his father. The expanse of Croftsburg sprawled in a vertigo-inducing abyss beneath the bright blue sky at his back, and his lips curled into a warm smile as he met his son's eyes.

Cole barely kept from bolting as he fled the room.

— ◆ —

Brogan watched the boy leave the lobby. Pale didn't begin to describe Cole's complexion. Dead would have been more accurate.

Letting the door close behind him, he crossed to Jamison's desk. "You told him the plan for the girl?" he asked, though he was fairly certain of the answer.

Jamison turned to the window, regarding the world below.

"Clearly he took it well," Brogan commented.

Silence answered him. A grimace touched his expression as the seconds slid by.

"He is more attached to the child than I anticipated," Jamison said quietly. "But Cole will come around. He agreed to the possibility of the Merlin queen's death. He'll agree to this."

Brogan didn't respond.

"That being said," Jamison continued, his thoughtful tone fading. "There is still the interim."

The king turned back from the window.

"Watch him. Let me know if his behavior becomes… concerning. But don't let him become aware of your attention. I will not risk alienating my son. Not if it can be avoided."

Brogan nodded and then drew out his phone. His gaze tracked the king as, ghosts of discomfort still clinging to his face, Jamison rose and headed for the conference room.

Chapter Eight

He needed to move. He couldn't stop moving.

His feet carried him into the elevator, and then the wall brought him up short. Spinning, Cole paced back, but then came the door.

He'd hit a button. He couldn't remember which. Blinking, he looked down, but then the door was open again and he didn't care anymore. The hall blurred around him, as did the doors and walls and things that didn't matter like people who were waiting at the end. Stopping sharply, he stared at them. They were guards. The guards on his apartment. He was on his floor.

His eyes went to the door beside him, and he blinked at the brass handle. He'd never given much thought to the only other doorway in the hall.

He'd just thought it was a storage room.

For some reason, the thought seemed excruciatingly ironic, though he couldn't figure out why. With trembling fingers, he reached up and tugged the latch down.

The door swung wide.

It was pink. The room. Like a nightmare of flowers and fluff stripped from the pages of a girlish decorating magazine. An oversized pink butterfly made up the thick rug on the floor, and a multicolored butterfly mobile dangled from the ceiling and gently twisted in the air from the hall. An enormous mural of clouds and smiling butterflies filled one wall, with several of the creatures escaping into the bathroom as well. White wrought iron twisted in abstract loops around the king-sized bed, framing the vividly pink quilt and the profusion of flower-shaped pillows, while sheer pink curtains filtered the light from the windows.

She'd probably love it.

The thought hit him and he choked. On unsteady legs, he walked into the room, and his shoes sank into the butterfly rug before it occurred to him he was probably getting the enormous thing dirty. His gaze ran over the idiotically grinning creature and slowly, he felt his heart start to pound.

This couldn't be happening. This was… this was stupid. Absurd. Stupid and absurd and wrong…

Oh God, this was wrong.

He gasped, yanking his gaze from the bug, only to find that the room still surrounded him.

This was beyond any definition of wrong. This made what Ashe'd done look like the practice run before the actual show.

Though she would have done it herself. Or tried to, if not for the fact they'd probably end up killing her today.

His father's face rose in his mind. Cole sank onto the bed, trying not to be sick.

He hadn't even cared. He'd been careful and meticulous and patient in his explanations, but he hadn't actually given a damn that, in the midst of it all, Lily was a child…

Just a child…

Cole shook his head. She wasn't just a child. She was a kid he'd been shot, thrown into trees, and nearly killed by wizards for. And every step of the way, all he'd wanted was to make sure the two of them reached the end of this alive, preferably without scarring the girl for life.

And his dad would make her kill. Men, women, even children would die because of her. And it wouldn't be enough. Cole wasn't stupid. After this was done, once Merlin and Taliesin had capitulated and licked their wounds, they'd be back. They'd want vengeance.

And she'd have to do it all over again.

His fingers dug into his hair and he braced his elbows on his knees, fighting just to breathe.

It would destroy her. The minute she found out. The minute she learned that all those people on whom she'd pushed the spell just a *little* bit harder…

The people he'd told her to push it on.

He stared down at the big, pink butterfly without seeing it.

This had always been the plan. Bringing the girls in. Seeing if they could 'help the Blood negotiate'. It was why his father sent the Blood after them. Why they'd needed only one. Two would have been better. Of course it would have been better. It meant the Blood had a backup as well as leverage, and that was probably the goal. But in a pinch, they really only needed one.

If Ashe hadn't become a murderer with the Merlin, his dad would have just made her one for him.

A gasp escaped him, the sound garbled and choked. His hands trembled on his scalp as the enormous, stupid bug became a pink blur beneath his feet.

Everything the Taliesin said… everything the Merlin said… everything *anyone* said…

His father surpassed them all.

Victor had started the war, but he'd made it make some sense why. He'd destroyed the councils, but of course there'd been a reason. His men were possibly going to kill Ashe today, but she was a monster, so for the sake of everyone, they might not have any choice.

Nobody ever had any choice.

Numbness spread through him, drowning the horror in a blanket of shivering cold.

Every single second, he'd been used. By the Smiths for protection, by the Taliesin for the same. And now by his father for everything he could convince an eight-year-old kid to believe.

Because she was so trusting.

And he was too.

His father said bloodshed wasn't his goal, and it wasn't. It was his means to an end. He said he wanted to create peace, and he would. By destroying an innocent little girl. And Cole couldn't for one minute believe it'd matter if he said no. Not after the look he'd seen in his father's eyes. His dad would do it anyway, and heaven help Lily for what she'd go through.

Heart pounding, Cole lifted his gaze to the door.

He couldn't let him do this. Not to her. Not to anybody. And he had to stop them now. Waiting till Simeon and the others brought Lily back would be too late, because by that time, his dad would have her on such lockdown that, while getting in to see her might not be a problem, getting her out of this room would probably take an army.

He didn't have any choice.

Nobody ever had any choice.

He'd be leaving his father to the war. All the other people in this building too. Ashe's people, the Taliesin, all of them. They'd have to slug it out for however long it took one of them to come out on top, and hundreds would die in the meantime. But he couldn't be responsible for that. Not given the alternative. And they could make peace. They didn't have to fight forever. For all he knew, when all this was said and done, the Blood would still have won, peace would be a reality, and maybe… maybe…

He closed his eyes, hating how much he'd simply wanted his dad to be right. To be the one he could trust and the man he remembered, and not this other thing he'd somehow become.

Maybe his dad would understand someday.

He drew a breath and opened his eyes. Maybe was good. He could hold onto maybe.

Running a hand over his head, he looked around. He needed to get out of here, and not just this monstrosity of a room. But the underground tunnel the Council had mentioned weeks before did him absolutely no good since he didn't know how to access it, and the parking garage was fifty floors of wizards away. Wizards who'd be watching his every move, all to learn how best to serve him – a desire that probably didn't include helping him steal Lily away before the Blood could get their hands on her.

He'd need a distraction. Or at least a cover that would allay their suspicions, which was basically the next best thing.

His gaze hopscotched across the butterflies and the smiling flowers, and he shook his head, coming up with nothing. A cover would have to involve other people, and no one here was exactly on his side. Forcing them was out of the question, since from Brogan all the way to the janitor, any of them could simply use their magic to swat him like the proverbial fly.

He paused. Almost any of them.

Exhaling, he pushed away from the bed and then pulled out his cell before he could reconsider. It was a long shot, and in no way resembled a full plan. It wasn't even half of one, since it hinged on being able to grab a weapon from a trained police detective and then keep that weapon long enough to force the man to get him out the door. It was ridiculous.

But it was the only option.

He flipped past the screens on the phone and then froze as Rupert's voice carried down the hall.

"Yes, Mr. Brogan?"

Silence followed. Cole's brow furrowed warily.

"Yes, sir, he's down in the girl's—"

Cole's lungs forgot to work. In the hall, Rupert cut off sharply, and when he continued, he sounded as though he was trying to keep the giant from reaching through the phone. "No, I mean, yes. I do. I didn't – Yes, sir. I–"

A moment passed, and then the man muttered something inaudible to Jerome. Cole's gaze twitched to the phone, his fingers flipping through the screens faster as he cursed the time it took just to reach the contacts page. Footsteps squeaked on the tile, coming his way.

"Sire?"

He reached Harris' name and smacked the button to dial the number, praying that Brogan hadn't called the man yet. Maybe that he wouldn't at all. Lifting the phone to his ear, he listened to it ring the other line.

Rupert leaned his head cautiously around the doorframe. "Sire, are you–"

"Hey, Detective?" Cole said over the guard's words as Harris picked up.

Uncertainly, Rupert paused.

"It's Cole. I was wondering if you'd grabbed breakfast? I just caught up with my dad and…" He let his voice trail off, hoping the detective would read into it. "You know, you'd said if I wanted to talk…"

By the door, Rupert shifted uncomfortably and Cole glanced over, giving him an irritated look as he waited for Harris' surprised agreement.

"That's great. Meet me at the elevator? Great."

He stuffed the phone back in his pocket as he headed for the door.

"Can it wait, Rupert?"

The man faltered. "Of course, sire. You'll be going to the cafeteria then?"

"Yeah."

He could feel the guards' eyes on him all the way to the turn of the hall.

They'd call down there. He could guarantee it. Which meant he had precious little time before the staff downstairs realized something was wrong. But the cafeteria was only two floors from the parking garage, and he remembered overhearing Simeon telling another wizard that keys were kept in all the cars.

This would work.

Hopefully.

Grimacing, he punched the button for the elevator and then glanced over his shoulder as he waited. The guards weren't following. The door rolled back, revealing no one inside. Taking a breath, he walked in and pressed the button for Harris' floor.

One hurdle down. God knew how many to go.

The elevator descended, and then slowed almost imperceptibly as it reached the proper floor. Forcing himself to breathe, he pushed a composed expression onto his face.

Mud grinned at him as the door pulled back. "Hey kid! You getting food?"

Cole's eyes went from Mud to the detective in alarm.

"He was in the hall," Harris said, his voice so neutral, it left little doubt of his opinion.

Stepping back to give the smelly man as much room as possible, Cole didn't answer, trying to stay calm. This wasn't good, but… he floundered and gave up, unable to find a bright side. His gaze twitched to the detective. At least the man had his gun. He always had his gun. Even if it was mostly useless against wizards, Harris kept it with him constantly, as though finding comfort in its proximity.

Cole glanced back to Mud. He had to keep going. There wasn't any other option.

"You waiting for something, kid?" Mud asked as the door slid closed. "Push the button already."

"Sorry." He drew a breath and smacked the button for the parking garage.

"Wait, what–" the detective started.

Cole spun and shoved Harris hard, sending him into the side of the elevator car. Reaching down, he ripped the gun from its holster and then retreated, aiming it at both men equally.

"Really sorry," Cole said, breathing hard. "Just… don't move."

"Cole, what're you–" Harris began, struggling up and bracing himself on the handrail.

He tightened his grip on the gun and the detective froze. In the corner, Mud stared, his yellowed eyes wide.

"You don't need to do this, Cole," Harris tried cautiously. "Just tell me what's going on."

He ignored the man. From the corner of his eye, he could see the numbers scrolling down, racing for the lowest floor. The parking garage had cameras, but they were mostly focused on the main gate. The magical barriers, however, would be more trouble. He'd figured on hiding in the back of the car and having Harris drive, but corralling both him and Mud presented much more of an issue. The little man was unpredictable at best, and would probably bolt the minute they reached the parking garage.

He really hadn't planned on shooting anyone, even the filthy little lump of…

His gaze darted back to Mud.

It was stupid. Ludicrous. The smell alone might kill him.

But it could work.

"Take off your coat," he ordered the man.

"Huh?" Mud said.

"Coat. Now."

Harris' brow drew down. His mouth twisting sourly, Mud looked from the detective to Cole and the gun, and then began shrugging out of the oversized and arguably brown floor-length coat.

"Did you actually talk to your father?" Harris asked, ignoring the grumbling noises Mud made while peeling the sleeves from his arms. "Did he say something that prompted this?"

Cole didn't answer, keeping the gun on Harris while he reached out for the coat. Beneath his stained gray t-shirt, Mud's bony shoulders hunched like a turtle stripped of its shell.

"You won't get away with this," the little man groused as he extended the enormous coat with a pale hand spotted by erratic sprigs of dark hair.

Ignoring him, Cole pulled the coat closer, fighting not to balk at the way the smell made his eyes sting. Harris hadn't taken his gaze off him, and he could tell the detective was just waiting for an opening that wouldn't result in a bullet ricocheting around the elevator.

The door dinged.

"Stay here," Cole ordered Mud. He glanced to Harris. "You're with me."

Backing up, he kept the gun aimed at Harris while he slung the coat over his shoulders with one arm. Unidentifiable bits of something he tried not to think about rained down as he tugged the hood over his head.

"This way," he said to the detective, jerking his chin toward the cars.

Watching him carefully, Harris started toward the vehicles. Tucking the gun under the coat, Cole cast a swift look back. Mud glared balefully from a corner of the elevator.

Attempting not to breathe too deeply, Cole turned away as the elevator door closed. Slouching as low as he could, he dropped his head to hide his face and let his steps shuffle in imitation of the little man's gait as he trailed after Harris.

Along the walls, the security cameras panned over the garage. Eyeing them cautiously, Cole cleared his throat and then nodded toward the nearest car when the detective glanced back.

"Get behind the wheel."

Harris paused and then headed for the dark green sedan. "Why are you doing this, Cole?"

"Shut up and get in."

Harris pulled open the door and slid inside. On the passenger side, Cole did the same, his skin crawling at the feeling of the coat pressing between him and the seat.

"Keys are in the visor. Drive."

The detective didn't move. "I'm going to need more of an answer than that."

Cole cocked the gun. Harris looked from him to the bulge of fabric concealing the weapon.

"You won't shoot me," the detective said quietly.

"You're not giving me a whole lot of choice."

Harris studied him a moment. A muscle twitched around his eyes, and the certainty in his expression faded ever-so-slightly. Slowly, his hand reached up and tugged the visor, letting the keys fall to his lap. Still watching Cole, he inserted the key in the ignition and then started the car.

"Did she put you up to this?" Harris asked, something dark entering his voice.

"I said drive."

The detective put the car into gear and eased his foot down on the accelerator. The sedan crept toward the exit.

"Faster."

The car sped up infinitesimally.

Breathing hard, Cole watched the detective as the vehicle climbed the slope to the gate. Muscles jumped beneath the man's jaw and his hands on the steering wheel were white. As the sedan pulled to a stop beside the small callbox by the gate, the man did nothing but stare at the road beyond the magical barrier.

"Put in your access code."

"I don't have one."

Heart pounding, Cole floundered and then regrouped. "Roll down the window," he ordered, trying to keep his face from view of the cameras. "Tell them… tell them it's your partner. Something's wrong and you need to see him."

Harris didn't move.

"Dammit, now!"

The detective's eyes slid to Cole and then back to the street. Expressionless, he rolled the window down and then reached over, pressing the button on the callbox.

"Harris here. Lower the barrier."

"Purpose?" came the reply.

The detective paused. "Malden's in the hospital. I need to see him."

"Access code?"

Irritation showed on Harris' face.

Cole exhaled furiously, his hand tensing on the gun. "Enter it or I shoot, Detective," he whispered desperately.

Harris glanced from him to the weapon. He typed in the code and then pressed his thumb to the scanner mounted nearby.

A moment crawled past.

"Clear."

The detective sent the car rolling forward.

"Head for the highway," Cole said.

Harris turned east.

Eyes stinging from the stench of the coat, Cole risked a swift look back as the sedan pulled around the corner. No one emerged from Chaunessy, and the pedestrians striding down the sidewalk were ignoring their car and all the rest of the morning traffic completely.

Returning his gaze to the road, he fought the urge to rip the coat off, knowing it'd just give Harris an opening. A few more miles and he'd throw the damn thing out the window. He just needed to get the other man out of the car first.

"She won't reward you for this," Harris said darkly. "Whatever this is about, whatever she promised… I guarantee you it's not going to end well."

"This isn't about Ashe," he said, scanning the street for signs leading to the interstate.

Harris' gaze went to him and then back to the road. "Then what?"

"Drive faster."

Muscles clenched tighter beneath the detective's jaw. The car accelerated, slipping past a yellow light just before it turned red.

"I didn't take you for a liar," Harris said scornfully.

Cole's gaze twitched back to the man.

"If this isn't about Ashley, then what?" the detective continued in the same tone. "Did you actually talk to your father or were you just making that up?"

Cole didn't answer. On the side of the road, a blue sign pointed the way toward the interstate.

"Pull over here," he ordered.

Harris grimaced, his derisive expression fading as if he'd realized contempt wasn't changing anything. The car slowed.

"Out," Cole said, motioning with the gun as the sedan came to a stop.

The detective looked at him consideringly. "This is about the little girl, isn't it?"

"I said get out."

Harris' eyes narrowed. "It is."

"Now!"

Face darkening, Harris shoved open the door. Keeping the gun leveled at the man, Cole backed out of the passenger side and then circled the car.

"Cole, whatever's going on, this isn't the way to fix it," Harris said, stepping back as Cole gestured him away from the door. "I'm trying to protect that kid too, so talk to me. Or, if not me, then at least go back and talk to your father. You know he wants to help her same as you."

Despite himself, Cole scoffed as he lowered himself into the car. Tugging the door shut, he glanced up through the open window, and a sickened twist of irony moved through him as his dad's words were all he could think to say.

"You shouldn't believe everything you see," he told the detective as he put the car into gear.

In the rearview mirror, he could see Harris staring after him as he sped away.

———— ◆ ————

"…totally insane! You should've seen his eyes. Bloodshot! And his mouth! Foaming! The boy's gone rabid, I tell you. And now he's got a hostage. Probably already shot him. I mean, I barely made it out and—"

Harris could hear Mud long before he reached the entrance to the parking garage, and as he rounded the corner, the little man's face was nothing short of amazed.

And a bit disappointed too.

"H-he didn't kill you?" the lump sputtered. "I mean… thank God! You're alive!"

Harris ignored him. Expressionless as a wall, Brogan stood to one side of the scrawny man with a cluster of very uncomfortable-looking wizards nearby.

"What happened?" Brogan asked shortly.

Harris let the walk down the slope buy him time as he tried to sort out what to say.

He didn't fare any better than he had the whole way back to Chaunessy.

On the one hand, Cole hadn't said much. The boy just looked like he'd found the edge and was staring over it. Something had obviously threatened the little girl, but if it'd actually been anything to do with Ashley, or even anyone here, Cole surely would have gone to his father.

So it was something Jamison had done. Something that scared Cole enough that he'd felt the need to go after the kid the moment he'd heard it. Something that made Cole question whether his father wanted to protect the girl at all.

Harris eyed the wizards as he came closer. If anyone had reason to trust Jamison, it was his son.

There could have been a misunderstanding.

He couldn't make himself buy that. Not with the look in the kid's eyes.

"Detective?"

"He surprised us," Harris answered succinctly. "Grabbed my gun and then forced me to drive a few blocks from here before taking the car himself. He didn't say why."

Brogan paused, and then turned to the wizards behind him. "Call

Simeon."

Harris glanced after the men as they hurried away. "He didn't tell us where he was heading."

The giant smiled, cold humor in his one good eye.

"We already know."

Chapter Nine

Her hand gripping Lily's, Ashe stepped from the portal and instantly the silence of the empty apartment in Banston was replaced by the rush of wind over the airfield. The hot afternoon sun beat down from a brilliant blue sky, glaring off the hangar at her side and glinting from planes parked by the terminal almost half a mile away. Flight crews like stick figures hurried around the planes, and the beeping noises of their vehicles carried thinly over the distance. A barbed-wire fence separated her from the service road and woods ringing the airfield, though for the moment, both the road and the stretches of tarmac were empty.

She glanced back as Elias emerged from the portal. Ignoring the vanishing gray shadows, he looked immediately to Nathaniel.

"Anything?"

She could see the large wizard's frustration as he shook his head. Wizards they could detect. The Blood were a whole other matter entirely.

Gravel crunched behind them. Her heart hitting her throat, she spun.

Cornelius walked around the rear of the hangar, and then jerked his chin back in the direction he'd come. "This way."

Drawing a steadying breath, she ordered herself to keep calm as she followed him. Lily didn't need to see her panicking. The girl was scared enough as it was. And for her part, she needed to stay focused anyway. In a few minutes, when the screaming began, she'd need all the composure she could muster.

Aluminum siding stretched ahead of them, interrupted only by narrow doors and by braces where one hangar ended and the next began. She could hear muffled voices inside, though from the way Cornelius ignored the sounds, she could only assume he'd already confirmed the people weren't a threat.

She flinched as Lily shifted her grip. She couldn't bring herself to look at the girl, and the small reminder of Lily's presence sent her pulse spiking again.

No matter how many times she ran the plan through her head, it never made anything better. She was going to bind her sister. The moment Lily climbed on the plane, just before she realized Ashe wasn't coming too, she was going to steal the girl's magic and let Cornelius take her away, hopefully before anyone could hear Lily scream.

And after that, she might never see her sister again.

She wasn't stupid. In the hours after she'd ordered Cornelius to get Lily away from the war, she'd had to admit the truth to herself. This war could kill her. Probably would kill her, if she wanted to be morbid about it. And if that happened, Lily's enraged, hurt and screaming face would be the last of the girl she'd ever see.

But there wasn't any alternative.

She couldn't keep Lily near her, not when together they made a larger target than they'd ever be separately. And she had to take the girl's magic. Lily would be furious when she realized her sister wasn't coming, and because of that, she might lose control. In the past few days, Ashe'd been trying to teach her how to use magic, but Lily was scary powerful and had a long way to go. She couldn't risk the very real possibility of the girl blowing up the plane and killing herself, just because her anger momentarily overrode her control.

And it wouldn't be forever. It probably wouldn't even be for a day. Once the plane landed and Cornelius called to say they were safe, she'd let the girl's power go. She wasn't going to leave her sister defenseless. She was just trying to make sure Lily stayed alive.

The aluminum siding came to an end. Turning the corner, Cornelius dropped the magic around himself between one step and the next, bringing him instantly into human view.

Her breath caught, the small shift of energy snapping her back to the present. Regrouping swiftly, she followed suit, trying not to let on how much she wished she could hang onto even a shred of defensive magic, as Elias and Nathaniel were doing. But that wasn't the plan. And the pilot would probably have a problem taking Cornelius and the little girl with him if he had to watch Lily scream at thin air.

Swallowing, she shoved the thoughts aside as they reached the edge of the hangar. Hesitating in the shadow of the building, Cornelius scanned the area, and then continued around the corner into the sunlight. Keeping Lily behind her, Ashe followed.

"Hey there, Mike!"

At the disembodied voice, she froze. Metal jangled on asphalt and then footsteps clunked down the ladder on the other side of the small plane in front of the hangar. Stained work pants hurried along the length of the aircraft and a moment later, a bald head popped into view.

"These them?" the man called cheerfully, a bright grin on his glistening face.

Lily ducked behind Ashe.

"Yep, these are my stepdaughters," Cornelius replied easily, all traces of formality gone. He nodded to Ashe and then to Lily. "Sarah and Emily."

Wiping his hands on an oil-smudged rag, the man continued around the nose of the plane. Twisting slightly, he shoved the rag into his back pocket and then extended a grimy hand to Ashe.

"Jerry," he said, shaking her hand. Still grinning, he bent to catch Lily's eye. "Shy, isn't she?"

Ashe tried to give him something approximating a smile, though the expression couldn't quite get past her discomfort at his proximity. Pulling her hand back, she fought the urge to glance over her shoulder to Elias and Nathaniel.

"So what's the deal?" Jerry continued, turning to Cornelius. "When you called, you didn't mention you were bringing two gir–"

"I didn't think it'd be a problem," Cornelius interrupted smoothly while Ashe's heart jumped.

"It's not. There's just only so much fuel and if they're both–"

"It'll be fine."

Jerry paused. At her back, Ashe could feel the confusion radiating off Lily.

"Okay…" the man allowed. "Then, uh, I've just got a couple things to finish up and we can be on our way."

Hesitating a moment more, the man glanced between the girls and the plane as if trying to calculate how to fit them and Cornelius together, and then gave up and headed back toward the ladder.

"What'd he mean?"

Ashe froze at the sound of Lily's voice. Possible answers raced through her head, though from the mixture of suspicion and uncertainty in Lily's tone, she wasn't sure any of them would work.

"Huh?" she tried, turning back with a baffled look.

"Hey, Mike?" Jerry called, clambering back down the ladder. "I wanted to say how much I appreciated that thing you did for me in Baltimore."

She glanced over as the man jogged around the nose of the plane.

The gun went off before she could do more than register it was there.

Cornelius stumbled back, his hands clutching at the blood soaking his trench coat.

Jerry smiled. "But they paid me a hell of a lot of money to tell them where you were."

Magic burst from the forest on the opposite side of the field.

Striking Elias and Nathaniel, it hurled them into the hangar and tore through the plane. The metal body disintegrated as the fuel tank exploded, engulfing Jerry and hurling fire into the air. Cornelius staggered away, his magic rising, and then flaming shrapnel drove him to the asphalt, where he didn't move again.

The blast wave punched her shields, throwing her down and sending Lily tumbling to the concrete. Without hesitation, Ashe scrambled toward her.

"Watch out!" Lily cried.

She looked from the girl to the forest, and then flattened herself to the ground. Magic streaked over her head. Beneath the protective cover of her arms, she twisted and then gasped.

Elias was rising to his feet. Energy burned the air around him as debris rained from his shoulders and Nathaniel struggled up at his side.

Magic slammed into them, hit the hangar wall, and then exploded, shredding the siding and sending the roof down on the wizards like molten tinfoil.

A choked noise escaped her, and then she was moving. Shoving off the asphalt, she sent a rapid-fire blast of magic racing toward the trees and then snagged Lily's arm, hauling her up. Behind them, people screamed as they fled the collapsing hangars and, across the field, airport security vehicles were rushing toward the scene. Dragging Lily with her, she ignored them all as she flung more magic at the forest and ran for the terminal a million miles away.

Either side of the field erupted. Electricity and fire pounded her defenses, hammering at her till she stumbled and crashed to the ground. From every direction, wizards emerged from the forest, tearing down the fences ahead of them as they came. Fighting to reach her feet, she ripped the magic from the nearest and sent it roaring back. A dozen fell, but more were behind, and pain buckled her legs as their magic slammed into her weakened shields.

"Run!" she yelled at Lily as she stripped the magic from another wizard and then hurled it back.

Whimpering, the little girl shook her head and pulled on Ashe's arm, her eyes on the people closing in on all sides. Blue-white light rose around Lily, tremulous and unsteady, and then it burst across the field, mowing down the wizards as it passed.

Ashe stared for a heartbeat, and then tore her gaze from the airfield. Digging her hands into the ground, she propelled herself back up, sucking air between her teeth as pain seared through her at the motion. Ignoring the blood running down her arm, she grabbed the girl's hand and took off for the terminal again.

Lily choked. Ashe's gaze darted over.

From the grass and tarmac, the survivors were rising.

A green sedan careened down the service road behind the wizards, a cloud of dust swirling in its wake. Swerving madly, it bounded off the path and tore over the fence, racing into the airfield.

The wizards turned. The car barreled through them.

Magic slammed into her from behind, tossing her through the air and ripping Lily from her grasp. Pain exploded through the side of her head as the asphalt met her and lights splintered her vision. Gasping, she rolled, trying to find Lily in the haze. Running toward her, the little girl shrieked and then tumbled sideways as magic roared past her to shatter the tarmac inches from where Ashe lay.

"Get up!" Lily screamed.

Dirt scattered as the sedan whipped around, screeching to a stop a few yards away.

"Lily!" Cole shouted through the open window.

With a relieved cry, Lily spun, grabbing Ashe. "Come on!"

Blood dripping down her face, Ashe struggled up from the ground. Clutching Lily, she didn't move as her eyes met his over the little girl's head.

Cole's face darkened.

"Ashley, please!" Lily cried, hauling on her arm.

Lightning crackled past, frying the trees on the far side of the field. The terminal was surrounded by flashing lights and gawkers watching the hangar blaze, all of them hundreds of yards away.

Snarling a curse, she ran for the car. Lily yanked open the passenger door and tumbled inside, colliding with Cole. Ashe swung into the back seat, but he hit the gas a mere second after she made it in. Grabbing the headrest, she hung on as momentum shoved her toward the open door and then sent her crashing back in the other direction.

The door slammed closed. Wizards leapt from their path as the sedan raced for the service road.

"I knew you'd come back," Lily told Cole. "I knew you would."

Ashe glanced over. His lip twitched into something that might have masqueraded as a smile, and his eyes didn't leave the airfield.

Drawing a breath, she twisted toward the rear window. The wizards were running for the security vehicles, and as she watched, magic struck the driver of the nearest pickup.

Metal screeched as the sedan tore across the fence and onto the road. Hitting the brakes, Cole hauled the wheel around, snapping the car through the tight turn.

Her gaze caught on the hangars. Flames engulfed the buildings and black smoke poured into the sky. On the ground near the wreckage, motionless bodies lay.

The air was thick and hurt to breathe. Pulling her gaze from the destruction, she stared at the seat fabric, fighting back a scream. Of its own volition, her hand reached up, gripping her wounded shoulder. The pain helped her focus and swiftly, she sent a rush of magic through the bleeding gash and up to the wound on her head, healing them as best she could.

Cole swore. Her eyes snapped back to the field.

The wizards had gained control of the security vehicles. And they were coming.

"Hang on!" he called.

With a jolt, the car flew past the broken gate of the service road and bounced onto the main airport thoroughfare. Horns blared in Doppler shift around them as the sedan darted between cars screeching to a halt and pedestrians scrambling to get out of the way.

The security vehicles skidded onto the road behind them.

"Faster!" she yelled.

"Trying!" he snapped back.

A minivan pulled from the parking garage ahead, its driver jerking to a stop in the middle of the road at the sound of all the honking. Swearing, Cole accelerated hard, jumping the sedan over the curb and onto the grassy hill by the roadside. The car tilted as it rushed up the slope, while in the lane below, the other driver never glanced their way.

She looked ahead. Over the rise, the elevated interstate arced above the airport road and, as the car surged forward, she could tell Cole had seen it too. Gripping the wheel harder, he raced the sedan down the incline and onto the street, veering around the cars paused by the exit road stoplight.

Fire erupted beyond the hill where the minivan had been.

Lily gasped. Ashe turned to see the girl clambering up on her knees to stare out the rear window.

"Get down!" she ordered.

She spun back to the road while Lily dropped low in the seat.

Half a dozen white security trucks flew out from behind the rise. The sedan took to the on-ramp, racing for the highway.

Lightning sped toward them. She gasped, her defenses rushing through the metal and the glass to surround the car.

Energy glanced from her shields and propelled the sedan sideways. Metal squealed as the rear panel slammed into a guardrail, and then they were on the interstate, leaving shards of the taillight scattered behind them. Snarling, Cole yanked the wheel around as the car careened across three lanes of traffic and then straightened out, snapping back onto the road just shy of the metal pylons at the center of the highway.

"Was that you?" he called, swerving to avoid another car.

"Just the shield."

Gripping the back of the seat to keep her balance, she looked over as he cursed, pain twisting his face. "Can you handle it if I attack them?" she asked.

A chuckle escaped him, the sound not remotely friendly, and she couldn't tell if it was intended for her or them. "Just make it quick."

She eyed him for a heartbeat and then turned to the rear window, dismissing her confusion as deeply irrelevant. Her gaze locked on the on-ramp and her fingers flexed unconsciously with the pressure of the magic beneath her skin.

Three white trucks charged up the ramp.

The rear window of the sedan exploded outward. Rushing over the distance, her magic punched past the wizard's defenses and into the grill of the foremost truck, carrying the engine back through the cab and out the rear wall. Swerving wildly, the truck collided with the pickup behind it, sending them both through the guardrails and onto the roadway far below.

"Son of a–" Cole shouted. "What the hell was that?"

Ashe drew a breath and struck out at the third truck. The pickup veered sharply as the wizard's shields crumpled under the blow, but a blast of magic followed the moment the driver gained control.

She ripped the energy from the air and threw it back. Rubber burst across the concrete as the truck's tires disintegrated and the pickup fishtailed madly through the lanes.

A gasp escaped her. Frantically, she flung her magic across the distance, but it was too late. Careening out of control, the truck caught the rear of the small car in front of it, shoving the vehicle into a spin even as the pickup kicked over itself and rolled.

Her magic hit the truck, propelling it backwards while the little car smashed into the metal pylons in the center of the interstate. As the truck tumbled to a stop, Ashe stared at the car.

The driver pushed open the door and stumbled out, gaping around in shock. Ashe remembered how to breathe.

"Ashley!" Lily cried.

She spun, looking from the girl to Cole. White-knuckled, he grasped the wheel, pain clear in every tense line of his face. Drawing air between gritted teeth, he whipped the sedan around another car.

"Any more?" he growled.

Turning, she checked the distant on-ramp. Her brow drew down. Midday travelers and semis occupied the interstate for miles.

But of the other three security vehicles, there was nothing.

"No," she answered warily.

He swallowed hard and swiped a hand at the sweat dripping into his eyes. "Good," he replied, the word sounding as though he'd just as soon it be a curse.

Scanning the road, she ignored him. On a lazy curve, the elevated highway swept toward the heart of Banston, most of which was veiled by a haze of smog. Beyond the guardrails edging the interstate, concrete drainage slopes led to deep ditches and a line of ragged trees trying unsuccessfully to shield the older sections of town from view.

White metal flashed at the corner of her eye, and her gaze snapped back to the highway. Half a mile ahead, three security vehicles sped down the off-ramp and charged into the oncoming traffic.

Her eyes darted from the trucks to Cole.

And then their magic was coming.

Electricity lashed across a semi ahead. The tires exploded, sending the truck careening, and then the semi jack-knifed hard. The front whipped back toward the trailer, catching on the blown tires. With lethal speed, the truck slammed down and ground across the width of the highway in a fountain of sparks and screaming metal.

Cole hit the brakes.

Two security vehicles raced around the ends of the skidding semi.

Swearing, Cole looked from the white vehicles to the semi-truck.

"Go!" Ashe shouted.

He crushed the accelerator to the floor.

The sedan surged toward the semi. Pulling in sharply, the security trucks veered toward the center of the road.

Ashe stretched her hands out to either side.

The car shot between the white pickup trucks.

"Now!" Cole yelled.

Her magic obliterated the windows and the vehicles beyond.

Spinning in her seat, she watched as the trucks tumbled across the interstate, the vehicles flying apart as they rolled. Twisting the wheel sharply, Cole raced the sedan through the narrow gap between the semi and the metal pylons dividing the interstate.

Lily screamed.

Cole slammed on the brakes.

She turned.

There was a car.

Propelled by magic, a blue sports car flew through the air like a child's toy, heading straight toward them, and she had no time. Metal howled as the car slammed into them, the destruction racing her magic to reach the occupants of the sedan.

Her shields enveloped them.

Glass exploded as the hood crumpled and the whole world went sideways. The magic behind the impact threw the green sedan backwards, and the steel pylons dividing the highway vanished as the car plowed over them and began to roll. Concrete flashed past the windows, grating and screaming and kicking up shattered glass to fly through the chaos in the car.

And then they were airborne.

Gravity vanished and Lily screamed. Ashe's stomach climbed into her throat, trying to escape, and breathing was an impossibility. Frantic, she poured everything she had into the shields as the world tumbled down and down and down.

Into the ground.

Chapter Ten

Glass tinkled like rain and smoke burned her nose.

Ashe opened her eyes. She was on the roof. Metal and fabric were pressing her cheek, while her shields still flickered weakly around her.

And the car was on fire.

The realization hit her as hard as the ground and she gasped, shoving away from the roof. Pain radiated through her, emanating from every muscle and bone in chorus, and she choked on it as she shifted around to see the front of the car. Pebbles of faintly green glass tumbled from her bloodstained clothes, and in her pocket, the crushed remnants of her cell phone grated as she moved. Beyond the headrest, she could see Cole dangling, his body suspended by the seatbelt still connected to the side of the car, and as she looked over, he groaned.

Lily lay on the roof by his side.

Breath catching, Ashe reached for her.

The girl moaned and opened her eyes. At the sight of her sister, she gasped. "You–"

"Are you okay?" Ashe interrupted, not caring what her injuries looked like.

Lily stared a moment more and then nodded.

Breathing again, Ashe echoed the motion. "We need to go," she said with meticulous calm.

Lily's nose twitched and then she looked sharply to the front of the car.

"Can you get him down?" Ashe asked in the same tone.

Wide-eyed, Lily nodded and then scrambled across the glass and debris to nudge Cole hard. "Wake up!"

Groaning again, the young man opened his eyes and then tensed, visibly thrown by finding himself upside down.

"Hurry," Ashe warned him.

He twisted in the restraints to look at her, and then nodded at whatever he saw in her eyes. Reaching down, he braced himself on the roof as Lily unfastened the safety belt. Controlling his fall, he tumbled sideways to the ground.

"Ready?" she asked as he pushed away from the ceiling.

Lily crawled over next to her, watching Cole.

He nodded again and started for the empty driver's side window.

Ashe grabbed his arm. "What if the wizards are waiting?"

He grimaced, stopping.

"Wait till I signal and then head for the trees," she told him.

She slid through the empty window and then rose swiftly, her gaze on the highway above the drainage slope. Smoke poured into the air, obscuring the view, though she could see the dim forms of people crowding around the broken barrier to scan the wreck below.

"Go," she hissed.

Glass and gravel crunched as Cole emerged. Quickly, he grabbed

Lily's hand, pulling her along as he took off for the trees. Her eyes on the interstate, Ashe backed away from the sedan and then turned, running after them.

Trees and bushes scraped her bloodied skin. As she pushed through to the other side of the hedgerow, her eyes swept the backyards. Chain-link fences separated each lawn from the next, with a few wooden fences thrown in for variety, and every one of the yards was still. A wall of houses blocked the road, but a few lots down, she could see a utility easement leading between two of the homes.

"Come on," she said.

Lily hurried after her, leaving Cole to follow.

Moving fast, she strode between the fences and the trees, her eyes twitching to the houses as she went. Dark windows stared out at them, threatening despite the fact no one appeared to be home. Somewhere in the distance, a lawnmower growled, the sound nearly obscured by the sirens rushing down the highway. At the end of the easement, she paused, scanning the street. Nothing moved and most of the driveways were empty, their owners long since gone to work.

She had no idea where to go.

A quiver shook her aching muscles at the realization. Miles of labyrinthine residential streets twisted away in front of her, leading to a city she knew nothing about. They'd only arrived in Banston a short time before, and hadn't hardly stopped long enough to do more than wait for the next portal on the way to the airport.

She made herself breathe as she fought the burgeoning panic. It didn't matter if she wasn't sure where they were. She just needed a portal to get them enough distance from here, and then it'd simply be a matter of finding a phone, calling Katherine and meeting up wherever the woman happened to be.

It was going to be fine.

Though that didn't bring Cole into the equation.

"Where to now?" he whispered, as though in answer to her thoughts.

She swallowed, not looking at him. Cole didn't matter; Lily did. Getting her away from here did. The boy was irrelevant, and if leaving him behind was what it took to keep Lily safe, then that was damn well what she was going to do.

Exhaling sharply, she raked her gaze over the houses, seeking a deep enough doorframe.

She froze. Between two homes down the street, the edge of a pastel pink house could just be seen. Magenta trim and purple shutters completed the image, rendering the garish house utterly out of place among its neighbors.

But she recognized it. She'd seen it from the apartment window when they first arrived in town.

She grabbed Lily's hand and darted from the cover of the houses.

"Where are we going?" she heard Cole call furtively.

She ignored him, her feet picking up speed as she ran across the road. A brief flicker of magic took out the lock on the fence blocking her way, and another removed the latch beyond. Barely pausing at the next street long enough to glance around, she started down the sidewalk, her shoes hitting the pavement at a rhythm a thousand times slower than her pounding heart.

The wizards would be coming. It wouldn't take them long to backtrack into the neighborhoods. She had to be quick if she wanted to get them out of here.

In so many ways.

Gritting her teeth, she pushed the thought away as she raced past the pink house. Lily would be upset. She knew that, and she'd deal with it later. But right now, the preset portal in that apartment was the best chance they had of reaching someplace actually safe.

She just needed to get it open fast enough to put the girl through before either Lily or Cole realized what was happening.

The tan brick of the apartment building came into view at the end of the next street. Her eyes sweeping the neighborhood, she ran down the sidewalk and then jogged up the entrance stairway, staying close to the wall. At the door, she paused, peering through the grimy window to the hallway beyond.

Stillness greeted her. Gray light shone through the glass onto the scuffed floor, and as she tugged open the metal door, the clank of the latch echoed in the silence. Her shoes squeaking on the tile, she pulled Lily behind her as she hurried across the hall to the stairs.

"Are the others here?" Cole whispered.

Halfway up the first flight of steps, she glanced back. His hand gripping the end of the banister, he seemed reluctant to move any farther, and though he never looked at the girl, it felt like he was focused on Lily all the same.

"What?" she asked, confused.

"The other Merlin. Did any of them stay behind here?"

She stared at him, incredulity warring with the memories. "Why?"

His face shut down as well as any wizard's, and ice crept through her, joining the magic twisting beneath her skin and making it hard to breathe.

"Just want to know what's up there," he said neutrally.

"They–" Lily started, her voice choked.

Ashe jerked the girl's hand and kept climbing, tugging Lily along.

It was a moment before she heard him follow.

Three flights up, she abandoned the stairs and ran down the shadowed corridor, making a beeline for the apartment at the end. The door flew back, the handle banging into the wall as she raced past, and to one side of the empty living room, the closet waited, a few bent hangers dangling within.

Her hand hit the closet doorframe. Blue letters chased themselves across the wood.

"Wait," Lily cried. "What–"

She turned and grabbed the girl as, in the closet, the hangers and the back wall vanished into a gray vortex.

Cole ran through the apartment doorway.

Lily's fist hit her shoulder, sending pain shooting through her arm, and for a second, her grip slipped. Shoving away from her, Lily tumbled to the carpet and then backpedaled.

"What're you doing?" the little girl exclaimed, retreating to the far side of the living room. "We can't leave Cole!"

Skidding to a stop, Cole's face tightened with discomfort.

Lily waved her hand at him anxiously. "Stay away from it!"

His gaze darted from the girl to the door, and then came to rest on Ashe.

"You're not taking her," he said.

From behind his back, a gun materialized.

Her magic met it before he'd done more than bring it into view.

He gave a pained cry as the weapon went flying, but he recovered fast, moving for Lily as the gun clattered to the floor. Ashe raced to intercept him. Swinging hard, her fist connected squarely with his jaw. He staggered to one side, and then turned quickly to knock her away.

"Stop it!" Lily yelled.

He shoved her hard, sending her crashing into the wall. Hot blood soaked her shoulder as the wound from the airport ripped open. Gasping, she pushed herself upright as he rushed past her, heading for Lily.

Her hand burst into flame.

"*Stop!*" Lily screamed.

Bracing herself on the red-streaked wall, Ashe looked over at him. "Don't touch her," she ordered, her voice ragged with the effort of speaking through the pain.

One hand gripping the little girl's arm, Cole didn't move.

"Ashley, stop this!" Lily pleaded. Ripping from Cole's grasp, she looked between them as she backed away. "Both of you. Stop!"

"You're not taking her to him," Ashe said.

Cole gave a cold scoff. "Wasn't planning on it."

Her brow twitched down.

"Please, Ashley," Lily begged. "Put the fire out. Please."

Her gaze flicked to the girl and then back to Cole. Tense, he watched her, and she was painfully aware of the gun resting in the kitchenette nearby. If she went for Lily, he'd go for the gun, and then there wouldn't be much she could do.

Besides kill him.

And she could tell he knew it.

She shook her head, the flames unchanged. "We're leaving. You can find your own way out of here."

"I'm not going anywhere without him," Lily protested.

"And if I try to stop you?" Cole asked, his voice becoming contemptuous.

Her hand trembled. "Don't," she advised.

His gaze twitched to Lily, calculations racing behind his eyes.

"You won't do anything in front of her."

Quivers shook her and she fought to keep from giving any sign. Everything hurt, the air was like ice, and braced on the wall, her arm was going numb.

She made the flames grow higher.

"Just get out of the way," she told him.

"Hey!" Lily snapped. "I said I wasn't–"

"Shut up!" Ashe yelled, her voice breaking.

Shocked, the girl fell silent.

"Get away from her," Ashe continued to Cole.

He paused. "No," he said carefully. "I'm getting her out of here. Away from you, him, all of this. And if you care about her at all, you'll let me. Understand?"

Ashe stared at him.

"Come on, Ashe," he finished. "You don't want her to be a part of this or you wouldn't have been trying to put her on that plane today. Let me help you."

A choked noise escaped Lily. The girl looked between them in horror.

Ashe swallowed hard. "That's why you came back?"

He nodded.

"Y-you were going to–" Lily sputtered, staring at her.

"What about your dad?" Ashe asked, unable to bring herself to look at the girl.

"Lily's safer away from him too," Cole said flatly.

Her brow drew down, and for a moment, she desperately wanted to believe he was telling the truth. Lily could be protected and nothing had changed, even though the whole world had changed because Cornelius and the others were lying dead in a field after she'd asked them to do the exact same thing.

She shuddered, memories flashing through her mind. Everything hurt so much.

"The Blood are coming, Ashe," Cole pressed. "Please. Do the right thing. Let Lily go."

"I'm not leaving without Ashley either," Lily argued, her tone lost between anger and disbelief.

Ashe watched him glance to the girl, and slowly, the desire to believe him faded away. Cole wasn't Cornelius. He wasn't Elias or Nathaniel either, and he never would be. At the chance to run to his father, he'd willingly blown every scrap of trust she'd given him straight to hell, and for all she knew, he'd just turn around and do it again. He was nothing.

And she was the best chance Lily had right now.

She pushed away from the wall, fighting to keep her face from showing pain despite the fact she wanted to collapse. "No. Lily stays with me. And if you know what's good for you, you'll get the hell out of my way."

The flames on her hand leapt higher in warning as she walked toward the little girl.

"Ashley, you can't do this!" Lily cried, retreating till the wall stopped her. "He–"

Ignoring her, she snagged Lily's arm. From the corner of her eye, she saw Cole start toward them, and instantly, her other hand flew out. A small burst of fire charred the wall near his head, sending him flinching away. She kept moving, tugging Lily with her toward the portal.

"No!" Lily protested, digging in her heels. "I'm not going without–"

"Yes, you are," she retorted, yanking on the girl's arm hard enough to make Lily cry out in pain. Guilt tried to surface at the sound and she crushed it back. She'd apologize later. She'd apologize for every damn thing in this day later.

"I won't!" Lily shouted as they reached the portal. "I'm not going! You can't–"

The magic hit before she knew it was there. Air rushed around her, and then she collided with the refrigerator across the room and crashed to the floor. Gasping, she opened her eyes, choking as she tried to breathe around the feeling her body had finally been broken for good.

Her vision cleared. The first thing she saw was the portal.

It was rippling. Rumbling.

Roaring.

Her gaze snapped to Lily, but Cole was already there. Grabbing the girl, he lunged for the door.

Magic erupted like a gray geyser behind him. Twisting and snarling, it surged across the room, hit the wall, and took the side of the apartment with it. Her eyes closed as brick and glass exploded outward and the building rocked from the blast.

The quaking stopped. She could feel herself trying to breathe, every gasp halted by sharp pains in her sides. Someone grabbed her. Opening her eyes, she saw Lily crouched in front of her, hands shaking her hard, but the girl's words were garbled by the rushing in her ears.

Cole appeared. He reached for the girl, trying to pull her away, and Lily shrugged him off, snapping something over her shoulder which made him freeze.

Lily's blue eyes locked on her own.

Everything faded.

"You're okay," she heard the girl whisper imploringly. "You're okay."

Air entered her lungs. Blinking, she looked up to see Lily staring at her, tears in her eyes.

"I didn't mean to," Lily said. "I-I didn't…"

"It's alright," she replied, her voice hoarse.

As Lily nodded jerkily, Ashe's gaze moved from the girl to the hole where the corner of the apartment had been. The carpet was smoldering and charred brick framed the open space that used to be the wall. Through the gap, she could see out over every house on the street.

Her heart started beating harder. Any wizard in a twenty block radius could've picked up on that blast. And now all of them would be heading this way.

Swallowing, she moved to push herself from the floor, and then hesitated when nothing hurt. Her eyes flicked to her shoulder. Smooth skin. Drying blood without a trace of damage beneath. She drew a breath, burying her surprise as she rose the rest of the way to her feet.

"We have to go," she said, reaching for the girl.

"Cole too," Lily warned, retreating a step.

Ashe's gaze twitched to him. Gun in hand, he stood a few feet from the little girl, and behind his caution, she could read the readiness to fight her all over again.

She barely kept back a scowl. "Cole too," she agreed coldly.

He tucked the gun into the back of his jeans without a word.

Jaw tightening, she grabbed Lily's hand and headed for the door.

———— ◆ ————

With a groan, Elias opened his eyes.

Memory rushed back and he drew a sharp breath, trying to sit up, only to feel something stab excruciatingly at his side. A choked sound escaped him as he collapsed back to the ground, and instinctively, his magic coursed around the wound, slowly making the air easier to breathe.

He was under something large and, from the feel of it, recently on fire. Smoke was thick in the air and, in the distance, sirens wailed.

But he couldn't hear the queen, her sister, or anything resembling a fight still going on.

Swallowing against the residual pain, he reached up and shoved the sheet of metal, bolstering the effort magically. The sheet bent back, though the piles of debris behind it still fought to hold the metal down. Grudgingly, the covering moved out of the way, letting the smoke-laden air hit him in full force.

Coughing, he struggled to his feet.

The hangar was gone, as was the plane in front of it and most of the other buildings. The fence guarding the field had been shredded into chain-link tatters, and several of the trees were smoldering. Small fires still burned in the piles of decimated metal siding, and smoke had turned the sky gray.

His heart was pounding harder, but he didn't pay any attention. From a safe distance, fire crews were raining water down on the building's remains, while in the airfield, medical teams were helping the wounded.

And neither of the Merlin's Children were among them.

They could have escaped. Nathaniel may have been able to reach them, or the queen might have managed to create a portal to get herself and her sister away.

The thoughts were background noise while he scanned the wreckage and, as his gaze caught on a boot protruding from beneath a wing of the plane, one of the optimistic theories summarily died. Bracing himself on a piece of metal sheeting, he climbed out from the debris and negotiated his way across the unsteady piles.

Metal struts and shards of siding covered the plane wing. Quickly, he pulled them away, his magic sending the remnants tumbling onto the other mounds of debris. The plane wing was harder, its size ungainly to begin with, but as it finally scraped to one side, he paused.

Blood covered Nathaniel's head and marred his face in half-dried streaks. The man's arms were a mess, and his legs hadn't fared much better. Bending swiftly, Elias felt through the sticky blood for a pulse.

A breath escaped him. Hurriedly, he shifted around and put a hand to the man's chest. Light burned hot beneath his palm, racing to strengthen the faint heartbeat. He pressed his other hand to Nathaniel's head, his eyes darting across the injuries covering every inch of the man that he could see.

Bone knit and skin followed, and slowly the wounds faded away.

Nathaniel drew a sharp breath, his eyes opening wide.

"The queen," he said immediately.

"I don't know," Elias answered.

A dazedly intense look on his face, the wizard moved to push himself upright. Elias rose and stepped away, scanning the ruins as he gave the man room.

"They have her?" Nathaniel growled, his voice turning the words into a bizarre mix of question and promise of violent retribution should they prove true.

"We don't know that," Elias replied, but his attention wasn't on the response.

Across the field, two bodies lay. Too large to be the queen and her sister, they were also too nicely dressed to be airport personnel, and they were surrounded by emergency technicians who seemed to be trying to figure out how the pair came to be there.

But tire tracks carved a path through the grass between them, leading from the broken fence to the tarmac, while others traced lines alongside.

Possibilities flickered through his mind, each as unverifiable as the last.

"Councilman?"

"Try her phone," he ordered.

As the large man drew out his cell, Elias pulled his gaze from the tire tracks and then paused. The fire surrounding the plane had been mostly extinguished, but beyond the ruin of the aircraft, the edge of a familiar trench coat could be seen.

Behind him, Nathaniel made an infuriated noise and sent the cell clattering into the debris. Eyes still on the trench coat, Elias pulled out his own phone and handed it back before starting across the wreckage. The jets of water from the fire hoses moved away as he passed, and when he left the hangar debris, the emergency crews flowed around him without noticing he was there.

"She's not answering," Nathaniel growled.

"Keep trying."

Circling the remains of the plane, he paused at the sight of Cornelius and then crouched down and carefully pulled away the man's bloodied coat. The wizard's shirt was sodden red, but past the torn fabric, a faint glimmer of magic crawled around the edge of the bullet hole while, incrementally, the man's chest rose and fell.

Elias shook his head dryly and then glanced up at Nathaniel. "Still nothing."

His mouth tightened and his gaze returned to the airfield. Even if she'd made it away, that still left the queen and her sister out there alone, with only the hope that the Merlin would find them before the Blood.

And they had such a good track record in that regard.

Pushing aside the old frustration, he looked back to Nathaniel and extended a hand for the phone. "Can you?" he asked with a nod toward Cornelius.

Nathaniel gave him the cell and then bent down at Cornelius' side. As the large wizard's magic spread over the man's wound, Elias hit the speed dial, his eyes on the city skyline barely visible beyond the trees.

"Kat?" he said as his wife picked up the other end. "We're at the Banston airport. We've got wounded and we've got a problem. Contact everyone and get them here quick."

He grimaced. "We're going to need them."

Chapter Eleven

◆

Apartment doors opened in the halls above them and shouted questions filled the air. Adrenaline pounding through him at the sounds, Cole raced down the steps after Ashe and Lily.

"What're we going to do?" Lily asked, her voice low and scared.

Ashe didn't answer. One hand clutching her sister's, she left the stairs and rushed for the door, pausing only to cast a swift look down the street.

"Ashley?"

"Everything's going to be fine," Ashe said.

Without another word, she shoved open the door and hurried into the sunlight.

Cole grimaced. The Bloody Queen of Merlin was lying through her teeth and he knew it. After what Lily did to that portal, every wizard for a mile around was probably coming here.

Tires screeched behind them as they reached the sidewalk, confirming his thoughts. He looked back, catching sight of a white truck rushing around the corner a block away, and then the migraine from hell shot through his head.

The truck flew backward and broadsided a tree.

Gasping with pain, he glanced back, but Ashe was already running with Lily in tow. He muttered a curse, taking off after them.

He wasn't sure what he'd been expecting today, but this wasn't it. Saving Ashe's life at the airport, running from his father's people with her… that hadn't been part of any plan. Back in the apartment, he'd thought for a moment he'd been able to reason with her. That, for one second, she'd been willing to let the girl go. But she'd gone right back to being what the Merlin had made her, and pretty much confirmed that she'd rather let the kid die with her than give Lily a chance to survive.

And there wasn't a damn thing he could do about it.

Following them around another turn, he scowled, his jaw still aching from her punch and the gun pressing uselessly against his back. He couldn't take Lily from her, and he couldn't convince the girl to leave either. For better or worse, Lily had given no sign she knew what her sister had done, and thus she'd never believe him if he told her. Simply forcing her to go was out as well. When he'd tried to pull her away after her magic nearly put Ashe through the wall, the little girl's snarled threat had been more than clear.

For the moment, wherever her sister went, Lily was going too.

He winced as magic rushed from Ashe and struck a black sedan coming around the corner, propelling it into the vehicle directly behind. Without pausing, Ashe turned, yanking Lily along as she bolted between a couple of nearby homes.

Grimacing, he ran after her, hoping that'd been a wizard and not just some human who'd happened to glance her way.

The neighborhood vanished between one block and the next,

becoming a commercial district that deteriorated the farther the three of them ran. Chic cafés gave way to seedy-looking bars, and trendy stores surrendered to pawnshops. The buildings grew older, their sides marred by graffiti and water stains, and For Sale signs began to appear in every window he could see. Weathered cars crawled along, and if any of the people wandering down the sidewalk ever looked up, they never seemed to care about the three of them running by.

Ashe made a choked noise and stumbled to a stop, her eyes locked on the massive building occupying the entire block across the street.

Coming up beside her, he scanned the building for threats, seeing nothing except boarded-up windows and doors, both covered in tape that warned that the five stories of carved stone were condemned. Baffled, he looked over, and alarm shot through him at the emotions racing across her face.

Shock. Disbelief. And then something so lost between hurt and hope, he couldn't have untangled it if he'd had a year.

Without a word, she took off running.

Brow drawing down, he glanced around and then followed. Darting across the road, she circled the side of the building and sped past three identically boarded windows before skidding to a stop. Swiftly, she reached for the plywood, only to freeze mid-motion.

Her eyes twitched to Lily. Worry flickered through her gaze.

"Stay behind Cole," she ordered the girl tightly, and then she tugged the plywood aside. The board swung out as though on a hinge.

"What is this?" he asked, his alarm growing.

"Get inside."

"I'm not—"

"Now."

Her voice was a growl and at the sound, he hesitated. The options weren't good. Arguing in the open like this was stupid, and they really did need to hide, but doing so in a place where Lily could be in danger should have been out of the question.

The look in her eyes was as uncompromising as stone.

His jaw tightened and he reached up, hoisting himself onto the ledge. The old wrought iron window frame was already open to the inside. Quickly, he swung over the stonework and dropped into the room beyond.

Room wasn't quite the right word, he realized. Cathedral would have been closer, though the thing wasn't a church. Marble floors stretched away in front of him, their patterns barely discernible in the thin, gray light filtering through the dusty windows fifty feet above. Graffiti-covered columns lined the left side of the space, the tall pillars surrounded in shadow and supporting the cobwebbed arches of a gallery with stone balustrades on the second floor.

He blinked, reading the tarnished brass letters above the cubicles on the distant wall. Departures. Arrivals. The place had been a train station.

Lily whimpered behind him and he spun to help her over the windowsill. Shielding her from the empty space, he waited as Ashe climbed up and then dropped down inside. As her feet hit the ground, she looked instantly to the shadows in the galleries, watching them as though daring them to move. Not taking her eyes from the darkness, she left the plywood cover open, the sun backlighting her as she carefully walked away from the window.

"What—" he hissed.

She made an urgent sound, the noise barely audible. Still eyeing the shadows, she came up next to him, ignoring the wary look on his face at her proximity. Her shoulder pressed against his, further blocking Lily from view. He tried not to move instinctively away.

"Hello," she called to the emptiness, almost as if she believed someone was there.

Gun barrels appeared in every window of the gallery.

His hand went for the weapon tucked in the back of his jeans.

Ashe made a choked noise. "Don't," she whispered.

His eyes slid toward her. She was motionless. He couldn't even tell if she was breathing. And then the truth hit him.

He couldn't feel any magic coming off her. In the face of all these guns, she wasn't using a hint of defense.

His gaze snapped over as skittering sounded in the shadows on the far side of the room. Twin shapes bolted from the darkness, resolving into a pair of enormous dogs.

Ashe gave a tiny gasp. Anxiously, he glanced between her, the guns, and the animals.

The girl never moved.

Bounding over the distance, the dogs rushed up and around her, bumping her legs. Their tongues flashed over Ashe's immobile hands and then the animals continued on. Lily squeaked with surprise as they sniffed her curiously.

Two men stepped from the shadows, shotguns in their hands.

He glanced back to Ashe, hoping desperately there was a plan involved in this, and then paused at the sight of her face.

The wizard impassivity was returning, shielding the fleeting trace of anguish in her eyes.

"Seems they recognize ya," one of the men called, his thick Southern accent making the words drawl.

Ashe said nothing.

Twenty feet away, the man came to a stop, his burly companion doing the same. "Want to tell me what you're doing here?"

"Saw the sign," Ashe said neutrally.

Confusion moved through Cole and he fought not to let it show. At the words, however, the man's expression didn't change.

"Y'all look like hell," he commented flatly.

"Wizards," Ashe replied in the same tone.

The man's brow shrugged. "What's your name?"

From the corner of his eye, Cole saw her gaze flick to the gallery and the plethora of weapons there.

"Summer," she answered.

None of the weapons moved. He felt a breath leave her.

"And him?" the man asked.

"Snake."

Cole struggled to hide his growing confusion, despite feeling like the man and Ashe were speaking some kind of code.

"And the little one behind you?"

Ashe hesitated. "Requires explanation."

Cole saw her eyes dart to him. Cautiously, she inched to the side.

The men cursed, their weapons swinging up, while in the galleries the guns shifted on the balustrades as their owners tightened their aim.

Ashe stepped back in front of Lily and internally, Cole swore. Cripples. He was a moron. The whole damn room was full of gun-wielding cripples who'd obviously think the little glowing girl was a threat, and Ashe just…

Ashe just…

Oh hell.

His ears tuned back in as his heart tripped over itself to go faster. Ashe was telling them some story about finding the girl. About how the Blood had killed the kid's family. Which was true, and so very false at the same time. But the cripples' guns were lowering. Incrementally, but they were lowering.

They were buying her story.

Oh, oh hell.

This must have seemed perfect to her. She knew enough to spot their hiding place, and now she had a building full of people at her disposal. People she'd use to bolster her power so that every wizard in a hundred miles wouldn't stand a chance. It was why she hadn't shown any trace of magic, why she'd not flinched when guns were pointing at her head, and of course, why she hadn't dared tell them her real name.

She was working to get farther inside.

Exhaling sharply, he tried not to curse as the man motioned for the cripples in the gallery to stand down. Damn good liar that she was, she'd done it again. And he couldn't yell her identity any more than he could shoot her to bring this farce to an end. She'd kill him as readily as the rest, and in the ensuing gunfire, Lily would absolutely be the cripples' target as well.

He was trapped, just like everybody else in this building.

She wouldn't kill them in front of Lily, though. He paused at the thought, hoping more than ever that it was true. Lily loved her sister. Clung to her sister. Her world depended on Ashe being the good guy, and on some level, Ashe seemed to realize that.

Which might give everyone here a chance.

His jaw tightened as the man told them to follow. Irony didn't cover it. He wasn't sure what did. After everything he'd done, the crazy stuff he'd gone through to protect the little girl, the survival of everyone around him suddenly depended on keeping Ashe's sister as close to her as possible.

The gun in the back of his jeans feeling heavier than ever, his gaze tracked Ashe as she started after the man, pulling Lily along. The whole thing was sickening. Twisted and sickening.

But it was only for now.

— ◆ —

Shadows closed around them as they headed between the columns on the side of the room and overhead, Cole could hear the guns disengage as their owners retreated from the gallery. A thin layer of debris ground beneath his shoes as he walked farther into the darkness, and the crunch of the footsteps ahead of him were the only other break in the quiet.

He blinked as his eyes adjusted. A faint bluish glow paled the shadows, emanating from behind a black barrier that could have been a wall. Their guide, who'd enigmatically identified himself as Blackjack, walked toward it and Cole followed, pausing as the source of the illumination became clear.

A single, blue emergency light shone dimly at the base of a wide stairway. Blackjack continued down, the dogs trailing him, though at the top of the steps, Ashe hesitated. She drew a breath, as if considering whether to go on, and then she started after the man, keeping Lily close to her side.

Cole's gaze tracked her. There still wasn't any magic coming from the girl, and even with the wizard impassivity clinging to her face, she'd somehow contrived to look like a beaten-up teenager struggling

193

not to be afraid of following a bunch of strangers into the dark, rather than a mass murderer quietly working on a way to kill them all.

At his back, the burly man called Shale made an impatient noise. Fighting to keep his frustration from showing, Cole headed after the girls.

The steps came to an end, with an opening to the right as the only possible direction to go. As he rounded the turn, his eyes swept the eerily silent space of cement columns and cracked tile. His brow twitched upward. The abandoned subway station was utterly still, and thick shadows hung beyond the island of light by the stairs. Up ahead, he could faintly discern the ledge where the floor disappeared, and as he followed Blackjack, he caught a glimpse of dim orange emergency lights farther down the tunnel on either side of the platform.

Quickly, the man jumped to the tracks and headed left. Waiting for the dogs to go ahead, Ashe dropped down and then turned, bringing Lily after her.

Feeling like he was falling farther and farther into a mistake from which he couldn't escape, Cole slid off the edge of the platform and followed.

Rubble carpeted the ground, fallen in disconcerting chunks from the ceiling above, and occasional dust rained down as subway trains flew through the newer tunnels nearby. Gripping Lily's hand, Ashe continued ahead of him, her form silhouetted by the orange glow and flanked by the dogs. In the shadows between the emergency lights, larger pieces of debris began to appear, like boulders cast through the tunnel as though they were dice, and along the wall, crazed and gaping fissures marred the water-stained concrete.

The man turned and disappeared behind one of the boulders,

while the dogs took up positions by simply flopping to the ground and fastening their gazes on the tunnel's end. Cole's brow drew down. Cautiously, he walked closer, glancing uncomfortably to Ashe at her proximity and then returning his attention to the shadows behind the stone.

Only a lucky trick of physics had kept the boulder from falling farther and blocking the steel door by its side. Towering higher than the door itself, the mass of concrete was littered with graffiti and sprigs of rebar that protruded like antennae from its edges. Ignoring the precariously balanced slab, Blackjack knocked a quick rhythm and then pushed the door open, sending golden light spilling into the tunnel.

Cole blinked in the sudden glare and then tensed at the sight of the people standing around a table in the room beyond.

To a person, they were armed.

His gaze flicked to Ashe. With one hand holding Lily behind her, she scanned their faces, an intensity he wasn't sure he wanted to understand flashing through her eyes. But after a heartbeat, the impassivity crept back and with an expectant glance to him, she started inside.

Without any other option, he paced her, keeping Lily out of sight. The room had been a storage space once, or perhaps a maintenance area, if the dusty switches and dials along either of the side walls were any indication. But sleeping bags and backpacks filled the space now, and the only illumination came from the brilliant yellow utility lights strung between the struts overhead. Near the far wall, a ladder ran to the ceiling, ending in an access hatch to whatever lay above, and in the center of the room, an old metal table balanced on unsteady legs beneath the weight of weapons and maps of various parts of the country.

"We've got visitors," Blackjack said.

Silence made it clear that the statement was obvious. Turning, the man raised an eyebrow to Ashe, caginess slipping back into his gaze. For a moment, she hesitated and then eased over, bringing Lily into view.

Weapons came up around the room. Instantly, Ashe stepped back to Cole's side.

"Hold it!" Blackjack called, raising his hands to forestall any gunfire.

No one moved.

"This here is Summer and Snake. They found this little one hiding out after the Blood killed her kin. So take it easy. They say she doesn't mean any harm."

The guns lowered, though only slightly.

"Why would the Blood attack their own?" a scruffy-faced man growled distrustfully.

"She doesn't know," Ashe answered.

The scruffy man's expression didn't change.

"Look," Blackjack said, glancing to Ashe. "Why don't y'all just start at the top? Where–"

Metal clanked as the access hatch on the far side of the ceiling swung open. Boots appeared, and swiftly, a man slid down the ladder, turning as he hit the ground.

The gun went off before Cole could move.

Ashe's shields surrounded her instantly, sending the bullet ricocheting into the defunct monitors on the wall, and around the room, the other cripples stumbled away, their weapons coming up to aim at the wizard girl. Shoving Lily back, Cole retreated toward the corner, knowing that with Shale and the dogs behind them, they'd never make it out the door.

Magic still hovering around her, Ashe stood motionless.

His muscles tense beneath the barbed wire and chain tattoos twisting down his dark arms, the man lowered the gun, nothing but ice in his eyes. As boots clanked on the rungs above him, he walked away from the ladder, his gaze locked on Ashe as though she was the only person in the room.

"I almost didn't believe it," the man said quietly.

A girl in a white tank top dropped off the ladder behind him, a shotgun strapped on her back across an extensive tattoo of spider webs made into wings. Yellow light played over the thick, blonde dreadlocks of her hair and as she turned, her expression was as guarded as any Cole had ever seen from Ashe.

"When Spider told me you were back," the man continued. "I almost didn't think it was possible."

He stopped in front of her, and though her magic must have hurt like hell, his face gave no sign. "Ashe."

Grips tightened on the weapons all around. Heart pounding, Cole clenched Lily's arm, willing the girl not to move.

They knew who she was. What she'd done. His gaze slid to Ashe, dreading what she was going to do now.

"Hello Samson," Ashe said softly.

Rage seethed under the ice in the man's eyes. "Where are the others, wizard?"

Ashe's gaze didn't leave him. Cole couldn't tell if she was breathing.

"There are no others," came her reply.

"Bullshit."

She said nothing.

"You're dumb as hell, coming here," the man growled. "There isn't a person in this room who's going to let you leave this place alive."

Cole swallowed, his eyes flicking between the man, the wizard, and the cripples who looked ready to shoot the first thing that moved. He didn't stand a chance of reaching his gun in time, even if he'd been so stupid as to think it'd do a shred of good.

Or known who he'd shoot anyway.

Ashe was silent, as though she was trying to decide how to respond. "I didn't do those things, Samson. And I never ordered them."

Her gaze flicked from him to the other girl and back. "I went to the Merlin Council because Carter told me to. It's the only reason I left. And they took what I told them, and some of them…" Her jaw muscles jumped. "I didn't know."

Cole watched her, uncertain what to make of her words, but at the mention of the name Carter, the rage on the man's face grew stronger.

"You didn't know," Samson repeated, disgust dripping from his tone.

"They said it was Taliesin. They…" She stopped, and Cole could see the emotion on her face swiftly being smothered back inside. "I made a deal," she continued more levelly. "With Darius, the Council leader. He promised to work with the cripples to prove to the rest of Merlin that the Blood existed, but only if I stayed and tried to recreate the binding spell. I couldn't leave or fight, but I could do what Carter asked. Because of the trust I'd built with your people, I could bring our sides together to destroy the Blood once and for all."

Her expression tightened, old loathing surfacing briefly in her eyes. "So I agreed. And a few weeks later, Darius came to say it'd happened. A cripple shot at a Blood wizard, and when he defended himself, the Merlin were finally convinced the Blood were real. Darius told me the Merlin had started fighting them, and that they were working with the cripples side by side. He claimed it was brutal, but we were winning, and that even though I couldn't go out there, I could rest assured that everything Carter had wanted was coming true."

She paused. "Wizards are bastards, Samson," she finished, deep anger threading through her voice for the first time. "You were the one who told me that."

For a moment, the man said nothing, and then derision crept into his eyes. "Convincing. Really. Especially with the little Blood at your side."

His gun twitched toward Lily and Cole pushed the girl farther behind him as instantly, Ashe's magic strengthened. A few feet away, Blackjack winced.

"Don't," she warned.

Samson's eyes narrowed.

"She's not a Blood," Ashe said, an edge to her voice. "She's my sister."

From the corner of his eye, Cole saw confusion flash across the dreadlocked girl's face.

Samson scoffed. "And he's your long lost brother," he said with a jerk of his chin to Cole. "And we're all just supposed to believe the Bloody Queen of Merlin is innocent because, what? She looks like hell and claims to be the victim here?" He made a disgusted noise, the hatred in his eyes deepening. "Try something else, you lying bitch. As I remember, that was your act last time, and I think we all know what came of it. Or was Carter just one more dead cripple to you?"

Everything about Ashe went still, and then slowly, she began to tremble. Like a wall coming into existence in front of her, her magic intensified, till sweat dripped down Samson's face with the effort of not retreating from the pain. Around the room, the other men backed away, while by the ladder, the dreadlocked girl's grip on a metal rung tightened till her knuckles showed white. Behind him, Cole felt Lily start for her sister and he snagged her arm, watching Ashe in wary alarm.

From within its protection, her magic barely hurt at all.

A breath escaped Ashe and the magic dissipated. Still shaking, she blinked, looking to the other girl.

"I'm sorry," Ashe said tightly. "I… I'm glad you stayed away."

Turning, she took Lily's hand. Drawing the little girl along, she walked past Shale out of the room.

Cole glanced from the door to the cripples, and then headed after her.

Feet devouring the ground, Ashe strode down the tunnel, with Lily half-running to keep up. Over the distance, he could feel magic flickering fitfully around her, and despite the desire not to let Lily out of his sight, he couldn't help but slow to lessen its ache.

"Ashley," Lily said.

The older girl didn't answer. She didn't even seem to hear.

"Ashley!"

Flinching, Ashe stopped, and her gaze followed Lily's back down the tunnel. For a moment, she didn't move, watching him through the dim light, and he couldn't read the look in her eyes.

Slowly, the magic faded to a shadow of what it had been. He came closer. She was still trembling and before he got within a few feet, she seemed to balk at his proximity and swiftly turned to keep going.

His brow drawing down, he followed.

The platform came into view, its bluish lights ghostly against the darkness. Grabbing Lily under her arms, Ashe quickly hoisted the girl onto the tiled ledge, giving no sign of noticing the worried look on her little sister's face.

"Ashe," came a voice behind them.

He looked back as debris crunched in the tunnel. Gun bouncing against her shoulder, the blonde girl from the storage room jogged out of the shadows. Stopping at the edge of the light, she held up her hands peaceably, as though between her and the wizard, she was the one who somehow needed to appear nonthreatening.

"Hang on a minute?"

Ashe didn't move.

The girl's mouth tightened. "Look," she said, taking a few steps closer. "Sam was being an ass, alright? What he said…" She glanced away, irritation flashing across her face. "I'm sorry."

Cole looked to Ashe. Nothing but typical wizard impassivity showed in her eyes. One hand on Lily's leg, she waited, motionless and still managing to look as dangerous as ever at the same time.

The other girl didn't even seem to notice. "What're you doing here?" she asked, her tone vaguely incredulous.

"Saw your message outside."

Her voice was quiet, and almost pained, and he found himself wondering again what the hell she'd seen. But at the words, the girl just scoffed, her incredulity deepening.

"And what? You thought dropping in without warning would be a good plan?"

Ashe said nothing, and the other girl's humor faded as she glanced to the blood on Ashe's face and arms. Silence fell over the tunnel, broken only by the patter of dust raining down as a distant subway train rushed by.

"I didn't want to believe it, you know," the girl said after a moment. "That you were behind all that…" She shook her head. "Didn't make sense. Wizards being bastards, now," she chuckled dryly, "that I'll believe any day of the week. But the rest…" She shook her head again.

"When'd you find out?" she asked, her tone becoming serious.

"About three weeks ago," Ashe answered quietly.

The girl paused. "Did you try to reach us?"

"They told me they killed Carter's people."

"They must've meant Serenity's crew. She and the others died trying to reach a couple of their friends a few months back." For a moment, the girl's face tightened, and then she visibly pushed the memory aside. "So what about the ferals?"

Cole glanced between them, at a loss for what she meant.

Ashe hesitated. "The leaders are dead."

The girl's brow shrugged equitably. "And that?" she asked, jerking her chin toward the dried bloodstains.

"Taliesin. Maybe Blood too."

"Still alive?"

"Some."

"We'll keep an eye out."

Silence returned.

"Listen," the girl said. "I don't know what your plan is, and I know the others aren't exactly happy you're here, but would you stick around a bit? There's someone who's going to want to see you."

He saw Ashe swallow at the words. "Okay."

The girl nodded. Adjusting the gun strap on her shoulder, she started for the platform.

"I'm Spider, by the way," she said to him as she approached.

He paused. "Cole."

"Cripple?" she asked. Her gaze twitched to Ashe.

Hesitating again, he nodded, and then noted how she didn't really seem to accept the answer till it came from Ashe as well.

He struggled to keep the bafflement from his face, feeling adrift enough as it was without letting the others know. Calmly, Spider kept walking, giving no sign she cared that a wizard the rest of the world blamed for mass genocide stood only a few feet away.

"And you are?" Spider asked Lily, her friendly tone marred only slightly by the tension he could hear beneath the words.

"Lily," Ashe supplied quietly.

Spider looked from her to the little girl, and as he came up near them, Cole could read the questions in her eyes. But with another glance to Ashe, she seemed to push past the uncertainty to just give the kid a smile. "Nice to meet you."

Cautiously, Lily nodded, watching her as if waiting to see what she'd do with the gun.

"This way," Spider said, hoisting herself over the edge of the platform.

He stared at Ashe and Lily as they climbed up after the girl and headed for the stairs. None of this made sense. Ashe, Spider, the gun-wielding gladiator who'd tried to shoot her and accused her of getting some guy named Carter killed.

Every single shred of evidence Harris and his father had supplied.

The pieces didn't fit.

His brow twitched down.

He didn't know who to believe.

The girls were closing in on the stairway, and if he didn't want to be left standing in the middle of an abandoned subway tunnel, he really had no choice. Drawing a breath, he climbed up onto the platform and followed, uncertain when he'd ever felt more at a loss in all the six months since he'd first met Merlin's bloody queen.

Chapter Twelve

A she followed Spider up the steps from the tunnel and, when the girl headed through the shadows to a maintenance stairway, she followed her up those as well.

Somewhere in the past few hours, the day had become a ride. She couldn't stop it, couldn't get off, and had spent most of it just trying to figure out how to hang on without crumbling so they could reach the end alive. But suddenly, she'd found herself here and, on some level, this was the most unbelievable part of all.

Her gaze trailed Spider as the girl climbed, the clunk of her boots echoing strangely from the concrete walls.

She hoped she wasn't actually lying unconscious somewhere, imagining the one bit of amazing news in this hellish day.

Five stories up, the steps came to an end in a steel door. A broken light fixture dangled overhead, and in the dim glow of a bulb farther down the stairwell, she could just make out the words 'roof access' stenciled in red paint across the door.

Spider glanced back as Lily and Cole reached the landing, and then she hesitated, looking to Ashe.

"Sam would've called up here the minute I left," she said quietly.

Ashe met her gaze. "Hey, Lil?" she called over her shoulder. "Stay here a sec, okay?"

Brow furrowing in protest, Lily shook her head. "No, we stick together."

"It's just for a second."

The little girl's expression hardened.

"I promise."

Lily hesitated and then reached over, her hand finding Cole's. Pulling him along, she retreated a few steps and then came to a stop, giving her sister a stubborn glare.

Ashe glanced to Spider. The girl's lip twitched. Shrugging the shotgun from her shoulder to let it hang low by her side, she turned and inched the door open. Brilliant sunlight shone through the crack. Beyond the opening, heated voices fell silent.

"It's me," Spider called. For a heartbeat, she waited, and then continued onto the rooftop.

Light filled the stairwell and Ashe blinked against the glare. Gravel spread away in front of her, stretching to a parapet of rough-hewn granite that surrounded the broad roof. Schooling her face back into impassivity, she followed Spider through the door.

A trio of stone-like gazes locked on her.

But she really was only watching one.

As she walked onto the rooftop, Bus glanced from her to Spider, and she couldn't read anything past the guarded look in his bright blue eyes. On either side of him, the other men's faces darkened, their hands twitching as though they wished they had weapons and not just walkie-talkies nearby.

"It's alright, Bus," Spider said, glancing to the adjacent buildings as she lowered her shotgun by its strap to the gravel. "It was like you said."

The stone-like expression cracked into a slow smile. Ignoring the others, he strode across the rooftop, coming to a stop directly in front of Ashe. With rough hands, he grabbed her shoulders and, for a moment, his eyes ran over her like he was trying to decide what to say.

"Glad you're back, kiddo," he stated. "You look like hell."

An incredulous noise escaped her, and his smile grew. Tugging her forward, he pulled her into a hug.

"About time you got here, girl," he told her kindly.

He patted her back and then pushed her away again.

She swallowed hard, trying to return his grin when she felt like at any second, the people around her would shatter as she woke from this dream.

Spider cleared her throat.

Ashe glanced over, and then followed the twitch of her gaze to the stairs.

"I take it he called up here," Spider said.

As Bus made an affirmative noise, Ashe looked past him to the other men on the roof. Loathing radiated from them, but at her glance, they returned to their surveillance of the street, as if too disgusted to meet her eyes.

She shivered, the warmth of the moment before fading away. Drawing a breath to stay focused, she turned back to the stairwell door and, with a small jerk of her head, motioned for Lily to come out.

Cole by her side, the little girl stepped from the shadows, a trace of stubbornness still hovering on her face.

"Holy…" Bus started. He cast a glance to the other men, but they seemed to have decided nothing on the rooftop behind them existed anymore. Blinking, he ran a hand over his white hair. "Samson wasn't kidding."

"What'd he say?" Spider asked.

Bus looked over at her. "Well," he amended. "About…" He gestured to Lily and then paused, exhaling slowly. "Yeah," he finished, as though answering his own thoughts. Taking a breath, he walked toward the girl.

Ashe followed, Spider coming a step behind.

"Hey there," Bus said as he neared the door.

Lily looked to Ashe.

"Bus," Ashe said. "I'd like you to meet Lily… my sister."

He glanced from her to the girl and back, but whatever his confusion at her words, she could see him stifle it quickly. Bending a little, he cocked his head as though to catch the girl's attention.

"How're you doing, Lily?" he asked.

For a heartbeat, the girl eyed him, her brow furrowing cagily. "Bus?"

"Yep?"

"Why's your name 'Bus'?"

He chuckled, straightening again. "Because I'm the transport, kid. Ain't a one of these folks could figure their way out of a paper bag without me."

"Hey!" Spider protested.

Bus grinned. "Well, 'cept maybe her," he admitted with a nod to the other girl.

Spider rolled her eyes. Lily looked between them as if uncertain what to make of what she saw.

"And who's your friend?" the old man continued.

Lily glanced up. "Cole."

"Cripple," Spider commented.

Bus' eyebrows shrugged appreciatively and he extended a hand. "Good to meet you."

Cole hesitated, and then shook the man's hand briefly, his expression anything but warm.

"No sense in us all standing out here, eh?" Bus continued, motioning toward the door and giving no sign he'd noticed the pause, or the ice. "We've got food downstairs, and you look like you could use someplace to clean up."

He directed the last to Ashe.

She couldn't quite keep the dry look from her face, and at the expression, he grinned.

"Oh, hush, girl. You're just lucky Memphis let himself get distracted by some car wreck a few blocks away when you showed up earlier." He nodded toward a man by the front of the building. "Looking like that… it's a good thing you made it to the door."

He clapped a hand on her shoulder and then started for the stairs.

Keeping her gaze from Lily, Ashe followed, well aware it wasn't just because of her own appearance that they'd been lucky.

The ground floor was empty when they reached it, and the sound of the stairwell door opening echoed in the silence. Striding past the entrance to the subway, Bus led them across the massive waiting room and around the corner to a hallway beyond the ticket counter's end. Destroyed marble paneling lined the walls, though nearly every surviving surface had served as a spray paint canvas at some point. Narrow windows sat near the ceiling, pouring sunlight down on the graffiti as though lighting an art gallery. Halfway down the hall, Bus turned, pushing open a pair of swinging doors and then holding one for the others to follow.

Few chairs and tables remained in the expanse of the cafeteria, though most were broken in one way or another and looked forlornly tiny beneath the high vault of the ceiling. Columns lined the room, their marbled veneers shattered to reveal the struts underneath, and on the far wall, a long row of windows stretched to the ceiling, their surviving glass haphazardly guarded by crisscrossed boards. Letting the door swing closed behind them, Bus strode ahead, leading the way into the kitchen. Broken shelving and tapioca-colored counter-tops ringed the next room, with space left only for an old metal fridge and an enormous stove with generations of cobwebs trailing from its hood.

"Here you go," Bus called back as he snagged a tattered rag from a jumble of towels on a countertop. He turned, tossing it to Ashe as she came through the door. "You can use one of the blue buckets over there."

Catching the rag, she looked between him and the collection of five-gallon buckets just visible around the corner of the large island in the middle of the kitchen. Releasing Lily's hand, she headed toward them as Bus continued to the refrigerator, grabbing its metal latch and succeeding in hauling the dented door open on the third try.

"Blasted thing," he muttered. He glanced back at Lily. "What's your pleasure, kid? We've got grape, orange, and cherry… I think. Red's tricky, so don't quote me on the last one."

Lily's brow drew down, her expression lost between confusion and caution.

"Popsicles, girl," he explained as though it was obvious. "What's the matter? No one ever told you you're supposed to eat dessert first?"

An incredulous grin surfaced on Lily's face as if it wasn't sure it should be there. She cast a look to Cole, who was standing by the door, and then shrugged. "Grape?"

"Best choice."

Ashe suppressed a smile as she reached the other side of the room. A dozen buckets stood in two groups in the corner of the kitchen, with permanent marker scrawl on their sides denoting their purpose. Moving past the white buckets labeled 'drink', she dipped the rag into one of the blue containers of water intended for washing and then began cleaning her face and arms.

"So where'd that happen?" Spider asked quietly, coming up behind her.

Ashe paused halfway through wiping her arm and glanced over. Hoisting herself onto the countertop, the other girl grimaced as her hand landed in a patch of dirt. Wiping her palm on her jeans, Spider jerked her chin toward the smears of dried blood. Across the room, Bus seemed engrossed in entertaining Lily with descriptions of the military ration packs stored in the cupboards, but Ashe could see him watching her, listening between his comments for her response.

"Airport."

Spider nodded in understanding. "The terrorist attack."

"What?"

"On the airport," she elaborated and then twitched her head back toward the rest of the building. "One of the old offices still has a television."

Ashe hesitated. "What else did you hear?"

Spider shrugged, watching Bus insist Lily choose from the meal packets hidden behind his back. "The usual. The reporters say terrorists, but admit it might not have been. They don't know and it's under investigation, which means that by the time the police find anything – *if* they find anything – no one in the media will care enough to report much on it anymore." She grinned. "What else is new?"

Wiping the last of the blood from her arm, Ashe paused. It wouldn't have changed anything to know the cops had found the others' bodies. No one would be safer, or any less dead. She didn't know why it felt like it would have helped.

Though maybe it would have felt a little bit less like she'd just left them behind.

The sound of the cabinet closing pulled her from her thoughts. Studying the selection of meals in her arms, Lily trailed Bus from the kitchen, with Cole rolling one shoulder off the doorframe to follow as they passed. Spider jumped down from the counter and headed for the main room.

Ashe hesitated and then left the stained rag hanging on a pipe to dry before starting after them.

With a flourish that left Lily grinning, Bus sat the little girl down at one of the few surviving tables, and then proceeded to demonstrate how to heat the ration as though performing a conjuring trick. Joining her at the table, Ashe watched Lily laugh as he pretended to burn himself and then confronted the offending meal like it had injured him on purpose.

Her gaze caught on Cole. Seated a few feet away, he was studying Bus and Lily as if they were a puzzle to which he'd just discovered someone had stolen a piece. From time to time, his eyes would flick toward Spider, though only when he thought the girl wouldn't notice.

Pulling her meal closer, Ashe glanced to the wrapper to determine what she'd been given, and then slid her gaze to Spider. Perched on the edge of another table, her feet propped on either side of a broken-seated chair with her shotgun lying nearby, the girl gave every sign of being focused on the tray in her hands. And then her gaze twitched up just long enough to meet Ashe's eyes.

Ashe exhaled, going back to her food. Cole had no idea how observant the people around him could be.

As though proving her thought, Bus lowered himself onto a chair with a sigh and then glanced to the young man. "So how do you fit into all this, Cole?" he asked as he picked up a plastic fork.

Cole froze. Across the table, all the nascent relaxation in Lily's face transformed instantly to panic.

"Well…" he started. His eyes darted to Ashe. "I was just in the–"

"He saved us," Ashe interrupted flatly, watching Lily. "Back on the farm and then at the airport today."

The little girl's panic crumbled into relief when nothing else followed the words. Cole stared, as though uncertain why she'd done that, or if he'd trust any explanation he'd receive anyway.

She returned to her food, noting distantly that the grayish-brown substance tasted mildly better than it looked. From the corner of her eye, she could see Spider and Bus glance to each other before the old man spoke again. "Ah," he said neutrally. "Thought I remembered Ashe mentioning your name before."

Plastic forks clicked as they kept eating.

"How'd you meet Ashley?" Lily asked Bus.

Ashe glanced up. Eyebrow rising, Bus looked askance at the little girl, a smile pulling on his mouth. "What? Your big sister never tell you about us?"

Uncomfortably, Ashe looked back at her dinner as Lily shook her head.

Bus chuckled. "Saved that girl's life, we did. Or Carter and Samson anyway. Ashe here'd stumbled into a trap we set for a feral back in Utah. Guy would've killed her if they hadn't stopped him first. Tiny little ghost of a thing when Carter found her, wasn't she, Spider? Running for her life and looking like the hounds of hell were on her tail." He glanced over at Ashe. "Of course, that was then."

She hesitated, reading between the lines. "I'm sorry I didn't tell you. I just–"

"Eh," he interrupted kindly. "I forgive you, kiddo."

Watching him for a moment, she managed a smile.

"You didn't tell me you were their queen," Spider commented, her quiet words at odds with the hint of accusation beneath her tone.

Ashe glanced over. "Would you believe I didn't know?"

The girl paused as though weighing a response.

Ashe dropped her gaze to the table. "I found out from Carter, right before he died. I didn't say anything because…" She shook her head. "I thought maybe I'd misheard or something. It sounded crazy."

Consternation flickered over Spider's face. "But how did *he* suddenly know? Or had he known all along? That night at Twitch's, he just…"

"It was his cousin," Ashe said into the pause. "Cornelius. Carter met him downstairs that night, and I followed." A wry expression crossed her face. "The rats had been keeping me awake. But I over-heard them talking. Cornelius was looking for me… us." Her brow drew down at the memory, and the old question of how things might have gone. "Carter didn't tell him I was there."

"Was this Cornelius one of the…" Spider asked, gesturing vaguely to fill in the venomous description she'd probably have used if Lily wasn't around.

"No, he was a good one." Ashe paused. "The Blood killed him today."

Silence fell over the table.

"I'm sorry," Spider said.

Ashe nodded.

A moment slid by.

"So where'd you go?" Spider asked.

Ashe took a breath. "Croftsburg."

"Nice?"

"Not really."

The corner of Spider's mouth twitched and, in spite of everything, Ashe felt herself mirroring the expression. Shaking her head, she looked down.

A second passed and her smile faded, memories driving it away.

"What happened?" she asked. "After… after I left?"

Spider looked to Bus.

"That's not really important," the old man said, his tone making it clear a change of subject was probably in order.

"Why didn't you go?" she pressed.

Bus looked back at the other girl.

"Sam said not to," Spider answered.

Ashe paused, hit by the incongruity of feeling grateful to the man who'd tried to shoot her a few minutes before. "And so you just…"

Spider exhaled, her gaze on her food.

"Samson…" Bus began, and then sighed, revising whatever he'd been about to say. "Losing Carter hit him hard, in no small measure because he wasn't there. Blames himself, I think, for what happened."

"And me," Ashe added quietly.

Bus paused and then tilted his head in acknowledgement. "Even if he shouldn't. Carter knew what going after the Blood meant; we all did. And as for the wizard stuff…"

Face tightening, Spider looked away.

"You had your reasons for not saying anything," Bus told Ashe, and then he glanced to the other girl. "You both did. And you thought there'd be more time."

Spider didn't respond.

Bus watched her a moment longer and then went back to his dinner. "Regardless," he continued, dropping the topic, "the boy's been driving himself to fill Carter's shoes ever since. I mean, in our own ways, we're all trying to maintain what Carter left behind. But for Samson, a part of that was a hardcore distrust for anything wizard, including anything that involved you. So when the word came that you were looking for help fighting the Blood…"

"He thought it was the same thing all over again," Ashe said, only partially asking.

Bus shrugged equitably.

"But you guys…" she continued.

He drew a breath and then let it out slowly. "She argued till I thought she'd shoot him," he said with a nod to Spider. "And I–"

"Offered to?" Spider commented, her eyes on the slats covering the large window nearby.

Bus eyed her wryly. "I told you that was going to be your job."

The girl smiled, but her heart didn't seem to be in it.

"We were trying to stick together," Bus continued to Ashe. "After everything, we weren't quite in the position to be running back off again. I'd gotten pretty banged up getting out of Twitch's place, and the dogs weren't in too great of shape either. Add to that just losing Carter and Samson still being on crutches half the time and–" He shrugged. "—we waited. And just when I started getting back to my usual athletic self…"

"You heard what was really happening," Ashe filled in when he paused.

"Yeah."

She nudged the last few bites of food with her fork, her appetite long since gone. "And the others?" she asked, bracing herself.

Silence answered her and she glanced up.

"Bus. The others."

The old man looked away. "Jericho agreed with Samson, and because of him, Magnolia and their girls stayed put. But–" He grimaced. "–Belle and some of the rest…"

She dropped her gaze to the table, trying not to show any reaction as he trailed off, leaving little question of what had happened to the cook and everyone else. And she'd known anyway. She should have just let it go, because she'd damn well known. Spider and Bus were a miracle; Magnolia and the kids even more so.

But not everyone would have stayed away.

She swallowed awkwardly, working to keep her expression calm despite the fact her heart seemed to be pulsing so much harder than it should have been. "You're sure?" she asked, blinking as she looked up at Bus.

He nodded.

She looked back down.

"It wasn't your fault, Ashe," he said.

She made a noise to let him know she understood.

"Ashe," he repeated.

She glanced up.

"It wasn't your fault."

Her gaze went back to the table. It hurt, somehow. Their for-giveness. Their trust. So many people were dead, destroyed by ferals who never would have touched them if not for her. And Bus and Spider forgave her. Welcomed her back. They treated her like family, returning after a few months away.

Instead of Bloody Queen Ashe of Merlin, the monster who'd nearly gotten every cripple in a thousand miles killed.

She could feel shivers running through her, though she didn't know why. "You guys have so much faith I wasn't behind it," she said, the words feeling as though they belonged to someone else. "But you just knew me a month. I never even told you I was a wizard. And the Merlin, they–"

"You saved my life," Spider said quietly.

A laugh came out of nowhere, the sound harsh and teetering just this side of controlled. "And?" she retorted. "And *what?* So I stopped *one* feral. It could've been a trick. Hell, Spider, I could have been saving you for myself! And then Carter died. And Belle and all your friends, right after I just trotted off to the damn–"

"Hey!" Bus snapped.

Her breathing ragged, she fell silent, staring at him. Across the table, Lily watched her with wide eyes.

"We trust you because Carter trusted you," Bus continued. "And because we're not stupid. Yeah, we knew you a month. Day in, day out for a month, while you lived at the Abbey and could've killed us all in a single night. You're a *wizard,* girl. You think we don't know what that means? You think we haven't gotten *damn* good at reading people, doing what we do?" He paused, and when he spoke again, the edge on his tone was gone. "You didn't have it in you to be a feral, Ashe. You still don't. And you didn't kill our friends. Or yours.

A bunch of wizard bastards who were already ferals anyway did."

Still shaking, she looked back down.

"Let it go, kid," Bus told her gently. "Guilt over the dead won't do anything but hurt your ability to protect the living."

Her jaw tightened and she nodded, more for his sake than any belief she could actually accomplish what he said.

A moment went by. Softly, plastic scraped across the tabletop.

She glanced up.

With a hesitant smile, Lily nudged the wrapped cookie closer. "It's oatmeal raisin," she said quietly. "Your favorite."

For a heartbeat, she stared at the girl, dumbstruck in the face of the silly, simple gesture. Her hand trembling, she reached out and pulled the cookie to her.

"Thanks," she whispered.

Lily's expression didn't change.

Ashe's gaze fell away. Closing her eyes briefly, she drew a breath and then opened the wrapping.

"So…" she tried, her eyes locked on the nearly stale cookie. "This place."

There was a question somewhere in the words, but she couldn't quite bring herself to find it. The others didn't seem to care, though, and from the corner of her eye, she could see Spider shift slightly on the adjacent table.

"It's Blackjack's," the girl said, her light tone sounding more than a little forced after the tension of a moment before. "He got the whole thing set up after the latest developer ran out of money for repairs about a year ago."

Ashe swallowed. "It's nice."

Bus scoffed. "It's a condemned dump."

Spider gave him a dry look. "Please. With Blackjack's old army buddy giving him these MREs, and the local food bank getting a random donation of the popsicles you missed so much? There's water just down the street, which is a damn sight better than some places we've been, and even you had to admit the generators in this old wreck were in fairly decent shape for their age." She eyed Bus. "Come on. You remember Tucson?"

"I don't want to remember Tucson."

"Yeah. Thought so."

Ashe glanced between them.

"We're just here because Blackjack spotted a couple ferals in the area and we came to help out," Spider continued, looking back at her.

"Did you find them?"

Spider smiled. "Oh yeah," she replied, as though the alternative had never been in question.

Returning her attention to the cookie, Ashe nodded, relieved.

"Okay," Bus said, taking Lily's empty tray and setting it on top of his own. "Enough of ferals. Bastards yesterday left me sore, even if you seemed to be having a good time." He met Spider's incredulous expression with a mock-glare and then turned to Ashe. "What's the plan now, your highness?"

She tensed at the title, but he just grinned as though he'd expected the reaction. Wetting her lips, she hesitated, and then drew a breath, trying to refocus like she knew he wanted.

"Pretty much what it's always been," she answered, her voice a bit hoarse to her ears. She cleared her throat. "Take out the Blood, preferably before the Taliesin king who controls them figures out the spell to bind us all." She grimaced. "Even if I have no idea how to do that."

"My favorite kind of plan," Bus said dryly.

She couldn't quite manage a smile.

"So what would be a good first step?" he prompted.

Pausing for a second, she shrugged.

"Alright, we'll get to that later, then. So Taliesin's king runs them?"

She nodded, keeping herself from looking at Cole.

Bus whistled softly. "He got any weaknesses you know of?"

The urge to look at Cole became nearly overwhelming.

"Not exactly," she allowed. "He's a Blood too."

"The Taliesin king is a Blood."

She nodded again.

"This wasn't the turn of conversation I was hoping for, kiddo."

"Sorry."

He exhaled slowly, glancing to Spider. "Yeah, well," he said. "What can we do to help?"

She hesitated, her gaze flicking to Lily before she could stop it.

The little girl's face darkened warningly.

Ashe looked away. There were too many variables. She needed to get back to the Merlin, though she dreaded the prospect of telling Katherine that Elias was gone. And as much as she hated the idea, she had to bring Cole with her when she went. Letting him wander off with knowledge of where Spider, Bus and the rest were hiding was out of the question. To keep her sister safe, she'd leave Lily here, except that chances were before she even made it to the door, the little girl would lose control, blow something up, and probably kill whoever was nearby.

She could bind Lily. She'd been planning on it anyway.

And the first moment Spider or Bus were busy trying not to get killed by ferals or Blood or whatever else they ran into, Samson and everyone else in this building would make sure the little glowing girl just mysteriously disappeared.

There wasn't a choice. Not anymore.

She sighed. "Do you know where we could get a car?"

Chapter Thirteen

The uneven legs of the chair threatening to rock beneath him, Cole studied the other occupants of the silent wreck of a room. A few minutes had passed since the old man left to find them transport, and the words that'd been spoken since then could have been counted on one hand. Watching the table as though she could read answers from its scuffed surface, Ashe sat where she'd been all dinner long, while several yards away, Spider leaned on the frame of the enormous window, scanning the bits of the world visible between the splintered boards. Across the room, Lily was wandering along the wall, investigating the old lunchroom debris.

He wasn't sure why Ashe'd covered for him about his family, or what to make of her near-breakdown. Believing it'd all been for some good reason, some innocent reason, would have been nice. He could just let his guard down and trust that, no matter what the rest of the world said, she actually wasn't the monster everyone believed her to be.

And that'd gone so well last time.

Swallowing hard against his crawling skin, he shifted on the unsteady chair and looked away. He was tired of believing what people said about themselves despite the countless stories piled up against them, especially since it was the stories that kept turning out to be true. He was tired of being that naïve, or that much of a damned fool. He had to trust what he'd heard, what he'd seen with his own eyes, and what he knew. He knew his father was a man who'd been a good person, whatever he'd become, and maybe someday he could be again. And he knew going hysterical over the dead wasn't Ashe's style. She might be a good actress, but she was definitely a wizard to the core, and they possessed about as much compassion as chainsaws on autopilot. And he could trust that about her. He'd seen plenty of examples, from her emotionless mention of Cornelius dying at the airfield today, to the way she'd left God-knew-how-many Taliesin dead on the interstate a few hours before.

Which meant everything she'd said was suspect. Or, more likely, an outright lie to manipulate everyone here. And thus, he'd be an absolute moron to take his guard down or believe in her innocence for a heartbeat.

He exhaled, anger pounding on the base of his skull as his gaze slid to her again. Probably, she'd just covered for him because she wanted something. That seemed to be the theme for his life; why should she be any different? And it had to be something more than the obvious, since if getting more power had been her goal, the others would already be dead.

Maybe. Or maybe she was just hoping to keep him quiet, or at least scared of what she might say about his family – and of what her friends might do to him in response – until she worked out a way to use this latest development to her advantage.

His eyes narrowed. Well, he could just do the same. Calling her out was tempting, but probably not the best plan. Going at her directly wouldn't get him anywhere, and there really were her gun-happy friends to consider. But murdering cripples wasn't all she'd been accused of. And she'd admitted to being after the spell, which also gave him an opening. Even if Spider and Bus obviously weren't the type to be bothered by killing if it seemed like a fun idea at the time, Lily was still on the fence.

And maybe getting Ashe to talk about what she planned or what she'd done to Malden could push the kid over the edge enough that, when the opportunity finally presented itself to get the hell out of here, Lily would be willing to go.

His gaze slid over, finding Lily against the far wall. Using her fingers like tweezers, she was picking through a stack of multicolored food trays.

"So the Merlin Council killed all those people?"

Ashe flinched, as though he'd jarred her from whatever thoughts she'd been having. Blinking, she looked over at him. "What?"

"The Merlin Council," he repeated neutrally. "They killed all those people?"

She gave a cautious nod.

"And Malden?"

He saw her tense. "What do you mean?"

"Were they responsible for what happened to him too?"

At the window, Spider shifted slightly, not looking back at them though he knew the girl was hearing every word.

"Who told you about Detective Malden?" Ashe asked.

He paused, reading something strange in the edge in her tone.

"It was Harris, wasn't it?" she continued.

"Does it matter?"

Her face darkened. "What'd he say?"

"That you set his partner on fire."

Ashe hesitated. He could feel Spider's attention on them, for all that the girl had yet to turn around. On the other side of the room, Lily's orbit through the debris was slowly bringing her closer.

"Yeah, I did," Ashe said quietly, looking away. "It was an accident. I lost control."

His brow drew down at the discomfort in her voice. She'd burned countless Taliesin right in front of him. And now she looked unsettled by the memory of one guy she'd sent up in flames.

Yeah, right.

"You accidentally lost control of your magic," he repeated. "Ashe, come on. After what I saw at the factory, that seems a little hard to believe."

Her gaze snapped back to meet his. "The factory where I saved your life from the Blood, you mean? Or, you know–" She eyed him sarcastically. "–whatever."

He tensed, not looking away from her with all his might, despite Spider's curiosity beating down on him.

"The police arrested me for my family's murder," Ashe explained acidly. "They interrogated me and locked me in a cell. Then an FBI agent came. Turns out, he was one of the Blood. And when I heard his voice, I panicked and lost control. I didn't know what magic was, and bursting into flame and killing Malden like that scared the living hell out of me. But then Harris pulled a gun and tried to shoot me, so I ran."

She grimaced. "Even if I'd known what I was doing, I couldn't have saved Malden. I suck at healing, as you might've guessed from the fact I looked like roadkill not too long ago. And as for what you saw at the factory—" She gave him a scathing look. "—I've spent nearly every waking hour for almost half a year training with Cornelius. And I'm nothing compared to the skill he and the others had. Oh, and I had the staff of Merlin, which is why you're not dead from that portal right now."

Spider glanced back. "You got him through a portal?"

"Yeah. And destroyed the best hope I had of recreating the spell in the process."

He watched her as she turned away, seething. She thought she'd killed the man. And given how she looked at the moment, he wasn't sure she'd believe him even if he wanted to disabuse her of the idea.

His gaze slid to the other side of the room. Several yards away, Lily had moved on to a bunch of broken pieces of marble, and was steadily collecting those that interested her into a pile.

"And what're you planning to do with the spell?" he persisted, praying the little girl started listening soon.

Ashe gave him a disgusted look. His heart began to pound harder.

"Or are you afraid to just admit it?" he pushed.

"Excuse me?"

"Just tell the truth. What's the plan for the spell?"

"What the hell's your problem, Cole?"

He paused. "It's just a question."

Her eyebrow climbed. "And you really want to go *there*?" she retorted with an illustrative twitch of her gaze toward Spider. "'Cause I'm more than happy to, but I don't think it'll go too well."

"It's not about that."

"Then what?"

"I just know what you can do – *all* you can do – and I figure you should be honest about it."

Ashe paused. "All I can do."

"Yeah."

"And what exactly is 'all I can do'?"

"Oh, come on, Ashe. You really want me to be the one to say it?"

She hesitated again. "Since you know so much."

He stared at her. Tense and angry, she barely seemed to be breathing as she waited for him to speak.

Disgust made him shake his head. She had to know Lily would've found out eventually. And it wasn't like Spider would have an issue with her killing people, as long as they weren't on her side. And yet she was still trying to keep the act up.

"How many are you planning to kill, Ashe?" he asked with quiet revulsion. "Really? Every Taliesin on the planet? Anybody who doesn't swear allegiance to you as their god?"

He'd never seen anyone's face go slack with shock, let alone a wizard's, but at his words, everything melted from her expression but horror. Silently, her mouth worked, trying to find her voice or stop nausea, he couldn't tell, but after a heartbeat, she swallowed hard.

"Kill…?" she whispered. "How many am I going to…"

She choked and then shoved away from the table to stride across the room, raking a hand over her hair as she went. By the window, Spider stared after her, while by the wall, Lily stood immobile, the piece of marble in her hand forgotten.

His brow drew down. She said she'd studied for months on the spell. There was no way she hadn't known.

But he wasn't sure actresses on Broadway could make ignorance look that real.

"Does he know how to do that?" Ashe asked suddenly, spinning back to him.

Cole tensed.

"Does he know how to do that!"

He glanced to Lily and said nothing.

Fury rippled through her, making her tremble. "Cole," she snarled, stalking toward him. "I swear to *God*, if you don't answer me…"

He felt her magic flare and could tell Spider did too. With a pained noise, the girl backed away from them both.

"Ashley, don't!" Lily protested.

"*Does* he?" Ashe came to a stop in front of his chair.

Pain pounding through his skull, he glared up at her, but she only made the magic grow stronger. "No," he growled.

The magic died. Swiftly, she spun, striding back across the cafeteria with Lily staring after her.

"How exactly is Cole involved in any of this?" Spider asked the room at large.

No one answered. She turned to him. "How?" she repeated flatly.

He scowled, but there wasn't a way around it. Besides, if the girl wanted to kill him, at this point she'd probably have to take a number. "Because of my father."

Spider looked to Ashe incredulously. "Does he mean who I think he means?"

Ashe glanced back at her. "Yeah."

"And you were going to tell me this when?"

Uncomfortably, Ashe grimaced and then chose to ignore the question. "How close is he to figuring out the spell?"

Spider made an irritated sound.

"You really think I'm going to tell you that?" Cole replied.

"If you damn well want to keep breathing, you will."

Lily choked. Dropping the broken bit of marble, she hurried to his side.

Ashe's gaze tracked her and then she scowled, pacing away. "You told me you wanted to help Lily. You realize if he figures this out before me, she dies too?"

He didn't respond. Disagreeing would only lead her perilously close to the realization that Victor couldn't recreate the spell without her or Lily, and jeopardizing his father had never been part of the plan.

At his silence, she made a furious noise and looked back at him. "Or do you just not care? Was that all a crock earlier about coming back for her?"

His face darkened. "Yeah, I get blasted off interstates for fun."

"Then what the hell? He'll kill her and you're doing nothing! We need help here, Cole! If it wasn't for you, I'd still have the staff and we'd stand a chance. But instead, you're all we've got! So do Lily a favor and save her life, will you?"

"This is about the staff?" Lily asked.

Cole's heart clenched. "No."

Ashe rolled her eyes, turning away again.

"Ashley?" Lily pressed. "Is it?"

"Lily, I told you–" he started.

"It's about the fact some very bad people are going to hurt us if we don't start getting help from your friend, Lil," Ashe said without looking back. "That's what this is about."

His heart pounded harder as the little girl glanced between them.

"Lily," he urged quietly. "It's okay. Really. She's wrong. No one's going to–"

"Cole lied about the staff."

Ashe froze, and he was fairly certain the rest of the room did too.

Distant sounds of traffic filtered through the windows, tinny and strange in the silence, and broken a moment later by the soft scratch of debris as Ashe turned slowly back around.

"We," Lily amended. "We lied. We found the staff at his grandparents' house. They're historians. For Merlin. They have a whole bunch of old history stuff at their place."

"The Merlin historians," Ashe repeated flatly, and then she looked from the girl to Cole. "His grandparents are the Merlin historians? And you met them?"

Lily nodded.

Irate bafflement chased itself across Ashe's face, and then she shook her head as though to drive it away. "Does your dad know about this?"

Cole didn't move. She swore as she read the answer in his eyes anyway.

"How much of a head start does he have?"

He looked away. She snarled in frustration.

"Lily, where's this place?" she demanded.

"Washington. I… I think I could find it."

"Good."

Without missing a beat, she strode toward the little girl.

"Wait, what–"

"We're going." Ashe glanced to Spider and then jerked her chin at Cole. "Watch him. Shoot him if you have to."

Shaking her head, Lily backpedaled. "I'm not–"

He felt a flicker of magic and then it was gone, taking the glow around Lily with it. Gasping, the little girl skidded to a stop, horrified.

"You… you…"

"I'll give it back when we find Katherine."

A cry escaped Lily. She bolted for the far side of the room.

"Lily!" Ashe yelled.

The girl retreated through the piles of debris into the corner, staring at her sister as though she didn't recognize her. "That's… that's what you were going to do, isn't it? Take it away and put me on that plane. You–"

"We don't have time for this!"

"That's what you were going to do! You got all mad at him for lying and you were doing it the whole time!"

"I'm trying to protect you!"

"Hell you are!" the little girl shrieked.

Ashe stopped.

"You said we'd stick together, and you're leaving him again. Well, I'm not going. I'm staying with him. And if you don't like it, then you can just go on your own!"

Rigid with adrenaline, Ashe trembled. "Lil…"

"You heard me! Get out! Go!"

Ashe's brow twitched down, expressions chasing themselves over her face faster than he could read. For a heartbeat, she stood motionless, and then a flinch shook her.

Lily gasped as the glow around her returned like a switch had been flicked back on.

Without a word, Ashe turned and headed for the door.

"Ashley…" Lily cried.

The girl kept walking.

Debris clattered across the floor as Lily scrambled from the corner of the room. She raced after her sister, grabbing Ashe's arm as she reached the door.

"No," Lily begged. "Please, I didn't... I'm sorry. You just... you can't leave him, okay? You can't ever leave anybody. Please."

Ashe looked down at her.

"Please?" Lily repeated.

Carefully, so carefully it seemed her bones might break, Ashe nodded. Her hand shook as Lily took it and interlaced her fingers with Ashe's own, and when the little girl turned, her older sister followed.

And then Ashe looked up and met his eyes with so much hate it made his skin go cold.

Lily's hand held delicately in hers, she walked with the little girl across the room.

"Spider," Ashe said as they came closer.

"Yeah?" the girl replied.

"Can you tell Bus to hurry about the car?"

Spider nodded. She glanced from her friend to Cole, as though weighing whether he'd still be there when she got back, and then just as obviously deciding she didn't care.

He ignored her, watching Ashe. Wordlessly, she went to the window, bringing the little girl along. As Lily climbed onto the edge of the table, Ashe joined her, moving a moment later to put her arm around her sister's shoulders.

Her expression never changed. Still as stone, not a muscle on her face twitched as she turned to the window and then lifted a hand to nudge a loose board out of the way.

But he saw her fingers tremble, and watched her breath catch as Lily laid her head against her side.

Cole looked away as the silence of the building returned and the faint sounds of traffic drifted through the room. The uneven legs of the chair rocked slightly beneath him as he crossed his arms, and in the corner, bits of debris whispered as they settled to the ground.

Even monsters had people they'd do anything to keep from losing.

He knew that better than anyone.

Chapter Fourteen

⸻ ◆ ⸻

Seconds slid by, turning into irretrievable minutes that trickled away like water as she watched the world beyond the cafeteria window. Somewhere in the distance, sirens howled, rushing away from the building or toward it, she couldn't tell, and past the window slats, a pair of teenagers met in the shadows of the crumbling train sheds to swap a small package for money. Her lungs barely worked, and neither did her body, both of them choked by a hot swarm of things she didn't want to look at too deeply.

She wished Elias or Nathaniel were here. Even Cornelius would have been welcome in his way. It would've been nice to have someone else in the room, if only to give her the space to leave it while still keeping Cole under guard and Lily pacified. It was a stupid reason to want them back.

But it would have been nice all the same.

A shiver ran through her, distant and strangely anything but cold, and without even noticing, she suppressed the shaking. Once they got back to the wizards, everything would be easier. More focused, anyway. It was true there weren't that many Merlin left, what with councilman Arthur and his allies having been killed in Croftsburg a week ago and the fact Gavin, Ermengarde and most of the other survivors had gone so far to ground, she didn't have the foggiest idea how to find them anymore. But Katherine was still out there. The woman was the only wizard still living who was trustworthy anyway. She'd find the doctor, get Lily to safety, put Cole someplace he couldn't do any harm, and then head across the country to the historians.

And through it all, she'd be moving. She just desperately wanted to be moving.

By the train sheds, one of the teenagers ambled off. The sirens died without a cop car to be seen, giving a brief moment for the ever-present susurrus of traffic to whisper through the room before new sirens rose all over again.

And time crept on, giving Jamison the historians and bringing her closer to having to watch everyone she cared about die.

She closed her eyes, keeping her breathing steady by force of will-power alone. It wouldn't happen. She wouldn't let it. She didn't know how, but she wouldn't let it. She wouldn't lose her friends and she wouldn't lose her sister. Not again.

Footsteps echoed in the hallway. Swallowing hard, she schooled her face back to emotionlessness and glanced over as the cafeteria door swung open.

"Good to go?" she asked as Bus walked in.

He nodded. Quickly, she slid from the table and turned, waiting for Lily and then fighting the sudden desire to hurt something when the girl looked to Cole before following.

"Got a car for you," Bus said as they came closer. "Loaded it up with food and the like. Spider tells me you might be on the road a while, so I wanted to make sure the kid had enough to eat."

He grinned at Lily, who hesitantly returned the smile.

"Thanks," Ashe said.

Something must have been in her tone, because he glanced over questioningly.

Swiftly, she looked down. "Do you have a phone I could borrow?" she asked, working to keep her voice casual.

Bus paused. "Yeah." He reached into his pocket for his cell. "Who're you calling?"

She hesitated. "One of the Merlin."

He froze with his hand in his pocket. His jaw slid around as he mulled it over, and then he finished pulling out an old flip phone.

"Thanks," she said again as he handed her the cell.

She turned away, quickly dialing Katherine's number from memory. For security's sake, the wizards changed phones every few weeks, but the frequent new numbers hadn't stopped Elias from insisting she memorize each one. Trying to ignore the distrustful look Lily was giving her, she paced across the room, waiting for the call to go through. Her breath caught when a click sounded immediately on the other end of the line.

A polite message informed her that there was no voicemail for the number in question, and then hung up.

Heart pounding, she lowered the phone. The woman could be using a portal. It wasn't like signal was possible in those things anyway. Or she could have turned her phone off.

Wizards never turned their phones off.

Drawing a steadying breath, she waited a moment and then dialed the number again, taking care to punch each button correctly.

Nothing changed.

She stood, the phone at her ear though it had gone silent the moment before. Katherine had been shuttling between safe houses in Arkansas, Texas, and Oklahoma, helping those too injured to travel farther. She shouldn't have been in much danger, not comparatively anyway. And she wouldn't have changed phones this soon; she'd just gotten a new one a week ago. So perhaps the cell had just run out of power. Or maybe it'd broken accidentally, or just didn't have signal right now.

Or something.

She shivered. There was no way Katherine was gone too.

Glancing to the phone, she hit redial and then tried to keep breathing when the result was the same. Without Katherine, there wasn't anyone still alive that she knew how to reach. Which meant Lily would have to come with her. Cole too. She wouldn't have any backup, and if Jamison was waiting for them…

Lily's fingers rested on her arm and she flinched, not having noticed her come close.

"It's alright," the little girl offered. "Maybe they're busy."

Ashe looked down. Lily smiled encouragingly.

She made herself nod. Taking her sister's hand, she crossed the room and extended the cell to Bus, fighting to keep the fact she felt like screaming from showing in her eyes.

"Keep it," he said kindly. "I can get another."

She slid the phone into her pocket as she stepped around him, heading for the door.

"Hey, wait a second."

One hand on the spray-painted wood, she glanced back as Bus hurried after her.

"Sorry," he said to the strained impatience in her eyes. "It's just

Spider asked me to–"

He cut off as the door at the far end of the hallway swung open, banging into the wall as Spider strode through. A pair of black backpacks were slung over her shoulders and her shotgun had been replaced by twin handguns just visible under the edges of her jacket. She jerked her chin at Ashe in greeting. "You ready?"

Ashe's brow drew down. "Yeah," she allowed. "Why'd you–"

"Good, let's go."

"Wait, what–"

"I'm coming with you."

She stared at the girl, torn between equal parts relief and horror. She wanted to be grateful. She wanted to be thrilled. She just couldn't get past the fact that, if Spider came along, she'd most likely end up adding the girl's name to the list of all the people she'd gotten killed.

Again.

"Spider–"

"Look," the girl interrupted flatly as she let one of the bags drop to the floor. "You need help. There're Blood out there–" Her gaze flicked to Cole. "–and you need someone who'll watch your back."

"But it's just... I don't want–"

"I wasn't asking permission, your majesty," Spider snapped.

Ashe blinked. Scowling, Spider looked away.

"So I take it you talked to Samson," Bus said carefully into the silence.

Spider's mouth tightened in something that could have been a smile. "Ran into him downstairs."

Bus' eyebrows rose and fell in response as he glanced away.

Harsh expression fading, Spider sighed. "Ashe, I get it, alright? It's dangerous. You think I've missed that memo over the past eight years? But you need help, and I can't just sit here waiting for the Taliesin king to kill us all." Spider paused. "So are we going or what?"

She didn't answer.

Irritation flashed over the girl's face. Snagging the strap of the bag beside her, she swung it up from the ground, making Ashe catch it awkwardly.

"Clothes," Spider said. "Roadkill. Now come on."

Without another word, she headed back down the hall.

Desperately, Ashe looked to Bus, but the old man just held up his hands. "Don't think you'll get me to argue with her," he said, stepping around her to start after the girl. "I'd be coming too if she hadn't asked me to stay."

Ashe stared after them and then flinched when Lily made a small sound. Glancing to the little girl, she hesitated and then shifted the bag around onto her shoulder and followed them.

"You're wasting your time, you know."

At the sound of Cole's voice, she froze, barely having made it three steps. Shivers ran through her, fueled by the overwhelming urge to just stop the boy from being a problem once and for all.

"Cole," she warned without turning around. "Don't."

Debris crunching beneath his feet, he gave her wide berth as he circled her.

"What?" he replied. "I'm just saying. My grandparents won't be in Washington anymore. Things didn't go too well when Lily and I were there, and they're not exactly the calm type. Minute they picked up the pieces, they'd have hit the road."

Her gaze slid over to him, and the shivering grew stronger at the innocent look in his eyes. "And where would they have gone?"

"As far from Washington as they could get," he said like it was obvious. "*If* they're even still in the States, they're probably hidden away in Florida by now."

She paused. "So you're saying we should go there," she stated flatly.

He shrugged. "I'm just saying you shouldn't rush off. Aren't there other wizards you could contact? Maybe you could send them down south, see if they find anything. I mean, you don't want to just go hauling Lily across the country unnecessarily, right?"

Expressionless, she regarded him, wondering if he actually thought she was gullible enough to believe he suddenly wanted to help.

"We'll start in Washington," she said.

Pulling Lily with her, she strode past him, trying to ignore the worried look the girl gave Cole as she went.

"You're making a mistake," he called.

Trembling with rage, she didn't answer as she yanked open the door.

Bus and Spider were talking quietly halfway across the room. As Ashe and Lily emerged from the hall, Spider glanced over and then, with a final look to Bus, she turned and disappeared into the shadows.

With a sigh, the old man waited for them both and then led the way toward the stairs.

The lower level was silent, and the blue glow of the light did little to alleviate the gloom. Crouching, she braced herself on the platform ledge and then dropped to the tracks. Eyeing the pitch-black shadows that guarded the maintenance room and resisting the impulse to let her defensive magic rise, she helped Lily down and then turned, her skin crawling as she followed Spider and Bus toward the tunnel's opposite end.

Minutes passed, their monotony broken only by the infrequent lights revealing layer upon layer of graffiti above the train tracks. Old cigarettes peppered the broken concrete beneath their feet, and years of garbage bordered the wall, filling the air with the stench of decay.

And finally, a hint of daylight thinned the shadows as the tunnel began to climb.

On some unspoken signal, Spider and Bus slowed. Reaching into his pocket, the old man drew out a set of keys and then handed them to the girl.

"Third one on the left, yeah?" she asked.

He nodded.

Spider hesitated, and then echoed the motion. Briefly, her gaze went back to the shadowy tunnel, hurt flickering through her eyes.

"Take care of him for me," she said quietly.

Bus smiled. "You know I will."

Spider drew a breath, forcing her expression to clear, and she nodded again. Adjusting the bag on her shoulder, she gave him a small grin and then started up the slope.

The old man glanced over as Ashe followed. "Now don't you go keeping all the fun to yourself," he ordered. "You need anything…"

Ashe hesitated. "Thanks, Bus."

He chuckled, patting her shoulder. "See you when you get back, kiddo."

She nodded, hoping it would be true. Hanging onto Lily's hand, she continued after Spider.

"Bye, Bus," Lily said shyly as they passed.

The rushing sounds of traffic filtered down the tunnel as they climbed, and after a dozen yards, the tracks abruptly came to an end. An overgrown gate lay ahead, its base entrenched by mounds of garbage and dead leaves. Twitching the kudzu aside, Spider scanned the street, and then flipped around the keys to unfasten a heavy padlock and chain lashed around the gate. Sliding the chain through the bars, she checked the street again and then pulled one side of the fence back slightly.

"Hurry," she said and then slipped through the opening.

A thick carpet of kudzu choked the ditch beyond the tunnel, ending only inches from the sidewalk. Beat-up cars sagged next to old parking meters, waiting for their owners to return, while across the street, abandoned office buildings gaped. Barely giving Cole enough time to make it past the gate, Spider refastened the chain, and then tucked it into the vines before striding swiftly for the sidewalk. At an old bronze car three parking meters from the entrance to the tunnel, she unlocked the door and then reached around to pull the rear lock as well.

Ashe climbed into the back seat, her nose wrinkling at the musty smell of the overwhelmingly beige interior. Scooting to the far side of the vehicle, she unlocked the front and then bent over to help Lily tug the door closed with a screech of rusted hinges. As Lily eyed the dusty seatbelt, surrendering finally to buckling it over herself, Ashe turned, watching the street.

Police cars shot past an intersection a few blocks away, their sirens howling.

She swallowed and glanced to the front as Spider turned the key in the ignition, succeeding in starting the engine on the fourth try.

"Blackjack's got to get better cars," the girl muttered. Pulling down the gearshift, she winced as the car jerked, and then eased the vehicle out onto the potholed road.

"Well," Spider said dryly. "Here we go."

Chapter Fifteen

A block from the latest target, Harris pulled the rental car to a stop and sighed. Forty-eight hours had passed since the kids escaped the Blood in Banston, and in his opinion, the time had not gone well. Half of Jamison's forces were tearing the city apart, while the rest were chasing any lead they could find. A few stragglers like himself were still being sent to other cities to take down any additional Merlin hiding places Tanya recalled, in case they were locations to which Ashley would retreat, and over Chaunessy, there hung a cloud of silence no one wanted to be the first to break.

Brogan looked like cold violence waiting to happen. Simeon hadn't bothered and lashed out at anyone who crossed his path. Tanya was like a woman possessed, wracking her already questionably stable mind for any hideouts she might have forgotten, and Jamison hadn't left his office in two days.

And meanwhile, Harris couldn't get Cole's words out of his head.

With a scowl, he shoved the gearshift into park and then turned off the engine. Glancing to the passenger seat, he eyed the paper sack of groceries dubiously, and then hefted it up and shifted it around till he could climb from the sedan without contorting himself into too much of a pretzel. The wide street was mostly quiet, with only a few midday drivers cruising the roads, but even the silence set him on edge. Hoisting the bag higher in his arms, he surveyed the neighborhood as casually as he could manage, and then headed for the cube of cracked stucco walls and cheap metal windows optimistically called the Beautiful Acres Apartments.

It was hard not to be tense. The Merlin had gotten craftier in recent weeks, once they'd figured out their hiding places were compromised. Apartments were booby-trapped as often as not, and in the past two days alone, every place he'd gone had proven to be a setup.

No one had gotten killed. Not yet, anyway. But the possibility of another trap left him edgy every time he walked into a building where Tanya said the Merlin had been.

With as pleasantly neutral an expression as he could muster, he pulled open the glass door and then strolled into the narrow hallway. Cracked tile popped beneath his feet, destroying any chance he had of approaching the apartments unnoticed, and through an open doorway, he spotted a young couple kissing goodbye before the man headed out.

He nodded to the guy as he passed and kept walking. It was a bit like the old days on the police force, running stealth reconnaissance like this. He got in, surveyed the area and then got out with the exact location of the targets in question. A squad would move in and subdue the threat, while he slipped off with none of the targets aware that the assumedly oblivious man who'd wandered by a few minutes before had actually given their position away.

Of course, it wasn't exactly the same. Back on the force, he'd known pretty much where everyone stood on things.

Fighting off a grimace, he pushed the thought aside and doubled back toward the stairway. He didn't know what had spooked Cole, but it wasn't something he could worry about right now. Everything else aside, the Merlin had proven time and again to be a clear, violent threat with an utter lack of concern for whom they hurt. That was reality, and he needed to focus on it if he wanted to keep the wizards from knowing he could see them, and if he wanted to make it back to the car alive.

But for the addition of an old woman sweeping her doorstep, the second story was identical to the one below. Narrow brown doors bearing tarnished brass numbers lined either side of the corridor, ending in a permanently sealed window that overlooked the parking lot. The door shut behind him as the old woman returned to her apartment and at the end of the hall, he could hear a television playing cartoons.

Confusion hit him, followed by a rush of recognition for the eye-crossing feeling he'd come to know so well. He forced his feet to keep moving. There were four doors on each side of the hallway, but to his right, his gaze was hell-bent on sliding past one.

Breathing slowly, he strolled past the magic to the last apartment and knocked.

The noise of the television clicked abruptly off. A few childlike voices protested, only to fall silent at a sharp reprimand, and then the door crept open.

"Yes?" a weathered-looking young woman asked, eyeing him from behind the security chain.

Harris smiled. "Hi, I'm from North Falls Presbyterian," he said, pulling from memory the name of a church he'd passed on the way here. "One of our members put down your family for a gift from our food pantry and I'm just coming by to drop it off."

The woman hesitated. "Who gave you our name?"

His smile took on a rueful cast. "I'm not really allowed to say."

"Are there cookies?" came a little boy's voice from inside the apartment.

"Stay in there!" the woman snapped without looking fully away from Harris. For a moment longer, she paused, and then she twitched her chin toward the floor. "Okay, just leave it by the door."

He didn't let the smile flicker as he set the bag down. "Have a nice day," he said as he straightened again.

"You too," she offered cautiously as he walked off.

No sound emanated from the other apartment as he passed it on his way back to the stairs. His eyes slipped over it, his expression blankly pleasant, and his heart picked up speed as he spotted shadows moving behind the peephole.

He kept going. The clatter of his footsteps on the stairs felt deafening and, by the time he finished sweeping the third floor, his heart was drumming fit to choke him. Jogging back down the steps, he headed out onto the street, fighting the urge to look back at the second story all the while. Continuing across the road, he thumbed the key fob for the rental and then slid into the driver's seat before finally allowing himself to survey the building.

Nothing moved. He pulled out his cell phone.

"Second floor, north side, halfway down the hall in apartment six," he said when Brogan picked up. "But we have a problem. There's people all around them. Kids too."

The wizard paused. "Understood. Head for the airport. We'll be there shortly."

Silence replaced the faint hiss of the phone call.

Harris set the cell aside. His gaze returned to the building as he started the car.

The fact he'd made it back meant that, like every place before it, Ashley probably wasn't in there, though other equally vicious wizards could be. But Brogan and the rest knew what they were dealing with when it came to the Merlin, if only by the number of people they'd lost fighting them. Meanwhile, however, he was sitting here when he needed to drive, because if any of the Merlin survived, spotted him elsewhere, and then remembered he'd been gawking at their window right before the Blood showed up, he'd really be screwed.

He grimaced and pulled the car away from the curb.

Why would Cole think his dad didn't want to help a kid?

He flipped on the radio in exasperation. Jamison made clear when they first met that the little girl's safety was as important as Cole's own. At the police station, Brogan had indicated much the same thing.

And people never lied.

He came to a stop at a red light and rubbed his face, a familiar ache beginning to throb in his temples. The Blood wanted to stop Ashley and everyone like her. They'd taken apart the ones who'd occupied Chaunessy before them solely to keep those wizards from ever hurting anyone again, and they were damn close to doing the same to Ashley's people. And beyond that, he really didn't care. Someone had to protect the innocent from her kind, and since no one in the so-called human world even believed wizards existed, the Blood were the best chance anyone had.

So why the hell hadn't Cole seen it that way?

A horn honked and he flinched, realizing the light had long since turned green. Exhaling in frustration, he waved apologetically as he glanced to the rearview mirror.

He froze. Above the apartment building, black smoke billowed into the sky.

A curse escaped him. Hitting the accelerator, he cranked the wheel around, spinning the car through a tight turn and leaving the drivers of the other vehicles staring. His hand reached for a siren before he remembered it wasn't there and then the next stoplight was behind him, with traffic screeching to a halt in his wake. A turn came and went as he raced the car onto the apartment building's street, and when he hit the brakes, the rental careened onto the curb before reaching a stop.

The second floor was in flames.

He jumped from the vehicle and took off.

Residents flooded out the door and others stood in the street, their eyes locked on the flames licking up the stucco walls. Sirens wailed in the distance and the wizards were nowhere to be seen. Skidding to a halt, he skimmed his gaze over the crowd.

The old woman and the couple were there. Dozens of other people too.

But not everyone.

He looked to the second floor.

A small hand pounded on the window of the endmost apartment.

He ran.

People stumbled from his path as he shoved through the doorway and rescued belongings went flying as he barreled between the crowd on the stairs. Protests followed him past the second story door, the noise dismissed as irrelevant the moment it reached his ears.

Smoke poured across the ceiling. Flames were devouring the walls.

Harris wrapped an arm across his mouth and nose, and ran for the end of the hall.

The heat was incredible. Everything on his body felt like it was cooking, and he could hardly breathe for the smoke. Amid the flames chewing through the cheap plasterboard, crazed scorch marks covered the walls, and charred drywall and insulation rained from holes blown in the ceiling.

He slowed, placing a hand to the door of the last apartment before grabbing the handle and hurrying inside.

Two wide-eyed faces stared up from beneath the layer of smoke, both of them crouched around a figure lying just inside the doorway.

He cursed, recognizing the young woman from a few minutes before. A gash covered her forehead, the ragged edges swelled tight, and blood laced her face till it was lost in her hair.

A shiver shook him despite the heat. She'd gone to get the groceries he'd left for her.

And then she'd gotten in the way.

Drawing a rough breath, he bent and scooped her up from the ground.

"Come on," he ordered the kids. "Stay low and–"

"What the hell?" came a muffled voice.

He looked up to see two firemen in the doorway, their equipment covering them from head to toe. Without waiting for an answer, the nearest strode forward, taking the woman from Harris' arms and jerking his head back toward the hall.

"This way," the man barked from within his helmet, while his partner rounded up the children and led them from the room.

Harris didn't argue.

Coughing hard, he rushed after them through the burning

hallway. Apartment doors had been kicked open, and living rooms filled with smoke and abandoned belongings gaped back. The floor groaned beneath him, the sound almost drowned by the growl of the flames, and beyond the walls he could barely hear the sirens screaming.

Prone figures caught his eye and he slammed to a stop. His confused gaze went from the firemen to the apartment, and then his mind caught up with where he was standing.

The door had been blasted inward. He could see that from the chunks of wood flung all over the place. And the Blood had gone in fighting, given the fact the bodies hadn't made it much beyond the living room. From the way the corpses lay, they looked like they'd tried to flee, and based upon the destruction in the hall and the residual blur of magic in the apartment, a few others had probably survived, though he couldn't say if they'd ultimately managed to escape.

But that wasn't the point.

He was shaking. He couldn't stop shaking.

Five bodies. Burned. Blackened. Charred beyond recognition by the assault they'd taken.

And three of them were painfully small.

The floor cracked warningly beneath his feet, jarring him as it started to give way, and he gasped, taking in a lungful of smoke before he realized what he was doing. Choking, he stumbled from the apartment, his legs carrying him to the stairwell door. A firefighter grabbed him, muscling him down the stairs and out onto the street, and when an oxygen mask appeared in front of his face, it was all he could do to breathe.

Children.

They'd killed children.

Hands grabbed him as he tried to rise, holding him on the ambulance step.

The Blood had killed children.

"Sir? Sir, can you hear me?"

He blinked at the woman as she put a hand to his head and then flashed a light across his eyes.

Children.

"Sir, are you hurt?"

His gaze slid to the apartment building, watching the fire hoses rain torrents of water down on the blaze.

"Sir?"

He shook his head slowly and didn't notice when she finally went away.

Emergency crews swirled around him while smoke billowed into the midday sky.

He pulled the mask from his face. Leaving it on the ambulance step, he walked back to the rental car. The door opened and let him into the driver's seat, and then closed again.

His gaze fell to his jacket and the space where it hid his gun.

He couldn't shoot them. He knew how that scenario ran. And arresting them was as much a joke now as it'd been with Ashley.

They'd murdered kids.

His eyes closed and his brow furrowed as his head began to pound.

The kids he'd led them to. The kids they must have seen when they'd come into the room and whom they could have avoided hitting if they'd really wanted. They hadn't needed to kill them. The adults weren't even anywhere close; not based on where the bodies lay. The Blood could have taken the children with them or, at a minimum, left them after everything else was done.

But there was nothing like the slaughter of kids to undercut your enemy's will to fight. Sometimes, anyway.

He shook his head, the thoughts beating against the pain in his temples.

And he'd made it happen. He'd set it up. He'd used the woman being rushed to the hospital right now as a cover, as if he hadn't known that leaving her to step into that hallway would never be safe, and he'd given up the location of a bunch of children without ever considering they might be the ones behind that door.

But he hadn't cared. He'd just assumed…

He'd always just assumed…

That wizards could ever be the good guys. That people didn't lie. That ninety-nine percent of their world wasn't solely focused on their own advantage, regardless of how many innocents they had to crush beneath them along the way.

And he was so, so much smarter than that. At least, he should have been.

A rasping breath escaped him as he opened his eyes, his gaze landing on the apartment building and its wreath of hoses and spinning emergency lights.

He'd wanted to keep people safe. To protect those whose only crime was being in the wrong place at the wrong time. And instead, he'd ended up helping a group every bit as vicious as Ashley's had ever been.

He wondered how many others the Blood had killed, while always telling him the Merlin were the only ones to blame.

Dragging in another breath, he looked away, his gaze tracking across the oblivious crowd watching the blaze. He didn't know how to make it right. He was only here because no one believed him anyway. Just saying Ashley went up in flames had gotten him driven off the police force, and if he ever tried to tell anyone about the things he'd seen since, a straitjacket and a rainbow of pills would only be the beginning.

He couldn't touch them. They operated with impunity based upon the simple fact they couldn't be seen. And he couldn't change that. He couldn't make the world look past their magic, or stare at supposedly blank video for however long it took for the static to give way. Recording a confession was useless, as was filming one of their fights, and with how far off the grid they'd made themselves, he'd be hard-pressed to find anything linking them to their continent-wide swath of crimes.

His head throbbed as his gaze ran over the crisp interior of the sedan without seeing the upholstery and plastic at all.

He had nothing. Absolutely nothing. He had…

Harris paused, the tiny blur in front of him resolving into the rental company sticker at which he hadn't realized he'd been staring.

Incredulity nearly made him laugh.

He was an idiot. The answer was right there.

Based on everything he'd seen, he had to assume the Blood used shell companies. Fake names and identification were probably considered basic necessities. In all their dealings, they'd undoubtedly been meticulous to avoid any trace that would connect to them directly, and their underworld contacts would likely put a mob boss to shame.

But everyone left a trail. Following the dead had led him to Ashley, for all that it hadn't gone according to plan in the end. And trailing Cole's friend had gotten him closer to finding the boy than anyone else in eight years. It hadn't been perfect, and it hadn't brought him success overall, but that wasn't the point.

It had worked. And there was one small, terribly important difference this time.

He was on the inside. He wasn't reading case reports or looking at evidence months after the crime. He was in their building, going on their raids, doing their dirty work and being ignored throughout every other part of the day.

Air escaped him as he looked back at the crowd still watching the flames.

A paper trail of private flights and car rentals between their murders could be enough to start the police looking for them. Eventually, it might even put their faces on the internet and TV. And while that wouldn't bring back the kids they'd killed or the others who'd gotten in their way, it would make life difficult to an extreme. Every time they set foot outside the door, they'd be at risk, because even if regular folks didn't necessarily see them, other wizards would recognize them immediately.

Though maybe, just maybe, if enough people started paying attention, they'd break through that damn invisibility.

A small chuckle slipped out and he drew a breath, reining the sound back in. Finding evidence wouldn't be enough. He'd need more than just what the Blood had on hand if he was going to piece their little empire together in a way the rest of the world would see.

Glancing down, he picked up his phone and then hesitated.

There wasn't an alternative. He didn't have the resources to do this alone.

His thumb hit the speed dial.

"Hello?"

He drew a breath. "Hey, Scott."

"John?"

"Yeah."

The man paused, and Harris could almost picture the expressions that would have been running across his face, if not for the scars. "It's been a while," Malden said carefully.

"I know. I'm sorry about that."

"You alright?"

It was his turn to pause. "I need to ask you something."

"You should come back in, John."

Rubbing his eyes, Harris didn't answer. Silence hung between them, and then a squeaking sound carried across the line, followed by the clunk of a closing door.

"You still in the wheelchair?" he asked uncomfortably.

"Another few weeks." A moment passed. "I take it you were getting Rhianne's emails, then."

"Yeah."

The hiss of the phone connection became deafening.

"Listen, if you'd rather I not–" Harris started.

"What's the question?"

He hesitated. "Do you still have access to the department databases?"

"You can't–"

"It's about the girl."

Malden went quiet. "She's the FBI's problem, John," he said with tight control. "Let them handle it."

Harris' gaze skimmed the crowd as he tried to figure out what to say.

"You find her?" Malden asked, an edge to the words.

He hesitated. "Close."

A moment passed.

"You going to bring her in?"

He grimaced. "If I can."

Malden let a breath out slowly. "Alright. What do you need?"

Harris' eyes closed in relief. "You got a pen?"

He could hear rustling on the other end of the phone. "Yeah," Malden said.

"Okay, take these down. Victor Jamison. Mason Brogan. Simeon Cavanaugh. Isabella Marceau. Mark Keller. I want everything you can find."

"These people connected to the girl?"

"Very."

"I'll see what I can do."

"Thanks, Scott."

Malden scoffed. "I'll treasure your gratitude when we're in jail."

In spite of himself, he chuckled before he hung up the phone. Sliding the cell into his pocket, he glanced back at the crowd.

News crews surrounded the building now, filming the destruction and interviewing firemen who would only have mundane and mistaken answers to give for the blaze.

But maybe that could change.

He started the car. Checking the traffic briefly, he pulled the vehicle from the curb and headed back for the airport.

Brogan would want to know why he was covered in soot, and the wizards would be furious he was so late, but he wasn't concerned. Like everything else, he'd just come up with a cover story.

Harris smiled. After six months of tracking wizards through a world where no one else believed they existed, he'd gotten really good at those anyway.

Chapter Sixteen

———◆———

"**I** *thought* it was this way…" Lily said worriedly as she stared out at the spruce trees crowding the roadside. "Past that big boulder that looked like a house."

In the seat behind her, Cole made a hedging noise. "I don't remember any boulder, and I'm pretty sure their place was a lot farther west than this. Over near Bellingham, maybe."

Her grip on the steering wheel tightening, Ashe glanced to Spider in the rearview mirror. The girl rolled her eyes. In the two days since they'd left Banston, the boy hadn't quit trying to slow them down. If it wasn't comments that they were going the wrong way, it was possible attempts to sabotage the car. More than once when they paused for gas, she or Spider had spotted him lingering near the vehicle, eyeing it as though trying to figure out how to break it without either killing them all or leaving too much of a trace. Between the two of them, they'd swiftly taken to never letting him out of their sight, although that hadn't brought an end to the incessant commentary.

Twisting in her seat, Lily looked back at him. "Really?"

Cole made a rueful noise. "I think so."

Ashe gritted her teeth, biting back two days' worth of frustration. With how he'd been steadily undermining the girl's confidence, there was a good chance they were on the wrong road anyway.

"You're doing fine, Lil," she said, her eyes on the gravel track.

The little girl glanced between them and then turned back to the road. "I… I didn't think it was too much farther."

"Lily, I'm sorry, but I really mean it. We're wasting our time. That turn back at the highway was a lot more familiar than–"

"Please shut up," Spider sighed, not looking at anyone in particular.

Ashe fought back a grin. More than just for being able to trade off driving with the girl, Spider had been about the only thing that'd gotten her this far, mostly by keeping her from going insane. Katherine had yet to answer any calls, though that hadn't stopped Cole from badgering her about asking the wizards to search the southeast. The car had barely held together over the past thousand miles, and lately emitted smoke from beneath the hood whenever they stopped. She was fairly certain Cole wasn't to blame for it, though holding him responsible anyway was tempting. They had little if any plan to speak of, and no matter what Cole said, there weren't any Merlin left that she knew how to reach.

But they were close. And as naïve as it seemed, she still had to hope that counted for something.

"Slow down," Lily said.

Ashe slowed accordingly and winced as the engine shuddered.

The little girl leaned forward in her seat. "There was a gate…"

"I'm telling you, Lily," Cole said with frustration. "We should go back. There's nothing down–"

Ashe hit the brakes as the car came around the curve. Black and imposing, a metal gate stood a few feet away, with petite security cameras mounted on either side. Near the edge of the gravel road, a decorative pole stood, a small speaker box mounted to its top.

Spider looked over at Cole dryly. "Obviously, your sense of direction sucks."

He didn't respond.

Creeping the car forward and trying to ignore the wisps of smoke already rising from beneath the hood, Ashe eyed the security cameras as she pulled up next to the speaker. Their lenses focused on the forest, neither device moved.

She glanced back at Spider in the rearview mirror. The girl shrugged.

The window crank squealed as she wound the glass down. Cautiously, she pressed the microphone button. "Hello?"

Silence answered her.

"Turn around," Cole ordered, all trace of theatrics gone from his tone.

She glanced back at him and then looked to Lily and Spider. "Stay here."

"Ashe–" Cole protested.

The hinges screeched as she pushed open the door. Watching the forest, she climbed out and approached the gate, letting her magic surround her. Birds chirped in the distance, joining the growl of the engine and the crunch of her shoes on the gravel as the only sounds. Ahead, the path twisted around a blind turn and disappeared into the thick cover of pine trees. Cautiously, she put a hand to the black metal fence, and then tensed when it yielded instantly to her touch. Still watching the forest, she pushed the twin sides of the gate open, and then retreated to the car.

"– try that again!" Spider snapped as Ashe pulled open the door.

She looked from the girl to Cole. Her hand on one of the weapons under her jacket, Spider was eyeing the boy as though she'd like nothing more than to shoot him, while Cole just looked as if he wished he still had the gun Spider had taken from him two days before.

"What happened?" Ashe asked as she climbed back in.

"Your friend tried to make a run for it."

"I wasn't–"

Scowling, Ashe shut the door on his words and then put the car back into gear.

Shifting position, Cole started forward and then halted at a warning noise from Spider. "Ashe," he urged as the car rolled past the gate. "Think about this for a minute. Something's wrong here. Turn around."

Watching the gravel road, she didn't answer. There wasn't any point.

"Dammit!" he snapped, ignoring Spider as he leaned forward again. "Listen to me! My grandparents would *never* turn off their security. They're the most paranoid freaks in the world. And you know who else was headed here. Please, just stop the car and–"

"I'm not leaving her with you," Ashe said, glancing to the motionless security cameras hanging in the trees.

He made an infuriated noise. "This isn't just about her, alright? You both–"

The car came round the turn and his words died.

Lily made a small noise, but Ashe didn't look over. Her irritation drained away, leaving a void. On autopilot, she let the car come to a stop.

Beneath the cloudless blue sky, pulverized bricks lay everywhere, crumbled into enormous mounds or scattered across the yard as though backhanded by a giant. Blackened struts of wood protruded at odd angles from the heart of the fallen house, along with twists of pipe that looked as though they'd been ripped in half. Ruts showed in the grass where emergency vehicles had come and gone, and at the edge of the yard, a single lamppost stood incongruous watch.

She pushed open the door.

Cool wind swept around her, making a half-broken pipe in the wreckage creak as it swayed in the breeze. She pulled her jacket closer and stepped away from the car as, behind her, she heard the others shut the doors.

Gravel crunched as Lily circled to her side. "I-I didn't..." she whispered, taking her sister's hand. "It wasn't like this..."

Ashe looked back.

One hand on top of the car and his face bloodlessly pale, Cole stared at the destruction. On the other side of the vehicle, Spider was watching them and the forest equally, her guns already drawn.

Ashe headed for the house.

Charred shingles littered the bright green grass, the pieces cracking beneath her shoes. Blackened clusters of twigs showed at intervals where bushes must have been, and broken stumps of metal and wire stood where other lampposts had once circled the yard. Through the trees ringing the property, the wind returned, stirring the ashes and sending the acrid stench of old smoke into the air.

She closed her eyes, faltering as the smell brought back the memory of another place the Blood had taken away.

The wind died. Tightening her grip on Lily's hand, she walked closer to the wreckage.

Bricks had crushed the house when they fell, and fire had taken care of whatever survived the collapse. Several yards in, a sudden drop showed where the basement lurked, though the majority of it was choked with debris.

Her eyes ran over the ruins as she circled the perimeter of the massive house. A bit of charred paper was caught between two bricks, the beautifully calligraphic writing saying nothing sensible, and half-crushed beneath a ceiling strut, the arm of a display stand twisted upward, its occupant long since gone. More remnants of the historians' archives met her gaze, from picture frames blackened by fire to warped leather backings for books whose contents were only ash.

She slowed, drawing an unsteady breath. She'd known there was a strong chance he'd get here first. She'd known it before the four of them ever left Banston, though she'd still had to try. And it was possible Jamison hadn't done this. The historians had pretended to be dead before. After Lily and Cole left, they could have razed the place and run, just like Cole claimed.

Her gaze landed on the charred scrap of a painting, its edges eaten by fire till all that remained was the desperate image of an old man, his lifted hands pleading with the sky.

She strode back to the car.

"What now?" Spider asked quietly.

Ashe didn't respond. "Do you know where they would've gone?" she asked Cole shortly.

Blinking, he pulled his focus from the wreckage. "Sorry?"

"The historians. They faked their deaths before, so…"

He paused, his gaze sliding to the house, and then he drew a breath, nodding. "Right," he said, returning his attention to her. "They, um…" He trailed off, his brow drawing down as though something about her upset him. More than usual, anyway. He blinked, looking away again. "I don't know."

She grimaced, clinging to the surge of irritation to stave off the powerlessness she was trying to ignore. "Then who would? Neighbors? Other relatives? You have to know something."

He didn't answer. His eyes were back on the rubble.

"What about Ben and Sue?"

Cole flinched at the soft sound of Lily's voice, and Ashe saw him hesitate.

"Who are Ben and Sue?" she asked them both.

"They're people we stayed with for a while," Lily explained. "They knew his grandparents."

Spider cast Cole a disgusted look. He didn't seem to notice.

"Would the Blood know about them?" Ashe asked.

"I'm not sure," Lily said.

Ashe glanced to Cole. His gaze on the ruins, he gave no sign he'd heard the exchange.

Irritation increasing, she made herself look away from him. It wasn't like he'd tell the truth anyway. And as far as everything else was concerned, they didn't have a whole lot of choice, given that none of them could exactly go to the cops for answers and they hadn't seen a neighbor for twenty miles.

"Where are they?" she asked.

"Um… back down the highway," Lily answered, eyeing Cole worriedly. "Maybe a few hours south."

"Alright," Ashe said. "Let's go."

The little girl hurried around to the passenger side while Spider tugged open the door.

Ashe drew a breath, reaching for the rusted handle, and then paused. Cole hadn't moved.

"After you," she said acidly.

He blinked again and looked over. Her eyebrow twitched up, and a flicker of anger tightened his expression in response.

And then he got in.

She closed her eyes, willing herself not to hurt him, and then climbed into the car.

⸻ ◆ ⸻

The engine clanked and smoke rose from beneath the hood. Every light on the dashboard had given up hours before, though the temperature gauge was still screaming bloody murder. Behind the wheel, Ashe looked like she'd come to the conclusion she was holding the bronze clunker together by willpower alone, while in the seat beside him, Spider occasionally muttered something about thanking Blackjack for his generosity in giving them the car.

As the vehicle shuddered over another bump, Cole shifted on the musty seat and returned his gaze to the window. In the time since they'd left the manor, the landscape had slowly flattened around them, with the familiar spread of farmlands gradually replacing the spruce-covered hillsides the Carnegeans had called home. Cows and harvested fields surrounded the country road, both of them touched with gold by the sinking sun.

And no matter how he tried, he couldn't let himself be calmed by any of it.

He didn't know why the deaths – possible deaths – of the Carnegeans bothered him so much. His grandparents had been monsters. Egomaniacal to an extreme, they hadn't cared about their own daughter, let alone the rest of the people dying while they hid in luxurious safety. And that didn't even bring into it the fact they'd tried to kill him and Lily.

But for some reason, that reality wasn't making his discomfort go away.

His dad might not have killed them. Ashe could be right – about that, if nothing else. They'd hidden once. And they must've made it look convincing that time too. For all he knew, the bastards actually were living it up in a mansion in Orlando or wherever, just like he'd been trying to make Ashe believe.

He shifted on the seat. Though, what the hell did it matter if the Blood *had* killed them? His dad still didn't have Lily or Ashe. Wouldn't, if Cole had anything to do with it. The rest was immaterial. The world was better off without them.

And Lily's family. And the councils. And his…

He shoved the thought away swiftly. He didn't know anything about his mom. Clara had been a victim of the war, according to his dad. That didn't mean Victor had killed her too. And just because he'd never answered any questions about it, and just because his people had possibly wiped out her parents like a demolition team from hell, didn't mean she was gone.

Drawing a breath, he forced himself to refocus. He was getting upset over nothing.

Except having handed them over to his father.

He paused in the middle of reading a billboard for an apple farm, the words becoming instant gibberish. He'd told his dad about the Carnegeans. About their location, their archives and everything he knew. And, two days later, they were possibly dead. Very, very possibly dead.

Breathing hard, he turned his gaze from the window, though it just caught on Ashe. Gripping the wheel, she was trying to give Lily a reassuring smile as an engine belt squealed, but even he could see the worry fracturing her expression.

She wasn't a good person either. She *wasn't*. She'd killed people, untold numbers of people, and there was still every chance she'd do worse than his dad if she got her hands on the spell. Just because he'd given up information on her too didn't mean he'd been wrong.

His stomach rolled. He pulled his gaze back to the window, silently cursing it.

The Carnegeans *weren't* good people, though. For pity's sake, they'd tried to kill their own grandson. Surely that counted for something on the grand scales of the universe? Made this karmic justice in a way.

That argument settled even worse than the previous one.

He scowled. He just needed to get over it. Chances were, the bastards were fine. They were probably tucked away in a palace somewhere, whining about their deplorable conditions and suffering, and if they'd known he was beating himself up over their possible deaths, they'd have just chalked it up to his cripple inferiority and laughed.

Really, he should hope they were dead.

The car bounced over another pothole, sending a spring jabbing into his leg.

"Much farther?" Ashe asked Lily tensely.

Clutching the door and her seat as though to keep from falling from the car, Lily shook her head. "Uh-uh. It's just a– there. See it?"

She pointed toward the pinnacle of a brown-shingled roof beyond the trees, and then gripped the seat again.

"You'll like Sue," the little girl added hopefully. "She kind of reminds me of Rose."

Ashe glanced over, giving Lily a smile, though the expression didn't touch the fleeting pain he saw in her eyes. Returning her attention to the smoke separating them from the road, she eased the car around the turn into the long driveway.

The engine shuddered, growling in time with the gravel beneath the wheels. He barely noticed, his gaze locked on the white farmhouse. A large autumn wreath had been added beside the wooden screen door since last he was there, and the oak tree in the front lawn now wore brilliant shades of red and gold, but otherwise, nothing had changed.

He felt like he was looking at the memory of a dream.

With a diminishing growl, the car pulled to a stop a dozen feet shy of the house, and with effort, Ashe shoved the gearshift into park.

"Stay–" she started, turning to Lily.

The little girl was already halfway out the door.

With a furious noise, Ashe spun and followed Lily from the car, and over the hood, he could hear her berating the girl while he and Spider climbed out.

The screen door swung open, and Ashe cut off, her gaze snapping toward the porch as though pulled by a string. An overloaded bag of vegetables in her arms, Sue backed awkwardly out the door and then turned.

She froze.

"Hannah?" she gasped. "Paul?"

He could feel the other girls' caution, for all that the woman didn't look like a Blood, and he saw Ashe glance to Spider swiftly, seeking confirmation.

"Ben!" Sue yelled over her shoulder. "It's Paul and Hannah!"

Not waiting for her husband, she plopped the bag by the porch swing and then ran down the stairs, ignoring the vegetables as they toppled to the ground. Ashe started forward, making it a few steps before the woman reached Lily and fell to her knees to wrap the girl in a hug. Eyes widening, Ashe went rigid, and furtively, he motioned to her, trying to forestall any explosive intervention.

The girl glanced to him. Drawing a microscopic breath, she shifted her weight slightly, as though forcing herself not to strike out.

"We thought–" Sue started, and then she gave another gasp. "Oh, it doesn't matter what we thought. I'm just so glad… so, so glad…"

She looked to him and her words trailed off, the relief on her face transforming into concern. Letting her grip on Lily relax, she began climbing to her feet, only to glance over her shoulder as the screen door opened again.

"Ben," she said, and Cole could hear the gratitude in her voice. She turned back to Lily, and then paused as she suddenly seemed to notice the other two girls. A doubtful look flitted through her eyes, strengthening as she took in Spider's appearance.

"You kids alright?" Ben called.

Cole nodded. "Yeah."

"Who are your friends?" Sue asked.

He could hear the careful treatment she gave the description, despite her pleasant tone. Her hand closed around Lily's shoulder, pulling the little girl a bit nearer to her side.

Ashe tensed all over again.

"Uh, right," Cole said, watching Ashe as he wracked his brain for names. "Sue, Ben, this is, um…"

"Jane," Spider cut in easily.

"Sarah," Ashe managed after a moment's hesitation.

"Nice to meet you," Sue said, still eyeing them both. "I'm Sue Summers, and this is my husband, Ben."

"Pleasure," Spider replied respectfully.

Sue gave her a polite smile.

"So, um, we were out camping," Cole offered into the brief silence, hurrying to prevent any more questions. "And we just got back to the, uh, Redmond's…"

Sue's guarded expression melted back into concern and she looked to Ben for help.

"What happened?" Cole asked.

Ben hesitated. "Maybe you kids should come inside, eh?"

"Are they dead?" he pushed.

"Paul."

At the iron in the man's voice, Cole paused and then looked away in frustration.

His gaze landed on Lily.

The tension leaked from him, leaving only a feeling of stupidity. No matter what'd happened, it probably hadn't been pretty. And thus Lily didn't need to hear about it. She already had enough nightmares.

"Okay," he surrendered, motioning to Sue and Lily and then trailing them to the steps.

Gravel crunched immediately as Ashe followed.

The familiar smells of apple and cinnamon hit him as he came through the door, emanating from the homemade satchels hanging from the hooks on the entryway wall. Through the open space leading to the living room, more country crafts met his gaze, from the afghans Lily used to curl up under on cool nights to the handstitched pillows Sue favored so much. A bouquet of mums had taken the place of the summer flowers in the bay window at the front of the house, and a stack of wood waited by the fireplace, ready for the coming winter.

It all felt alien after the past few weeks.

"Oh!" Lily cried, coming to a stop. "Is that Butterscotch?"

He glanced over, spotting the potbellied tabby flopped behind the flower vase on the windowsill. At the sight of Lily, the animal rolled to her feet and then lumbered down from her post to bump her head against the girl's leg.

"She's gotten so huge!" Lily exclaimed, crouching to scratch the loudly purring cat.

"I think she missed you," Sue answered with a smile.

The woman looked to Cole and he could see the request.

"Hey, Hannah?" he said. "Why don't you take Butterscotch over to the couch before she hurts herself? We'll just be in the kitchen."

Lily glanced up, instantly reading between the lines. "I can–"

"Please?"

The little girl paused, her eyes flicking between him and Ashe. "Fine."

Scooping up the purring creature, she headed for the sofa.

Sue gave Cole a grateful smile and then continued down the hall.

"You want me to stay?" he heard Spider ask Ashe quietly.

He looked back. As tense as ever, Ashe looked from the large window to Lily, and then glanced to the archway at the far end of the room that afforded a view of the brightly sunlit kitchen. "No," she said tightly. "Thanks. I'll just…"

She motioned to the opening haltingly and then headed after Sue.

Cole glanced to Spider, but the girl just lifted an eyebrow at him, waiting.

He followed Ashe. In the kitchen, the wizard girl leaned against the archway, her arms crossed and her gaze darting from the Summers to Lily and back. For their part, Sue and Ben were retrieving refreshments from the refrigerator, while awkwardly trying to pretend that having an edgy teenager watching their every move was remotely ordinary.

Fighting back a grimace, he sank onto a barstool by the island at the center of the room. Spider immediately took the seat next to him. Her gaze twitched across the windows above the kitchen sink and in the mudroom and, after she moved slightly to have a better sightline on both, she turned a look on him that made only the barest pretense of being a smile.

He shifted in his chair, fighting the urge to scoot farther from the girl, and forced his attention to the couple by the refrigerator. "So what happened?" he asked.

Sue paused in the middle of pulling out a bottle of orange juice and looked to her husband.

Reluctance flashed across Ben's face. "Sheriff said he thought it was probably a break-in," he said. "Just based on what they found and…"

He trailed off uncomfortably.

"What do you mean?" Ashe asked.

Ben glanced over at her. "That's not really important."

Cole could see the muscles in the girl's jaw jump. "We need to know—"

"When?" Cole interrupted.

Ashe's gaze darted to him, but she stayed silent.

"About two days ago," Ben said.

Cole looked down, his brow furrowing as he processed the information and all it meant.

"Did they find any bodies?" Ashe asked.

He glanced up in time to see Sue's eyebrows rise.

"Young lady, don't you think you're being a bit–"

"Sue," he cut in.

The woman looked to him.

"They might not have been home."

Sue hesitated, her indignation fading, but by her side, Ben just grimaced. "They did," the man said.

Cole's gaze found its way back to the tabletop. He shouldn't be upset. It didn't matter if they were dead or why. They hadn't been good people. The world was better off with them gone.

The nausea eating his stomach didn't quite see the value of his reasoning.

"Are they sure it was them?" he heard Ashe ask after a moment.

By the counter, Ben shifted uncomfortably. "Yeah. I… I identified them."

Cole looked up. "You were there?"

Ben's jaw worked around. "Sue and I…" He glanced to his wife. "We were curious–"

"Worried," the woman amended as she poured orange juice into a set of tall glasses.

Ben's mouth tightened. "When we didn't hear anything from you kids after that first phone call. We rang up there a couple times, but Geoffrey always answered. Just said you were having fun and not to worry." Ben looked to his wife. "Didn't seem quite right. So two days back, Wally and I – he's one of the new guys I got working for me since you left – we headed up there on pretense of delivering some samples of Sue's newest recipes and…" He grimaced. "We got there in time to see the fire engines heading out."

He sighed. "Sheriff's an old friend of her dad's," he said with a nod to Sue. "When he realized we'd been doing business with the Redmonds, he asked me to take a look. Make sure it was them."

Ben paused. "I'm sorry, Paul."

Cole looked away, and from the corner of his eye, he could see Ashe do the same.

"We're just glad you kids weren't there," Sue said, putting a hand on his shoulder as she set the orange juice down beside him.

Taking the glass, he managed a nod, though the motion was only for show. Fact was, he and Lily wouldn't have been there. And if they had, it wouldn't have happened in the first place. Of course, then he and Lily would also be dead.

The Carnegeans hadn't been good people. They'd deserved what happened to them. They'd been horrible, wretched excuses for human beings, and –

"The break-in," he heard Ashe begin. "You said something about what they found."

And he'd killed them.

He tensed. His father's people had killed them. They'd murdered his grandparents, whom he didn't even like.

But they'd done it because of him.

All because of him.

"That's not–" Ben protested again.

"Ben," Cole interrupted, his heart pounding. He looked up, meeting the older man's eyes. "Tell me what they did."

"I don't think we need to go into that."

"Ben."

"It's not important," the man tried.

A chill moved through him, distant and strange. "Yes it is," he said quietly.

For a moment, the man watched him, and slowly, his stubbornness drained. Carefully, he set down his glass. "The bodies…" He exhaled. "Paul, they showed signs they'd been tortured. Electrocuted and the like. Sheriff said the thieves probably wanted the safe combination, and then burned the building to try to cover the evidence."

Cole swallowed.

"And you're absolutely certain it was them?" Ashe asked, a hint of desperation in her tone.

"Their faces had been left untouched," Ben told her reluctantly.

His lungs still seemed to be operating, though Cole couldn't figure out why. He knew Brogan. Simeon too. Even tangentially, even just a bit. But enough to see what they'd done. The message they'd left, after getting all the information they needed. The Blood had known – they had to have known – that the Merlin would come looking for their historians. Now that Cole had gone after Lily, now that Ashe was still alive, they would have anticipated the queen learning the Carnegeans' location.

And they'd made certain there'd be no doubt of the historians' fates this time.

"Did you know the Redmonds too?" he heard Sue ask gently.

He glanced up. Her hands gripping the archway behind her, Ashe was staring at the floor, though her attention seemed far from the cream-colored tile. At the girl's silence, Sue turned to her husband, and Cole could feel the concern aimed at him and Ashe alike.

Uncomfortably, he looked down, grasping after something to keep their questions at bay. "Do they have any suspects?"

"Not at the moment," Ben admitted, "but they have a lot of people working on it. There were even some feds at the scene, helping the sheriff investigate."

Cole's head snapped up, and he saw Ashe's do the same.

"Feds?" he repeated.

Ben nodded. "Three of them. I'm not sure what agency, though I'm guessing FBI." He paused. "Maybe you could help them, though? Were there any odd folks hanging around, or…"

He trailed off hopefully.

Cole hesitated, and then shook his head. "No."

Ben sighed.

"These feds," Cole continued, his eyes twitching to Ashe. The girl's gaze was locked on the bay window and its view of the road. "Did you tell them about us?"

Ben looked uncomfortable. Cole's heart began to pound harder.

"I had to ask the sheriff, Paul. Just if he'd found… well, bodies. But I only said that I thought the Redmonds had some kids up there; nothing else. And I didn't talk to the feds. Wally did, but he doesn't know you all anyway, so…"

Cole returned his gaze to the table, trying to look reassured despite the fact breathing was really starting to become an issue. There was a chance Wally had overheard something. Knew something. There was a chance of a lot of things. And if they involved the Blood, anywhere near those chances was nowhere he wanted to be.

He hated to do it, didn't even know how he was going to explain it, but the four of them had to get out of here. And now.

"So," Sue said into the silence. "Where'd you go camping?"

He blinked, thrown by the sudden topic change. "Um…" he stalled, scrambling to remember a single campground within a thousand miles.

"Up near Glacier National Park," Spider filled in. "My family has a cabin there."

"How nice," Sue replied.

Spider smiled.

"You girls are from the area then?" the woman continued.

Glancing to Ashe and Cole, Spider drew a breath. "I am," she answered casually. "Sarah's from back east. Met in college over at Oregon State. Roommates, you know? But as for how we ended up camping with Paul and Hannah…"

She gave Cole a smile.

He cleared his throat, trying to keep pace with the girl's effortless lies. "I know Sarah's family," he said with an uncomfortable look to Ashe. "I just hadn't seen her in a long time."

Spider turned her friendly expression back on Sue. "Crazy how you can run back into people online, eh?"

The woman smiled at the girl pleasantly. Cole tried not to stare.

"Look…" he tried awkwardly. "This… it's been kind of a rough day, and Jane and Sarah really need to get back to class so–"

"Nonsense!" Sue interjected with an incredulous look to the kitchen window and the sinking sun. "You can't leave at this hour; you won't get there till past midnight! Besides, you kids have had a real shock today, and I won't have you out driving in this condition. You're staying here till you've had a chance to rest, end of discussion."

"That car looks ready to fall apart, Paul," Ben added.

He hesitated, knowing that for the last, at least, the man was right.

"If the girls need to get back, you can take my truck," Ben said. "But tomorrow. Okay?"

Cole glanced over to Ashe and Spider. Still gripping the archway wall, Ashe was watching Lily, and he couldn't tell what was racing behind her eyes. For Spider's part, the girl just hesitated a heartbeat, and then gave Ben and Sue an apologetic smile.

"That's very kind of you," she said. "Really. But my sociology professor is a total jerk. If I'm not there–"

"Don't be absurd," Sue interrupted. "I'm not letting you risk your life over a class. I'll call your college in the morning and explain the situation. Surely, they'll–"

"You don't have to do that," Ashe said, turning back from the living room. She looked to Spider, her face deadpan, though her voice was more so. "Doesn't your uncle know your professor's boss? We'll just call him. He'll pull some strings."

Spider watched her for a moment. "Right." She affected an embarrassed expression as she glanced to Sue. "Wow. I guess today messed me over more than I thought. I mean…" She trailed off, swallowing hard. "Seeing somewhere people just *died*…"

She shook her head, looking for all the world like she was trying not to cry.

Sue came over to pat her shoulder sympathetically. "That would mess anyone over, sweetie. Now come on. Paul and Hannah can take their room upstairs, and we have some nice sleeping bags we can put down in the office for you and Sarah. In the meantime, you kids just focus on getting cleaned up and I'll have dinner ready in about an hour, alright?"

The girl smiled tremulously.

Sue glanced to Cole. "Can you help Ben get the office set up?"

Blinking, he pulled his gaze from Spider. "Sure."

He slid off the barstool and started for the hall. Behind him, he could hear the chair scrape back as Spider followed.

"Hannah," Ashe called.

Lily set the cat aside and hurried to join them. "Are we–"

She fell silent at the sight of Ben. Her eyes darted between them as the man slid by, and she said nothing else as she followed them all upstairs.

"This way," Cole said as he rounded the landing and headed toward the office halfway down the narrow corridor. As Ben struggled with the stuck closet door at the end of the hall, Cole paused, waiting for Ashe to go past him into the office.

The girl stopped just outside the door. "Can you get his keys?" she asked softly.

He glanced over. Her gaze twitched from him to Ben, monitoring the man as he wrestled the sleeping bags from the shelf. A few feet away, Spider leaned against the wall, watching them.

"I'm not stealing his truck," Cole growled.

Ashe blinked fast, forcing back an expression that he would have almost sworn was discomfort. "We need to get out of here."

"I *know* that, but I won't–"

He cut off as Ben returned. Two bundled sleeping bags in his arms, the man maneuvered around them on his way into the crowded office. Plopping the bedding down beside the stuffed bookcases lining the walls, he eyed the file boxes and the partially unpacked pieces of a desk in the center of the floor.

"Sorry this place is such a mess," Ben said with an abashed smile. "Keep meaning to get this together every year, but I just always end up falling back into the habit of working from the dining room table each time spring rolls around."

The man motioned for him to come help and then bent down,

hefting a box from the floor. Pausing, Cole eyed Ashe and Spider, and then looked to Lily waiting uncomfortably behind them.

"Hannah," he said shortly. "Help me with the blankets."

Lily slid past her sister and went into the room.

He watched her go, and then glanced back at the other girls. "We're not doing that."

"What do you think is going to happen tomorrow?" Spider asked, nothing but stark reality in her tone.

He glared, knowing he had no answer and hating the fact.

"We're not," he repeated.

Without another word, he followed Lily into the office.

A few minutes later, he was almost surprised to find the two of them still waiting when he emerged again.

"Bathroom's on the first floor, left of the kitchen," Ben said, slipping around them on his way to the stairs. "And if you need anything, Sue and I will be just down the hall."

"Thank you," Spider said.

The man smiled and then jogged down the steps.

"Other room there?" Ashe asked tightly, jerking her chin toward the door by the landing.

Cole nodded.

She turned, heading for the bedroom. "I'm taking first watch."

He watched as Spider followed, and then closed his eyes, grimacing tiredly.

It was going to be a long night.

Chapter Seventeen

From the shadows beside the bedroom window, Ashe watched the darkness. Stars scattered the cloudless sky and beneath the moon and the autumn breeze, the oak tree quivered in shades of silver. On the horizon, the security light of another farm glowed, while around her, the Summers' house creaked as it cooled for the night.

Ben and Sue had gone to sleep hours before. In the twin bed on the far side of the room, Lily was curled into a ball beneath patchwork quilts. Cole sat on the matching bed nearby, his back against the headboard and his eyes on nothing she could see. Spider had brought in the sleeping bags from the office and taken the floor, and though Ashe knew the girl could sleep in the midst of anything if necessary, she wouldn't have put bets to Spider actually doing so tonight.

Jamison had the historians' information. At this very moment, while the cats skulked through the shadows and the wind dislodged the first autumn leaves, he could be putting the finishing touches on the spell. She knew it wouldn't take him long. She could hope it would, pray it would, but in the end, he had a lifetime of experience on her, not including the past eight years of even knowing there *was* a war. He'd have prepared for this. And if he'd killed the historians – especially like that – it meant he'd gotten exactly what he was looking for.

Her gaze slid to Cole. She wished she knew how the affiliation thing worked. If Jamison could reach them here, or if distance would affect the spell at all. If staying by Cole – affiliated with Cole – would spare Lily's life, or that, if she left the girl behind to go after Jamison and he got his hands on her, she'd condemn her sister no matter where Lily tried to hide.

But then, Merlin had bound every wizard who'd sided with Taliesin, regardless of where they'd been at the time. This would probably be the same.

Her eyes found Lily in the darkness. Furrows wrinkling her brow, the little girl was staring at the blankets of the bed next to her.

Ashe looked away. She didn't know where she'd send the girl, or where they would have gone if Cole'd agreed to steal Ben's truck anyway. But ultimately, she had to go after Jamison. One Merlin wizard in his hands would be enough for him to kill them all, and even though most of the Merlin were already dead, that didn't mean he'd never encounter another in her lifetime.

It was a long shot, and probably suicide, but she had no choice. Anything else just meant living every moment knowing it brought her closer to the one in which she'd have to watch her sister die. And while Lily would never forgive her, and would always think she'd abandoned her, she couldn't let that change her mind.

No matter what it took, she was going to get Lily to the end of this alive.

Her eyes tracked a tabby cat as it skirted the blue-white glow of the security light. It really was nice here. The farm, the cats, and all the crafts everywhere. Maybe after this was over and the Blood weren't a threat anymore, Lily could come back. She could be happy in this place.

It was so very much like home.

Her gaze lingered on the edge of the light's glow, though the cat had disappeared moments before. She missed them. Her father, and his beaming smile every time he had the chance to come see them. Jonathan and Rose, and the way they'd teased her while still teaching her everything from driving to baking pie. She missed the other farmhands, despite the fact they'd never really been close. In retrospect, she supposed it'd been the royalty thing. She even missed crazy old Thelma, who'd kept life interesting and who, in the midst of hell, had sat in the ashes to comfort her with gibberish, all because she'd wanted to help.

It felt like someone else's life. It had *been* someone else's life. She wasn't that girl anymore. And for all that it had only been a few months, it still felt like she hadn't been for a very long time.

"Did the Blood kill them?" Lily whispered.

Ashe blinked, pulling her gaze from the window. Eyes wide, Lily stared at Cole.

His brow furrowed as he looked over. "What?"

"The bad men… the Blood. Did they kill them?"

She saw him swallow uncomfortably. They hadn't told the girl everything. There really wasn't any need for her to know.

"Yeah," Cole admitted quietly.

"Why?" Lily asked.

He hesitated, and his gaze dropped to his hands. "I don't know."

"But how could they just–"

"They weren't good people, Lily," he said harshly. "You shouldn't feel sorry for them."

Ashe eyed him, disgusted. Across the room, she could see Spider watching him too, though otherwise, the girl hadn't moved.

Lily faltered. "I-I know. But they still were–"

"Were what?" Cole snapped. "My grandparents? Lily, they wanted to kill you. They *would* have killed me. They locked us up with their propaganda of Merlin and his two lackeys binding my ancestors, and you expect me to–"

"What?" Ashe interrupted.

He turned to her, fury hot in his gaze. "Excuse me?"

"What did you say?"

"They tried to kill us."

"No! The other part. The propaganda thing."

"Why do you–"

"Just tell me!"

His brow drew down. "They had a lot of paintings," he said meticulously, rancor dripping from his tone. "One was of Merlin. He was on a cliff, posing with two of his disciples and his staff, while all the nasty little Taliesin got bound below. Why? You want to go get yourself a copy?"

She ignored him.

"Ashe, what is it?" Spider asked, propping herself up on an elbow.

She didn't answer, her gaze tracking across the hardwood floor without seeing it at all.

It was mad. More than mad. Losing the historians had pushed her over the edge.

But try as she might, she couldn't stop hearing the ramblings of a crazy old woman from a lifetime before.

A crazy old woman who'd wanted to help.

"There were three of them?" she asked, feeling like the ground was falling out from under her. "In the painting of the binding… in the *beginning*… it was Merlin and two others?"

"Need me to repeat it again?"

"Yes! There were three of them. Three. You're sure it was actually three?"

Cole nodded, eyeing her like she'd gone insane.

"Ashe…" Spider pushed.

Unable to respond, she looked away. Her hand pressed against her face and, a moment later, she made an incredulous sound as she glanced back to Cole.

"Did one of them look like Elvis?"

———— ◆ ————

"Ashe, this is nuts," Spider insisted quietly. "Just because some crazy old lady said—"

She fell silent as a man walked around the corner of the Summers' house, a crate full of dirt-covered vegetables in his arms. Standing by Ben's red pickup truck, Ashe glanced over as the flannel-shirted man sidled past, his eyes darting from the gravel walkway to them and back. Continuing on, he set the basket down by the porch steps and then, with a look to Lily and Cole by the front door, he circled back around the side of the house.

"I know," Ashe answered, her gaze tracking him.

From the corner of her eye, she could see Spider studying her. And then the girl turned back to the house. "Just making sure."

The screen door swung open and Sue hurried out, a paper bag full of food in her hands. "Now you have directions, right?" she said to Cole and Lily. "And don't forget to call if you need anything. I don't care what it is. You go ahead and call."

Ashe looked away. She really did sound like Rose. And she was so visibly worried for Lily, it was uncomfortable to watch.

But then, Lily could come back. Eventually, anyway.

"You realize he's going to have to be the one to drive us out of here," Spider commented as Ben pulled out his keys and handed them to Cole.

Ashe glanced to her.

The hint of a smile pulled at the girl's mouth and she didn't say anything more.

"Just watch out for each other," Sue ordered as she trailed Lily and Cole down the steps.

"We will," Cole replied. He glanced to Ben, and Ashe could see his discomfort from a dozen feet away. "You're sure it's okay if we use your truck, though? This isn't going to be a short trip and I don't want to—"

Ashe tensed, but Ben just smiled. "Got the old clunker in the barn, which is still in better shape than that thing you have there," the man answered, clapping him on the shoulder. "We'll be fine. Just drive safe, eh?"

Cole nodded. Taking the bag from Sue, he headed around the truck. The discomfort in his eyes strengthened at the sight of her and Spider, and without a word, he opened the rear door and then set the bag on the floor.

"It was nice to meet you girls," Sue said, coming up to them.

"You too," Spider told her as she put her backpack in the pickup, nothing but polite sincerity in her tone.

Ashe managed a smile and then climbed into the back seat.

"And if you need extra time, don't worry, alright?" the woman continued as Cole shut the door. "Don't stress yourselves to hurry back on our account. We'd rather you be safe."

He nodded. "Thank you."

The engine turned over easily, and in the front seat, Lily swiftly buckled herself in.

"So when *are* we coming back?" the little girl asked as they pulled away from the house.

No one answered as the truck turned onto the road.

———— ◆ ————

"And the southern contingent?" Jamison asked.

"We've had run-ins with Merlin in Banston and the surrounding area, sir," Simeon replied. "Including at several locations we believe they were using as hiding places. From what we can tell of their movements, they appear to be searching the city as much as we are." The man paused. "But no. Nothing on the Children or Cole."

From his position by the bookcase on the far side of the office, Brogan watched Jamison look away.

"Have any been taken alive?" Jamison asked.

Simeon hesitated. "Not yet, sir. The Taliesin seem to have an opposition to–"

In his pocket, Brogan's phone buzzed. Turning from the attempted explanation, he drew the cell out and eyed the unfamiliar number.

"Yes?" he answered.

"Mr. Brogan? This is Wally. From Washington? Remember, we

talked back–"

"I remember, Mr. Dodd. To what do I owe the pleasure of your call?"

Across the room, the king ordered Simeon into silence.

"Uh, yeah," Wally said. "You remember how you asked me to call if I saw those kids again? The ones staying with Redmond?"

Brogan waited, but nothing more came. "Yes?"

"Right. Well, uh, they were just here. At the farm, I mean. The Summers' farm? In Washington?"

It took actual effort to keep the tired note from his tone. "I remember, Mr. Dodd. Please continue."

"Yeah. They were here. A guy and a kid who looked just like the descriptions you gave. Had two others with 'em too. Blonde chick, looked like she might be a gangbanger or one of them Rasta people you hear about, and then a black-haired girl."

Brogan's eyebrow twitched up. The queen and her sister were possibly on their own, save for a single guard? Matters for the Merlin were worse than he'd thought.

He glanced to the king, covering the mouthpiece of the cell. "Washington," he relayed quietly. "Cole, the Children, and only one bodyguard."

Jamison turned to Simeon. "Plane. Now."

"Uh, Mr. Brogan? You still there?"

Releasing the mouthpiece, Brogan returned to the call as behind him, Simeon dialed the aircrew for the late Council's private jet. "Of course. So no one else was with them?"

He could almost hear Wally shaking his head in response, for all that the man was on the other end of a phone. "Uh, nope. No one else."

"And where did they go?"

"Headed for the highway about five minutes ago."

"The highway."

"Uh-huh."

Brogan waited. "Do you have any more *specific* information, Mr. Dodd?"

"Yeah, sure. They were in a red Chevy Silverado. Crew cab, chrome bumper with standard wheels and a small dent on the right rear fender. Oh, and Washington plates too. Number three-three-something. Seven, maybe. Or four."

"Is that all?"

"Uh…" the man drawled helplessly. "The blonde girl did mention something about a crazy old lady. Or something a crazy old lady said." Wally hesitated. "You know, the highway's only about twenty miles from here and if you hurry you could probably–"

Brogan hung up. For a heartbeat, he paused, and then turned back to face the room.

The king was watching him.

"Simeon," Brogan said.

The gray-haired man told the person on the other end of the line to hold on.

"There was an old woman… mentally unstable… associated with the Children…"

"The neighbor in Montana," Simeon confirmed with a nod.

Brogan glanced to the king.

Jamison smiled.

Chapter Eighteen

———— ◆ ————

The truck came to a stop and, with more effort than she would have expected it to take, Ashe pulled her gaze from her lap.

Six months hung like decades on the bungalow.

Half the porch railings had fallen, victims of decay or a summer storm, and one of the support posts had cracked, leaving the porch sagging precariously. Cobwebs clung to the surviving rails, and on the house itself, what shutters were still attached dangled wildly askew. Moss-covered shingles littered the ground, and by the base of the house, the wooden screen door moldered among the weeds.

Spider glanced back from the driver's seat, which she'd taken from Cole the moment they'd lost sight of the Summers' farm. Wordlessly, Ashe pushed open the door and climbed out.

She could feel the farmhouse like a physical pressure past the rise behind her.

Carefully, she walked toward the bungalow, avoiding the broken steps that had given way an unknown amount of time before. Reaching the weathered door, she drew a breath and then knocked.

A solitary meow answered her.

She swallowed hard.

Seconds crept by. She knocked again.

Nothing changed.

Her lip slipped between her teeth. Gingerly, she reached out and tried the door handle.

The door swung open with a rusty creak.

She flinched as a cat shot past her feet. Bolting down the steps, the animal cut a sharp turn and then vanished through a hole in the crisscross siding that skirted the base of the house, where frantic squeaking rose a heartbeat later. Remembering to breathe, Ashe grimaced at the sound and then turned back to the room beyond the open door.

Old blankets were draped over everything from the worn furniture to the cracking hardwood floor. Tattered sheets covered the windows, dampening the light and leaving the whole space feeling as insulated as a padded room. The stale smell of dust and cat hung in the air, and empty tin cans were scattered across the otherwise barren countertops.

The place could have been abandoned for years and no one would've been able to tell the difference.

"Thelma?" she called.

The silence remained.

Her eyes closed briefly, and then she turned from the door.

At the base of the steps, Lily watched her, Cole a few feet behind, while from her place by the truck, Spider just looked away.

And behind them, the countryside spread toward the horizon till it ran headlong into the dark line of trees.

She pulled her gaze back to the porch steps, shivering though it wasn't cold. Struggling to force as much expression from her face as possible, she headed back down the stairs.

"Spider," she said. "Could you–"

A rustle of leaves by the bungalow made her turn. From around the corner of the house, a scrawny woman and a sea of cats came into view.

Cole grabbed Lily, shoving her behind him as Spider drew her guns.

"Wait!" Ashe cried.

The girl froze, both weapons trained on the wide-eyed woman clutching a bundle of sticks in her arms.

"It's okay," Ashe continued. "This… this is Thelma."

Spider looked incredulous. "She's a *Blood*?"

The air froze in Ashe's lungs.

"Sort of a Blood," Cole amended warily. "Sort of… like her too."

He jerked his head in Lily's direction, though his eyes didn't leave Thelma. Spider hesitated, her brow twitching as if she couldn't figure out what she was seeing or why, and then she allowed a careful nod.

Ashe looked back at the old woman. Bark flecked her wild gray hair and her bony fingers were white around the twigs. The months had been as good to her as they'd been to her home, leaving a fog in her eyes thicker than any Ashe had ever seen. Uncomprehending, she stared at them while, oblivious to the standoff, the cats melted through the broken siding to join their counterpart below the house.

Slowly, Ashe exhaled, ordering herself to stay calm. Thelma had lived near her family for almost eight years. And the night the Blood came, the woman had distracted them to give her time to escape.

She couldn't be one of them, no matter what she looked like.

"Thelma?" she tried.

With eyes too vacant for comfort, the old woman turned toward her.

"Do you remember me?"

Seconds passed. "Ashley?"

Ashe nodded.

A happy smile crept through the uncertainty on Thelma's face. "Ashley burning bright."

Ashe's brow twitched down.

"You found the little flower," Thelma continued, her smile growing as she looked to Lily.

"That's right," Ashe said, forcing herself to stay focused. "And now I need to ask you something, okay?"

"She's pointing guns at me," Thelma said, staring at Spider in bewilderment.

Quickly, Ashe motioned for the girl to lower the weapons. Glancing between them, Spider hesitated, and then made the guns vanish beneath her jacket.

"See?" Ashe said. "The guns are gone. Everything's fine. But I need you to concentrate now."

Thelma blinked as if she'd already lost track of the thought.

"Do you remember the night…" Ashe grimaced, making herself go on. "The night the firemen came?"

"I didn't know. I–"

The old woman glanced to Spider and Cole, blushing with apologetic embarrassment.

"I… I know you didn't," Ashe said, confusedly following Thelma's gaze to the others. "But you said something to me. Something about there being three at the beginning. Two others and one who looked like Elvis."

Her gaze on the mossy shingles beneath her feet, Thelma sighed. "Elvis…"

Ashe paused, feeling every ounce of the absurdity of the question. "Thelma, were you talking about the spell to bind Taliesin? The spell Merlin did in the last war?"

The woman hesitated, a hurt expression moving over her wrinkled face. "I was just trying to help," she said defensively, and then began to turn away.

"No, no," Ashe said, stepping forward hurriedly. "I know. I–" She drew a breath, forcing herself slow down and working to ignore her disbelief at the same time. "I know you were. But I need you to tell me again."

"There were three."

"Yes. I remember that part. But who were they? Can you tell me that?"

Thelma's brow furrowed in confusion. "The paladins should know." She looked over at Spider and Cole. "She even looks like him."

"Who?" said Spider.

"Elvis," Thelma replied as though it was obvious.

Ashe saw Spider glance to her incredulously.

"You do," Thelma insisted. "Like his eyes… and maybe his eyes…"

Spider's brow rose higher.

"Why should they know?" Ashe pressed.

"They see the differences. Or did. Still do, I guess. At least with the ones they haven't given the differences to anymore."

Ashe tried to ignore the incredulity she could feel radiating off the others. "Okay," she allowed. "But–"

"They'll help you," Thelma continued. "They know what it's

going to cost now. And the flower's here. I would, but with her…
it's why I stayed. Why I looked for you. Didn't know you'd have
her." The woman's gaze drifted toward the ground. "Should have
said something, though. Would have. It was just so bad last time,
and it started to look the same way again, and if it really had been, I
just… I couldn't be sure…"

She trailed off, gazing at the ground mournfully.

Ashe blinked.

"Are you getting any of this?" Spider asked.

Ashe shook her head, watching Thelma mumble to herself. She'd
been clutching at straws, coming here. Thinking that a mad old
woman, whether or not she apparently looked like the Blood, could
possibly have the answers when no one else had managed to find
them in five hundred years.

She just didn't have any other options left.

"Thelma," she said as the woman nudged a shingle with her mud-
covered shoe.

"I wanted to help," the old woman responded firmly, as though
someone had asked.

"You did," Ashe assured her. "But can you tell me about the
spell?"

"What spell?"

A desperate gasp escaped her at the woman's puzzled expression.
"The spell that bound Taliesin. The spell their king broke when he
killed my grandfather."

"Nobody broke any spell."

"Oh sweet…" she heard Cole mutter behind her.

"They didn't!" the woman protested. "Fractured, yes. Cracked a
bit. But the spell's not *broken.* Just look at her."

Ashe couldn't keep the confusion from her face as the woman gestured to her, losing a few sticks in the process. "What about me?"

Thelma studied her briefly and then turned to Cole, disapproval in her eyes. "You should know better," she admonished him.

"*What* should he know better?" Spider demanded.

The old woman gave Cole a last glare and then turned to the girl. She went still for a moment and then her brow furrowed. "What happened to your hair?"

"Okay!" Ashe cut in as the woman reached for Spider's dreadlocks. Drawing a quick breath, she tried to refocus. "How do I fix the spell, then? Put it back?"

Thelma stared as though she'd asked a strange question. "You?"

"Yes." Ashe said with frustration. "Me."

"You can't."

She could feel something drain from her, and it seemed a lot like hope. "I can't," she repeated.

"You can't fuel the canyon on your own."

Wondering if this was what a yoyo felt like when it was jerked around, Ashe closed her eyes. "Canyon?"

Thelma nodded. "He always had it. After, I mean. Not before. But after… always after. All around him. All around everyone, though not in the same way." She shook her head ruefully. "They couldn't see it like he could. Feel it like he could. And even with his toys to help, nothing was ever really better. The canyon was still there."

"Who?"

"Merlin."

Ashe sighed. Merlin and a canyon. She felt a grimace coming onto her face, and then she paused as suddenly, the gibberish clicked.

The abyss. The black void at the edge of her power.

"I have to… fuel that? Like with something like Merlin's staff?"

"Staff?"

Thelma sounded like she'd never heard of such a thing. Of course, Ashe reflected, that didn't mean much.

"Yes," she persisted. "The staff only the Merlin's Children could use. The staff that glowed when they touched it and made them stronger. I need something like that?"

The old woman's bafflement melted into derision. "Toys. Push the canyon back, but never *fix* anything. You have to fuel it. Toys won't do that."

Ashe closed her eyes again. The staff was gone anyway. On some level, the answer was almost a relief. "Okay, then what will?"

"I told you."

She exhaled sharply. "Can you tell me again?"

Thelma pointed to Cole and Spider. "Them."

Ashe froze.

"You take from them. Like Merlin did. You need her," Thelma glanced to Lily. "And then you need them. The power they have. What they are. You take it from them and make it yours."

A rough breath escaped her, and she felt her head shake back and forth.

Thelma met her shocked gaze confusedly. "It's how he made the spell."

Another breath slipped out. It was hard to pull them back in. Things seemed to shift around her and she felt her hand grasp instinctively onto the banister, steadying her as the ground moved.

"Okay, you crazy Blood bitch," Spider snapped. "Enough. Who the hell are you? Why do you look like them and how the *hell* do you know anything about this anyway?"

Thelma blinked at her. "I was there."

"What?" Spider demanded.

The woman's brow furrowed. "You pointed a gun at me."

An infuriated noise escaped the girl.

"Ashe…"

She flinched at the sound of Cole's voice, and she couldn't bring herself to look at him. At any of them. Fighting for air, she turned away, her hand still gripping the banister as if it was the only stable thing in the world.

"Ashley?" Lily called worriedly.

Her eyes darted to the bungalow, to the yard and the land beyond, and her legs trembled with the need to run. To climb out of her skin. To vanish instantly.

But she couldn't even breathe.

"Ashley, you can't make the spell without taking–"

"Shut up!" Spider yelled at the woman. "You *want* a gun pointed at you again?"

With a gasp, Ashe shoved away from the banister.

"Ashley!" Lily cried.

She didn't turn back. Striding fast, her feet carried her away from the truck and the house till she reached the far side of the overgrown backyard and her legs wavered beneath her. She stopped, staring unseeing at the crabgrass.

Birds chirped in the distance. The wind rushed past, cold and fresh with autumn, while overhead, distant cloud wisps drifted across the brilliant blue sky.

It was everything she could do not to scream.

Gravel rumbled in the distance. Her breath catching, she spun.

Shouting broke out beyond the house, followed instantly by

gunfire and a blast of magic so strong, it could only have come from her sister.

She ran.

Magic hit the bungalow, taking part of the roof with it, and she dodged wood and shingles as they pelted the ground. Sliding on the grass, she skidded around the side of the house.

Thelma was standing in the middle of the yard, arms outstretched.

Half a dozen sedans were racing down the road.

The old woman's arms slammed to her sides.

Magic roared from her, instantly disintegrating the gray sedan rushing toward them and sending metal debris strafing through the cars behind. Careening wildly, the surviving vehicles veered around the wreckage and kept coming.

"Ashley!" Lily yelled.

She gasped, her eyes sweeping the yard. From the cover of the porch steps, the little girl started toward her, only to have Cole grab her and yank her back as magic smashed into the house. Ducked behind the truck, Spider turned her face away as a second blast shattered the passenger window and sent the pickup rocking hard.

Thelma stumbled weakly, her hands catching on the tree nearby.

"Come on!" Spider shouted, grabbing the door handle above her head.

Ashe darted forward as Cole swung Lily into his arms and bolted for the truck.

Simultaneously, magic rushed them from the cars. Swiftly, Ashe stripped the nearest attack from the air and sent it back at the sedans, while Thelma's defenses rose to take the other blast.

She wasn't fast enough.

Magic hit the old woman, sending her flying into the side of the bungalow.

Ashe skidded to a halt, looking between the woman and the truck. Stirring weakly, Thelma struggled to rise, and then her arms gave out beneath her, sending her crumpling back to the ground.

Snarling a curse, Ashe ran toward her.

Chunks of siding pelted her as she reached the old woman, and she ducked, one arm protecting her head as the other snagged Thelma's bony elbow.

"Move!" she yelled.

Gasping in pain, Thelma shook her head. "Can't…"

Ashe flung her magic at the approaching cars, propelling one of them sideways into a telephone pole, though the vehicle behind just kept coming. "You have to!"

Thelma shook her head again. "Go."

"I'm not–"

Light swelled from the old woman, and then Ashe was flying. Crashing backwards to the ground, she gasped as air rushed from her chest and the world shuddered back into place in a staccato of color and sound.

She was beside the truck, Lily was shouting, and by the bungalow, Thelma was deathly still. Over her head, the rear door of the pickup flew open and then Cole was there. Leaning out, he grabbed her arm, hauling her from the ground.

With a gasp, she scrambled up and tumbled onto the seat as Spider hit the accelerator. Scattering dirt in its wake, the truck whipped around and then raced for the road.

A sedan was right in front of them.

Spider swore and yanked on the wheel, sending the truck swerving wildly into the ditch. Snagging the headrest, Ashe pulled herself up from the seat, flinging magic at the passing car as she moved.

The sedan went sideways, caught on its own momentum and barrel-rolled into the air. More magic rushed them, coming from the wizards struggling from the damaged cars ahead, and quickly, her defenses swelled around the truck, taking the blows.

"What the—" Spider cried.

"Just go!" Cole yelled.

The girl didn't hesitate. The engine roared as she sent the pickup surging out of the ditch.

Cole looked from Ashe to the wizards on both sides of the road, and then threw himself to the floor.

Her magic raced out and punched into the damaged cars, propelling them into the fields.

The wizards fell behind them and the tires growled as the road began to climb. Spinning on the seat, she looked through the rear window.

No one could follow.

A gasp escaped her as she stared down at the valley. Cars and pieces of cars littered the ground in a path of destruction from the base of the hills to the crumbling bungalow. Wizards ran for the tiny house, and a few already circled the space where Thelma lay.

And less than a mile from the chaos, an old pile of rubble marked her home.

The adrenaline drained as her gaze lingered on the ruins till trees swallowed the view and the truck swerved onto the higher reaches of the mountain road.

"A-are we okay?" Lily asked, clutching the front seat and staring between her, Cole and Spider as Ashe turned back around.

She didn't answer.

"Ashley?" Lily pressed, and then tried again when a moment went by. "Ashley?"

Wordlessly, Ashe looked away.

———— ◆ ————

Blood dripped from shrapnel wounds covering him from head to toe, and his dislocated arm dangled uselessly. Smoke billowed from the wreckage of the sedan before him, though it didn't obscure the bodies of the two wizards inside.

Grimacing, Brogan tugged a shard of fragmented car from his forearm and tossed it to the ground. Reaching up again, he gripped his shoulder, drew a short breath, and then shoved it hard.

A snarl escaped him as the joint snapped into place.

He scowled, exhaling as the pain subsided to a level he could more readily ignore.

The day they were done with the Merlin queen couldn't possibly come soon enough.

Rolling his shoulder slightly, he eyed the destroyed vehicles scattered over the fields on either side of the road, and then turned back to the decaying house. They hadn't given much consideration to the old woman six months ago, and certainly had never thought she could be like the Blood. How it was possible was a mystery, though thankfully, one the king would likely have the leisure to explore.

Motioning the wizards aside, he studied the old woman propped against the crisscross siding. Thick blood plastered sections of her wild gray hair to her head and stained the colorless fabric of her clothes. Bony legs stuck out from beneath her tattered skirt, one of them twisted awkwardly. But past the survivable wounds, age seemed to be bearing down, till only the shortest of breaths moved her lungs.

He nodded to the wizard crouching beside her.

A short pulse of healing magic sped through the old woman.

She gasped, her eyes flying open. "Firemen," she croaked.

The wizard glanced back, questioning.

Brogan ignored him. "Do you know why you're alive?" he asked her calmly.

She nodded, certainty in the feeble motion. "Won't tell you though," she whispered.

He paid no attention to the deranged response. It was enough at the moment that she was capable of giving one at all.

"You will tell us everything you told them, why she came to you, and all that you know. Do you understand?"

A strange smile crept onto the old woman's face.

"Yes," she answered simply. "Do you?"

Chapter Nineteen

S ilence hung heavy on the truck cab, and through the shattered windows, the wind blew with the icy bite of altitude. Broken glass grated beneath him and, rising slightly from the bench seat, he brushed the blue-green bits toward their innumerable counterparts littering the floor.

Several pieces flew haphazardly to hit the girl at his side, and Cole glanced over. Staring out the broken window as the wind tossed her hair, Ashe gave no more sign of noticing the glass than she had anything else over the past few miles.

He hesitated. Whether or not the old woman was right about the spell didn't really matter. He could tell Ashe believed it.

And it kind of looked like it was killing her.

The air seemed too thin and he turned away, suddenly working to take in a breath despite the wind whipping it away from him. Blinking, he scooted forward and wrapped an arm around the headrest to steady himself as the truck bounded over the rough country highway. In the seat below him, Lily glanced up, and then returned her gaze to the window like a small twin of her sister.

"Where are we going?" he asked, his voice tight.

Silence met the question.

"Spider."

The girl's eyes went to him briefly. "We need to lose the truck," she said quietly.

Cole tried not to scowl, despite the fact he knew she was right. A big, red pickup wasn't subtle on a good day, and that didn't even bring into it the resources Brogan had at his disposal. Half the state would probably be looking for the Chevy within the hour, based on God knew what ridiculous story the Blood came up with this time.

He just hated what it would do to Ben and Sue, learning that not only were he and Lily hundreds of miles from where they said they'd be, but they were missing from a truck that looked like it'd gone through a war.

"Yeah," he agreed.

Spider glanced to him and then returned her eyes to the road.

Looking out the window, he studied the valley below. Farms were scattered across the landscape to the horizon, and the afternoon sun picked out the houses and the vehicles next to them in brilliant relief.

He had no idea how they were going to get another form of transportation, short of theft.

Again.

Sighing, he shook his head. "So what's the plan, then? Don't suppose you know how to hotwire cars or something?"

Spider was silent for a moment. "Yeah."

He paused. Of course she did.

Minutes passed and gradually, the highway descended. Houses and shops appeared among the trees crowding the roadside, and traffic picked up as blue signs for the interstate came into view.

"There," Spider said.

He glanced over as she steered the truck toward a small gas station set back from the road. A yellowed marquee hung below the sun-faded station sign, and from the abbreviated words crowding the letter slots, he could only garner that something was on sale. Rusted siding dangled loose from one side of the pump shelter, and so many neon advertisements crowded the windows, it was almost impossible to see inside.

His eyes scanned the lot again before he realized what the girl must have noticed.

A dark green SUV sat in the shadow of the station, by the restrooms and far from any other cars. Meanwhile, only a single security camera was attached to the building, and it was pointed squarely at the pumps fifty feet away.

Spider guided the truck off the road and through the parking lot. Pulling around to the rear of the building, she brought the vehicle to a quick stop, threw the gearshift into park and then pushed open the door.

"Stay here," she said over her shoulder as she climbed out.

He didn't bother to answer as she shut the door and strode toward the SUV, her gaze sweeping the surrounding area as she went. At the side of the vehicle, she paused, checking the interior, and then tugged the handle.

The door opened easily.

With a glance to the restrooms and the front of the station lot, she slid into the SUV and then ducked sideways, vanishing from sight. He waited, barely breathing as his gaze twitched from the vehicle to the restroom door and back.

The engine of the SUV kicked over. Swiftly, the girl rose into view and put the vehicle into drive.

"Come on," Cole said.

Ashe was already moving. Snagging the bags from the floor, she paused only long enough to be sure Lily climbed out before she pushed open the door and ran for the SUV. Quickly, he followed. Lily scrambled into the back seat after her sister, and he grabbed at the passenger door while Spider shoved it wide.

The restroom door opened.

Cole swung in as Spider hit the accelerator.

The SUV surged forward, pushing him back into the seat, and suddenly, a spike of pain rushed past him, fading almost as fast as it came. He twisted in the passenger seat, looking back to the gas station. By the restroom, a scrawny teenage boy gaped at the lot as though he couldn't see his SUV racing away.

Cole glanced at Ashe. Staring out the window, she seemed oblivious to everything, but as the vehicle shot past the trees and left the station behind, he felt the faint buzz of magic disappear.

He turned back in the seat and looked to Spider. Her eyes on the reflection of her friend in the rearview mirror, she said nothing.

"You never answered my question," he told her.

She didn't respond.

"Where are we going?"

Spider's gaze returned to the highway. "I know a place south of here where we can stay."

He watched her for a moment, but something made it clear he wasn't going to get more. And maybe it didn't matter. It wasn't like he had a suggestion for where to head anyway.

Miles slid by in silence as the sun gradually sank below the horizon. Signs for Yellowstone began to dot the sides of the highway, growing more frequent the longer they drove. Cars sped past in blinding flashes as darkness took hold, and on the hillsides, light glowed from the windows of distant cabins.

Spider kept driving.

As the mountains fell behind them and the sky opened into an expanse of stars, he blinked tiredly, realizing they were leaving the country road they'd been following for longer than he could recall. A small town lay ahead, almost lost in the darkness and barely large enough to have a few streets to its name. A handful of decaying businesses peppered its sidewalks, joining the houses in having their windows darkened for the night.

At a street like any of the others, the girl turned and, half a dozen houses later, she pulled the SUV to a stop.

"Give me a second," she said.

Pushing open the door, she climbed out and headed for a two story block of house that could have been cloned from any neighborhood in America. Climbing the steps to the porch, she reached the door and then hesitated, almost as if preparing herself, before lifting a hand to knock.

A minute passed, followed by another. She knocked again.

Incrementally, the door crept open.

The first thing he saw was the barrel of a shotgun.

His hand went for the door handle, though he knew he'd never reach her in time.

Spider didn't move.

Neither did the gun.

Heart pounding, he watched as the girl said something to the person beyond the door. A moment crawled past after she spoke and then, ever so slowly, the barrel retreated into the darkness.

Spider walked back down the stairs.

"They'll let us stay the night," she said flatly as she reached the SUV.

An incredulous noise escaped him.

"It's the best option," Spider snapped.

Roughly, she grabbed her bag from the footwell and then slammed the door.

His eyebrows rose as she strode away. Exhaling, he glanced to the back seat.

Ashe hadn't moved. Her gaze on the middle distance, she gave no sign she'd noticed they'd stopped at all. Resting her head on her sister's lap, Lily was asleep, and absently, Ashe was running her hand over the child's hair.

He paused, seeing for the first time something of the girl he'd rescued six months before.

Discomfort grated through him. He turned and climbed out of the vehicle.

A moment passed and then he heard her follow.

Evenly cropped bushes fronted the house and a tall wooden fence blocked any view of the backyard. No light was visible through the thickly curtained windows and the porch was bare except for a faded welcome mat whose message belied everything he'd just seen.

Carefully, he pushed past the front door, half expecting the shotgun to reappear.

Instead, there was only a couple who, like their house, could have been cut from a mold for stereotypical white, middle-class Americans from anywhere. A terry-cloth robe of pale pink covered the woman, with a corresponding one of dark blue hanging off the man, and while their hair was neither curly nor straight, it was such a completely unremarkable shade of brown, the effect was a bit incredible.

He suddenly found himself thinking that his adoptive mother, Melissa, would have been jealous as hell.

Tension charged the air like an electrical hum, though the yawning golden retriever lumped in the corner didn't seem to care. As Cole and Ashe came in, the couple ran their eyes over them in mirror image of one another, and when Lily peeked around her sister, their faces went rigid with alarm.

"Annie, Gary. Summer, Snake and Flower."

Spider motioned between the two groups by way of introduction, and then crossed the entryway to the stairs.

"We'll be gone by tomorrow," she called tersely as she climbed the hardwood steps.

Uncomfortably, he followed Ashe and Lily after the girl.

The couple's gazes tracked them the whole way.

A small lamp sat in the bedroom at the far end of the hall, casting dull light on the flowered wall paintings and providing the only illumination for the corridor. Ignoring it, Spider rounded the landing and headed into the first room by the stairs. Bringing Lily, Ashe trailed her, while by the doorway, Cole paused.

Holding aside the edge of the curtain, Spider swiftly scanned the neighborhood, though from the way her gaze flicked back to her friend almost immediately, he could tell her attention to the street was on autopilot. In the glow of a nightlight, Ashe led Lily to the bed and helped her climb beneath the cream-colored quilt. As Lily situated herself, Ashe sank down beside her and, when the girl's eyes finally closed, she gently resumed running her fingers over the kid's hair.

There wasn't a trace of expression on her face the entire time.

Stepping farther into the room, he glanced around, searching for somewhere to be. The staid block of a dresser met his gaze, with closet doors framing it on either side, and except for the additional blankets hanging from the bed's footboard, the rest of the room was bare. Without options, he crossed to the second window and joined Spider in watching the sleepy town.

Minutes passed. Outside the door, the floor creaked as Gary and Annie crept to bed.

"I need you to do something for me," Ashe said softly.

He glanced over to see her watching Spider in the darkness.

The girl's brow drew down. "What?"

"Take Lily."

Spider's expression cleared. "No. Ashe, *no*. You're not doing what I–"

"I have to stop him."

"So stop him!" the girl hissed, trying to keep her voice low. "But not like this. Not without any backup or–"

"You're not coming with me."

"I'm not letting you do this alone!"

"You're not coming with me, Spider."

The girl made an incredulous sound. "And you're going to stop me?"

He saw Ashe's gaze twitch toward the door.

Spider scowled. "You…" she started furiously. "You can't do this, Ashe. Just because some old woman–"

"He'll kill her, Spider. And you. And everyone I…"

Ashe grimaced, looking away.

"He can't."

She turned back sharply.

Cole blinked, the words feeling like they'd come from nowhere. Uncomfortably, he hesitated.

She had to know. If he wanted to keep her from going after his father, if he wanted to stop his dad from doing what he thought he needed to do, she had to know.

Because she wouldn't ever have done the same.

He shivered. She wouldn't, and he should have known it. Trusted it. Seen it at all, when it'd been in front of his face so many times. But he just hadn't wanted to risk it. To believe he'd been that horrifically wrong.

To believe he'd actually given a girl who was just fighting to hang on in this nightmare, a girl who was just struggling to survive the same as he was, up to die.

For things she'd never even done.

He blinked hard, trying to find words and not be sick at the same time. She never could have done it. Not what she'd been accused of, nor what the old woman insisted she had to do to end the war. He'd read it on her face the moment Thelma told her, and watched it in the way she bolted at the words.

Mass murderers didn't react like that. Not when offered absolute victory for the cost of only one victim more. Mass murderers wouldn't have even batted an eye.

He knew. He'd seen the alternative.

And he should have known.

Cole swallowed. "He can't do the spell. Not without you. He researched it with my mom, back before the war, and learned that what Merlin did… it's something only your family can control. That's why they needed you. Or Lily. They were going to force you to do it, once they found my grandparents and got their information too."

Ashe stared at him. "You… you *knew* that?" she whispered. "And you never said–"

"Why do you think I was trying to make sure his people didn't get Lily that day?"

Disbelief flashed over her face and then she paused, her brow furrowing as she processed what he'd said.

He cursed internally, realizing it too.

"You son of a bitch," Spider growled.

"What was that day, Cole?" Ashe asked, her quiet voice unsteady. "In Banston, when the others died?" She hesitated. "Was I supposed to be dead too by the time you got there?"

He looked away.

"Was that your plan?"

A heartbeat passed.

"It was," she said, her voice gaining strength. "Wasn't it?" She gave a choked gasp. "What else did you tell him while you were there? Did you tell him where the Merlin were hiding? What our defenses were? Where to find those kids who died in Austin, or those families who burned alive in Omaha? *Huh*? What'd you say?"

Trembling, she stared at him, her face a picture of old horrors and hurt gone on too long.

He shook his head, not taking his eyes from her. "No."

She waited.

"I told him…" He swallowed again. "I just told him about those three wizards and Katherine. And you."

"*Why?*"

"I thought…" He drew a breath. "I thought you'd killed all those cripples. That they'd made you – taught you – to do it. I thought…"

Cole looked away, his skin crawling at the pain-filled incredulity in her normally so expressionless eyes. "I heard what everyone said you'd done. The stories Harris and my dad told, and I thought you were a monster. A–" He glanced to Spider and then regretted it. The girl looked like she was trying to decide which of his limbs to shoot off first. "A feral."

"But–"

"You torched people in front of me, Ashe."

"I was trying to protect my sister!"

"I-I know. I get that. I just…" He grimaced. "When I heard the stories they told–"

"You thought you'd just have them kill me?"

"I was trying to protect people too!" he countered desperately, fighting to keep his voice low. "The other cripples and Lily–"

"You thought I'd hurt *Lily?*"

"No! I thought you'd–" He grimaced again. "I thought you'd make her like you."

A gasp escaped her. Rising, she walked away from the bed.

"They made it sound convincing, alright? And how was I supposed to know they were lying when even your own people claimed it'd all been okayed by you!"

She spun toward him and then paused. Her brow drew down ever-so-slightly as her gaze slipped from him to the floor.

"You really wanted to trust him," she said quietly. "Didn't you?"

"He's my father."

Ashe's gaze climbed, meeting his own. "He killed my family."

Cole looked away.

"Why'd you go back there?" she asked.

"I told you."

"You–"

"I didn't know. About you or the others. And he…" Cole's mouth tightened. "I just wanted his side."

"But you didn't try to take Lily."

The words were as much statement as question, and at them, he glanced up again.

"He killed your family. I wasn't going to risk her. Not till I knew what was going on."

She stared at him for a moment. "Elias said that, you know," she told him, her voice tight. "That maybe you were trying to protect her. That we shouldn't assume the worst of you."

He turned away, the words hurting like she'd probably intended them to.

"They were good people, Cole."

His jaw clenched. "Just stay away from him, alright? Take Lily and run to the other side of the world if you have to. Just don't let my dad get his hands on you."

He looked back when the girl didn't answer.

She was watching Lily.

"Ashe. Please."

A moment slid by.

"Okay," she whispered.

He let out the breath he hadn't realized he'd been holding.

Pulling her gaze from Lily, Ashe blinked as though trying to refocus her thoughts. Wizard expressionlessness gradually reasserted itself over her face as she searched the room, only to falter as her gaze caught on Spider.

For a heartbeat, neither girl spoke.

"The ferals will still be out there," Spider said, a note of apology in her voice.

Ashe looked away and after a moment, Spider did the same.

"I'll think about it," she added quietly.

Ashe hesitated and then nodded. "We, uh…" Her brow furrowed as she regarded the floor. "We should probably head back to Banston then. Just in case Bus…"

He could read on her face what Spider thought the answer would be, but the girl nodded anyway. "Yeah."

Silence filled the room.

"I can take watch tonight," Spider offered.

Ashe didn't look up as she shook her head. "You need sleep too."

"Wake you in a few hours then?"

"Sure."

Ashe walked to the bed, pausing before she lay down at Lily's side. By the window, Spider returned to watching the street.

Cole closed his eyes with relief before looking back outside. It wasn't much, getting Ashe to agree to leave the war like this. It didn't mean everything was fixed or that his dad's plans would suddenly disappear. But it would keep Lily safe, and Ashe, and protect his father too.

And that counted for something.

So much more than anything else thus far, that definitely counted for something.

———— ◆ ————

Sunrise crept over the horizon, brushing the little strip of neighborhood with soft colors and lighting the haze on the fields at the end of the road. In the guest room, shadows clustered behind the thick curtains, and only the thin strip of light slipping past her broke the gloom at all.

On the bed, Lily rolled over in her sleep and sighed.

Ashe glanced back. Bundling the blanket tighter beneath her cheek, Lily settled into the covers and didn't move again.

For a moment longer, she watched the girl before turning back to the window. It was odd to think that in a few days, they'd be escaping the war together. The whole world felt like an option, barring those places she knew the Blood were hiding and that she wouldn't have wanted to go to anyway. It was strange. She knew she should be excited. Happy, even.

Instead, she just felt numb.

For the past six months, all she'd wanted was for this to end. First with the Merlin, and later when she discovered Lily was alive, her only goal had been to stop the fighting so they could live without constantly worrying about who else might try to kill them each day. She'd thought the spell would do it, and when that wasn't an option, she'd still been ready to let go of everything to give Lily that chance. No matter what, she'd at least wanted Lily to be able to go somewhere and rebuild a semblance of home.

But that wasn't ever going to happen. She'd have a life with her sister now, of course, but it wouldn't be like before. They'd spend every day looking over their shoulders, never getting close to anyone because, at any moment, Jamison might find out where they were and they'd have to cut ties all over again.

And it would never change.

Against the window frame, she shifted uncomfortably, her gaze tracking a woman walking a dog through the faint morning light. Whatever happened, she'd handle it, and if this was what it took to keep Lily safe, then it was what she'd do.

She'd just really wanted to go back to having a home someday.

A creak sounded behind her and she turned. One hand gripping the doorframe, Gary was watching her, his wife peering warily over his shoulder. Tension lined his face, while Annie fingered their dog's collar as though wishing she could convince the placid animal to attack.

Ashe glanced to Spider, but the girl's eyes were already open as though she'd never been asleep at all.

"You said tomorrow," Gary told her.

Spider's gaze twitched to the bedside clock. With a contemptuous look to the couple, she pushed back the blanket and rose to her feet.

"Can you have one of them pull the car closer?" the man persisted with a halting gesture toward Ashe and Cole. "Since they're less–"

Spider leveled a flat look at him and he fell silent. With a quick motion to Annie, he retreated to the stairs.

Shaking her head, Spider exhaled and then caught sight of Ashe watching her.

"You should've seen how they reacted to having two black guys around," she said, irritation thick in her tone. She snagged her bag from the floor. "Didn't matter that Carter'd gotten them set up here. They just worried over whether they'd have to explain him and Sam to the neighbors."

"Sounds familiar," Cole muttered as the girl disappeared down the hall toward the bathroom.

Ashe glanced over as he shoved the blanket aside from the space he'd taken on the hardwood floor. Rubbing his eyes tiredly, he drew a breath and then moved to stand, only to pause as he noticed her.

"We leaving?" he asked, his voice tight.

"Soon as she gets back."

He finished climbing to his feet. Scrubbing a hand over his hair, he crossed to Lily's side to wake the little girl.

Ashe turned back to the window. As always, Cole presented his own problems, in so many ways, she was starting to lose count.

"Time to go?" Lily asked, a weariness in her voice that Ashe could tell had little to do with being woken so early.

"Yeah," Cole said.

"Where?"

Cole paused. "Back to Banston. We're going to meet up with Bus."

Blankets rustled as Lily clambered hurriedly from the bed.

Down the hall, the bathroom door opened. Sighing, Ashe checked the street again and then turned to grab her own bag before following Lily and Cole from the room.

Gary and Annie were waiting at the base of the stairs.

Wordlessly, Spider stepped around them, ignoring the angry noise Gary made as she did so. Tugging open the front door, the girl glanced down the road, and then walked outside, leaving the others to come after her.

The door slammed the moment they made it through.

"Friendly," Cole commented.

Lily made a disgusted noise.

Scanning the street, Ashe didn't say anything as she followed Spider to the SUV. Pulling open the door, she waited for Lily to climb in while Cole circled to the other side of the vehicle and Spider swung up into the driver's seat.

The hair on the back of her neck rose and she glanced to the house. At the front window, the barest edge of the curtain was tweaked back. Suppressing a disgusted sound of her own, she got in after her sister as Spider turned the key in the ignition.

She could feel the couple's gazes trailing them as the SUV drove away.

Chapter Twenty

As the elevator slowed, Harris sighed.

He couldn't believe he was doing this.

In almost a week of searching Chaunessy, he'd gleaned precious little information on how the Blood ran their empire. Their security was extensive, ranging from magical barriers around any sensitive location to a central monitoring station on the fifteenth floor that scrutinized every other level. The wizards weren't particularly talkative either, at least to him, and from the few conversations he'd managed to overhear, he'd only gathered a handful of names for Malden to run. He was getting nowhere slow, and after days of putting it off, he'd finally surrendered to the fact he needed to use every resource at his disposal.

No matter how irritating that resource could be.

The elevator door slid open, rewarding him with the sight of the squat little man sidling along the cafeteria deli counter. His pale hands shooting out from the voluminous layers of his coat, Mud snatched a pair of sandwiches from behind the back of the counter attendant and squirreled them away with lightning speed.

Drawing a breath, Harris made himself leave the elevator before he could change his mind. "Hey!" he called as he strolled into the cafeteria.

The man dropped the sandwich and turned to bolt before he realized who had spoken. Recovering quickly, he plastered his dirt-smudged face with a smile. "Hey, buddy!" he cried. Exaggerated bafflement furrowing his brow, he picked up the plastic-wrapped sandwich again and returned it to the tray as though he couldn't understand how it had fallen. "What brings you down here?"

Harris shrugged. "Just stretching my legs."

Mud looked like he wouldn't have seen the appeal of such a thing even if he'd been in chains for a year. "Uh-kay," he allowed, his smile faltering a little.

Harris leaned over slightly, casting a look to the attendant. "She noticed," he whispered.

If he hadn't been gambling on his own ability to get the arrogant little man to talk, the gamut of expressions would have made him laugh, shooting as they did past alarm, fear, and then stuttering into a sort of ingenious confusion so transparent, it wouldn't have fooled a child. "Huh?" Mud asked, seeming to notice the woman behind the counter for the first time. "I, uh…"

He trailed off as the attendant glanced back at her tray of sandwiches and then looked to him, her face darkening.

"I was going to have a seat, if you'd care to join me?" Harris offered.

Mud edged toward the door. "I should probably get–"

Harris made a cautioning noise, his eyes sliding meaningfully toward the attendant.

The little man made a beeline for a table.

Theatrics fading, Harris glanced to the woman. "I'll pay for the sandwiches," he told her tiredly before following.

By the time he reached the other side of the cafeteria, Mud had already managed to devour most of what he held in his hands. Plastic wrappings lay in shredded pieces all over the small, round tabletop, interspersed with smatterings of lettuce and tomato.

Harris repressed another sigh.

"Thanks for that," Mud said between bites as Harris sat down. "Regular bunch of Nazis, they are."

"Wizards," he agreed, ignoring the fact the man's comment didn't remotely approach logical.

"No kidding."

The conversation fell flat and the sound of Mud eating filled the room.

"So what gives?" Harris tried. "I thought you were out on patrol?"

"Got me watching prisoners now."

"They agreed to that?"

He couldn't keep the surprise from his tone, but it didn't matter. Mud just smiled, sandwich and all. "Gave 'em a good tip and got paid," he replied.

"Oh yeah?" Harris managed, looking away quickly.

Mud returned to his sandwich, radiating self-satisfaction.

Harris waited, but nothing more came. "Too bad," he commented.

"Huh?"

"Oh, nothing. I just can't imagine guard duty's very interesting. No news, no information. Just watching folks all day. Leaves you out of the loop entirely."

Derision twisted through Mud's expression. "I hear plenty."

"Come on," Harris chided. "It's not like wizards talk much. Not to the likes of us, anyway. Besides, I've been here just as long as you, and I still haven't even heard how Jamison manages to pull it all off."

"Pull what off?"

"His money, for starters," he said as though it was obvious. "How does he keep the lights on around here? Or the jets and cars and hotels damn near everywhere. How's he pay for all that and still keep every Merlin and Taliesin with a laptop from tracking down where he's hiding? It doesn't make sense."

"Well, that's your problem right there, isn't it?" Mud countered superciliously. "It's not Jamison who's doing it."

Harris didn't have to work hard to look skeptical. "Excuse me?"

"It's not Jamison," Mud repeated. "Oh, it's his money. But Brogan's the one who set it all up. The mansion in upstate New York, the cars and fake IDs and all the crap here. He even took the company Jamison's great-granddad founded, broke it up and turned it into a whole bunch of new ones without the Taliesin Council being any the wiser. Morons just thought the damn thing went bankrupt after Jamison supposedly died. But the money's still there, boatloads of it, all funneling back to them a dozen different ways. Brogan's just got it so covered in paperwork, anybody on the outside doesn't stand a chance of seeing how it all fits together."

Harris paused, filing the information away and then refocusing. He gave an amused scoff. "Yeah, right."

The little man's brow furrowed. "What?"

He shrugged. "Seems a bit farfetched, is all. I mean, 'boatloads' of money? Secret companies? Hidden mansions? You have any proof that's not just something the Blood dreamed up to make Jamison sound more impressive?"

"Why would they? You said yourself the man has tons of cash. Hell, most of the higher-up wizards do. Being outsiders like them tends to lend toward long-term thinking, so the bastards and their ancestors have been investing and building up money for years. Why should Jamison be any different?"

Harris chuckled dismissively. "Because having cash and having all of what *you're* talking about are two totally different things. If you haven't heard of any proof, let alone seen any…"

He let the scorn hang in the air and waited.

"And what the hell would you know, *Detective*?" Mud retorted, his tone twisting the last word into an insult. "Six months ago, you thought the damn queen of Merlin was some teenage delinquent you could *arrest*, for pity's sake. And now you want to pretend you know more than me about what's going on?" He scoffed. "Please. Did you know Jamison used to be married to a Merlin? Until he killed her, that is. Or that they brought in some crazy old lady and stashed her in Jamison's office the other day, but nobody dares ask why? No. You didn't. 'Cause I know things about this place that'd make your skin crawl off. And as for the setup Brogan made… they've got all the proof you need stored up at that mansion of theirs. Jamison stayed in that house for eight years. You don't do that and not leave a trace."

Harris couldn't stop the internal cop from kicking in. "Jamison killed his wife?"

Mud shrugged enigmatically. "That's what they say."

"When?"

"Back before the war."

"How do you know?"

The little man snorted. "Oh, they don't pay attention to the likes of us, remember?" The amusement in his beady eyes took on a patronizing cast. "Obviously, I just listen better than you."

Harris ignored him. His earlier words aside, truth was no one could miss Mud. He lived at the heart of a putrid fug of month-old produce and dirt. In all likelihood, the lump had bribed wizards for information, or else gotten into places he shouldn't and lived to tell the tale.

"And the old woman? Who–"

He cut off as his phone buzzed. Pulling it halfway from his pocket, he glanced to the number and then drew it swiftly out.

"Excuse me," he said to Mud as he rose.

The man was too busy tearing into his third sandwich to respond.

Walking to the windows several yards away, Harris thumbed on the phone. "Hey, Scott. You find anything?"

"Nothing on a Charles Brentworth," Malden answered. "I have a Lucas Brentworth that turned up at Croftsburg Memorial Hospital about a month ago. Unconscious, heavily injured, possibly the victim of a hit-and-run. Records show he skipped out after receiving treatment, though, so there's not much to go on. But that's not why I called."

"What's up?"

"Had a question. You heard anything about a missing old woman?"

Harris froze. "I'm sorry?" he managed.

"Just got word of a missing person's report from Montana that I thought might interest you. Remember that farm where the girl lived? Well, the power company headed up that way about three days ago on a report of some outages. Turns out the stretch right by the girl's house looked like someone went through with a wrecking ball. Poles down, wires everywhere, ground torn to pieces. Neighbor's house was a mess too. State records have an old woman living there, but no one can find her. Locals say some fairly strong windstorms came through the area right around that time, and the police are worried she might've run off when her roof collapsed. Search and rescue hasn't turned up anything yet, though. But it got me thinking. No one knows for certain when the old lady disappeared. So what if she didn't run off in the storm? What if that's just the reason anyone noticed she was gone, and she disappeared a long time ago? After all, God knows what she might've seen, living so close to the girl. So I wondered if maybe you'd come across anything that meant I should point the Montana cops that way?"

Harris didn't answer, his gaze skimming the concrete park below the windows. The old woman had been deranged. She'd talked about flowers and Elvis and panicked when he told her Ashley killed her family.

And yet the Blood had torn the countryside apart just to bring her back with them.

"John?"

He blinked. "Not really."

"Ah."

"So the house was a mess?" he pressed on, trying to pull his thoughts back to the present.

"Yeah. Though from the conditions inside, that could've just been normal decay."

"Huh."

"You sure you don't know anything about this?"

Harris glanced to the table. "Not yet," he replied, and then paused. "Thanks, Scott."

He hung up. Returning the phone to his pocket, he walked back to the table and sat down.

"So," he said to Mud. "About this old lady you *claim* they have upstairs…"

"So Bus has everything ready?" Ashe asked as the SUV pulled to a stop.

Spider nodded. "Much as can be, according to what he told me on the phone a few minutes ago. Jericho and Magnolia will meet you in San Antonio, and he's talked Blackjack into helping with some IDs. That part'll take a day or two, but Bus has a setup for you away from the others in the meantime."

"These IDs," Cole asked dryly as he pushed open the passenger door. "They're going to be better than Blackjack's cars, right?"

Spider gave him a flat look and then shut off the engine. "Yeah."

Ashe said nothing as she climbed out. Two days of driving, and she still didn't know what to do about Cole. Lily wouldn't want to leave him behind, though whether Cole would even want to come with them was its own question. But in either case, she wasn't certain how she felt. On the one hand, he'd tried to have her killed and for that alone, she'd love to find the nearest ditch and throw him in it. On the other, he could see the Blood wizards and had as much reason for keeping her sister safe from them as she did.

The same factors that made him an asset were tangled up with the ones that made him a liability, and no matter how she turned it around, she couldn't find a solution for that problem.

Taking Lily's hand, she scanned the street as she trailed Spider, leaving Cole to fall in behind. A trio of homeless men sat by an abandoned flower shop a block away, though none of them looked up from the sidewalk. Tired vehicles sagged into the parking spaces along the otherwise empty road, while a half mile off, a few cars rolled past the dim stoplights.

The chains hidden in the kudzu clunked as Spider pulled the lock around, and the rusted hinges creaked a moment later when she tugged the gate aside. Twilight surrounded them as they slipped into the tunnel and continued on, till the thin sunshine pushing past the vines faded, leaving only the intermittent glow of utility lights.

"Bus is going to meet us at the subway platform," Spider said quietly. "Some of the others aren't exactly thrilled you're back, so he thought an escort might be best."

Ashe's mouth tightened.

"On the bright side," Spider continued. "He did say Magnolia and the kids are really excited to meet Lily, so–"

She saw Spider's expression change, and then the attack was there.

A wave of air smashed into her, propelling her into the wall. Blackness surged across her vision, bringing pain on its heels and revealing the tunnel in a blur of concrete and graffiti and people charging by.

She struggled up blindly from the ground.

Something struck her head.

Concrete met her and wet heat spread across her face. Gunfire rang through the rushing in her ears, and then gave way to the sound of Lily screaming her name.

The screams went silent. The gunfire cut off. She gasped, choking on rocks and dust, and fumbled up from the ground to see a mob of wizards retreating toward the tunnel's end.

One of them had Lily slung limply over his shoulder.

Magic left her, rushing at them in a wave of fire. Wizards fell, howling.

The one with Lily never looked back.

She lunged to her feet and took off, reaching for his magic as she ran. The man behind him stumbled, his power rushing into her, and without hesitation, she flung it at the wizard with Lily.

Another man staggered between them, taking the blow.

A cry escaped her as electricity scattered across her defenses and blasts of nothingness sent her stumbling. Fire mowed down her attackers and cleared her path, but the tunnel entrance was light-years away and the man with Lily had already reached it.

The gate burst open ahead of him, letting in blinding sunlight.

Frantic, she raced from the tunnel and onto the street.

There were wizards everywhere.

Magic hit her defenses, driving her back past the gate, and chunks of ballistic concrete sliced the air in front of her as blasts of energy pounded the entrance walls.

Shouts rose. The attacks diverted from the tunnel.

Shoving from the cover of the wall, she bolted into the open, her eyes sweeping the buildings and the road as magic rained down on the wizards around her.

The man with Lily had reached an abandoned storefront a block away.

She ran.

Endless blackness swirled in the doorframe ahead of him. One hand gripping the little girl, he glanced back at the street.

Melted skin met her gaze. Through the chaos, he spotted her, and a cold smile pulled at his scarred face.

He stepped into the portal and she screamed. Wizards fell around her as they tried to attack. She barely noticed them disappearing. The portal began to swirl into nothing, and she flung herself at it, racing the fading darkness.

Wood slammed into her, throwing her to the street as the magic vanished. Gasping, she rushed back, pounding her fist at the surface and then fumbling madly at the doorframe, seeking any trace of the portal that remained.

There was nothing. With a choked shriek, she stumbled back. "Ashe?"

She spun toward the sidewalk, fire rushing up her arms.

Coming to a stop a few yards away, Cornelius stared.

"Your majesty?" he tried.

She choked again, looking between him and the impossible wizards running toward her.

"Is she–" Elias called, cutting off as he came closer. "Holy…"

Jogging up behind him, Katherine's eyebrows rose at the sight of her, while across the street, Nathaniel swiftly dispatched a pair of wizards and then continued after the councilwoman. Dozens of other Merlin were scattered through the area, fending off the Taliesin and driving them from the neighborhood.

Staring at them all, she fought to breathe around the words lodged in her throat. "You… you're here… how are you here…"

"We were following the Taliesin," Cornelius said.

She barely heard the words. "T-they have her. They have…" She turned back to the doorframe. "Can you track it? Can you–"

Running out of air, she looked between Cornelius and the door. Stepping around her, he placed a hand on the splintered wood.

His expression told her everything. She felt herself start to shake.

"Your highness," Katherine began, coming up beside her. "You need to–"

She pushed the woman's hand away, her gaze darting around frantically. "There has to be something. They can't–"

Her eyes caught on Cole emerging from the tunnel, his attention on the dead bodies lying on the street.

"Cole!" she shouted.

Shoving past the others, she took off. He turned sharply and then froze, his brow furrowing at the wizards coming behind her.

"They have Lily," Ashe gasped. "He – where is he? Where would he take her?"

Cole refocused on her with alarm.

"Please!"

For a heartbeat, he stared at her. "Chaunessy," he said as though the word was pulled from him. "They're at Chaunessy Tower in Croftsburg."

A breath escaped her. "Okay. We need to–"

Her gaze snapped over as Spider stepped from the tunnel entrance, guns in hand.

"Don't!" Ashe yelled as the weapons swung toward them.

The girl froze, murder in her eyes as she scanned the wizards. Guns still raised, she headed back inside.

Blinking, Ashe looked between the tunnel and the storefront door, guilt trying to war with the panic steadily overriding everything. "W-we have to go now… we can't…"

"We need a plan, your highness," Elias said carefully. "We rush in there, we'll be killed."

She shook her head, not wanting to hear the words. "There's no time. We–"

"Ashe," Cole interrupted.

Her frenetic gaze went to him.

"Let me help."

She stared, uncomprehending.

"I can go there. I can talk to him–"

A laugh escaped her, the sound nearly hysterical. "You think he'll *listen?*"

She spun, racing for the nearest door.

"Ashe!" he yelled, running after her. "Dammit, wait!"

He snagged her arm, pulling her around and then letting go before her hands caught fire. "Just… wait. I'll get you inside, okay? Past the barriers and the guards. Just slow down."

"How?" Cornelius demanded, striding up behind them.

Cole glanced toward him uncomfortably.

"Okay," she agreed breathlessly. "Fine. Do it."

"We need a car first," Cole said, his voice taking on an edge of measured calm.

Panic surged at the miles growing between her and Lily with every second.

"Your highness," Cornelius argued, "let us contact the guard. They can go to Chaunessy and find a way past the defenses themselves."

The words were eating time and she ignored them, her eyes sweeping the street. Cars lay wrecked and smoking by the sidewalks, and a few were smashed into the abandoned buildings.

Her gaze twitched to the subway. She started running.

Dead wizards filled the tunnel and the walls were blackened above most of them. Ignoring it all, she pounded over the concrete, barely slowing to scan the platform as she passed.

Gunshots echoed down the tunnel.

Magic rising around her, she fought to run faster.

Light poured from the maintenance room, burning her eyes as she darted around the boulder blocking the doorway.

Shale and several others lay dead in the middle of the floor. By the side walls, a pair of men were slumped, the bullet wounds through their heads leaving wide splatters of blood on the controls nearby. Across the room, Spider was crouched by the others, and as Ashe skidded to a stop, the girl yanked the gag from Bus' mouth.

"Damn you're good, girl," he told her as she undid the ropes on his hands.

Spider didn't respond as she moved on to Samson. "How many more?" she asked, tugging his gag away.

Samson's eyes went to Ashe and the wizards behind her.

"Dammit, Sam!" the girl snapped. "How many?"

"Not sure," Bus supplied. "Couple dozen originally. Bastards swooped in not ten minutes ago, locked up a few of us for information and used the rest for, uh…"

The old man glanced to the bodies in the center of the room.

"Target practice," Samson finished with a growl. Rubbing his wrists, he rose to his feet, his gaze returning to Ashe. "And you're at the heart of it again."

"Shut up," Spider told him. "She didn't do this."

"I need your help," Ashe said.

Samson's face darkened. "Go to—"

"Son," Bus interrupted. "I'm fairly certain your lady just told you to shut it."

Bracing himself on the ladder, the old man climbed to his feet.

"Alright, your majesty," he said, icy resolve in his blue eyes. "What can we do for you?"

Chapter Twenty-One

——◆——

The little girl slumped in the wood-framed chair, the black waves of her hair obscuring both her face and the red welt left on her neck by the tranquilizer. From the opposite side of the desk, the king regarded her, fingers folded in front of him and nothing in his face to give hint to the thoughts passing behind his eyes.

But it didn't matter. Brogan could guess. With a few rather notable exceptions, they were presumably similar to his own.

Overall, the operation had gone exceptionally well. At first blush, Mud's joy at spotting one of the so-called Hunters near where the Children had disappeared seemed insignificant. But when he'd added the queen's apparent penchant for trusting street cripples over her own kind, matters had entirely changed. Subduing the refuse had taken a matter of moments, and for her to return to the area only minutes later had been fortuitous indeed. In the end, he couldn't help but be pleased with the result.

The expression on Ashley's face when he took her sister hadn't hurt either.

A corner of his lip gave a minute twitch and the king looked up at the motion.

"The queen," Brogan explained.

Jamison's brow shrugged. "She will be coming for the girl," he reminded him.

The nascent smile broadened infinitesimally and brief humor touched the king's expression in response.

A clatter rose behind the conference room door, followed by indignant protests and the sound of a chair being dragged back upright. A squawk came on the heels of the noise and a moment later, a wizard slipped around the door. Struggling to conceal the harried look in his eyes, he grimaced in apology and then strode from the room, muttering something about bandages and crazy old women who refused to be healed as he went.

Jamison's gaze tracked the wizard and then returned to the conference room. "Is there any indication they are related?"

Brogan didn't need explanation. "None." He paused. "Though obviously, the woman has been less than forthcoming."

The king looked back at the girl, the fingers of one hand drumming lightly on the other.

A knock sounded on the door.

"Come in," Jamison called.

The door swung open at Isabella's touch. Stone-faced, she crossed to the desk and then stepped to the side to afford the king full view of the woman trailing her heels.

With her daughter partially hidden behind her, Tanya shifted uncomfortably under the scrutiny of the three Blood wizards, a hint of defensive pride twisting through her expression. Her gaze skimmed the office, and then alarm suffused her face as she caught sight of the little girl in the chair.

"Is that–"

"What is wrong with her?" Jamison interrupted coldly.

"What…" Tanya repeated. "*I* don't know. Howard just–"

"Did he tell you the nature of her condition?"

"I don't think he knew," she retorted, her annoyance for the interruptions clear. "She just lost most of her magic the night the war started. That's all he'd say."

Brogan saw Isabella glance to them, but the king ignored her.

"She was there?" Jamison asked.

"Yeah. Council kept it hushed up, but Howard said they found her in the house." She looked between them. "Why?"

No one answered her. For a moment, Jamison regarded the girl, and then glanced to Brogan and Isabella.

"The old woman," Brogan reminded him.

Jamison looked away.

Tanya's brow drew down. "What old woman?"

"Was there anyone associated with the family who shared the girl's condition?" Jamison asked. "Perhaps someone who was also there that night?"

"No," Tanya replied, her tone narrowly avoiding outright disrespect. "She was the only one at the house who survived. And nobody ever ended up looking human from an explosion." She paused, seeming to realize who she was talking to. "I mean…"

Her gaze flitted uncomfortably over them.

Jamison didn't take his eyes from the conference room door.

The silence stretched, interspersed with the rustle of Tanya shifting her weight and the quiet sucking noises of her daughter investigating the taste of her thumb.

"Would you like me to remove them from the room now, sire?" Isabella asked carefully, an eyebrow arching over her pale blue eyes.

For a moment longer, Jamison studied the door. "Not yet." He glanced back to Tanya. "You say 'most of her magic'. She still possessed some?"

"Patrick bound something."

Again, her tone edged toward insolence, and Brogan could see Isabella tense in response.

"Don't," Jamison ordered without looking at them. "It will help the girl to see a Merlin with us." The barest hint of a smile touched his lips as he watched the woman. "But make certain she stays silent."

Indignation tried to surface in Tanya's eyes, but at a look from Isabella, it withered. At the Blood's direction, she retreated with her daughter to the far corner of the room.

"Wake her," Jamison said.

Brogan stepped from the girl's line of sight as Isabella reached over, briefly resting her fingers on the child's neck.

The little girl gasped, her eyes flying open. Swiftly, she looked around, her gaze lighting across Jamison, Isabella, Tanya and the other child.

"Wha– where–" she started, her magic flickering up in response to her fear.

And then it was gone.

Her attention snapped back to Jamison.

"Hello, Lily," he said gently.

The girl trembled.

"I'm sorry for that," he continued. "I promise I'll give it back soon."

"You're Cole's dad," she whispered.

He nodded. "I can't imagine he's said too many nice things about me lately. We kind of had a fight, you see."

She didn't answer. He smiled anyway.

"Cole misunderstood something and it made him angry at me. But sometimes that happens in families. You get into fights. But in the end, you still love each other. You'd still do anything to keep each other safe."

She barely seemed to be breathing.

"Kind of like he'd do anything for you," Jamison finished.

The girl didn't move.

"He wanted to bring you here. Did he tell you that? This was his plan to keep you safe."

She shook her head. "He doesn't want to come back."

"I'm sure that's what he said. People say a lot of things when they're upset. You know that, right? How you can say stuff when you're fighting that you don't really mean?"

Distrust radiated from the girl in waves, but in the seat, she shifted uncomfortably.

"He told me himself that he wanted you to stay with us," Jamison continued. "How he hoped you'd help us. We even have a room set up for you, right by his. Does that sound like something we'd do if he didn't want you here?"

She looked away. Brogan moved silently to stay out of her view.

"Ashley said you killed my mom," she replied after a moment.

Jamison grimaced ruefully, playing along with the topic change. "Ashley's right," he admitted with difficulty. "I did. It was a mistake, Lily. In a war, people sometimes make horrible mistakes. And I know I can't just say I'm sorry and make it go away. But I am. Sorry, I mean. I just…"

He shook his head, seeming for all the world as if he was at a loss for words. Brogan suppressed a smile.

The king drew a breath. "Cole said you were a smart girl, though. He said you could understand. We never wanted to hurt you. Or your family. We wanted to make peace, but things… they just got out of hand. And I am sorry for that. Truly."

Lily said nothing.

"Could you help us, Lily? We just want peace. That's all."

For a moment, the girl remained silent. Briefly, she turned to look at Isabella, Tanya and the child.

"They said you wanted to kill everybody."

The shock on Jamison's face appeared nothing but genuine. "*Kill* everybody?" he repeated. He closed his eyes as though pained. "Is… is *that* what Cole thought?" He exhaled, seeming appalled. "No wonder he left."

He looked at her imploringly. "We want to stop the people who like this war. The ones who won't quit fighting. We just need to take their magic so they can't hurt anyone."

She paused. "What about you, then?"

His brow drew down confusedly.

"You keep hurting people."

"No, no. We're not like that," he countered, his tone almost begging for her to understand. "We don't want to hurt anybody. Really. To be honest, we're a lot like your sister. After all, isn't Ashley just trying to stop the war?"

The king waited. Her head gave a hint of a nod.

Jamison smiled. "That's all we're doing too."

"But you're not like her."

"How so? Your sister defends the ones she loves, doesn't she?

That's all I'm trying to do. And the people who've died…" He grimaced reluctantly. "Well, the people Ashley's killed…"

He trailed off. "You know she's killed people, right?" he asked awkwardly.

The girl shifted uneasily and Brogan read the fact that she did from the compassion that filled Jamison's eyes.

"I really believe she's just doing it because she's trying to protect you," he said as though searching for the bright side of a tragedy. "And I'm sure she's only hurting the people she thinks are a threat. But we can help her not need to do that anymore. We can stop the war and… and maybe Ashley can just be Ashley again. I mean, I have to think all the stress of worrying for you has left her not quite the same as she used to be." He waited a heartbeat. "Right?"

She shifted in the chair again.

"You can help her, Lily. I know all she wants is not to be afraid for you anymore. We can give her that, me and you."

For a long moment, the child said nothing, her eyes on her arms clutched tightly across her stomach, and Brogan could only gauge her expression by the beseechingly hopeful look that remained on Jamison's face.

"Ashley stops the bad people," the girl said, almost more to herself than the king. "She just wants us to be safe again."

"And all we're asking is for you to help us make that happen," Jamison urged gently. "For Ashley and Cole, and all the *good* people out there."

The little girl didn't answer, but Brogan could tell what was happening anyway. With every second that slid past, she seemed to shrink further in on herself, while slowly, the king's lip crept toward a smile.

And then she shook her head.

"No," she whispered.

Jamison's brow twitched up.

"You're a liar," she continued softly. "That's why Cole left. He didn't want me here, and he's probably coming to get me right now." She trembled. "And Ashley will *never* be like you."

"Lily, that isn't the truth. Please, we want the same–"

"I know the truth," the little girl interrupted.

She looked up at the king.

"I know my sister is going to stop you too."

———— ◆ ————

Car doors slammed and the murmur of hurried conversation rose and fell in sharp waves. Tension traveled with the sounds, growing stronger as more cars arrived in the parking lot of Joe's new restaurant.

Climbing from the back seat of the fastest vehicle Bus could steal, Ashe barely noticed. On the outside, she supposed the time between Banston and Croftsburg looked like it'd done a lot toward calming her down, though she wouldn't have actually described it that way. Focused was more like it, and she could feel it in the fact she couldn't take her eyes from the place they'd been for the last twenty miles.

There wasn't anything remarkable about Chaunessy. There never had been. Maybe seventy identical stories of steel and mirrored glass, ending in a flat roof, the building was as uninspired as they came. Other skyscrapers surrounded it, topped with enough tiered crenellations to make a gothic architect weep or sheer asymmetrical slopes that looked designed to cut the air. Dozens of lighted pinnacles glinted faintly in the afternoon sun, all promising multicolored splendor when night finally came.

Among them, Chaunessy was nothing.

Except that it had her sister inside.

"He won't hurt her."

Ashe looked over, not having noticed Cole come up. Expressionless, he was watching the skyscraper as though he could see through its walls to his father.

"Why are you helping us, Cole?" she asked.

For a moment, he didn't move. "I can't let him do this," he answered quietly.

Her brow flickered down as he glanced to her, and when he looked away again, she couldn't bring herself to speak.

He still hoped he could change his dad's mind. She could tell it as clearly as if he'd said the words aloud.

And after everything else the man had done, she couldn't see how that would be possible.

"Your highness," Elias called.

She blinked, looking over her shoulder. Halfway across the restaurant parking lot, Elias waited, other wizards filing past him to head inside.

Doubt moved through her as she glanced back to Cole, but there wasn't anything for it. She didn't know how this was going to go, or whether *not* killing Jamison would even be an option. But it wasn't important. Not really, anyway. She was going after Lily and she was going to get her sister back from that man.

No matter what it took.

Without a word, she turned and crossed the parking lot to join Elias.

It was a moment before she heard Cole follow.

Joe's new restaurant was going to be even nicer than its predecessor; that much she could tell despite the unfinished construction. Large double doors of dark wood and beveled glass fronted the building, giving access to a high entryway. Manufacturer's stickers still dotted the windows on three sides of the building, and through the reflective glass, she could only see suggestions of the space inside.

Noise hit her the moment Elias opened the door.

The dining area lacked tables or chairs, and the plastic-wrapped fixtures had no bulbs, but the room's occupants didn't seem to care. More of the Merlin than she'd known survived filled the space, and portals brought further arrivals through every available door. A corner of the bar was occupied by the cripples, and behind Spider and Bus, she could see Samson muttering dark comments to Blackjack, the content of which she could guess from across the room. Shouted instructions surrounded her as she followed Elias through the crowd, mingled with greetings to her from wizards nearby. At the center of the throng, Cornelius glanced over as she approached, though the guard, Gavin, didn't look away from the city map lying on the stack of boxes in front of him.

"…wizards patrolling a half mile out," Gavin was saying. "They're within visual distance of each other at all times, so grabbing one won't work, and a direct approach has to deal with the cameras. But if diversionary squads draw their attention at these locations–" He pointed. "–we should have enough cover that they won't be able to get a count on our numbers, which should provoke them into over-committing reinforcements from Chaunessy. Plan is then for a small squad to infiltrate the building and take down the shields, allowing our forces to…"

"Your highness," Cornelius said as he left the group and came toward her. With a slight bow, he motioned to one side, and then waited for her to precede him away from Gavin. "Katherine has requested your assistance. The wounded–"

"No," she interrupted. "I'm not staying behind. Elias and I already covered this on the way here."

The wizard looked beyond her to the councilman, and from the way his jaw muscles jumped, she could guess at the exasperated look that must have been in Elias' eyes.

"You are not a soldier," Cornelius said, returning his attention to her. "You are the queen. If we lose you–"

"He has Lily. Chances are, he knows how to recreate the spell. If we don't stop him, it won't matter what protections you put around me. I'll be dead all the same."

The man looked away. News that the spell could kill them hadn't hit well among the Merlin. Most seemed to be determined to ignore it, though the tension around her had a different flavor than what she'd become used to over the past few months. Battles against the Taliesin were one thing. But fights where the enemy could kill you, your loved ones and anyone else you knew, no matter where they tried to hide, were something else entirely.

"I'm going after my sister, Cornelius," she finished. "End of discussion."

His gaze slid back to hers, and her chest tightened at the fury she saw in his eyes. Determinedly, she kept herself from looking away as the seconds stretched on.

"You said you could gain us access to the building?" Cornelius asked icily as he pulled his focus from her to pin it on Cole.

A breath escaped her. Working to hide the reaction, she turned to the boy. Standing a few steps behind Elias, Cole looked between her and Cornelius, misgivings flashing over his face.

"Cole?" she pressed.

His mouth tightened. "A tunnel," he surrendered. "Beneath Chaunessy. The Council tried to get us out through it when my dad, um… came there."

"How do we reach it?" Cornelius asked.

"I'm not sure."

Her brow drew down, and Elias' wasn't far behind. "Then how does this help us?" the councilman demanded.

"I need to make a call," Cole explained.

"What? Who?"

Cole's gaze flicked to her uncomfortably. "A friend."

Elias glanced at her.

She didn't take her eyes off Cole.

He'd lied to her so many times. He'd wanted her killed. And if she let him direct the wizards' strategy, she was putting the life of every person she knew squarely in his hands. But a clock was ticking in the back of her head, and she could see the same in his eyes. They'd be dead soon anyway unless they did something, and all the Merlin's plans were also going to cost lives.

And he wanted to save Lily. Despite everything else about him, she had to hope that was something she could trust.

"Do it," she ordered.

He drew out his phone and headed for the front door.

"You're putting a lot of faith in him, your highness," Elias said neutrally as he watched Cole leave. She tried not to grimace when he looked back at her.

"I know," she answered, and then followed the boy outside.

On the sidewalk, Cole was thumbing through screens on his

phone. At the sound of the door, he glanced over and his face tightened at the sight of her.

She stopped a few feet away, waiting.

He turned back to the phone and then paused as he reached the screen he needed. Drawing a deep breath, he hit a button and then raised the cell to his ear.

Her eyes slid to the horizon as the seconds crept by.

"Um, it's Cole."

Her gaze snapped back to him.

"Look…" he said, hesitant contrition in his tone. "I-I've been thinking about what you said, and I think maybe you were right. I shouldn't have–"

He cut off sharply and she tensed.

"Uh…" Cole hedged, the theatrics melting away. He looked back to her, caution taking the place of everything else on his face. "Okay… it's like this. My dad has Lily. He's going to use her to kill a lot…" He studied her for a moment. "A lot of innocent people."

Alarm moved through her at what she could have sworn was sincerity in his eyes.

"I need your help to stop him. If you could tell me–" Cutting off, he grimaced. "We don't have a lot of time," he tried quietly. He paused. "Okay. Thank you."

He hung up the phone.

"Twenty minutes. Parking garage near Hillsdale and Grand, fourth level."

Questions pressed on her, but before she could speak, his gaze went beyond her. She looked back to see Nathaniel and Elias watching them from either side of the restaurant door.

Her heart picked up speed, the questions instantly becoming a distant second on her list of priorities. "Ready?"

Elias nodded.

She made a beeline for the car.

The miles blurred in a stream of roads and lights she didn't notice passing. On his cell, Elias conferred with wizards taking up positions around the parking garage, while silently, Nathaniel wove their speeding vehicle after Cornelius'. By the opposite window, Cole stared out at the city, lost in thoughts of his own.

"Your majesty."

She blinked. In the front seat, Elias was looking back at her.

"Once we reach Chaunessy, you stay with Nathaniel," he ordered. "Anything happens, get out of there and head for Joe's. Backup to that is his house, and backup to that is the abandoned meat-seller's shop on Fourteenth and Polson. Understand?"

At her silence, his grimace deepened.

"With all respect, your highness," he said, each word tight. "I don't care what the Blood king plans. We will stop him, and we will keep you safe while doing so." His eyebrow rose pointedly. "End of discussion."

"You know I'm not going to do that."

"You will if you want to do Lily any good. Getting yourself killed won't help anyone."

She looked away, tired of an argument that he had to be aware wouldn't change anything. "What happened at the airport last week?" she asked, and when her gaze twitched back to the front a moment later, she could see his irritation at the response.

"We got lucky," he replied. "Minus the rather large issue of losing you and Lily. Point is, we're not doing that again."

"Why couldn't I reach Katherine?"

He exhaled. "Because her phone was destroyed," he answered sharply. "Half our people in the city were destroyed too. It was a mess, tearing Banston apart to find you while tracking the Taliesin in case they got you first. A few pieces of equipment were the least of our concerns."

She couldn't stop herself from glaring at his acid tone. "I would've called, Elias. You think I didn't want to? I was just kind of under the impression you were all dead, so I didn't figure there was much point in trying."

In the driver's seat, she could see Nathaniel glance at them both, and behind him, Cole did as well. The wind of the car's passage along the street became the only sound.

Nathaniel cleared his throat, breaking the awkward silence. "We're here."

Her gaze returned to the road. Beyond the car, downtown Croftsburg surrounded them, and a block ahead, the neon sign for a parking garage protruded from high on a wall. Guiding the car after Cornelius' around the turn, Nathaniel eased over the bump of the entrance and then slowed further as the close air of the garage enveloped them.

The cars continued upward through the tight confines of the tunnel, the sounds of their tires bouncing strangely from the ceiling and walls. At the beginning of the fourth level, Nathaniel pulled the car to a stop after Cornelius', the others behind them doing the same.

"Where's your friend?" Elias asked.

Cole eyed the vehicles dotting the mostly empty rows, and then shook his head. Without a word, he climbed from the car.

Before Elias could protest, she followed.

The smell of oil and wet concrete hung heavy on the air, and somewhere below, tires squealed as a vehicle descended to the street. Up ahead, a wall bearing a lit exit sign separated the garage from the elevators and stairs. As Cornelius and Gavin got out, she glanced back, seeing Spider and Bus standing by their own vehicle a few yards away, with Samson glowering behind. Katherine waited beyond them, and a host of guards took up the rear.

Footsteps echoed from behind the stairwell wall.

Harris came around the corner.

She tensed, but Nathaniel was already moving. Stepping in front of her, his magic beat hers in rising to their defense, and in response, the cripples' guns materialized, aiming for the detective.

"Wait!" Cole cried as Harris froze. "This is—"

"We know him," Elias snapped. "The son of a bitch put a bullet through the queen."

Heart pounding, she kept her eyes on Harris as Cole looked back at her in alarm.

Swiftly, Gavin strode forward, a pair of guards at his back. One of them grabbed the detective, pinning him as Gavin patted him down. A scowl twisted Gavin's face as he located a gun beneath Harris' coat. With a dark look to the detective, he handed it off to a guard and then grabbed Harris' shoulder, giving him a rough push toward the wizards.

Rocking from the shove, Harris eyed the man briefly and then started across the garage.

"You didn't tell me you were working with them," he growled to Cole as he came closer.

"I didn't think you'd help if I did," Cole answered.

Harris' expression made it clear he'd been right.

"Put him in the car," Cornelius ordered, ignoring the exchange.

"We will handle him later. And call–"

"No," she interrupted, striding past Nathaniel. "If he knows how we can get inside, then–"

"The boy is one thing, your highness," Cornelius protested. "But this man shot–"

"How can we get in there?" Ashe demanded, turning to Harris.

The detective's face tightened.

"You can't trust–" Elias started.

"*How*?" she snarled, flames racing up her arms.

"Whoa!" Cole broke in, rushing between them with his hands raised. "Hang on! Just…" He swallowed and then looked back at her, an insistent expression flashing across his face. "Back off."

Trembling, she eyed Cole and then eased away, her gaze twitching from him to the detective.

"You shot her," Cole continued to Harris. "And my dad has her little sister. So she's pissed, alright? But she's not what they said. And she's not what you think. She didn't mean to hurt Malden. It was an accident." He glanced back at her. "And you didn't kill him, by the way. Malden's alive."

She blinked, her anger faltering with confusion. "What?"

"Malden's alive," he repeated. "He's in physical therapy. He's going back to work for the department soon."

A breath escaped her. Reeling, she looked away.

"Malden?" Elias asked.

"A… another detective," she managed. "In Utah."

She looked up to find Harris watching her guardedly.

"Ashe isn't a killer, Detective," Cole said. "Not like my dad claimed. She just wants to protect the innocent in this, same as you. So please… help us."

For a moment, Harris didn't speak, his eyes running over her as though he couldn't decide whether to trust what he saw. "The man in the boathouse a few weeks ago," he said, his tone giving nothing away. "What was that?"

She swallowed, struggling to bury every trace of her reaction that she could. "He said he'd killed my friends," she answered, nodding toward Spider and the others.

"Cripples," Harris said, a hint of a question in his tone.

She glanced back in time to see Spider's eyebrow twitch coldly at the man in response.

Harris ignored the girl's expression.

"My dad is going to kill everyone here if you don't help us, Detective," Cole said. "And he's going to use Lily to do it."

Harris' gaze flicked to him, and she couldn't read what was going on behind his eyes.

"Your family," he continued to her. "What happened that night?"

She paused. "Brogan killed them."

His mouth thinned at her response and he looked away.

"Detective," Cole urged. "We're running out of time."

For a moment, the man didn't respond. "You really think your father's going to do that to the kid?"

"I know he is," Cole replied.

Harris' gaze returned to her. Slowly, he drew a breath. "What do you need?"

Cole exhaled, the tension almost visibly leaving him. "The tunnel below Chaunessy. I need to know how to reach it, what kind of defenses it has, everything."

Harris' brow drew down. "Tunnel?"

"Yeah."

The man shook his head, his eyes flicking to the wizards. "I've never heard of any tunnel."

"What?" Cole said incredulously. "No, the Council – the Taliesin Council – they had a tunnel under the building. They…" He trailed off at the blank look on the man's face, and then turned to her helplessly.

She hesitated. "Are there other ways we can get in?" she asked Harris.

"Your highness," Elias protested. "This man isn't–"

Her hand twitched, cutting him off, and though her gaze never left the detective, she could see Elias and Cornelius share a dark look from the corner of her eye.

Harris paused. "The wizards monitor everything. I have access codes to the doors, but they've got cameras and guards on each one."

She grimaced, looking away. That was it then. They had to go and the wizards' backup plans were the only ones left.

Even if there was no chance they wouldn't be bloody.

"Call the others," she said to Elias, her voice hard. "Have them get ready to–"

"Who's Charles Brentworth?"

She glanced back to Harris.

"What?" Cole asked.

"Why?" she demanded.

Harris looked between them. "Is he connected to that Council?"

She nodded carefully.

"I heard some wizards talking about him several days ago. Sounded like he was one of their prisoners, somebody important." Harris paused. "If there really is a tunnel below Chaunessy…" He shrugged noncommittally.

She looked to Cornelius and Elias, and watched the former's expression go stone-like, while the latter just turned away. Behind her, displeasure radiated off Nathaniel in waves.

"Do you know where the prisoners are located?" Cornelius asked tightly.

Harris eyed the wizard. "A few miles from here in an old hardware store on the edge of downtown."

She fought back a grimace, feeling like she was being dragged farther from Lily with every second.

"And how do we get inside?" Cornelius pressed in the same tone.

"Access is restricted to just those in charge of the prisoners," Harris answered. "And they don't share the codes with anyone. Though…"

He paused, and she glanced back to see him studying her again.

Her brow drew down warily. "What?"

"Mud got moved to guard duty yesterday."

Elias scoffed. "Oh, great. Him again."

"Wait, did you say *Mud*?" Spider said, coming closer.

"You know him?" Ashe asked her.

Spider tossed a glance to Samson. "You could say that. Bastard found Sam and I when we were kids, said he'd help us, and then tried to sell us out to the first bunch of ferals he saw. Would've thanked him for it, if he hadn't slipped away while we were busy trying not to die. How'd you meet him?"

"Sort of the same way," Ashe replied dryly. She turned to Harris. "What're you thinking?"

"You can't trust that weasel to help us," Spider argued, and her eyes flicked over Harris as though to include him in the epithet.

Harris met her gaze. "I'm not that stupid. I'm just going to get him outside the building and then–" He glanced across the Merlin, distaste for them all still lingering in his expression. "—you ask him about getting to the prisoners. The Blood and the Taliesin never come out of the building. They use portals to travel to just outside Chaunessy. But Mud can't do that, so he'll know what you need to get past their security."

"Fine," Ashe said. "Let's go."

Cornelius gestured to Gavin, who jerked his head at the detective in a wordless order to get in the car. Doors opened and then slammed around her while the others did the same.

"Ashe."

She glanced over at Spider. Giving Cole an oblique glance, Spider grimaced as she came up beside her. "Look," she said, keeping her voice low. "Far be it from me to agree with wizards, but... you sure about this? You're risking a lot based on the word of a guy who tried to kill you." She paused. "Two, actually."

Ashe hesitated, feeling her expression mirror the girl's own. "You see another option?"

Spider looked away. "It just sounds like a trap. Claiming not to know about any tunnel, getting you to head for their prison rather than the main building..." She shook her head. "He works for the Blood, and they would've had more than enough time to plan something between when Cole called and you showed up here."

Ashe exhaled, her gaze sliding to the vehicle holding Harris.

She knew they were right. Elias, Cornelius, Spider, all of them. Harris couldn't be trusted, and there wasn't a shred of evidence to say he wasn't just trying to finish what he started a few weeks ago. And Cole wanted to save his dad. It was incredible he'd helped them get this far.

A phantom ache throbbed in her chest, and her hand twitched

with the impulse to rub at it, if only to make it go away.

Harris could be leading them into a trap, and everyone here could wind up dead as a result. But at the same time, her only other option consisted of throwing what Merlin were left at Chaunessy and hoping any of them made it inside the walls alive.

"We have to try."

"And if he's lying?"

"Then you shoot him," she answered, her voice tight. "And make sure to aim for his heart."

Without another word, she headed for the car.

Chapter Twenty-Two

"You sure this is the right place?" Cole asked.

"They didn't want the prisoners near Chaunessy," Harris replied. "Security risk."

"No, it's just… a hardware store? How's that useful?"

"Apparently the former owners left lots of material for building cages behind," Harris responded wryly. "And from what Mud said, the old security was still in place, so it worked well."

Barely listening to them, Ashe tilted her head around the corner of the alley to get a better view of the squat building nearly two hundred yards away. Hemmed in by newer structures, the one-story block of brick sat trapped at the rear of a weathered parking lot. Cameras were mounted on each corner, however, keeping every angle covered without a blind spot to spare.

Behind her, Nathaniel made an annoyed sound, and she closed her eyes briefly before pulling back. Because of the cameras, the Merlin wouldn't be able to get close, and the magical defenses on the building meant an outside attack could never be fast enough to beat the wizards inside to an alarm. There wasn't a better plan than the one they had, but that didn't stop it from leaving her sick to her stomach at its risk.

At the other end of the alley, the chain-link fence clinked as Spider and Samson slid past to join them. "Bus, Memphis and Blackjack have the next street and the vehicles covered," the girl said quietly as they came closer. "So what's the plan?"

Fighting the urge to let her gaze go to Nathaniel, Ashe didn't answer. "Everyone else in place?" she asked Elias.

He nodded. She echoed the motion, pretending not to see the wary look Spider was giving her.

"Make the call," she told Harris.

The detective eyed her briefly and then turned away, drawing out his cell.

A moment crept past. Her eyes slid toward the rooftops as though she could see the wizards hiding there.

Harris cleared his throat. "It's me. Yeah. Because you gave me the number. I–" He grimaced. "Listen, I think I might've spotted someone connected to the queen, but it'd be better if you identified them too." He paused. "Because if I go to Brogan and I'm wrong..." He waited. "Fine, I'll share credi– no, just share." Another moment passed. "Fine."

He hung up the phone. Drawing a tired breath, he scowled. "It worked. He's coming."

"Get him in the car so he can't run, and we'll take it from there," Elias reiterated.

The detective just headed for the sedan parked inside the alley entrance.

Trying to ignore the look that passed between Elias and Nathaniel, she followed the others back into the shadows. Dumpsters and moldering cardboard boxes crowded the rear of the alleyway, while decomposing trash plastered the concrete. Her nose wrinkling, she stepped carefully around the overflowing garbage to hide behind one of the rusted bins.

"Awesome," Cole muttered, and she glanced over to see him extracting his foot from an unidentifiable substance on the ground.

"Quiet," Elias ordered from across the alley.

Cole shot him a dark look.

She turned back to the entrance, sparing a glance for the doorway just beyond the garbage bin. They had options in case this went wrong, so there wasn't any reason for concern. Not yet, anyway. Either the path through the building or the one past the fence would get them out of here.

Assuming they could extricate themselves from the garbage in time to escape.

Grimacing, she pushed the thought away and tried to focus on how little she could breathe and remain conscious. The seconds were like a physical pressure, filled with eye-stinging fumes and the instinct to draw more air, and just when she was certain the little bastard wouldn't show, the sound of shuffling footsteps carried down from the street.

She fought the urge to sigh in relief. It wouldn't go well, and she needed all the oxygen she could get. Shifting slightly for a better view, she peered through the gap formed by two of the dumpsters.

An oversized coat drawn around him till he looked like an anthill with a head on top, Mud edged into the alleyway entrance, his gaze twitching around on overdrive the entire time. Looking first one way, then immediately the other, he barely paused at the sight of Harris before continuing his scan of the alley and the street.

"Where are they?" he asked. "The people you saw?"

"A couple blocks from here," Harris answered. He gestured to the sedan. "We can take my car."

Mud started down the alley. From the corner of her eye, she saw Spider and Samson shift position, getting ready to move.

"So what'd they look like?" Mud asked.

"Eh, African-American guy, maybe early twenties or so. Thought I remembered him from Utah."

Mud froze. Across the alley, Ashe heard Samson give a low growl of irritation that would have put Nathaniel to shame.

"Really?" Mud asked, suddenly thoughtful. "You saw him here?"

"You know someone who looks like that? Good, then you'll–"

"Anyone else with him?"

Harris shrugged. "We'll see when we get there, right? Hop in."

Mud didn't move. "You sure you didn't see anybody?"

For a heartbeat, Harris eyed him, and when he spoke again, she could almost hear the cop in his voice. "Why?"

"No reason."

Harris paused, and then dropped his hand from the door handle. His brow furrowing, he circled around the front of the vehicle, nothing in his demeanor to indicate any awareness he was blocking Mud's exit.

"What's going on, buddy?" Harris asked, his tone concerned. "You don't tell me what's up, I can't help."

Mud hesitated and then glanced around furtively. "Okay, look," he confessed. "That guy? Two problems. One, if he's here, it means the good ol' bloody queen probably is as well. And two, he's supposed to be dead. Brogan promised me after I tipped him off about that train station where he and his little 'Hunters' were hiding that he'd have his people kill them all."

"Oh, that son of a…" Samson snarled under his breath, his hand tightening on his gun.

"Really?" Harris asked, sounding worried. "Well, I'm not sure it's the same–"

"I'm not going to find out," Mud interrupted, ignoring the other man's motion to get in the car. "The guy's a cold-blooded killer, Detective. His whole group are. And that bitch girlfriend of his…"

He gave an exaggerated shudder and started back for the street.

"Wait," Harris protested, keeping himself between the man and the exit. "We still need to check before telling Brogan."

"You check," Mud snapped, trying to shuffle around the detective.

Elias glanced to the others. "Move!"

She fled the stench of the dumpsters on the heels of Nathaniel, with Spider and Samson barely a heartbeat behind. At the sound of their footsteps, Mud looked back, his beady eyes going wide, and then he spun faster than she'd have imagined the little man could move. Reacting quickly, Harris darted between him and the street again, his hands raised to stop Mud from escaping.

A gun appeared in Mud's hand like a conjuring trick and Harris barely had time to tense.

Fire left her, charring the man's fist and knocking the gun wide. Bullets struck the brick wall as the weapon went flying and Mud collapsed to the ground, clutching his hand and howling.

Nathaniel strode up to Mud and hauled him from the concrete to slam him into the brick wall. Moving past them, Elias headed for the alley entrance to check the street, while Spider and Samson watched the little man as though waiting for the moment when the wizards would be done with him. To one side, Cole scanned the ground for the gun, and then scowled when he realized it'd fallen through a grate to the sewers.

Harris just stared at her.

Uncomfortably, she avoided his stunned gaze as she came up behind Nathaniel.

"You… you…" Mud panted. "She–"

"How do we get inside the prison?" Nathaniel demanded.

"She burned my hand!" Mud shrieked into the wizard's face.

Nathaniel grimaced at the man's breath and then pressed him harder into the wall. "I won't ask again."

Mud just choked, his focus returning to his blackened skin. Nathaniel growled in annoyance, casting a glance to Elias.

"Switch," Elias said, jerking his head at the street.

Nathaniel waited for the wizard to join him and then promptly dropped Mud to the ground. Ignoring the cry of pained alarm behind him, Nathaniel headed for the alley entrance.

Disgust tingeing his expression, Elias crouched down in front of Mud. "You have a choice," he told the whimpering man. "You help us, and maybe we'll heal your hand. Or you don't help us–" He glanced over his shoulder. "–and we leave you with them."

Mud's beady gaze went to Spider and Samson.

"What's it going to be?" Elias asked.

Contempt twisted through the pain on Mud's face. "I'm not afraid of them."

Expressionless, Spider drew her gun, letting it hang by her side, and instantly, the little man went pale, his scorn melting.

"Uh-huh," Elias agreed. "I can see that." He sighed, pushing back to his feet. "Guess we're done, then."

He motioned to Spider and Samson as he started to turn away, only to stop at an inarticulate gurgle from Mud. Elias glanced back.

"W-what do you want to know?" Mud asked, his eyes locked on Spider and the gun.

"How do we reach the prisoners?"

"Prisoners?"

"Oh, for pity's sake," Elias said, motioning to Spider and Samson again.

"No!" Mud protested. "I mean… you want the Taliesin? They're down the street. In the building down the street. Um, it's the–"

"We know which one it is."

"Oh. Uh…" Mud looked between the wizard and the cripples. "Can you just have them–"

"No," Elias replied. "What can you tell us about the security?"

Mud swallowed hard, his eyes darting around the alley. "They, uh… if they know I…"

Spider shifted position slightly.

"Oh-two-seven-eight-three," Mud said, the words tripping over each other to come out. "Code for the door. Access pad's behind the third brick left of the handle. The code is oh-two–"

"Fine," Elias cut in. "What other defenses are there?"

The little man looked desperate, his eyes twitching from Spider to the wizard and back. "Uh, guards?" he offered. "Four of them. Security cameras too. Three outside the building, two watching the side streets, and six inside."

"Are the cameras connected to anything at Chaunessy Tower?"

Mud shook his head. "Just the monitors inside the prison. They've got an alarm, though. If the guards trigger it, it goes off at the main building."

"Magical defenses the same?"

Mud nodded.

"What about guards on the surrounding buildings? Anyone watching for an attack?"

The man scoffed desperately. "They didn't think you'd come for the *Taliesin*. They thought your plan was to go after the kid."

Mud stared at him as though questioning why the wizards weren't doing that anyway.

Elias ignored the expression. Stepping away from the little man, he glanced briefly to Nathaniel and then drew out his phone. Dialing quickly, he kept an eye to Mud as he waited for the call to go through.

She turned away, her stomach beginning to churn again.

"Four guards," Elias said succinctly when Cornelius picked up the phone. "Eleven cameras. And we have the door code."

"Ashe," Spider said.

She hesitated, and then looked over. Behind her, Elias continued to relay the information Mud had given them.

"The plan?" the girl pressed.

Ashe's mouth tightened.

"Nathaniel's going in," Cole supplied. "They set it all up on the way here."

Spider looked between them. "He's a wizard," she said, as if uncertain why they weren't seeing the obvious. "The guards'll spot him a mile away and call the Blood."

Cole grimaced. "She's going to take his magic."

Spider's brow climbed.

"Bound wizards aren't visible the same as unbound ones," Ashe explained quietly. "Not as much, anyway. And he just needs to make Mud get him to the door. Once the defenses are dropped, Elias'll open a portal and we'll head in."

Spider watched her for a moment. "And if they do spot him?"

She didn't answer.

The girl rolled her eyes. "Screw that." Turning sharply, she looked to Mud. "Hey, scumbag. Layout of the inside."

"Huh?" Mud sputtered.

"Spider, what are you–" Ashe started.

"Guards, moron. Alarms." Spider continued, ignoring her. "Where are they?"

Across the alley, Elias cut off the phone conversation, his brow drawing down.

"I– uh," Mud tried.

"What are you doing?" Elias asked, covering the cell with one hand as he came closer.

"There's no way the guards'll buy that weasel capturing your friend on his own," Spider told him. "So we're changing the plan. I'm going."

Mud blanched.

"No, you're not," Ashe retorted incredulously.

"Spider," Samson said.

"Miss, you aren't–" Elias began.

"This isn't a debate," Spider said over the protests. "You need somebody they won't suspect, and I'm sorry, but your guy there isn't it." She looked to Elias. "You just make sure you get that portal open without hitting me and–"

"I'll do it."

Spider turned at the sound of Harris' voice. "Excuse me?"

The detective looked between them with varying degrees of discomfort. "I said I'll do it. I'll get the door open."

Spider scoffed. "No way. No offense, but we've known you for five minutes. And you tried to kill her. So you're staying."

"Of everyone here, I'm the least likely to raise their suspicion," Harris countered. "If for no other reasons than the ones you just named. And I'm not a wizard or a cripple, so it's not even going to cross their minds that I could be a threat." He paused. "It never does."

Spider's eyes narrowed, but Elias cut in before she could speak. "You said they wouldn't believe it if you just showed up there," the councilman argued.

"Alone, no," Harris allowed with a grimace. "But with Mud…"

Elias shook his head. "No," he stated. "For *exactly* the reasons she just named. We're doing this the way we planned. Nathaniel still has the best chance—"

"The hell he does," Samson interrupted.

"What?" Elias snapped.

Samson strode past him to Mud, and snagged the man by the collar when he tried to flee. "The Taliesin need to see a prisoner. But not your attack dog there; he'll just get you killed. Even if they buy the cop and that idiot capturing him, you're still risking everything on the hope your queen's infallible and the guards won't just see through whatever the hell she's planning to do.

"Now, normally," he added, "I wouldn't give a shit. But there's still a chance that king'll be able to hurt my people just because we've talked to you, so we really need to keep you lot alive till we can throw Bloody Queen Ashe at him and let them kill each other."

He hauled Mud up from the ground, ignoring the man's indignant squawk. "You told him you needed his help with someone connected to the queen," he continued to Harris, "and my guess is the twerp here shared that around before leaving. They won't believe for a minute that he'd bring you with him for no reason, but I doubt they'll buy him being tough enough to drag anyone in on his own either. So let's get this over with already. Escort your prisoner back."

"Sam," Spider protested.

He glanced to her. "Shoot the bastards if they try anything."

She paused, and Ashe couldn't tell if she was breathing. But after a heartbeat, the girl just nodded, whatever she'd been about to say vanishing as though it'd never been.

"Gladly," she answered.

"You are not deciding this—" Elias started, looking between the two of them.

With a shove, Samson sent Mud stumbling past Nathaniel into the street. Spider's gun rose instantly, tracking the little man.

"Sorry, wizard," he replied coldly. He looked to Harris. "Coming?"

Alarm in his eyes, Harris hesitated before nodding. Crossing the distance between them, he took Samson's arms, pinning them back as though handcuffed, and then led him after Mud.

"This is—" Elias started.

"Elias," Ashe interrupted tightly. "Just… get ready, okay?"

Incredulity showed in his eyes, but he buried it swiftly and looked to Nathaniel. "Tell me when they get close," he said, traces of disbelief still in his voice. He raised the phone to his ear again. "Never mind. Get ready to move on our signal."

He hung up and headed for the door near the end of the alley.

Ashe followed Spider to the entrance. Ignoring Nathaniel's dark glare, the girl sank down by the edge of the wall, her eyes trained on the men making their way down the street and her fingers playing over the grip of her gun.

"You didn't have to do this," she said to Spider quietly, keeping out of sight against the brick wall. "Either of you."

Spider didn't answer.

Ashe looked back to the alley. Halfway between her and Elias, Cole was watching them as though he didn't even know where to begin with all the things that'd potentially just gone wrong.

"No one's better with portals than Elias," she told Spider. "It'll be fine."

"It better be," the girl answered without looking away from the street, and Ashe couldn't tell if the threat in her voice was for the wizards or Samson.

Or both.

Ashe closed her eyes briefly and then turned away. Heading toward the door, she stopped a few feet from Elias, waiting.

Silence settled over the alley, undercut by the distant sound of traffic and a tension so thick, she could barely breathe. She wasn't sure what she'd do if gunfire came from down the street, though probably, that wouldn't be her first indication something had gone wrong. Her gaze slid back to Spider, watching the girl for any sign of change, while Elias stood nearby, one hand on the doorframe and his eyes locked on Nathaniel for much the same reason.

And the seconds dragged on.

Chapter Twenty-Three

Gripping the young man's arm, Harris made himself walk down the sidewalk as though he couldn't feel the gun aimed at his back or the cameras aimed at his front.

For all intents and purposes, he should have died five minutes ago, and the knowledge was disturbing to say the least. It wasn't really the gunshots or the near miss; those were upsetting, but he'd been shot at before, though never at that close of range. It was the circumstances around it, and the reason it hadn't gone the way Mud planned.

Ashley'd just saved his life.

He drew a breath, scanning the street and the intersection ahead as cars sped along both. Of course, she could have just reacted to the sight of the gun. Operated on instinct, as it were. That'd be a perfectly plausible explanation, given how tightly wound she obviously was right now.

Except Mud hadn't been aiming at her. And wizards weren't threatened by guns anyway. Not when they saw the weapon coming and could block the bullets, to hell with the ricochet.

He'd learned that after he shot her a month ago.

His shoulders twitched involuntarily beneath his jacket. At the motion, the young man glanced over, a question and a glare sharing space in his dark eyes.

Harris grimaced and returned to his surveillance of the street.

She wasn't a kid. She'd never been a kid, no matter what she tried to pretend. And there wasn't any way to prove that what she said was true. Blaming the opposition was the oldest trick in the book. She still could have killed her family, and the man at the boathouse could have been her victim, along with all the other bodies that'd littered the floor. For that matter, her cripple allies gave him the impression that, if he ran their prints through state or federal databases, they'd probably have more than a few unsolved murders of their own to their names. And Cole's faith she hadn't been behind any of it could simply be a wishful extrapolation from the fact that she did, at least, seem to care about the little girl.

Then again, he had to wonder how much more he was willing to chalk up to Cole just being confused. And that didn't bring into it the look on her face at the news Malden was alive.

He scowled. She could have been acting. They could have planned it, her and Cole, to allay his suspicions.

And this really was all about him.

He fought off another twitch, cursing himself for being so distracted when there was a gun pointing at his back. Most people, even a fair amount of cops, probably couldn't have hit him at his current distance from the alley. But there was something in the way the young man's girlfriend had taken the order to shoot him so dispassionately that left him reluctant to trust she fell into that group.

Besides, anyone could get a lucky shot. He almost had.

Letting out a breath, he pushed the thought away as he glanced to the young man. Everything else aside, 'allies' might have been a strong word, at least where this guy was concerned. Anger still etched his face, nearly unchanged since his abrupt resolution to the standoff in the alley, and if his words a few minutes before were any indication, he seemed only a half-step shy of shooting the Merlin queen himself. Given everything she might have done – things Cole swore she hadn't done – it raised more than a few questions.

And meant he possibly wasn't as mistaken in this as he was really starting to fear.

"You're one of the guys who helped Ashley back in Monfort," he said, keeping his voice neutral for all that he couldn't quite make his pulse slow down.

The young man ignored him.

"You're one of her supporters?"

A muscle of the guy's jaw jumped, but any answer was forestalled by a snort from Mud.

"Weasel," the young man snapped. "Shut up and hide your hand already."

A surly expression twisted Mud's face as he glanced back, but he tucked his burned hand into his coat nonetheless.

"Your name's Sam?" Harris pressed.

Briefly, the young man pinned him with a glare. "No."

Mud looked back with a smirk. "It's *Samson.*"

The young man's eyes took on a strong tinge of threat, and Mud swiftly turned away.

"Okay," Harris continued carefully. "Well, Samson, I just ask because, for someone who helped Ashley escape the police, you don't sound like you care for her that much."

He let the implicit question hang in the air.

"I never have," Samson said finally, his voice low as his eyes flicked over the open apartment windows above them. "I'm just here to keep my people from dying. Now shut it. The wizards might have spies in the buildings."

Harris glanced to him. "But you don't believe she was behind all those deaths earlier this year?"

The muscles in Samson's jaw jumped again, and he could see the young man draw a slow breath.

"I said shut up, cop," he answered shortly.

He studied Samson, his brow drawing down. He couldn't decide what to make of the response, any more than he could the expression on the young man's face or his tone. He almost looked like he *wanted* to be angry.

Of course, Ashley could have murdered some of his people. He could just be here to keep it from happening again. And Cole could've just been clinging to the hope she didn't do it because he wanted to save the kid.

And she could have just reacted to the sight of the gun.

He scowled. Four wizards ahead and nearly that amount behind, and he couldn't stop woolgathering. He'd agreed to do this so he could help rescue that little girl, because regardless, he had to hope an eight-year-old was still an innocent in this mess. But if he kept this up, he'd blow that goal and all the answers to his questions would be irrelevant, because he'd have long since gotten himself killed.

They paused at the curb as a car rolled past, its throbbing bass setting the looser bits of its body buzzing. He glanced over, catching sight of Mud shifting his weight as his eyes darted from the prison to the street.

"Spider *will* hit you," Samson warned quietly, his mouth barely moving. "And I'm still armed."

Mud scowled and headed across the road. His hand gripping Samson's arm, Harris followed.

Tall brick buildings flanked the empty parking lot, and tiny black cameras were mounted high on their corners. Faded yellow lines crisscrossed the cement, and the handicap spots closer to the old store featured only bare posts for nonexistent signs. The road seemed to extend infinitely behind them, and as he glanced over his shoulder, it took him a moment to find the alleyway where the others were hiding.

He drew a breath, moving to keep himself between the cameras and Samson's unbound hands as he trailed Mud across the lot. Brown paper covered the inside of the windows and door, blocking any view of the interior, and as the little man came up to the entrance, a camera above the doorway turned to track his progress.

Mud paused. His gaze crept toward the camera staring down on them like a glass eye.

Harris' pulse accelerated and he fought to keep from looking up as well. "You think the Blood will give a rip you don't want to help the Merlin?" he murmured tensely. "Just standing here means you're in too deep in their eyes."

Mud's beady gaze slid to him and a sneer edged onto his dirt-smudged face.

The door flew open. Harris jumped, his hand flinching for the gun he no longer had.

"What the hell is this?" a bulky wizard demanded, eyeing Mud briefly before turning a baleful look on Harris and Samson. "Who gave you permission to bring them here?"

Mud swallowed, his arrogance vanishing. "Uh, they made–"

"He asked me to come," Harris cut in hurriedly, jerking his chin toward Mud.

The wizard's gaze panned to the little man growing steadily antsier on the concrete stoop.

"You think he could bring this one in on his own?" Harris continued with a scoff. "He spent half the trip back panicking that the guy'd get free and kill him." He glanced past the wizard to the building's interior. "Come on. Move back so we can get this guy inside. We look suspicious enough without standing out here like kids doing a fundraiser."

The wizard didn't move, the muscles in his jaw flexing. "Leave him," he ordered. "Head back to Chaunessy."

"And what?" Harris retorted. "Watch you fry him when he tries to escape? We think he's got information on the Merlin queen; he's not going quietly. And Brogan'll like us heading in there a lot more than he'll like this loser ending up dead."

For a heartbeat, the wizard eyed him, as though blatantly questioning what Harris could possibly do that he could not. A smirk twitched his lip.

Swiftly, he reached out and snagged Samson's arm. Magic flared around him briefly, making the young man gasp in pain, and then the wizard flung Samson through the doorway.

"Hey!" Harris snapped, starting after him, only to run into the wizard's grasp. "You–"

The gunshot sounded all the louder for the close walls of the hardware store and suddenly, the wizard's eyes went wide. Gasping wetly, the man lurched forward, his grip clenching painfully tight and his weight pinning Harris to the doorframe.

From within the store, he could hear Samson firing at the wizards. The dead man sagged, crushing the sharp edge of the doorjamb into Harris' spine.

A bullet ricocheted from the wizards' defenses to hit the wall inches from his head.

"Move!" Samson shouted.

With a grunt, Harris shoved the body away and then stumbled into the store.

Three wizards were staring at him. More crowded a caged-in area on the far side of the room. Monitors were scattered across the counter to the right of the doorway, each screen showing black-and-white segments of the store. Hands raised in front of him, he straightened, hoping the plan hadn't changed even though he and Samson were now inside the building.

"I don't want any trouble," he said cautiously as he inched away from the open door.

The closest wizard flung up a hand and he barely had time to leap aside as a blast of electricity scorched the wall behind where he'd been standing. He crashed to the floor, pain shooting through his arm at the impact and gritty linoleum ripping at him as he slid.

Someone shouted. He twisted on the ground to see the three wizards' magic lash out at the door. Elias' defenses took the blast, the electricity chasing across the shield surrounding him like lightning over glass.

Ashley stepped through the portal and the nearest man stumbled as though something had been physically ripped from him. At the sight, one of the wizards went for the counter, his fingers outstretched for a button beneath the red laminate top.

Fire hit him before he made it two steps.

Eyes wide, the other wizards spun, tearing for the door at the far end of the room.

Elias' magic propelled them into the wall, where they crumpled to the floor and didn't move again.

Nathaniel emerged from the portal, the eye-crossing shadows vanishing behind him. He scanned the fallen wizards briefly, and then turned his attention on Ashley.

An uncomfortable look flashed across her face. "We couldn't wait," she said, almost as though defending herself. "Go see if the others–"

She cut off, and Nathaniel glanced back and then stepped aside as the girl calling herself Spider drove Mud ahead of her into the room. With a shove, the girl sent him to the ground to one side of the door, giving no sign of hearing his pained cry as he crashed to the tile, and then she headed for Samson.

A step behind her, Cole came inside. "Everyone alright?"

Ashley didn't answer. For a heartbeat, she watched Samson climb to his feet, and then she started for the cage at the opposite end of the store. The wizards followed, leaving Cole to come behind.

Carefully, Harris rose, wincing as an ache throbbed through him. Brushing grit off his arm, he trailed the others across the room.

In a twenty-by-thirty-foot rectangle, the cage occupied one large corner of the store. Metal pipes stretched through the drop ceiling to the floor, their bases driven into the ground so hard, debris from the concrete foundation surrounded them. A barred door interrupted the cage halfway along its longest side, the hinges melted to a pole and a hefty lock holding it closed.

But no one was paying much attention. To a person, their eyes were fixed on the men and women watching them from behind the steel-barred walls.

Not one of them was untouched. Scorch marks covered faces and broken blisters left red tracks across arms and legs alike. Makeshift bandages wrapped their wounds, the bloodstained fabric torn from their shirts and pants and tied over burns that seemed to be festering.

A small breath escaped Cole.

"Open the door," Ashley ordered, her eyes never leaving the people in the cage.

Elias paused, scanning the bars, and at his hesitation, she looked over.

"Security," he explained. "If the door's wired to any alarms…"

"Hey, Mud," Ashley snapped over her shoulder. "Any alarms on the door?"

On the ground, Mud glared.

Ashley's hand burst into flame.

"No," Mud said grudgingly. "Jamison took the Taliesin's magic. Why would anybody need alarms?"

Her eyes weighed him briefly, and then she turned back to Elias.

The wizard fried the lock with a single touch. The door swung open.

For a moment, no one inside moved, and then a few turned as a rustling came from the shadows in the back corner of the cage. Favoring his right leg heavily, an old man limped into the light. Dark circles hung under his eyes and the button-down shirt beneath his torn jacket was brown with old bloodstains, but when he came to a stop at the center of the cell, he straightened as though none of it was real.

"Hello, your highness," he said neutrally.

"Councilman Brentworth," Ashley replied. Her eyes flicked over the other prisoners. "Your people can go. We're not here to hurt them. We just…" An ironic expression tried to push onto her face, succeeding for only a heartbeat before it vanished. "We need your help again."

Harris' brow drew down at the last word.

Brentworth regarded her. "Who are your companions?" he asked casually. "Those two, I recall, but the others…" His gaze skimmed almost dismissively over Spider, Samson and Harris before coming to rest on Cole. "I confess, they are not as familiar."

Ashley didn't move. "They're friends."

Brentworth's face took on a patronizing cast. "You want my help, your majesty, and yet–"

"Cole."

Brentworth's gaze returned to the young man.

For a moment, Cole watched him, something strange in his expression. "My name's Cole," he repeated.

"Cole Jamison, I presume?" Brentworth elaborated.

The rise of tension was almost palpable, and Harris felt himself shift his weight in response, for all that he had no idea what he would do. The prisoners had no magic, that much Mud had said.

But an angry mob didn't really need that anyway.

"Stop it, Brentworth," Ashley said, moving slightly as though to put herself between them and Cole. She looked to the prisoners. "Jamison's got what he needs to recreate the spell, and he's going to push it until it kills everyone who gets in his way. And it won't just be you. Your families. Your friends. Anyone, no matter where they're hiding. We're here because we want to stop him, and because I don't really give a damn about the war. I want it over. So does he." She twitched her head toward Cole. "And if you're smart, you will too."

She glanced to Brentworth. "We need to get inside Chaunessy to stop Jamison. We want you to help us do that."

Harris watched the man as he paused, weighing her words.

"You're one of the Taliesin Council?" Cole asked into the silence.

If possible, Ashley seemed to grow more tense. Harris' eyes narrowed warily.

"Retired," Brentworth said.

"Were you retired eight years ago?"

"Cole," Ashley interjected.

The young man glanced to her.

"Lily," she said quietly.

His face tightened. He looked back to the councilor, and then his gaze seemed to catch on the prisoners.

"Heal them," he said tensely.

Ashley hesitated, something almost like guilt flashing over her face. "We don't have–"

"Have a guard come back and heal them," Cole ordered. He glanced to Nathaniel. "Someone you can spare." He looked to Brentworth. "And you guarantee the guard's safety."

The old man eyed him up and down, but after a moment, a bit of the regal arrogance seemed to fade from his expression. Carefully, he nodded once.

"Ashe," Cole continued.

Ashley hesitated. Her eyes flicked over the wounded and Brentworth, and then she nodded as well. She turned to Nathaniel. "Do it. Have the guard get them out of the city when they're done."

The wizard's face darkened, but he drew out his cell phone. A moment later, shadows swirled in the store doorway. A stockily built man emerged from the grayness and, as the magic disappeared behind him, he nodded to Nathaniel and Ashley and then took position by the door, waiting.

Ashley looked to Brentworth.

"Very well," he acquiesced. He limped closer. "What do you require?"

"The tunnel beneath Chaunessy," Cole said flatly. "How do we access it?"

Brentworth's mouth tightened. "You will do best to have my assistance with that."

Elias scoffed. "Again?"

"*That* was not my fault," Brentworth replied.

"You could've said something about not recognizing those guards."

"The Council possessed hundreds–"

"Point is," Elias interrupted. "We're not dragging you along again. Tell us where this tunnel lets out and we'll handle it from there."

"Happily," Brentworth said. "One mile west of Chaunessy, subbasement of the Presidio Hotel, hallway on the southernmost side. But the *point*, sir, is that the tunnel is hidden. You will not locate it without my help."

"Fine," Ashley cut in before Elias could speak. "Heal his leg and let's get out of here."

Without another word, she walked away from the cell.

Harris watched her go. Expressionless, she stopped beside the open door, staying to the shadows with her eyes on the horizon toward Chaunessy. Stoic as ever, Nathaniel came up behind her, saying nothing and watching the road, while Mud scooted away from them both.

"Out of curiosity," Brentworth began.

Harris glanced over. The man's tone was idle, though pain fought through his casual demeanor. Limping from the cell, he crossed to a plastic chair a few feet from the bars and then lowered himself carefully down. Behind him, the prisoners started to slip from the cage, staying widely clear of everyone else in the room. Silently, the guard by the door went to join them.

"My nephew, Lucas," the old man continued.

Ashley looked back at him.

Brentworth's eyebrow climbed questioningly. "Have you any word of him?"

He could have been asking about the weather, but Ashley tensed all the same. She glanced to Elias.

The wizard shook his head. "I didn't see," he said quietly.

Brentworth hissed as Elias did something to his leg. "I understand," he replied when the pain seemed to clear.

Harris glanced between them. "Lucas Brentworth?"

Everyone looked over at him and he tried not to grimace at the scrutiny. He really hated being the focus of so many people's attention, especially when most still looked on the fence about killing him.

"He's okay. At least, last time I heard. He was checked into Croftsburg Memorial about a month ago, assumed to be the victim of a hit-and-run. He disappeared after the doctors patched him up."

"How do you know all that?" Ashley asked.

He paused. "Malden's been looking into any names I overheard. He didn't find Charles Brentworth–" He nodded toward the old man. "–but Lucas came up."

She turned away. He hesitated, and then walked closer till a glare from Nathaniel stopped him.

"Ashley," he said.

"Ashe," she countered.

The sharp response seemed almost reflexive. His brow drew down.

She glanced back at him. "It's Ashe," she repeated firmly before looking away again.

He nodded carefully. "Ashe," he amended. "How–"

"Back off," Spider growled behind him.

He turned, not having heard her come up.

"Ashe," the girl continued, slipping a cell phone back into her pocket. "Bus and the others are ready with the cars, whenever you want to go."

Drawing a breath, Ashe nodded. Behind them, Brentworth rose, stretching his leg and then walking over with only a shadow of his former limp.

"After you, your highness," the old man said.

Ashe paused, and then glanced up at Harris.

"We survive this," she told him. "We'll help Malden too."

He stared after her as she followed Nathaniel out the door. He hadn't been intending to ask that. It hadn't even occurred to him, since no one had ever suggested it and he hadn't thought it was possible anyway. Not so long after the fact, and with as much damage as she'd done. He'd just wondered what'd happened to make the Queen of Merlin and a retired member of the Taliesin Council work together.

"Hey," Spider snapped.

He blinked and turned to see her looking at Mud. Weapon in hand, she jerked her chin toward the empty cell.

"Go," she ordered.

Mud glared.

Across the room, Samson drew his gun, his eyes showing only ice and a serious evaluation of the benefits of just shooting the little man.

Spider glanced to him, her own expression nearly the same.

Mud climbed to his feet and inched toward the cage, still watching them both.

"Wizard," Spider called to Elias. "Care to help us out here?"

Elias snorted, and then slammed the door behind Mud. Magic flickered over his hand, melting the lock to the metal around it and then racing across the bars, leaving them shimmering as though faintly electrified.

He looked to Spider. "Good enough for you?"

A smile twitched her lip and she nodded. The gun disappeared back beneath her jacket as she headed out the door.

Samson followed, with Elias coming behind. Several yards away, the guard moved among the prisoners, triaging their wounds and then bending to heal the worst of their injuries without a word. Tense and expressionless, Cole watched him, and then turned, striding quickly from the room.

A noise like a bug zapper came from the cell, followed by a screech of pain.

Harris glanced over. Sucking his fingers, Mud eyed the bars hatefully before his gaze caught on him.

"Hey," the little man said, hope practically dripping from his tone. "Hey, buddy. Look, I–" His eyes darted to the wizards and then he lowered his voice, inching as close to the bars as he dared. "We're together in this, right? I mean, I know you're just playing along with them. Waiting for their guard to go down. So come on. Now's your chance. Alarm's right over there. All you gotta do is press it and we're golden, right? Blood'll come, get us the hell out of here, and stop that bitch at the same time."

Harris didn't move.

"Okay, forget the Blood," Mud amended. "Screw the bastards, right? But they'll get us out of here, and then we can head for the hills. Just push the alarm, okay? Come on."

Harris glanced to the street. By the curb, three sedans were pulling to a stop.

"Dammit, Detective!" Mud snapped. "You owe me! I got you away from them! It's your turn now! And think about who you're dealing with here. That's Bloody Queen *fucking* Ashe! Don't you remember what she's done? She'll burn you alive the second she doesn't need you anymore!"

He looked back at the little man trapped behind the melted lock and the electrified wall. Red-faced, Mud quivered, his fists clenched as though he was fighting the urge to punch the bars.

Harris shook his head. "Go to hell, Mud," he said, and then followed the others out the door.

Chapter Twenty-Four

The Presidio Hotel rose twenty stories from the street in a wall of dark brick and ornately trimmed windows. Revolving doors of mirrored glass allowed no glimpse of the world inside the hotel, though the arched window towering above the entryway revealed a daunting chandelier and levels of marble-pillared galleries, while the red Lamborghini pulling into the drive hinted at the customary clientele.

In the back seat of a stolen sedan, Ashe tensed as a valet glanced toward their car. For a moment, the man paused, his brow furrowing, and then he shook his head at himself and pulled his attention squarely back to the Lamborghini.

She exhaled, her nails working tightly into her palm as her magic faded back inside.

Spider and the other cripples in the car ahead would have already been getting out of here if they'd seen any Blood around. She knew that. She'd been reminding herself of it for the past fifteen minutes. But so close to their goal, only a mile from Chaunessy and her sister and everything that would entail, little things like logic didn't make her feel better.

Or address all the other allies Jamison had at his disposal.

Her gaze slid back to the nearby buildings and the painfully ordinary skyscraper hiding beyond their walls.

"Still clear?"

She flinched as Elias spoke. Studying the hotel, he made a sound of acknowledgment at the response from the wizard on the other end of the line.

"Rear entrance's still good," he told Nathaniel as he hung up.

The large wizard didn't respond, but he followed the lead vehicle into the service drive alongside the hotel. Brick walls closed claustrophobically around them, and when they arrived in the tiny lot behind the hotel, Gavin and five other guards were waiting. As the cars pulled to a stop, Gavin gestured to the guards and quickly, two of them broke off from the group and hurried back down the alley to check the street.

"Inside," Gavin said shortly as they climbed out. "First left, rear entrance to the ballroom."

Nathaniel nodded and headed for the door. Striding after him, Gavin took up position by the steps, watching the rooftops before following them all inside.

The plush hallway was eerily silent, the noise of the lobby lost this far into the building. Dense maroon carpet deadened their footsteps, while the gold-rimmed light fixtures seemed to leave too many shadows in the richly decorated corridor. Scanning it all guardedly, Nathaniel rounded the first turn and strode toward the ballroom. The handle clanked as he twisted it open and then the door swung back with a pneumatic hiss to reveal two dozen Merlin standing beneath the chandeliers hanging above the pale marble floor.

Cornelius looked over as they came in, his hand rising to halt the words of an anxious-looking guard. Anger simmered beneath his impassive expression, though it faltered into swiftly hidden relief as he spotted her.

"You are unharmed? The guard just informed me there were wounded."

"Prisoners," Elias supplied.

Cornelius said nothing, his gaze running over her as if to ensure that the other wizard wasn't lying. She looked away uncomfortably.

"Taliesin?" Nathaniel asked, curtailing any further questions.

"On the streets and rooftops a quarter mile from here," Gavin replied as he pulled the ballroom door closed. A brief flash of magic twisted over the lock and then he turned, walking back toward them. "And every block farther on to Chaunessy."

With barely concealed gratitude for the topic change, the guard by Cornelius nodded. "They appear to be concentrating on holding the perimeter. Sentries have doubled in the past hour, but we've seen little sign of patrols farther into the city."

"Not like they don't know where we're headed," Elias said dryly.

Gavin bowed his head in acknowledgement. "Though hopefully not how."

"Your team ready?" Nathaniel asked.

"Soon," Gavin replied.

The other guard's gaze twitched toward the cripples. Discomfort flashed through his eyes, swiftly buried.

Nathaniel's face darkened at the sight. "Go," he ordered both men. "I want you on the streets in five."

"Yes, sir," Gavin said.

The other man was already heading for the Merlin guard.

"This tunnel," Elias said, looking to Brentworth. "Where does it come out?"

"The lower basement of Chaunessy, below the parking garage. The level primarily consists of service areas for water pipes, so I doubt they will have bothered to upgrade security with cameras and such."

"You heard of them doing anything like that?" Elias asked, turning to Harris.

Standing by the door, Harris blinked, pulling his gaze from the guards. "Nothing in the basement, no."

"What about elsewhere? What emergency measures do they have prepared?"

The detective's mouth tightened.

"Look," Elias snapped. "While it's nice that you agreed to use your thumbprint to get us in the door and all, what we really need is the Blood's current security layout. So..." He gestured impatiently.

Harris exhaled. "Like I told you, cameras on the doors, with guards and alarms as well. Entry's controlled with codes and biometrics. As for emergencies..." He shrugged. "The Blood learned from the way they took Chaunessy. They made changes everywhere. Biggest are the barriers between every few floors, in addition to the one outside. Jamison also controls a separate one around the penthouse. If they find out we've gotten past their outer defenses, the security office will enable the barriers to keep you from using those portal things to maneuver within the building. Then they'll relay the location of the tripped defenses to their troops and send them to, well–" He grimaced. "–kill you."

Elias ignored the comment. "Where's the security office?"

"Fifteenth floor."

"How many stationed there?"

She turned away as the barrage of questions continued. Cole had wandered to one side of the ballroom, his gaze on the floor as if reading meaning from the flecks in the marble. Closer to the door, the cripples were ignoring everyone. Blackjack had dropped the large duffle bag he'd been carrying and Spider was crouched over it, checking the rifles inside. Bus and Samson stood with several others nearby, conferring quietly with short glances to the walls as though they could see through them to the buildings beyond.

"And you are *certain* they will not have shields on the basement floor?" Cornelius interjected behind her. "It may be underground but that does not mean–"

She headed toward Spider. The tunnel had to work. She couldn't contemplate the alternative anymore.

Samson fell silent as she came closer, his face darkening, though Bus pretended not to notice.

"Your boys there don't trust us," the old man commented.

Spider glanced up, a dry note in her eyes, and Ashe tried not to grimace. Observant as hell, of course they'd seen the guard's expression a moment before. "You're Hunters," she explained awkwardly. "They've seen you as a threat for about half a decade now."

Bus' eyebrow twitched with amusement and Spider returned to the weapons, but not before Ashe caught the satisfied look on her face.

"You guys okay with this?" she asked.

"Being your decoys, you mean?" Samson retorted. "We've been sniping your kind for eight years, your majesty. We're pretty good at it."

"This is the easy part," Spider said quietly.

"The Blood are going to send everything they've got after you–"

Ashe started.

"So you make sure those wizards of yours stay out of our way," Samson finished.

Watching Spider, Ashe didn't respond. Still examining the guns, the girl didn't look up.

"Your highness," Elias called. She glanced back to see Gavin and half the guards heading for the rear door. "We're ready."

The air pressed from her chest, but she nodded. Keeping her face as blank as possible, she turned back to the others.

"See you soon, kiddo," Bus said before she could speak.

Words failed. Blinking, her eyes flicked over Samson and Blackjack before lighting on Spider.

The girl never looked away from the rifles.

Swallowing, Ashe nodded. "Yeah," she said to Bus.

Drawing a breath, she turned and walked back toward the wizards. The remaining guard flanked Cornelius and Elias as they headed for the main entrance to the ballroom, leaving Cole, Harris and Brentworth to make do on the fringes of their protection. By the rear of the group, Nathaniel waited, and she fell in beside him without a word.

"Ashe."

She glanced back.

Tossing a quick look over her shoulder to the cripples heading for the other exit, Spider jogged a few steps closer.

"You…" Spider started, and then trailed off, dropping her gaze to the floor with a frown. "Just watch your back, alright? And…"

She reached beneath her jacket and drew out one of her handguns.

"Take this," she said, roughly pushing it into Ashe's hands. "In case he gets your magic or… whatever."

For a heartbeat, the girl paused and then, with a nod more for herself than anyone, she turned and strode back toward the others. The door swung shut behind them as they disappeared into the hall.

Ashe blinked. Her brow twitched down, the reactions choked before they could fully emerge.

"The others are waiting," Nathaniel said quietly behind her.

She nodded. Automatically, her hands tucked the gun into the back of her jeans.

"Your highness. "

"I know," she snapped, the words harsher than she'd intended. She drew a breath, struggling to sound calm. "I'm coming."

She turned and started back toward the wizards.

Nathaniel's hand caught her arm. She looked up at him in shock.

"That is not what I was going to say," he told her carefully, his deep voice barely more than a murmur. "You must focus now, your majesty. The target ahead must be your only concern. Your friends chose their path, and the enemy will soon take its attention from them anyway. And until that time–" He paused. "–I have ordered each of the guard to protect the Hunters with their lives."

She stared at him. "T-thank you."

He bowed his head and then met her eyes again. "Focus," he repeated.

She took a breath and then nodded, glancing to the door. "After you."

Nathaniel paused, his lip twitching in the closest she'd ever seen him come to a smile. Without a word, he headed back toward the others, leaving her to fall in behind.

———— ◆ ————

The lobby beyond the ballroom bustled with ringing phones, luggage carts clattering over tile and a dozen different conversations mingling to form an incomprehensible din. Staying close to Nathaniel, Ashe hurried after the others, drawing a breath of relief when they finally slipped around the door to the stairs. The brightly lit concrete stairwell gave way to an equally bright hallway, where panel lights glinted off the pale linoleum and the white cinder block walls. As she stepped from the stairs, her nose wrinkled at the sting of industrial detergent hanging in the air and from the end of the long hall, multiple voices yelled over the dull roar of dryers and the rush of washing machines.

"Tunnel?" Elias asked Brentworth.

Silently, the old man moved past the guards to take the lead. Rounding a corner, he continued to a point halfway down the corridor and then stopped, regarding the wall.

Ashe watched him, her brow furrowing. The painted cinder blocks were unremarkable, though that wasn't surprising. No trace of magic lingered on their surface, however, and Brentworth didn't seem to think he needed any from the Merlin either as he pushed his fingers into several of the many indentations mottling the wall.

Nothing happened.

Her heart beginning to pound harder, she glanced to Elias, and Brentworth caught sight of the look. He gave her a humored smile, and then pressed his fingers to the indents again.

His smile faltered as nothing changed.

"Councilor," Elias started.

Brentworth pressed harder.

A faint thunk sounded within the cinder blocks, and then a section of the wall swung back, revealing nothing but the dank smell of water-soaked stone.

Brentworth's smile returned. "Magic can be such a giveaway, really," he commented, a hint of condescension returning. "Imagine, after all, the trouble we could have had if one of you walked past and noticed it?" The smile broadened. "Sometimes, it's better to hide things the old-fashioned way."

She suppressed a scowl as the old man turned back. Worries about what Jamison would do to her sister, and about what the Blood would do to her friends, and about how many people with her might die were all enough. Worry that they wouldn't even make it into the damn tunnel was more than she was ready to handle.

Exhaling slowly to calm down, she trailed Nathaniel through the narrow opening. Darkness waited ahead of them, with only the light from the hotel corridor letting her see enough not to trip as the rough concrete floor began to slope down.

Never taking his eyes from Brentworth, Cornelius waited till she passed and then raised an eyebrow at the old man. Without a word, Brentworth pulled the section of cinder blocks closed after him, killing every trace of light and sealing them inside.

Magic sparked to life in the hands of the wizards around her, illuminating the space in a pale blue glow. At a look from Cornelius, Brentworth slid past the group, leading the way by the glow of the lights behind him.

Their footsteps became the only sounds. After a while, the floor leveled out, though nothing else changed. Darkness pressed at them and the air felt too close, as though, if they weren't careful, it would run out. The concrete ceiling hung low, a thin sheen of moisture clinging to it and reflecting the blue lights.

"Who built this?" Harris whispered to Brentworth. "You?"

She closed her eyes briefly, fighting back the urge to snap at him to stop using the air.

"When we established Chaunessy as a possible hideout eight years ago, yes," Brentworth answered. "It seemed prudent that, in any given location, we create a method to evacuate those for whom portals are not an option, should they happen to be with us during an attack."

A few steps ahead, she saw Cole look away.

She tried not to wince. The math was obvious, the implication more so, and neither were the point. Not fully, anyway. The wizards were going to use portals to get through Chaunessy the moment they arrived. Meanwhile, Cole would be left in the basement, without any defenses to speak of, seventy-odd floors from where the Merlin would be trying to end the war.

But it didn't matter. Reality of the situation be damned, she knew that just like her, there wasn't a chance in hell he would've stayed behind.

"You sure it's still sound?" Harris pressed, interrupting her thoughts.

Brentworth gave him a wry look, but he didn't answer.

She swallowed and kept walking.

Minutes crawled past with all the energy of dying slugs, leaving cloying moisture that clung to her skin and slid in itchy droplets down her face. The air thickened, becoming hard to inhale, and on the shadows the blue glow danced, revealing nothing but the same endless stretch of concrete she'd crossed for the past thousand steps or more.

The floor began to slope upward.

A short gasp escaped her, and the others walked faster, even as she did the same. Climbing swiftly, they reached the top of the incline, where the tunnel came to an end in a featureless concrete wall.

Stepping around Brentworth, Elias reached for a hatch in the low ceiling.

His hand froze an inch from the handle. He swore.

"Barrier," he whispered.

Cornelius turned his face away as though restraining the urge to curse as well.

"I… why would they…" Brentworth started, his composure cracking as he stared at the hatch. "There's no reason for this. It's underground. No one could possibly get a portal around the wall defenses to–"

"Obviously," Elias interrupted. "They're thorough." He glanced to Harris. "Can you get us past it?"

The detective scanned the ceiling, a helpless expression flashing across his face. "No keypad. I can't–"

Elias cut him off with a gesture, already looking to Nathaniel, who glanced down at her.

"Like hell," she answered the implicit suggestion.

Cornelius closed his eyes, shaking his head at her, and then turned to Elias. "Break through it. We move quickly and bypass as many levels toward the security office as we can."

"They'll know the moment you do that," Harris protested.

Cornelius' expression made his knowledge of the fact clear.

"You don't have another plan?"

The wizard ignored him, turning to Brentworth. "How close is the nearest location for a portal?"

"About thirty feet down the hall in either direction," the old man answered. "Eastern door leads to the stairs. Western to a supply closet. Either are deep enough to hold a portal."

Cornelius nodded and looked back to Elias.

"Give me my gun," Harris broke in before he could speak.

The wizard regarded him flatly.

"Give me my gun," the detective repeated. "If you're bringing half the building down on us, I'm damn well going to need a weapon." He glanced to the guards, finding the one who'd been with Gavin when they searched him at the parking garage. "Well?"

The guard looked to Elias questioningly.

"Just stay out of the way," Elias said.

Harris scoffed incredulously, and then his gaze caught on Cole. "No," he stated, shaking his head. "You're *not* doing this and leaving us defenseless—"

"Give it to him," Ashe interrupted.

Elias turned to her. She didn't take her eyes from Harris. Breathing hard, the man looked like there were few worse things he could consider beyond being stuck in a hallway with wizards hell-bent on killing him and anyone else in their path.

"He has a point," she said quietly.

"Your majesty," Cornelius protested.

She looked down, the gun tucked in the back of her jeans feeling heavier than any weapon ever had. With a sharp breath, she tugged it out and extended it to Cole.

He blinked, his brow drawing down in wary surprise, but he took the gun.

"Do it," she said to the guard harshly.

The man looked from her to the councilmen, and then pulled out the weapon and handed it to Harris.

"So we going?" she asked Cornelius.

He stared at her as though he couldn't believe what she'd just done. She turned to Elias, arching an eyebrow in tacit repetition of the question.

Elias shook his head at her disbelievingly. "Punching past that thing won't hold long," he said to Cornelius.

The wizard grimaced. "As I said," he replied. "Quickly."

Elias met his eyes, and then his mouth tightened. "Yeah." He glanced to the others. "You heard the man."

He drew a breath and then lifted a hand toward the hatchway. A wry expression passed over his face.

Magic slammed into the hatch and crackled out across the ceiling, throwing sparks as it went. She ducked low, the others around her doing the same, as the electrical storm chewed at the invisible edges of the barrier, driving them back farther and farther till Elias finally dropped his hand with a gasp.

"Move!" he ordered.

Nathaniel didn't have to be told twice. Grabbing her arm, he hauled her toward the tunnel's end as a guard rushed the hatch and threw it wide.

The barrier was already expanding back toward them.

Like a tide sweeping in on all sides, the shield raced to fill the gap blown open by Elias' magic. She could almost see it coming as Nathaniel took her waist and hoisted her swiftly after the guards through the opening, and as she tumbled to the basement floor, she felt it rush by her through the dark concrete. Cornelius and Elias leapt after him, propelled by magic as much as muscle, with Cole and Harris scrambling through the hatchway on their heels.

A shriek rang through the hall. She shoved off the ground, staring in confused horror.

In the hatch, a guard hung suspended halfway through the blue-green pool of opalescent magic filling the opening.

Nathaniel snagged her arm, spinning her back toward him as the screaming began and the smell of burning flesh permeated the air. "Go!" he barked roughly.

The wizards ran past her, racing for the storage closet.

Shadows swallowed the doorway before they'd made it ten feet. The guards skidded, their magic surrounding them, as Cornelius turned for the stairs.

A portal was already appearing behind them.

Taliesin poured into the hall.

Magic flew at her from both sides, striking her defenses hard. Lightning came from everywhere, lashing out at the Merlin and ripping back into the Taliesin, and the cinder-block walls disintegrated into ballistic debris from the blasts. Bullets hit shields, ricocheting away to meet magic with explosions of their own, and all around her, people were yelling.

She looked back, spotting Cole and Harris crouched against the wall with Brentworth ducked nearby.

Electricity raced at them.

She ripped it from the air and threw it at the Taliesin by the stairwell.

"Run!" she shouted.

Harris grabbed Cole's arm and bolted for the stairs as the portal vanished.

Magic hit her from behind, crackling over her defenses and making her stumble. Immediately, Cornelius struck back, and she heard screams as the attackers fell.

"Get us out of here!" he yelled at Elias.

More Taliesin rounded the corners at either end of the hall.

She swore, setting them on fire as Elias flung a hand toward the closet doorframe. Shadows enveloped the doorway with impossible speed.

"Go!" Elias shouted.

The Merlin raced for the portal.

Chapter Twenty-Five

Taking the steps two at a time, Cole chased Harris up the stairs.

He couldn't believe they'd just left the wizards.

Grabbing the banister, he whipped around the landing and drove himself up another flight. Rough metal scraped at his palm and his legs already were beginning to burn. Endless steps spiraled away above him, twisting into oblivion like a surrealist painting from hell, and somehow, he had to make it to the top.

He hated wizards. Of course they'd come in on the bottom floor; they didn't have to worry about little things like gravity and distance with portals at their disposal. And it wasn't like elevators were an option. Not with the magic-wielding crowd tearing everything apart. He remembered how that went all too well.

He couldn't believe they'd just left.

"We get to the security office on the fifteenth," Harris called. "You don't say anything. Let me do the explaining."

Cole kept running. Harris wouldn't want to hear his response anyway.

An explosion reverberated up the stairwell as a door five floors below blew outward and tumbled to the basement, taking part of the banister with it. Debris strafed the walls and shouts rose, indistinguishable over the distance. Catching himself on the rail, he stared down for a heartbeat before realizing he'd stopped.

He couldn't believe they'd…

Ashe could take care of herself.

A ragged breath escaped him as he shoved away from the railing and propelled himself up the next flight of stairs. Ashe was a crazy-powerful wizard. For all he knew, that blast had come from her. Plus, she had over a dozen bodyguards at her side. She'd be fine.

And he had to stop this before things got any worse.

Air grated on his lungs as they passed another floor. People were killing each other down there, and more outside Chaunessy as well. People were dying all around him; people he knew. And while he wished he could just not give a damn about them, because God knew it would be easier, that didn't change the truth.

He couldn't let this happen. He couldn't let his dad…

The door on the level above burst open and slammed into the concrete wall.

"– the *hell* they made it to the seventh floor!"

He skidded to a stop at the sound of Brogan's voice and, a few steps ahead, Harris did the same. The detective looked back frantically, thoughts racing almost visibly across his face, and then he abandoned the stairs to rush down to Cole's side.

"Don't say a word," Harris hissed, grabbing his arm. "Just look angry."

It wasn't hard to follow the command.

"You get your people down there and kill the–"

The giant cut off, coming to a sharp stop at the sight of them, and the eyes of the wizards trailing him went wide.

"Found him running from the fight downstairs," Harris explained tersely.

His anger became anything but feigned, and Cole felt his face darkening.

Brogan's mismatched eyes narrowed at the reaction. Curtly, he motioned to the other wizards. His gaze never left Cole as they rushed past him, aiming for the destruction below.

"Is that true?" the giant asked, descending the stairs more slowly.

Silence was the only answer he could give. The alternatives would probably get him or Harris killed.

The wizard's lip twitched coldly.

"I was taking him to the fifteenth floor," Harris continued, and Cole could hear caution enter his tone.

"Why?"

"Safety. Seemed the most secure place, and I figured Jamison's priority would be to keep him protected."

The cold humor surfaced again. "Yes," Brogan agreed quietly. "Yes, it would be."

Something dark slithered beneath the giant's tone, and at the sound, Cole felt Harris' grip tighten on his arm. "I'll just get him up there, then," the detective said, starting toward the steps.

Brogan's hand shot out, snagging Cole and bringing them both to a halt. "No. Head back downstairs. I'll take care of the king's son."

Harris hesitated. "You're probably a lot more needed down there than I am…"

"Are you suggesting one of the Blood should guard a hallway rather than the heir to the throne?" Brogan asked, his gaze sliding to

Harris and his voice dangerously low.

The detective tensed. "No, of course not. I–"

He glanced over. Behind his eyes, Cole could see the calculations run, coming up with nothing.

"You know," Harris amended, "forget it. Sorry. The explosions…"

He gave a chagrined chuckle and then released Cole and stepped back, hands raised. "You're right. I'll get to it."

Brogan ignored him. Without a word, he turned, yanked open the nearest door, and then headed into the hallway. Cole stumbled after him, having no choice but to follow or lose his arm. He saw Harris staring after them both, his pretense of embarrassment melting into something far closer to an unarticulated curse, and then the door slammed closed.

With the intractability of a steamroller, Brogan strode down the hall, and Cole twisted in his grasp, trying to find his feet as the wizard plowed ahead.

"What are you–" he started.

Brogan walked faster.

At a speed barely short of a run, they rounded the corner and headed for the elevator. Cole exhaled sharply, wanting to balk and knowing there was no point. At the moment, he'd have better luck dislodging a pit bull from his arm.

Besides, beyond his magic, Brogan had well over a hundred pounds and damn near a foot of height on him. If the bastard wanted him dead, there were a lot more direct ways of going about it than sticking him in an elevator in the middle of a war zone.

At the wizard's summons, the door rushed open. Striding inside, Brogan ignored the elevator's controls, reaching instead for the maintenance panel, and the hinges broke as he ripped open the small door. Dismissively, he tossed the panel away, his attention on a keypad grafted to the multicolored wires. The buttons tripped over one another to beep in response to his jabs, and then a burst of magic left the wizard's hand, chasing across the wires to disappear into the walls.

The elevator took off.

Numbers flashed by faster than Cole could read and gravity pressed him toward the floor. The elevator shuddered and bucked as it rocketed upward, while overhead, the cables began to squeal. By the wall, Brogan stood immobile, giving no more indication that he noticed the turbulence than he did the fact he still gripped Cole's arm.

Another burst of magic left the wizard's hand. With gut-wrenching deceleration, the brakes dragged the elevator to a halt.

The door opened. The room beyond was empty, and the breadth of the building itself. Concrete pillars supported the ceiling, and nothing but grit and construction dust covered the bare floor. A bank of windows lined the far wall, giving a bird's eye view of the city that only his father's office rivaled.

Brogan hurled him forward.

He tumbled to the ground a few yards from the elevator, pain shooting through his shoulder as it took the brunt of the impact, and dust rose around him, choking his instinctive gasp. Coughing, he scrambled for his feet, trying to ignore the pain throbbing through his arm as he scanned the room for the wizard.

Hands clasped behind him, Brogan walked from the elevator.

Cole backed away. "Where are we? Why–"

"What is the Merlin's strategy?"

The Blood's tone was patient, as though despite the fact people were dying on the floors below, he hadn't a single concern.

"What's the…?" Cole repeated, retreating farther into the room. Emptiness surrounded him, and the exit to the stairs was a hundred yards away. Between him and the elevator, Brogan waited like a wall, his hands folded peaceably at his back.

Cole swallowed, suddenly feeling very aware of the gun tucked beneath his jacket, and how thin a line between him and whatever Brogan planned it really formed. The giant would block anything the moment he spotted the weapon. Bullets only killed wizards if they didn't see the shots coming.

And in Brogan's case, maybe not even then.

"I don't know what you're talking about."

"You have one chance to live," Brogan said. "Tell me the truth – the *real* truth this time – of all they intend and where I can find the queen, and I will take you to your father. Lie to me…"

A cold smile surfaced briefly before disappearing beneath the implacable ice of his face.

Cole shook his head cautiously. "I-I don't know."

"Do not waste my time, Cole."

He hesitated. "I'm just here to help my dad."

The smile reappeared, tinged with wry disbelief.

"I am," Cole insisted. "I want to help him. I… he can stop this."

"He will."

Cole couldn't bring himself to respond.

Drawing a contemplative breath, Brogan tapped his hands together as he paced away from the elevator. "It would be nice to trust you. To believe you truly have the king's best interest at heart. You are, after all, his only child and heir. Who else should be loyal to him, if not you?"

His gaze slid to Cole. "And I'm certain that's the point. Your father would do anything for you. *Has* done anything for you. He would burn heaven and earth for your sake and, despite all evidence to the contrary, he would still risk everything we have built for the hope his son could be saved. You know this." Brogan's face darkened. "And so does the queen."

Cole shook his head. "I'm not—"

In an instant, the wizard was across the room, his weight driving Cole back till he slammed into one of the concrete pillars. The air rushed from his chest with the impact, but before he could breathe again, Brogan's hand was around his throat. Instinctively, he grabbed the giant's fingers, fighting to break his grip.

He may as well have tried to bend stone.

"You fled to her," Brogan said. "You stole her sister away with her. You have travelled about in her company for the better part of these past weeks, barring the time you spent coercing your father into believing you were on his side. And now you are here, just as the Merlin are attempting to attack. Everything you have done puts your protests to a lie, and if you do not tell me what she plans right now, the king will be mourning your tragic death, which I was too late to stop from occurring at the hands of the Merlin queen."

Air came rough around Brogan's fingers while the gun pressed sharply into his spine, the weapon pinned between the concrete and the weight of the giant crushing him to the wall. Desperately, Cole swung hard toward the wizard's gut.

Brogan tensed as the blow struck, and otherwise barely moved.

"You can't—" Cole rasped.

"Yes," Brogan countered, utter certainty in his voice. "I can. I said your father would do anything for *you*." He paused. "Sometimes, even kings must be protected from themselves."

The giant's face drew in close. "Tell me where to find her."

Cole choked, one hand dropping to his side for the gun while the other clawed at the wizard's grip. "I don't–"

"Yes, you do."

"No… didn't tell me… don't…"

Brogan regarded him, paying no attention to the fingers grasping at his own.

And then his eyebrow shrugged equitably. "Very well."

Brogan's hand clenched tighter. Darkness and sparks of blinding light spread like wildfire across Cole's vision and blood throbbed in his head, unable to escape. His body panicked, screaming for oxygen and his fingers scrabbled for the weapon, scraping past the concrete till they wrapped around the gun.

Frantically, he yanked the weapon from behind him and then pulled the trigger.

The grip on his neck vanished. He crashed to the floor, his legs unable to hold him. Coughs wracked him as air burned over his throat, and he blinked hard, fighting to see past the darkness disappearing too slowly from his eyes.

Brogan lay on the ground a few feet away.

Trembling, Cole staggered to his feet, the gun still clutched in his hand.

Blood pooled beneath the wizard and red-soaked bullet holes clustered near the center of his motionless chest.

Eyes never leaving Brogan, Cole inched closer.

In Hollywood, the bad guy always got back up. In Hollywood, the monsters never really died. Even Ashe hadn't been able to kill Brogan. Neither had anyone else who'd come up against the man.

The gun shook as he lifted it, aiming at the wizard's head.

In Hollywood…

He turned his face away and squeezed the trigger again.

A rough breath escaped him. He lowered the gun to his side.

Adrenaline faded, leaving nothing but shivering. His fingers played over the grip of the weapon, as though uncertain whether to let go.

Seconds crawled by. His eyes crept up to the room, and the god-like perspective of the windows. The height was familiar. The view too. His father had to be close. Maybe only a couple floors away, if not closer still.

And Ashe would be coming.

He ran for the stairs.

———— ◆ ————

The door slammed closed on Brogan and Cole, and it was all Harris could do not to swear.

Whatever semblance of a plan anybody'd had in all this was disintegrating faster than a sandcastle in a hurricane.

Resisting the urge to punch something, he took to the stairs again. The boy would be fine. Trapped with the giant and his father, but fine.

It was the girl blowing up the building to rescue her sister who was in real trouble now.

Another explosion shook a lower level as he rounded the landing. Screams rose with the smoke this time, cutting off with a sickening sharpness that could only mean the wizard hadn't been able to fly. Gripping the banister, he ran faster and didn't look back.

It wasn't like there'd be any point.

The fifteenth floor came into view, the number painted large on the concrete wall by the door's side, and he skidded to a halt, trying to regroup. Barreling in wouldn't do any good. Whether or not the wizards saw him as a threat, startling them would probably still get him killed.

He drew a breath, running a hand over his hair and then straightening his sports coat. Habit drove him to check his gun in its holster and pure survival made him step to one side before punching his access code into the keypad. No magic flew out as he tugged the door open, and he couldn't hear any shouting coming from the corridor beyond.

Cautiously, he leaned around the doorframe.

Security cameras were locked on him up and down the hall.

Rapidly, he schooled his face into as purposeful an expression as he could manage, and then stepped through the doorway. A hall stretched in either direction from him, looping the circumference of the building with staid offices that barely interrupted the colorless walls. Another corridor ran directly ahead, peppered with more cameras and ending in a metal door, and only the hiss of the ventilation system broke the eerie quiet as the stairwell exit closed behind him.

A wizard leaned her head out of an office, and he barely stopped himself from grabbing his gun. Her cold expression became disgusted, and then she disappeared back inside.

Forcing himself to breathe and hiding an annoyed expression of his own, he started toward the metal door. Guards in the offices. Of course. The narrow hallway he was currently walking along would bottleneck any assault and the guards could cut off retreat, turning this little corridor into an instant killing ground.

It was a decent strategy, all things considered.

He wondered what other security measures they had up here that he couldn't see.

Drawing another breath, he kept going, trying to ignore the soft whir of the cameras as they turned to follow him. That magic was a part of the defense was obvious; a moment's thought on the subject made his eyes want to slide from every surface he could see. And the security codes for the doors would potentially slow *someone* down, though probably only someone like him. As it stood, he'd only made it this far because Brogan had long since given orders that, second only to the protection of Jamison himself, the last fallback for the building's defense was the outer hallway of this floor.

But that meant nothing for the protections they'd have in the office at the end of the hall.

He had no idea how he was going to get those shields down.

Another breath struggled into his lungs. The barriers were linked throughout the building by magic and computers combined and, barring the chance they'd just installed a big red button on the thing, both would present a problem. He couldn't do anything about the one, and had never exactly been a master of the other, and as nice as it would be to just pull out his gun and shoot something, he doubted that would actually accomplish anything.

His mouth tightened. It didn't matter. He'd just have to figure something out.

The security office door had obviously been purchased with the goal of withstanding a battering ram in mind. His knuckles hit the metal with a dull thud, and silence answered, unchanging as the seconds stretched and the cameras stared like gun sights at his back.

Trying not to grimace, he lifted a hand to knock again and then hesitated. Brogan was occupied with fighting the Merlin or protecting Jamison. The odds of anyone being able to confirm anything with him quickly were minute at best.

Hopefully, anyway.

He pounded on the door. "Open up! I have orders from Brogan!"

Nothing happened.

He hit the metal surface again. "I said I–"

The door swung back. His heart plummeted like a rock, hitting his stomach hard.

"What do you want?" Simeon snapped.

"I have–"

"We heard you. What?"

"I–" he started, and then faltered as his eyes went beyond the man. The gray office sprawled across the width of the fifteenth floor, excluding the space left for the outer halls, and little else filled the room. Guards stood around an area enclosed in green glass and shimmering magic at the center of the room, within which sat other wizards watching computer screens. More monitors lined the office walls, each of them scrolling images of every floor.

He fought the urge to curse. Of course they could see the halls. What'd he think they had cameras for? Which meant they would've seen Brogan take Cole and–

"Spit it out," Simeon ordered.

Hell with it.

"Brogan's got Cole," he said. "Found him downstairs. We need to get the boy to a secure location, and Brogan sent me to check if everything was clear to bring him here."

Simeon regarded him flatly. "Brogan sent *you?*"

Harris feigned an apologetic shrug. "He needed the wizards to hold off the Merlin. And he's protecting Cole."

Irritation and disgust flickered across Simeon's face in equal measure as he ran his gaze over Harris again. "Tell Brogan this location is just–"

Klaxons blared overhead.

"What the hell?" Simeon barked, looking beyond Harris to the hall and then turning to the office. "Where's the breach?"

"Northwest stairs, sir!" a woman shouted, her hand to an earpiece as she relayed the information. "Keller's on his way and the guards have them contained–"

The door on the far side of the room exploded.

Harris darted around the swiftly closing door as Simeon took off across the office, the wizards around the glass cube a step ahead of him. An onslaught of magic lashed out at them, cutting down four of the guards instantly and making Simeon falter, his defenses shuddering. Fire roared in the hallway and smoke billowed through the door, turning the Merlin into lethal ghosts in the shadows. Lightning raked the room and then struck the cube, setting the iridescent barrier alight. Blue-green electricity snarled as it spread like a web over the surface, engulfing each side and growing brighter by the second.

Till the glass shattered.

Harris hit the deck as shards exploded across the office to smash into the walls. Covering his head with his arms, he cringed at the sound of screaming and the sting of glass raining down.

Simeon gave an inarticulate snarl. Lifting his head from the protection of his arms, Harris only had time to see the defenses around Simeon go opaque, and then the wizard's magic rushed outward with a roar. Tiles stripped from the ceiling and floor as the magic passed, as did the glass and debris, and all of it lunged straight for the Merlin.

Amid the lightning and smoke, defenses glinted like crystal balls, but as the Blood's assault continued, some of them flickered and failed.

Shoving up from the ground, Harris bolted for the remnants of the cube. Glass crackled beneath his feet as he ran, the broken chunks skittering and slipping alarmingly, and an errant blast of lightning sliced the air above his ducked head. He could hear shouts coming from the Merlin, the words indistinguishable past the howling magic racing at them all, and behind the Blood wizard, the Taliesin paced like wolves, waiting to strike anyone who made it past Simeon's attack.

He reached the shattered glass door and his steps suddenly faltered, the memory of the guard caught in the barrier downstairs flashing through his mind. There wasn't any evidence the defenses on the room still stood; if anything, the destruction was a strong indication they were gone. But he wasn't a wizard. He couldn't be sure.

And to burn like that… like Malden had…

A cry rang out. It sounded like it came from a girl. Across the room, the Merlin were falling back, and he couldn't tell how many were still alive.

He lunged past the door.

The hairs on his arms rose, tingling as though electrified, and then he was through. Racing toward the desk, he leapt a fallen body and then slid to a halt before the bank of monitors. Only a handful still clung to their metal braces, while the rest lay shattered on the floor.

But the wizards hadn't had time to log out. They hadn't had time for anything.

And they'd been working on getting the lower floor barriers back online.

He bit back a laugh, the sound edging closer to hysterical than could ever be safe, and then he rushed for a chair. A grimace twisted his face as he pushed the glass-peppered body of a dead wizard aside, letting it tumble to the floor. Splatters of blood covered the mouse and keyboard, with more splashed across the screens nearby, and he swallowed hard, trying to focus on which of the meters on the monitor directly before him was connected to the barrier outside.

On the right side of the screen, he spotted it. In a gradient of green, the meter pulsed near the maximum of its gauge, although he had no idea whether that meant it was fully defended or under attack. Behind him, he could hear the fight fading, and he kept from looking back as he grabbed the sticky mouse and navigated to the bar.

A click brought up the controls, from startup to shutdown and everything in between.

He swallowed hard, feeling the laugh rise up again.

"What the hell are you doing?"

Simeon's voice sent his heart clawing for an exit from his chest. His gaze snapped to the other side of the room, and the Blood wizard standing there. The Merlin were gone and bodies lay by the door, though he didn't recognize any of them. The Taliesin were running for the hall while explosions echoed from deeper in the building, testimony that the surviving Merlin were still fighting for their lives.

"I asked you a question, human," Simeon demanded, striding toward him.

Harris struggled to breathe, his thoughts racing. No blur of magic surrounded the wizard, and no hint of defense either, because the danger had moved on and only the human remained.

And he wasn't a threat. He never had been.

A boathouse flashed through his mind, bringing with it the sight of a teenage girl falling bloodied to the ground.

Never, except to those he shouldn't ever have tried to harm.

He turned back to the desk, his eyes rising to the monitors overhead and the reflections caught in the gloss of their broken screens. Gently, his hand slid beneath his jacket as the wizard rounded the remnants of the shattered glass door.

"I'm making it right," Harris answered.

The weapon left its holster as the chair spun, and the rapid gunshots echoed in the empty room before Simeon's eyes went wide. The bullets ripped through the man's chest, driving him back into the wall, and glass crunched and broke and dripped red behind him as the wizard slid slowly to the ground.

Harris exhaled, briefly eyeing the fallen wizard, and then his gaze went to the hallway door. None of the Taliesin reappeared; amid the explosions, no one had heard the gun.

A smile lifted the corner of his mouth.

He turned to the controls and hit shutdown.

Chapter Twenty-Six

With a gasp, Ashe ripped the magic from another faceless wizard and hurled it into the endless horde. Howling, the man stumbled away, colliding with two others and then crashing to the tile.

She didn't stop. Three more wizards followed him screaming to the ground.

They'd made it fifteen floors, though it felt like more. With every inch of concrete and tile coming at a cost, the Merlin had carved a path all the way to the security office, only to find a Blood wizard inside. The fight had been manageable, and the barrier controls had been in sight, but when another Blood showed up behind them, the narrow hallway suddenly made every previous floor look like paradise.

And too many of their people had fallen before the Blood behind them died. Too many by far.

Swiftly, she drew in a blast of magic rushing for Nathaniel and flung it back. The large wizard didn't react as the Taliesin fell. He was used to it by now.

She swallowed down a breath and kept going. The surge of magic gave her strength and, though her muscles and bones still ached, she could see the difference the borrowed power was making for her in the exhaustion on the others' faces.

These were the strongest wizards Merlin had.

And without help, they wouldn't last much longer.

She bit back a curse as more Taliesin rounded the corner, reinforcements for wizards the Merlin had long since cut down, and a few steps ahead, Nathaniel snarled as another group at the opposite end of the corridor did the same.

"Get her out of here!" Elias shouted to Nathaniel.

"No!" she snapped back.

A blast of magic tried to race past her and, without looking from Elias, she stripped it from the air and threw it at the Taliesin. Lightning from Cornelius joined the attack, knocking the wizards into those following them.

Elias ignored her. "That's an order, Nathaniel!"

A pair of Taliesin rushed by their fallen counterparts, heading for Cornelius, and swiftly, she set them both on fire.

"We just need to get inside the–" she started.

Every surface seemed to shiver. In a heartbeat, all the barriers on the building fell.

"Signal the damn reinforcements!" Cornelius yelled.

Elias grabbed his phone, hit speed dial and then sent a burst of magic through the device so strong that the plastic melted as he flung it to the ground.

Portals opened. Taliesin flooded the hall.

"Son of a–" Elias swore desperately.

Magic slammed them from all sides. She stumbled, catching one blast of electricity as she dodged another flying past her head, and for a moment, she couldn't see the others to know if any of them were still alive.

More portals opened at the end of the hall. The Merlin guard rushed through. Screams and explosions surrounded her as the Taliesin surged forward, crushing against her as they fled the Merlin charging them from behind. She sent her magic rushing outward, shoving the Taliesin back and giving herself a fragile moment of space. Caught in the chaos, she could see Nathaniel struggling to reach her while Cornelius yelled for him to get her away.

Electricity snarled over her defenses and she turned, hissing with pain. At her back, the Taliesin were regrouping against the Merlin mowing them down.

And by her side stood an empty office door.

She gasped, glancing back to see Nathaniel fling a man bodily through the air, though two more just took the fallen wizard's place. Beyond him, Cornelius and Elias were surrounded by Taliesin, while the Merlin guard pressed in from either side.

They'd make her leave.

They were too tired to stand a chance.

And they were all running out of time.

Her hand landed on the doorframe. A portal swirled to life.

"Your majesty!" Nathaniel shouted.

She cast him an apologetic look, and then raced into the darkness.

———— ◆ ————

At the end of the stairs, Cole paced. Cold metal waited in front of him and beyond the banister, the stairwell stretched down into an infinity of dizzying shadows before ever reaching the ground.

He barely noticed.

"Dad?" he yelled.

There weren't any cameras. Nothing adorned the wall but the windowless gray door. He couldn't guarantee that anyone could hear him, but he didn't have another option. Even putting a finger on the metal had been excruciating.

A click sounded in the silence. The door swung open.

Hesitating before the doorframe, he eased a hand through, and then took off when he encountered nothing but air. Moving fast, he strode down the black-marbled corridor and barely paused as he rounded the lobby doors. Glass chimes clinked at his presence while reflected light from the panes danced across the white sofa to the delight of the tiny, blonde girl seated upon it, though her mother didn't seem to notice. As he came in, Tanya looked over, the repressed fury on her face almost as easy to read as the fear, while standing behind her, Isabella regarded him with all the warmth of marble.

He eyed the Blood wizard briefly, and then his gaze flicked up to the sunlit gallery and the closed double doors. No sound could be heard from the office, meaning nothing and worrying him all the same, and with a last glance for the ice queen, he headed for the doors atop the wide staircase.

Her gaze seemed to follow him all the way.

Pausing on the landing, he reached for the door handle cautiously, waiting for the bite of magic, but nothing came. Drawing a steadying breath, he pushed the door open and walked into the room.

"Cole," his father said, rising from behind the desk with a smile as the door swung shut again.

Seated before the massive desk, Lily turned, her eyes widening.

Swiftly, she shoved out of the chair and raced across the office, throwing her arms around him as she reached his side.

His arms wrapped around her instinctively, his gaze dropping to search every inch of her that he could see. She wasn't hurt. He'd been right. But no hint of a glow surrounded her at all.

Strange squawks came from the conference room. He looked over to the closed door, his brow drawing down.

The chair creaked as his father pushed it out of his way, and the sound snapped Cole's focus back instantly. Lily tensed, turning to keep the man in view as he walked toward them.

"I'm glad you came back," Victor said, clasping Cole's shoulder warmly.

A rough breath left his lungs. "Dad, I–"

"We were just discussing the spell."

His words dried up. Panic twisted through his chest as his gaze returned to Lily.

Fierce determination showed on her face, with a fair amount of anger as well.

He couldn't suppress a breath of relief.

"You don't need to do it," he said, looking back up at his father. "Really."

Victor's mouth tightened.

"I'm serious," Cole tried. "I've talked with Ashe. I've seen the Merlin and the Taliesin and…" He faltered, swallowing hard at the memory of the prison. "I'm telling you, it doesn't have to be like this. Really. Just let Lily go. Let her magic go. Talk to Ashe and you'll see."

"And what do you think that would accomplish, Cole?"

"Peace?" he offered desperately. "It'd stop this, Dad. I promise you it would. Ashe doesn't want this war. No one does. All these people are only here because they think you're going to kill them, and if you could just show them you're willing to try another way–"

"There is no other way."

Only pity showed in his father's eyes, mired in a conviction so cold, it made him want to break something.

"Unless we take control of the spell," Victor continued gently, "the inequality that started this war will always be a threat to us. As will the wizards who would do anything to recreate that disparity. You know this. Your grandparents alone were more than sufficient example of that worldview. And left unchecked, with the possibility of reinstating the binding forever at their disposal–"

"But Ashe wouldn't do that. She'd never–"

His father gave him a sympathetic look. "She is a Merlin."

"So *what*!" Cole cried. "So was Mom! So's the little girl you're trying to make *kill* half the damn world, but I'm telling you, you don't have to! Please! Whatever my grandparents were like, whatever they told you about the spell, it doesn't mean you have to do this!"

Victor paused, glancing to the conference room as something smashed behind the door. "The Carnegeans gave me nothing, because they had nothing to give," he said, turning back. "But that is not the point."

Cole stared.

"Controlling the spell – and doing whatever is necessary once it is in place – is the only way to create the stability necessary to ensure the security of our world. Compromise will not accomplish that, because compromise will never hold. Half measures never do. Unless we make the cost of opposition clear, the forces threatening us will only return later to resume the conflict."

"It's not like that," Cole tried.

"It always has been."

Victor turned away, pacing back to his desk.

"I am more than willing to release this little one's magic," he continued after a moment, absently rolling a pen across the desktop. "And could even do so now–" He looked up. "–provided she promises you that she will not touch me with it."

Swallowing, Cole glanced down to Lily. "Just promise," he whispered. "Please."

She hesitated, and then gave a small nod.

The glow around her returned like a switched-on bulb.

A nearly imperceptible smile flashed across Victor's face when nothing else happened, and Cole struggled not to be sick, reading his father's satisfaction at the confirmation of Lily's obedience to him.

"I am not the aggressor in this war, Cole," Victor said, his gentle tone returning. "I started it, yes. But I am not the reason it continues. The Merlin's Children oppressed our people for half a millennia. And the threat of their ability to do so again, whether they choose or even know how to use it, has perpetuated this war for almost a decade."

"But Ashe won't–"

"How can you be sure?"

Cole fell silent. If the Carnegeans had told the Blood nothing and Lily hadn't caved, then explaining about the cripples, the spell, and everything he knew of the Merlin queen would only give away the information that had most likely kept everyone alive thus far.

And that probably stood between Lily and his father forcing her to do the spell right now.

"That's my point, Cole. You can't know. You cannot guarantee that the forces around the young queen won't change her mind, regardless of what she currently claims to believe. And so," he said, his gaze falling to Lily, "we must control the situation. We must make certain they cannot harm us. We will never have peace any other way."

A chill crept through him and, involuntarily, Cole pushed Lily farther behind his back. His father didn't even seem to be looking at a person. Maybe not even an animal.

Just a thing. A weapon. Nothing more.

"Dad… "

"You will understand eventually. When this is over and you can finally see what I have worked so hard to create… you will understand. You'll see how all this, every part of it, has been to protect our family. To make the world a better place for our family. There has never been another reason."

"But," Cole floundered, "that's all *anyone* is trying to do here. Can't you see that? Ashe, the Merlin, all of them. They're only trying to stay alive and protect the people they love. And if you could just make them realize you want peace too–"

"Our versions of peace are not the same thing."

"They can be! You don't have to–"

A beep sounded on the desk. Glancing over, Victor regarded the monitor briefly before lightly tapping a key.

Cole's heart began to pound harder at the feeling of a barrier rising into place behind him. "Just try talking to Ashe," he urged. "She'll listen. If Lily asks her to, I promise she'll listen."

The dull thud of an explosion reverberated in the distance, and past the office doors, he could hear the tinkling of the chimes. A squawk arose in the conference room, indignant and vaguely wild.

"She's not a murderer, Dad," he pressed on desperately. "She was friends with those cripples who died. It was some bastards on the Merlin Council who took what she told them and used it to kill all those people in her name. And you know what that's like, right? Having a Council manipulate you and hurt people you care about?"

The pity in his father's eyes made him want to scream.

"She's been where you were, okay? So just *talk* to her! Make her understand that you only did those things to keep the Council from hurting your family! You can end this without–"

The conference room door burst open, chunks of the lock and wood scattering across the carpet. Dazedly, Thelma stumbled to a stop, a battering ram of a broken chair leg in her hand.

Cole stared, shock and panic hitting him in rapid succession.

Putting a hand to her head, Thelma blinked and then froze, her mad gaze locking on him.

"No," she gasped. She dashed forward, the chair leg slipping from her hand, forgotten. "No, no, no. You can't. You can't tell him how–"

She clutched him, her bony fingers clawing his shirt desperately till he pushed her away. With a wail, the old woman buried her face in her hands.

He barely noticed, looking back to his dad.

Victor was studying them. "Tell me how to what?"

Cole scrambled for an answer, but his father read one before he could speak.

"I see."

"Dad–"

"The old woman knows how to recreate the spell. And she told you." His gaze dropped to Lily, and the girl's fingers clenched on

Cole's side. "Both of you."

An explosion rocked the lobby. Someone shouted and the glass chimes shattered as they hit the ground.

"And the queen."

"It's not like that."

"Did it require Ashley to be here?"

"No. And it doesn't matter. Ashe won't do it. She *can't* do it. Recreating the spell means killing a cripple and she would never–"

"And yet she is here."

Magic hit the barrier on the office doors and Cole gasped, stumbling away with Lily as pain spiked through his head. "She's just here because she thinks you're going to hurt her sister and kill everyone!"

Victor glanced to him.

Everything in Cole's body went numb.

"I will do whatever is necessary," Victor said quietly, "for there to be peace."

A breath escaped him. "Dad, please. She'll try to kill you."

Around his father, the glow of magic increased till it rivaled the afternoon sun.

"Perhaps," Victor allowed. "But she will fail."

Chapter Twenty-Seven

Light and sound rushed past her, carrying flashes of running people and empty halls, and then she was through.

Her footsteps loud on the hard floor, Ashe skidded to a stop, her magic rising. The mist of the portal faded, taking with it the whisper of moving air and leaving only silence.

And darkness.

Her hands burst into flame, bringing the room into view.

Glossy black marble surrounded her, casting back strange reflections of the fire, and opaque glass sconces dotted the walls, though most were broken. On the other side of the room, a ten-foot high wall stood, with a few chairs behind the ledge at the top, while at her back, the empty doorway led to a shadowed hall.

She let out a breath, her eyes rising to the ceiling and the nearly physical pressure of the barrier she could feel there. She had no idea where she was, but it wasn't important.

It was just the closest she could come to where she needed to go.

With a last look to the room, she headed for the hallway. Orange light danced across the black marble walls and caught on countless broken tiles, but in the remnants of the glossy surface, fragments of her reflection kept pace as she strode down the corridor. A door came into view at the end of the hall, its dark surface dented terribly, though a small sign noting it as the stair access was still visible nearby. Moving faster, she pushed past the exit and took to the steps, racing upward till they came to an end at a plain steel door.

Her gaze skimmed over the metal. Like everything else, the door was guarded by a barrier, and there wasn't any way to know what was on the other side. Lily could be just beyond it. A hundred Blood wizards could too.

Briefly, she closed her eyes.

Her magic punched into the barrier. The defenses crackled, retreating into the wall, and swiftly, she switched attacks, letting the energy hit the door hard.

Metal flew back. She darted through the gap as the barrier rushed into place. Another hallway waited beyond the door, a twin of the one below but for the lack of destruction, and nothing like the utilitarian layout of the building's lower floors. Pale light came from crystalline sconces and barriers defended both walls, and the veneer of black marble blurred as it stretched away ahead of her, giving an unbroken and endless feel to the hall.

An angry voice came from down the corridor, the words indistinguishable, and then she heard a door close.

She headed toward the sound.

Halfway down the hall, the marble on the left gave way to black double doors so permeated with magic, their dark surface gleamed. Coming to a stop, she glanced in either direction, and then returned her gaze to the doors, praying Lily wasn't anywhere nearby.

Her magic hit the barrier and drove it into the walls. Pulling back quickly, she took aim at the doors.

She heard the attack coming. It roared behind the doors like a freight train.

Wood exploded around her. Magic rushed over her, through her, shielding her from the debris even as it burned like acid through her veins. She gasped, drawing it in and then sending it back with all her strength.

Glass shattered and a little girl screamed. White furniture erupted, the magic mowing over it and sending chunks of wood and stuffing flying.

Heart in her throat, she raced into the room.

A woman was crouched by the left wall. Someone small was beneath her.

Blonde hair flashed at the corner of her eye and then magic was coming at her again.

She spun, ripping it from the air, and then her own power raced outward, chasing it back to the source.

The Blood wizard froze, shock shattering her icy expression as her magic rushed away.

Ashe gasped, stumbling. The force of the woman's magic swept into her, nearly overwhelming her ability to hold it in, and heat built on her skin to compensate for its strength. Flames rose of their own accord as she straightened, the fire spreading fast over her body and burning the remnants of stuffing and fabric to dust around her as they fell from the air.

For a heartbeat, the Blood wizard stared, and then her gaze flicked to the double doors at the top of the stairway.

With a gasp, she fled the room.

Ashe turned, her eyes finding the woman still huddled against the wall.

Tanya was watching her. In her arms, she gripped a small girl, one hand turning the child's face to her side.

Ashe felt her blood go cold. The safe houses. The kids and families and everyone who'd run in the hope of finding safety, only to discover the Blood waiting for them when they arrived.

The urge to let the flames loose was unbearable.

Her gaze dropped to the little girl.

Blonde curls quivered with the child's sobs. Her hands were white as she clutched Tanya, and her grip readjusted with every few breaths as though to reassure herself the woman was still there.

Ashe's eyes rose back to Tanya.

"Run," she growled.

Tanya stared at her. Muscles twitched on the woman's face, chasing circles between hate and fear, and then she seemed to remember the girl. Trembling, she pushed to her feet, keeping one arm around the child. Her eyes never leaving Ashe, she backed toward the hall.

The sound of her running footsteps faded down the black marble corridor.

Ashe looked to the double doors at the top of the steps.

Magic glistened on the wood, surpassing the shine on the brass handles and the sunlight from the windows overhead. No sound came from beyond the doors, the barrier dulling any trace of noise.

She crossed the room and climbed the stairs.

The barrier radiated from the doors, pressing on her even from the lower reaches of the steps. The fire grew around her, pushing back harder and harder against the magic till the force of it transformed the flames into an iridescent haze. Beneath her, the wooden stairs burned fast, crumbling as her feet left them.

As she reached the landing, she hesitated, fear flickering through her. Lily would have gotten away from the barrier. She wouldn't be right on the other side. She'd be safe.

She had to be.

Swiftly, Ashe drew a breath and then let the fire go.

The barrier went white. Her magic spread across it, rippling it like waves on a pond and then growing steadily stronger, making the defense buck like the sea in a storm.

Till it broke.

The door flew inward, scattering wood shards everywhere, and she followed them inside, the flames still snapping and twisting from her skin.

Jamison stood on the far side of the office. Cole was a few yards to the right of the door, his body sheltering Lily and his expression tense as hell. A hand to her head, Thelma staggered to her feet beyond them, uninjured and impossibly alive.

Ashe looked back to Jamison.

His lips rose in a smile. "Hello, your majesty."

She went for his magic.

His power lashed out to do the same. A shock jolted through her, smarting over every inch of her skin as their magic collided and rebounded to smash into the walls. She regrouped fast, reaching out again.

The second attempt hurt more than the first. Gasping, she stumbled to the side, her muscles quivering as though electrocuted.

Jamison exhaled slowly and straightened. His mouth curved back into a smile.

Gray flashed at the corner of her eye. Fingers splayed like claws, Thelma screeched and launched herself at Jamison.

He gestured as though flicking a bug. The old woman rocketed backward to crash into the couch on the far end of the room.

Lily gave a cry. White light rushed Jamison, slamming into him and sending him staggering. Wave upon wave of it swept over his defenses, making the shield around him flicker as it passed.

Fire flew from Ashe's hands to join Lily's attack. Jamison's magic began to falter as he stumbled and grasped at his desk to brace himself under the assault. He bent over, his breathing labored, and then his gaze snapped up.

Cole grabbed Lily and flung her to the ground as his father's shields burst outward. The impact threw Ashe backwards, smashing her into the wall as bookcases toppled and furniture went flying. The desk skittered and rolled, barreling toward her as she crashed to the floor, and protectively, she flung out a hand, her defenses swelling fast. Wood splintered as the heavy desk slammed to a stop against her shields.

She shivered, lowering her hand though her defenses remained, and on the carpet, the woodchips crept away under the pressure of her magic. Across the room, Cole was crouched behind a bookcase with Lily nearby. Thelma was nowhere to be found.

Magic hit the desk, pressing it harder against her defenses and sending wood scattering across her shields.

"Stop it!" Cole yelled.

Jamison made a short sound of acquiescence. "Very well."

She tensed, but no other attack came.

"Touch my son and Lily dies, your majesty," Jamison called in the same pleasant tone.

Her brow furrowed.

"Yes, I know about the spell. In fact, I wish to make you and your sister a deal. Bind the Merlin at my command, and you both will live. Refuse and, well…" He chuckled.

She shoved up from the carpet. Her magic struck out at him, scattering across his defenses.

His counterattack threw her back and nearly drove the desk through her shields.

"You cannot defeat me, your highness. Neither can that child. One of you *will* give me what I want; it's just a question of the price you wish to put on your temporary refusal." He paused. "Or do you think I am not capable of convincing you to do as I ask, even if your sister is dead?"

Magic lashed across the room like a whip. With a shriek, Lily collapsed as it cracked hard against her meager defenses.

Ashe gasped. Propelling herself from the floor, she rushed toward Lily and then skidded, retreating as bursts of electricity sliced across her path. She tumbled down behind the desk and then scrambled for her feet again, only to freeze at the sight of Cole helping the girl sit up.

"Damn you, stop it!" Cole shouted over the fallen bookcase.

Jamison ignored him. "I can kill her without touching my son, your highness. Bring this to an end before you lose the last family member you have left."

"She matters to me too, you bastard!" Cole yelled. "You can't—"

"Or would you prefer Lily to be the one who watches her family die?"

Magic slammed into the desk, crushing her backwards till only an inch remained between her and the wood.

"I can give you luxury and peace. A tranquil life of utter safety with all you and your baby sister could ever ask for. Or you can spend every waking moment learning the price of refusing me."

Lightning snaked around the desk, stabbing her shields. Sparks hit her, burning as they burrowed into her skin, and she choked, her fingers digging into the carpet at the pain.

"Goddamn it, Dad! You–"

"Quiet."

Another blast struck, raking over her shields as it sent the desk skittering away and left nothing between her and the Taliesin king. She gasped, tears stinging her eyes as she fought to hold her defenses against the sparks of magic crawling into her.

"It's your choice, your majesty," Jamison said calmly, watching her. "Like binding my people, like leaving us captive for half a millennia, like everything that has led to this point… it has always been your choice."

Lightning cut through her shields, and she screamed as it slashed her back, leaving hot wetness pouring down in its wake. Across the room, she saw Lily scrambling to reach her, her hands clawing at Cole as he held her back.

"Please!" Cole begged. "Stop it! You're not… this isn't you! You're not like this! You're not–"

"Quiet, Cole."

Another bolt hit her. She couldn't even scream. Her arm gave out, sending her crashing to the floor.

"What is your decision, your highness? I will convince your sister to help me. Your death will not spare her that."

The magic seared through her, setting every vein on fire, and lightning slashed her again.

"Ashe! Ashe, listen to me!"

She dragged her gaze from the bloodied ground.

"Just do it," Cole ordered intensely. "Do what he says."

Horror twisted through the pain as she read his meaning. Her head shook as sparks crawled over her skin.

He met her eyes. "Do it, Ashe."

She gasped, choking on a sob as another blast sliced her back. Cole's face crumpled at the sight and across the distance between them, she could see him whisper a single word.

"Please."

Tears fell on her scalded cheeks. Magic struggled up around her, dragging from the depths of all she had left as the lightning devoured the last of her defense.

"Do it!" he shouted.

She reached out, ripped the magic from Lily, and then flung it all at the young man who wouldn't look away from her eyes.

The air around him shattered like glass. Iridescent shards flew apart, hanging weightless for a moment before racing at her in a thousand pieces of color and light. Lily screamed, her fingers clutching Cole as Jamison started forward, his face white with horror and rage.

And time slowed. The fragments slid through the air, whispering like a fingertip across crystal as they came.

Cole collapsed.

She closed her eyes.

And the broken pieces struck her skin.

Energy flooded her, spreading like wildfire through her veins, and bringing Lily's magic on its heels. The abyss rushed in, eroding the island of her power like sand beneath a tide.

She unleashed the magic at the darkness.

The void hit.

And then everything was gone.

———— ◆ ————

Darkness surrounded her, perfect and still. She couldn't feel the ground, or any brush of wind. The air echoed in a muted scream and the sound of someone calling her name, but the noise was distant. Paused.

Waiting.

She drew a trembling breath and her gaze fell, finding her own body despite the black. Light glowed from her, as though the power she'd taken lit her from within. But frail, black lines traced jagged paths through the glow, like remnants of a lightning strike.

The ghost of a memory drifted past, vanishing before she could grasp it all. But it'd hurt. She remembered that much. There'd been a sudden darkness. And pain.

A flash caught the corner of her eye and she looked up. The world seemed to quiver and as she watched, a glimmer broke the black, faint and no larger than a grain of sand. Her eyes tracked across the void as others joined it, first a few, then more, each one pricking through the darkness like stars emerging in the night sky.

She paused. Not stars. Magic. Her skin shivered as more appeared, and the hairs on her arms rose, as if tied to the lights in the sky.

As if bound to them.

The stars grew brighter and the quivering became a low rumble, radiating from the heart of an earth she couldn't see.

A breath slid from her. They were wizards. Each light. Each star. Wizards bound to her, with their magic rushing down to course beneath her skin.

Just as it had always done.

In the darkness, the rumbling grew louder. The air shook, carrying a scream and the sound of her name.

She stared in awe. She'd lived at the heart of this. She'd just never been able to reach it. She'd never had the strength. But it was a part of her, just as it had been for her father and all her ancestors before him.

"I am the spell," she whispered.

The rumbling became stronger. The stars grew bright, burning away the darkness. She could hear Lily past the noise, and through the fading shadows, she could see Jamison. He was turning toward her, lightning leaving him slowly to strike her again.

It was so clear. The connection from herself to him, stretching out to the Taliesin through their king. She could feel the same within her to the Merlin and, with a thought, she could direct the light inside her to take any of them, bind them.

Even kill them.

She shivered, shying from the thought. Binding the Taliesin would be enough. The world just needed to be the way it had been. And it would be so simple. The magic beneath her skin connected her to them all.

Though none were like the stars.

Her brow furrowed. The magic of the Merlin and Taliesin was hazy, like moonlight pushing past a cloud, and while that of her own people glowed vaporously behind the mist, the Taliesin shifted in shades of transient gray.

And both felt wrong. There hadn't been anything like that around the stars. If anything, with their magic pouring into her, there almost hadn't been anything left beyond the fragile sphere of their light.

She blinked, her gaze going to Cole.

Realization settled over her like snow.

"Didn't know what it was going to cost," she whispered.

In the distance, Lily was screaming. Electricity crackled as it cut the air. She looked back to Jamison.

And she could hear the abyss roar.

She could send the magic through him. She could bind the Taliesin and the Blood, and give the Merlin the power to end the war. It was all her father had worked for, everything her people had fought and bled and died to achieve.

It would be so simple.

But the world needed to be the way it had been.

Light spread from her skin. Magic swirled around her, spinning faster and faster. The desk disintegrated as she rose to her feet, and the carpet shredded beneath the wind. The lightning of Jamison's attack scattered across the face of the whirlwind and as she straightened, she could see him stumble back, his rage transforming into horror.

He lifted a hand, and another blast rushed toward her.

She let the magic go.

The light erupted. Debris rushed away as though propelled by a hurricane, and Lily hit the floor, her fingers digging into Cole as it swept over them. Wood and stone strafed the walls and shattered the windows, but the magic continued on, rolling from the building to explode across the sky.

And like smoke, the abyss faded away.

A breath slipped from her. Glass tinkled down, pinging from the window frames to drop to the street, and a breeze drifted past the broken windows, carrying the distant sounds of the city as it twisted through her hair.

"What…" Jamison gasped. "What have you done?"

She looked over. On the other side of the office, he stumbled to his feet, staring between her and his shaking hands.

"Ended it," she answered.

A choked sound escaped him. Rage spasmed across his face, growing stronger with every heartbeat. Lightning gathered in his palms, and at the sight, triumph flared amid the fury in his eyes.

His gaze rose to hers. Slid to Lily. And his lips curled into a smile.

"Don't," she warned.

His hand flung outward.

Her defenses were faster.

White light rushed from her, shattering the blast. In a wall of wind, it slammed into him and threw him back. He gasped, his hands flying out to claw for the window frame as his eyes went wide.

And then the world was at his feet.

Forever at his feet.

She closed her eyes as his screams faded from the sky.

Chapter Twenty-Eight

—◆—

"A shley?"

She opened her eyes. Crouched a few yards away, Lily was staring at her. Woodchips and carpet fibers flecked the girl's hair and her face was bloodlessly white. On the floor beside her, Cole lay motionless, and the little girl's fingers trembled as they clutched him.

Ashe exhaled, an ache twisting deep in her chest. And she knew it would grow. In the next days, in the next moments when reality sank in, what she'd done was going to hurt like hell.

She swallowed and crossed the room to lower herself down by the young man's side. "Lil," she said quietly, reaching out to wrap her fingers around the girl's hand.

Cole stirred beneath them.

Ashe jerked away, her gaze going to Lily. "How did you—"

Lily shook her head. "I-I didn't. Did you…?"

Ashe looked back down, shaking her head as well. All around him, the strangely missing feeling she'd grown so accustomed to with the cripples was gone, and nothing was in its place. No crystalline glow like the Merlin. No shadow.

Just… nothing.

"A-Ashley?" Lily tried again.

She glanced up to see her sister staring at her, one hand hanging timidly in the air as though afraid to touch her.

"I'm fine, kiddo," she assured the little girl, returning her attention to Cole. She didn't want to think about it. About the pain or what Jamison had done. Nothing hurt anymore, despite the blood she could feel drying on her back. And Cole was alive. They all were.

That was enough.

Cole coughed. His brow furrowing, he rolled to the side, pain clear on his face.

"What…" he managed hoarsely. Coughing again, he shook his head and then pushed away from the ground.

Ashe reached down, helping him sit up. Breathing hard, he blinked as if trying to focus.

His gaze went beyond Lily and found the windows.

For a heartbeat, he froze. Haltingly, his gaze scanned the room, and his brow twitched down, as though contending with something he didn't want to believe.

"He…" Cole began, and then he swallowed hard. "He, um…"

"I'm sorry," Ashe said quietly.

The air seemed to press from his lungs. With an anguished expression, he closed his eyes.

She looked away, silent as the minutes crawled by.

Cole cleared his throat. "I, uh… I thought I was dead," he said, his voice tight with the effort at normalcy.

"Me too," she replied.

He paused and then drew a breath, visibly pushing the pain aside.

He glanced back at her.

For the second time in as many minutes, he froze. "Holy…" he started, shock washing every other expression away.

She stared at him. "What?"

His gaze darted from her to Lily and back. "You…"

She glanced at Lily. The little girl was watching her too. "*What?*" she pressed.

"You look like her," he explained. "I mean…"

"N-not like the Merlin," Lily finished warily. "Human."

"*Glowing* human," Cole added.

Ashe paused. "What?" she said again.

A groan sounded behind them. She turned sharply, her hand tightening around Lily's as shredded sofa cushions rolled back from their mound by the pockmarked remnants of the wall.

Thelma sat up. Her eyes blinked blearily and her bony hand lifted to pat uselessly at her wild gray hair. Dazedly, she looked around the room and then paused as the three of them came into view.

Her mouth dropped open.

"It…" She gasped. "It's gone!"

Her skeletal fingers clawed at the cushions as she scrambled to her feet.

"She talking about the Merlin thing?" Cole asked, watching Thelma warily.

Ashe gave a careful shrug, not looking away from the woman either.

A smile broke out across Thelma's face. She stumbled from the pile, only to halt in shock as she saw the blood on the tattered back of Ashe's shirt.

"Hurt?" the old woman cried. "Hurt you?"

"I'm fine."

Her own tone was guarded, Ashe could tell. But she couldn't bring herself to change it, any more than she could decide what to think. They wouldn't be here if not for Thelma.

In how many ways, she wasn't sure.

Tripping over the last of the cushions, the old woman came closer and then sank down beside them. The smile returned to her wrinkled face as she looked between the three of them, and then Cole flinched as her arthritic fingers wrapped around his hand.

"Did so well," she told him approvingly. "My little one. My brave paladin."

"You keep calling him that," Ashe said before Cole could speak. "What does that mean?"

"Defenders. Ones who gave the magic you gave back."

Ashe's brow flickered down. "You knew about that?"

"Excuse me?" Cole cut in.

"Of course," Thelma replied.

"But how?" she asked. "No one's ever—"

"I'm sorry, can we go back for a sec? Gave *what* magic?"

Thelma turned to him, looking mystified. "Your magic."

"I don't have any magic."

The old woman blinked perplexedly.

"Ashe?" Cole tried.

She swallowed. "Actually, you do."

"Uh, no…" he corrected. "Pretty sure I'd remember that."

"Didn't know?" Thelma asked Ashe, pointing to Cole in baffled surprise.

Ashe shook her head. "Nobody did. That's why everyone calls them cripples."

The old woman's eyebrows rose.

"Ashe," Cole said, sounding more than a little unnerved. "Look, you realize who we're talking to, right? You can't just–"

"I'm not," she interrupted edgily. "And you do. I don't know how, but you do. Merlin bound it. He took what you have and bound it to make his family into the spell." She paused. "And I have no idea how, or why, or what the hell that means."

For a heartbeat, he watched her.

"What the hell's a paladin, Thelma?" Cole asked, turning to the old woman.

Ashe exhaled, her heart slowing again.

"Defenders," Thelma repeated. "Watchmen on the hills. The ones who saw how people fit together, connections they shared. Weren't like the firemen, destroying and burning and creating all those wars. Wouldn't light the night sky or make wet wood burn. But saw the differences, the samenesses, and protected those they served. Those they loved. Guarded them against what they couldn't see."

She paused. "But you gave it up."

As Cole's brow twitched down, she shrugged. "Didn't mean to, I know. Plan was only to help. Give the connections to make the spell and share the sight of who was who, so people didn't have to be afraid anymore. So many betrayals, back then. So many families lost when friends didn't turn out to be friends. Paladins couldn't stop it. Couldn't protect everyone. So you shared the sight. The connections. Let the others see what you saw, let him use the connections you could feel so he could take the magic from the ones who started wars. Let him use all of it.

"Didn't think it would take it away."

The old woman picked at the debris beside her crossed legs.

"Never knew he'd need to keep it forever, either," she mused. "And Merlin didn't want to. Poor man. Hated what it did. Knew you accepted it, though. Saw the good it made, the lives it saved, even if it cost you. Even if you couldn't be near your friends anymore. Hurt so much. The magic. Pulled and burned and caused so much pain. Spell did that. Took all your beautiful protections and sight, and made them all backwards. Gave nothing but a view of your world that hurt when you came too close to anyone who wasn't outside, and used the spell to give your last strength to wolves when they attacked." She shook her head sadly, her gaze going to the broken windows. "So horrible. So high a price."

She sighed. "Cost you too, though, I guess," she continued, looking back at Ashe. "Cost everyone. Nothing without a price. Not like the paladins, of course. Nobody paid like them. But weakened the others. Differences weren't natural, and needed strength to see. Drained them to see it, though they didn't really care. Eventually forgot life before the differences came along. Forgot so much when all the pieces tossed up by the war finally came down. Just glad to be alive. Didn't seem important that everything was out of balance. That new things were over them now, making them strange. Birds fled. Dogs barked. All so very strange. So weak. So much a shadow of what they had been."

The old woman shrugged again. "Not the same for you. Made you different than them all. Could still fight and bind like Merlin, but had to stand in the middle like him too. Had to hold it all together, both sides. Conduit for the spell. Made you look like them, but not be them. Weakened, but not as much as them. Become the spell, while they were under the spell. Nothing strange on you, no dogs barking at you, because the spell *was* you. What you were. The link for it all." She paused, the sad expression drifting back across her face. "Hurt so many of my little ones when it fractured all wrong, though. Took so many of them away, when it never should have. But it left you. Her too."

Thelma gave Lily a tender smile. "Scary, I bet, when you slipped outside," she added to the little girl. "Even if it was good. You could help. Especially since those bad men slipped outside too."

She returned to picking at the debris, her smile fading.

Ashe stared, and she could see Cole doing the same. Questions pushed on her, each more incredulous than the last, and for the life of her, she couldn't seem to find words for any. Brow furrowing, she floundered through the flood of information and, in desperation, latched onto the last thing the woman had said.

"Outside the spell?" she hazarded.

Thelma nodded, seeming confused by the question.

"And is that what happened to you? Were... were you there that night?"

The confusion didn't fade. "Always been outside."

"Since you were a kid?" Cole tried.

Thelma looked at him oddly. "Since we made the spell."

Incredulity bubbled up, hitting Ashe with the sudden urge to laugh. They were talking to a crazy woman. Someone who chatted with her cats in fragments of poetry and used to call the farmhands' truck a Jabberwocky.

Someone who'd known exactly how the spell worked, had an explanation for why cripples had magic, and possessed more detailed information about the last war than anyone else she'd ever met.

The urge to laugh melted away, leaving her with the sense that her grip on reality had suddenly become unstable.

"Thelma," she asked delicately. "What exactly does that mean?"

"Just," Cole added, "*assume* we don't know."

Thelma paused. "Made the spell," she said again. "Didn't want to. None of us did. But didn't have any choice. He wouldn't listen. Always so headstrong, even as a little boy. So talented, but so terribly headstrong. And to have him take the world…" She shook her head. "Couldn't let him do that to people. To humans. To us. We'd have to hurt them eventually. Always more of them than us."

"Who wanted the world?" Ashe asked faintly, afraid she might know.

"Taliesin."

Ashe swallowed hard.

"I would have done it," Thelma continued. "Bound my little one, but Merlin wanted to protect me. Always so protective of family. Worried the spell might not work and kill whoever took it on. I argued, but he was the stronger one. Both were. Took after their father. If anyone had a chance, Merlin did. And he wouldn't help unless I was the one who stayed outside. Unless I was the one who stayed behind."

She glanced to Lily, the smile returning with a touch of melancholy. "Couldn't know you'd get outside too."

Ashe shivered.

"Anybody remember where reality was?" Cole murmured. "Because I think we've lost it."

"You were *alive* back then?" Lily asked, putting words to at least one of the questions Ashe could no longer bring herself to raise.

Thelma nodded pensively. Her gaze drifted to the side, losing focus as it went.

"That's not possible," Cole said.

Lily looked at him, tremulous credulity in her eyes. "Ashley catches herself on fire and you say people glow," she pointed out.

"Well, yeah, but–"

"Not common," Thelma said as if answering him, though her gaze never left the carpet. "Took so much to do. But necessary." She nodded to herself. "Part of the plan. One spell to bind and one to stay, in case the binding weakened before peace came. Elvis wanted to just pass the spell's secrets down. To tell the little ones how to do what we'd done. But what if the spell didn't end the war? What if we failed? What if later someone pushed it harder… and killed?"

She shook her head. "Needed someone to stay. Someone to be strong enough because they were outside. To know the secrets in case the spell had to be put back again, and to guard the secrets so bad people couldn't use them to kill. And I had to be the one. No one else could."

The old woman paused, her brow furrowing distantly. "Never knew what it'd be, though. To watch people fade. Babies' babies fade. To change names over and over to hide, while things went and went and went… and never came back again…"

Her voice trailed off.

Gingerly, Lily reached out and took her hand.

Thelma drew a breath, the ghost of a fond smile rising again. "Always meant for the spell to end eventually, though," she told the girl quietly. "Wouldn't have left you with the canyon forever. To bind him and his friends forever. Just had to wait till they'd listen. Till they saw they didn't need to run the world to be happy, and could have power without burning everything down."

From the corner of her eye, Ashe saw Cole look away.

"But… it didn't go like that," Thelma said, her smile melting.

"Made sense at first; so much blood on both sides. But then, when the Merlin's little ones grew old, and more grew old, and more… it got worse. Cruel. Became everything we tried to stop. They took pleasure in the power. Pleasure in the hurt." She closed her eyes. "So, so much hurt."

Ashe shifted uncomfortably.

"And then it fractured," Thelma sighed. "And I couldn't do it again. Couldn't help if it would be like last time. So many of my little ones were gone that night, but… hoped maybe the rest would work it out this time. Even if there was fighting, even with all the blood and hurt between them… still hoped maybe it would be okay."

She glanced to Ashe apologetically. "Never meant to let them take everything but the little flower."

Ashe looked away.

She wanted to be angry, and deep down, she could feel it bubbling inside. The rage at what could have been. Maybe even should have been. The things they could have been spared, and all the things that wouldn't have been this way. She wanted to be furious.

But it wouldn't change anything, or bring anyone back again.

Somewhere in the distance, sirens echoed, the sounds faint and meaningless on the wind. Bits of paper fluttered over the carpet from the destroyed books scattered across the office floor, and beyond the shattered glass, wisps of cloud drifted through the darkening blue of the early evening sky.

"You want to get out of here?" Cole asked quietly, his gaze on the windows.

She nodded.

Silently, they climbed to their feet and helped Thelma rise. Papers scattered away as the four of them made their way to the door, the white flecks sweeping out with the wind to float over the city and leave the office behind.

━━━━◆━━━━

Defenses rising, Ashe left the portal with Lily at her back. Cole followed, dizzily stepping away from the old conference room door and ignoring Thelma's quizzical stare.

The Merlin guard filled the first floor lobby, their identity recognizable only through vague familiarity, since they felt nothing like they had before. Strain lined their faces, along with a lack of surprise at the sight of Cole coming through a portal that left her unnerved, and as they spotted her, the nearest of them simply turned away and lifted his phone to his ear.

"She's here," he said tersely.

Ashe's brow drew down and warily, she looked back at Cole.

He didn't notice. Bent with a hand to his head, he blinked as though trying to steady the floor beneath him.

"Leaning on the wall helps," she murmured, keeping one eye to the guards.

Cole glanced up at her. She gave a small shrug.

Closing his eyes briefly, he drew a breath. "I'll be alright," he said, straightening. "It's still better than last time."

His gaze went to the wizards at the end of the elevator corridor. His expression tightened.

"Glowing?" she asked under her breath.

He nodded.

"Good, though?" Thelma interjected. "Not working for the bad ones?"

Cole paused, his gaze flicking from the woman to the guards, and Ashe could read his discomfort at whatever it was he saw. "I guess so," he allowed.

Ignoring Thelma's smile, he headed toward the guard, looking as though the wizards were far preferable to the old woman right now. Taking Lily's hand, Ashe followed.

A portal opened in the conference room door behind them.

"Your majesty!" Elias called, rushing from the shadows with Cornelius and Nathaniel a step behind. "Are you–"

He paused, catching sight of her back. Behind him, she could see Nathaniel register the same. The large wizard's face went dark, though she couldn't tell if the anger was for her, the bloodied rips in her shirt, or just both.

"We're fine," Ashe said before they could speak. "We're all fine."

Swiftly, Nathaniel shrugged off his jacket and swung it around her shoulders, his expression practically daring her to protest.

"We've been trying to reach you," Elias said. "We–"

"Yeah," she interrupted, shifting uncomfortably in the enormous coat. "I'm sorry. I just…"

She didn't know how to finish the sentence. They'd been exhausted after fighting their way through the building, and they were protective as hell. In trying to defend her and Lily from Jamison, they almost certainly would have been killed.

But she couldn't tell them that. The insult wouldn't even be the half of it.

"Where is the Taliesin king?" Cornelius asked flatly into the awkward silence.

She hesitated. "Dead."

Cole looked away.

"What's going on?" she asked, jerking her chin toward the guards.

Elias glanced to Cornelius and Nathaniel. "You should probably just come with us," he told her.

She tensed, struggling not to show nervousness at the words, and followed him. The guards surrounded them all as the three men headed around the elevator island for the door to the concrete park at the building's side.

Her footsteps slowed as the windows came into view. Up ahead, Nathaniel pushed open the glass door and then stepped back, waiting as the others continued through.

The Merlin guard ringed the park. At least, she was fairly certain it was them, based on how the others weren't reacting. Brentworth and Blackjack were there as well, sitting among the wounded beneath the trees at the edge of the concrete, with Katherine and Ermengarde nearby. On the broad steps of the building, Spider, Bus and Samson watched the crowd, nearly motionless and ignoring Harris as he studied them all from a few yards away.

And in the center of the concrete expanse, over a hundred people stood, eyeing the guards and casting furtive glances to her as though waiting for the moment when she'd try to kill them all.

"Whoa, this is weird," Cole said, coming to a stop behind her.

Spider glanced back, tense agreement in her eyes. "I'm assuming you did this?" she asked Ashe.

Walking up next to her, Ashe couldn't respond. Everyone looked the same. As human as Harris. As unremarkable as the Blood had appeared to be. The instant recognition of Merlin and Taliesin and cripple was gone, leaving nothing to differentiate them from any of the ordinary people strolling obliviously past on the sidewalk.

"All wizards once," Thelma murmured.

She looked back. By the doorway, Thelma smiled.

"So," Elias began uncomfortably. "We're pretty certain these are all allies of–"

"They are."

Spider's voice was flat and tight, and when the others glanced to her, the girl didn't take her eyes from the park.

Irritation flickered across Elias' face. "How do you–"

"Get away from me!"

Ashe turned.

In the lobby, Tanya stood, a disappearing portal and a little girl both at her back. Guards circled the woman, and sparks flew from their defenses as Tanya threw bursts of magic to hold them at bay.

"Well," Elias commented, watching her. "Guess we know who sold us out." He paused. "Again."

"She was upstairs with Jamison," Ashe said quietly.

"Put her with the others," Cornelius called to the guards.

Tanya's eyes went wide and her gaze snapped over, spotting them beyond the glass door.

Magic raced from the woman.

And died as it passed Cole.

Ashe blinked. Her attempt to intercept the attack faded as the guards snagged Tanya and shoved her to the ground. Distractedly, she took the woman's magic, ignoring the shriek it elicited from Tanya, and turned to Cole.

He looked as confused as she felt.

"Bastards!" Tanya shouted, struggling in the guards' grip. "You killed him!"

The woman choked as the guards hauled her up from the tile. Muscling her forward, they headed for the door, one of them bringing the little girl behind.

"I'll make you pay," Tanya snarled as she came closer. "I know what you had planned for us. How the king wanted to have us killed and how his guards murdered Howard that night for showing the Blood how to find them first. I know *everything*, and I will see you burn in hell before you lay a hand on my daughter!"

Ashe's brow furrowed. "What?" she asked, glancing to Elias.

"Just get her out of here," he sighed tiredly, motioning to the guards.

Holding Tanya, the guards started forward, only to come to a stop as Thelma wandered into the doorway. "A friend came with the bad firemen?" the old woman asked.

Thelma looked between Tanya and her daughter in confusion, and then she paused, cocking her head.

"Dead man by the road," she said slowly, studying the child. "Glasses. Heavy. Her eyes."

She blinked at Tanya. "Never came near the farm. I went out when the Jabberwockies left and I saw him… saw him lying by the roadside. Bullet in his back and hands all clawed up with dirt like he'd tried to crawl away." She paused. "Had to hide as the firemen came to drag him back when they were burning the house down."

Tanya stared. "No," she whimpered. "No, that's not true. They–"

"Get her out of here already," Elias ordered the guards.

Ashe came over, taking Thelma's arm. The old woman blinked again, and then obediently followed her aside.

"No," Tanya said again. With her gaze locked unseeing on the ground, she kept repeating the word as she stumbled after the guards.

"There's not a chance…" Ashe started, looking to Cornelius and Elias.

"Your father valued the Bartlow family's safety almost as much as your own," Cornelius replied. "No."

Ashe exhaled. Her gaze returned to Cole.

The confusion on his face hadn't changed.

"Yeah," Elias said, reading the young man's expression. "About that." He glanced over as Spider came closer. "Guards figured that out real quick a few minutes ago. One second they were covering your friends here on a retreat from the Taliesin, and the next…"

"It appeared magic could no longer touch them or those they were near." Cornelius supplied into the pause. "Magic intended for harm, in any case." He hesitated. "We are not certain what this development entails."

Spider scoffed. "Says the guy suddenly glowing like a damn Christmas tree."

Cornelius eyed her. "Or that as well," he acknowledged.

Ashe glanced between them, but no one seemed to want to continue. "Well, um," she said to Cole awkwardly. "Thanks for that."

He seemed at a loss. "Anytime."

She paused. Clearly uncomfortable, Cole turned back toward the park and after a heartbeat, she followed his gaze.

"So, your majesty," Spider said dryly. "Now what?"

For a moment, Ashe didn't respond, her eyes on the people filling the park beneath the shifting colors of the setting sun.

"Now," she answered. "We end the war."

Epilogue

Three months later

"The worst was one called Penguin Rally," Lily said.

"Penguin Rally," Ashe repeated.

The little girl nodded. "You had to race these really ugly penguins around this ice-rink thing, and Travis kept insisting I play it because then he could tell his Aunt Mauve he'd gotten to the end. He even emailed Cole last week wanting to know if I could remember a certain part, because his five-year-old cousin wouldn't stop asking about it."

Ashe laughed as she pushed aside a low-hanging tree branch. The ice on the wood melted at her touch, sending fat drops of water down into the snowbank below.

"And you had to do this for how long?"

"Like a month!" Lily replied incredulously, and then she paused, amending the statement. "Well, I mean, not every day. I did get to make some stuff while I was there. Not like I did at Sue and Ben's, though. They had so much stuff for making things. Craft paper and beads and yarn like she used in that blanket she sent. You liked that one, right? I thought it was so pretty."

Ashe nodded, but Lily had already moved on to talking about their plans to visit the Summers' farm. Clambering over a snow-covered log, the little girl continued down the path through the trees.

She shook her head in amusement. No matter what was happening, no matter how busy they became, she always tried to make it back to spend some time with Lily. It helped that the joint headquarters for all the wizards had been placed in a city not too far from their new home, and that with their stronger powers, the wizards had discovered they could push the distances of portals farther than before. So far, she'd managed not to miss a day, even if sometimes she had to resort to playing the trump card of the whole queen thing.

Life had become so different since the end of the war. Politics now dominated everything, and demanded balancing acts that sometimes even Elias and Cornelius couldn't believe. Half the Merlin still wanted the Council to speak for her, while the rest wanted each former member removed. The Taliesin were much the same, despite Brentworth's agreement to acknowledge Cole as heir to the throne, though they had the added trouble of some among their number who still believed the Blood had been right all along. Maintaining the peace process was hard, especially in light of those who'd rather do anything but compromise, and it had swiftly become a full-time job that, if they weren't careful, would perpetually keep her and Cole away from home.

It made them both crazy, even if she knew he was as grateful as her that they'd at least reached the point where their people were talking, rather than just trying to kill each other all the time. And though they technically represented what most continued to view as different sides, it was still a relief to be able to come home and vent like the close friends they were becoming about all the stupidities they both perceived.

There'd never really been a discussion of the three of them not staying together. Lily wouldn't hear of leaving Cole now that, like them, his family was gone. Within a week of the war's end, they'd moved to the manor in rural upstate New York that, along with the rest of Jamison's property, now belonged to his son. It'd been hard for her, at first, to stay where the man who killed her family had lived, but with the constant flow of wizards coming and going and the pressure of day-to-day needs from all sides, the discomfort was slowly beginning to dissipate and just leave the place feeling like home.

Overall, she had to admit the changes had mostly been for the better – not counting the politics and nonsense that seemed to accompany it. The threat of the ferals had vanished overnight, owing to the fact their prey could not only spot them a mile off, but had become magically impervious to boot. Those who could be identified had been taken into custody, and plans were in the works to try them according to the laws that existed before the war. And of the rest still out there, the advantages of seriously considering a new lifestyle seemed to be quickly sinking in.

For their part, the former cripples kept their distance from the wizards, though Spider and Bus had still been by to see her plenty of times. Their work kept them both busy, as most of their efforts now were focused on setting up shelters where their own people could come and start rebuilding their lives after the war. Nothing much identified the buildings beyond the symbol of Bus' own creation that he said meant 'nice place, bring food', but when they'd last stopped by, they'd told her they already had twenty such locations throughout the country, mostly courtesy of the network Carter had built. And although they still tended to go silent whenever someone else walked into the room, they didn't let their feelings toward the majority of wizards stop them from helping her from time to time. Two months back, they'd uncovered the Blood, Isabella, hiding in a five-star hotel in San Francisco, and every few weeks seemed to bring another short phone call to tell her where more troublemakers could be found.

Thelma had been given a new home in the care of some of Katherine's best healers, and gradually, she was rediscovering life among her own. She still clung to her cats – though most of the wizards had taken to owning a pet or two, simply for the novelty – and occasionally drifted into talking about the distant past like everyone else had been there, but she was steadily becoming a favorite of the historically inclined on both of the former sides, and was loving every minute of the attention.

Harris had moved into an apartment not too far from the manor and spent most of his time flying around the country, helping Cole piece together his father's empire and locate the money Brogan had hidden away. The detective had only returned to Utah once, owing to difficulties with his department about which he'd never really gone into detail, but after the short trip with Katherine, a weight seemed to leave him, and lately he'd looked more at peace than she'd ever seen.

"I can still bring back a few of Butterscotch's new kittens, right?" Lily asked.

Ashe blinked, the question pulling her from her thoughts. "Yeah, Cole's already warned the pilot he'll be taking them back for us on the plane."

"Cool," Lily said, her lips twitching with an excited grin.

She buried a smile as the girl kept walking. It'd been a good three months, despite the stress of working out some new issue between the wizards every day. And if negotiations and politics were the worst things she ever had to deal with again, there was no way she'd claim to be anything but happy.

The trees parted as the path came to an end, leaving them on the broad swath of grassland leading to their home.

"So where to tomorrow?" Lily prompted.

Ashe smothered a chuckle. Miles of forest and hills surrounded the sprawling manor, and she was developing the sneaking suspicion that Lily planned to explore every inch of them.

"There's the path south of the conservatory that we haven't tried yet," she offered.

"Perfect! But can we start early? I think I saw a family of deer not far from–"

A crash from the house brought them up short. The door to the patio flew open and Cole raced out, his feet skidding on the ice and snow.

His eyes swept the yard and then went wide at the sight of them.

"He lied!" Cole yelled.

Ashe didn't move, her shields dropping cautiously. Behind her, Lily began to squirm in her grip.

"What?" she shouted back.

He didn't answer as he rushed down the steps. "Come on!" he called, waving an arm at them.

With an uncomfortable noise, Lily broke out of her grasp and started through the snow.

Warily, Ashe followed. "What's going on?"

"Nathaniel and Gavin are waiting at the portal," he replied, taking Lily's hand and hurrying back into the house. "I'll explain when we get there."

Brow drawing down, she continued after him. "Get where?"

He didn't respond. Swiftly, he helped Lily out of her winter coat and tossed it aside, and then turned, catching himself as if suddenly recalling that her sister rarely bothered to use one.

"Cole, seriously," Ashe stated flatly.

"Come on," he said again.

She followed him to the portal. Nathaniel and Gavin bowed at the sight of them, half a dozen of the royal guard at their side.

"The doctor has been told to expect you," Nathaniel said to Cole.

She looked up in alarm, but the wizard didn't say anything more as he headed into the portal. Exasperatedly, she went through after him.

Light and sound blurred, depositing them in city after city. Gavin and Nathaniel traded off, creating portals as the other stood guard, until finally they stepped out onto a sidewalk beneath a cloudless blue sky.

"Cole, where the hell are we?" Ashe asked, eyeing the palm trees swaying in the faintly salty breeze.

"San Diego."

Without another word, he started across the street, heading for a white mission-style building. An archway stood before the entrance, with gold letters glinting in the sunlight.

Her brow drew down at the words and she glanced to Cole. He seemed as tense as she'd ever seen him.

If not more.

"You said–"

"I found a journal," Cole replied without looking back. "There was a safe in the library floor, hidden under some carpets. We were moving the desks and…" He shook his head. "It talked about everything. *Everything.* What he did, what happened to her. Why he thought she'd…"

"Who?" Ashe asked when he trailed off.

He paused, his hand on the door handle. "My mom."

She stared as he yanked open the door and strode inside.

Cool air filled the lobby and sunlight streamed from the windows set high beneath the arched ceiling. Corridors stretched off the enormous room and on the other side of the expanse of earth-toned tile, the front desk waited against the wall. A man in a white coat stood by it, and as they entered, he turned.

"Welcome," he said with a smile. "Would one of you be Mr. Jamison?"

"Cole," came the short response.

Ashe glanced over. He barely seemed to be breathing.

The man gave no sign of noticing as he crossed the room and then reached out, shaking Cole's hand. "The director called to say you'd be coming." He gestured to the leftmost corridor. "If you'll follow me?"

At Cole's nod, the man turned, leading the way. Cole started after him and then hesitated, glancing back as though feeling the pressure of her gaze.

"My dad bound her," he whispered as they followed the doctor. "After… after he started the war. He told Brogan he'd kill her, told him he *had* killed her, because he worried that, as a Merlin, the Blood would see her as a threat to all they were trying to do. And he was afraid of what she'd think… how she'd look at him in response to what he felt had to happen. So he said he'd kill her himself, and then he bound her and took her away. He'd been paying for this place out of some account Harris and I hadn't found yet, and he told the doctors she was crazy. That she thought she was a wizard and had magic and all sorts of stuff, and then he paid them to have her stay here under another name. Claimed he didn't want to shame the family or whatever to keep them quiet. But he didn't kill her. He couldn't. He wanted her to understand. To see that what he'd done was right and made the world safe for… for us."

Cole paused. "He thought he could explain it to her someday."

The doctor came to a stop ahead. "Despite her medication, she's been relatively agitated these past few weeks, which forced us to sedate her several times. We took her off the current dose, however, when we received your call. She should be becoming more lucid shortly." He hesitated, looking to the door. "If you need anything, please let me know."

At their nod, the doctor walked away.

Cole didn't move.

"It's okay," Lily said quietly, taking his hand.

He glanced down, trying and failing to mirror her small smile. His eyes closed as he reached for the handle, and when he drew a breath, Ashe could hear it tremble.

Cole pulled open the door.

On a narrow twin bed, a woman was seated, her gaze on the window taking up the far wall. Sunlight poured through the glass, lighting on long brunette hair the exact shade of Cole's own and catching on her pale skin as she turned toward the sound of the door.

Tremulous shock and joy rose in her warm brown eyes. "Cole?"

"Mom."

He crossed the room as she rose, her hand clutching the bed for support, and when he came near, she reached out and then pulled him close, hanging on as though she'd never let go.

Ashe leaned on the doorframe, watching them both, and smiled.

The End.

Loved the book?

If you've enjoyed Wildfire and The Kindling Trilogy, please consider leaving a review on Amazon.com, Goodreads.com, and other book-related sites.

Hear about all the new releases!

Join Skye Malone's mailing list at
www.skyemalone.com/mailinglist

Other titles

The Awakened Fate Series
The Touch Me Series
The Kindling Trilogy

About the author

Skye Malone is a fantasy and paranormal romance author, which means she spends most of her time not-quite-convinced that the magical things she imagines couldn't actually exist.

A Midwestern girl who migrated to the Pacific Northwest, she dreams of traveling the world — though in the meantime she'll take any story that whisks her off to a place where the fantastic lives inside the everyday. She loves strong and passionate characters, complex villains, and satisfying endings that stay with you long after the book is closed. An inveterate writer, she can't go a day without getting her hands on a keyboard and can usually be found typing away while she listens to all the adventures unfolding in her head.

Connect with Skye

Website: www.skyemalone.com
Twitter: www.twitter.com/Skye_Malone
Facebook: www.facebook.com/authorskyemalone
Instagram: www.instagram.com/authorskyemalone

Acknowledgements

This series, The Kindling Trilogy, started out as a novella I wrote many years ago, and back then, it was known simply as Merlin's Children. Ashe, as well as Lily and Cole – who were, at the time, called Hannah and Paul – were characters that never left me through all the years that followed.

I'm so grateful I've had the opportunity to share them with you now.

My thanks go to you for reading this series, and to all those who have left such positive reviews, shared book news, talked about how much they enjoy these stories, and encouraged me in publishing this trilogy. Your support means more than I can say.

My thanks also go to my friends and family. You all are a gift for which I am immensely grateful and I am so glad you are in my life.

To my mother and sister, Mary Ann and Keri, you keep me going. You believe in me even when I don't always believe in myself. Thank you.

Avery Peterson, my wife and best friend, deserves so much credit for these stories. From talking with me through myriad plot points, to spending hours formatting the electronic editions, to even taking a jeweler's eyepiece to printed fonts just to learn their point sizes down to the millimeter, she has had a hand in almost every stage of this process. Simply put, these books wouldn't exist without her.